Martina Reilly is the author of eight successful novels: *Flipside, The Onion Girl* and *Is This Love?* published b- D-... and *Something Borrowed, Wedded B... is You* and *The Summer of Secrets* pu... worked as a columnist for the *Iris...* she writes a column for the *Irish...* on her novels. She is a mother of... teaches drama at the Maynooth ~~School~~ of Drama, writes plays and helps out with her son's under-11 soccer team! Look out for Martina's new novel, *Second Chances*, coming from Sphere in autumn 2008.

For more information on Martina and her books, please visit www.martinareilly.info.

Also by Martina Reilly

Flipside
The Onion Girl
Is This Love?
Wedded Blitz
Wish Upon A Star
All I Want is You
The Summer of Secrets
Second Chances

Something Borrowed

MARTINA REILLY

SPHERE

First published in Great Britain as a paperback original in 2004
by Time Warner Paperbacks
This edition published by Time Warner Books in January 2006
Reprinted by Sphere in 2007
Reissued by Sphere in 2008

A CIP catalogue record for this book is available from the British Library.

ISBN 978-0-7515-4102-1

Typeset in Baskerville MT by
Palimpsest Book Production Limited, Polmont, Stirlingshire

Printed and bound in Great Britain by Clays Ltd, St Ives plc

Papers used by Sphere are natural, renewable and recyclable
products made from wood grown in sustainable forests and certified
in accordance with the rules of the Forest Stewardship Council.

Mixed Sources
Product group from well-managed
forests and other controlled sources
www.fsc.org Cert no. SGS-COC-004081
© 1996 Forest Stewardship Council

FSC

Sphere
An imprint of
Little, Brown Book Group
100 Victoria Embankment
London EC4Y 0DY

An Hachette Livre UK Company
www.hachettelivre.co.uk

www.littlebrown.co.uk

This is dedicated with thanks to all those who have bought and read my books in the past – hope yez enjoy this one!

Acknowledgements

Thanks, as always, to my family for their support, for buying my books and for trying not to look too bored every time I talk about my writing. Thanks to Claire for reading and helping me proof the final drafts of *Something Borrowed*.

Thanks to all my mates, especially Margaret for her sales patter to the good folk of Tesco, Kathleen for her lovely peaceful house, Imelda who I miss, Irene who I met because of Imelda, and Mary, my lovely neighbour with the fab garden that keeps my daughter entertained. Also to Gaye for her belief in me and all my neighbours who buy my books and ask 'how's the writing going?'. Thanks too to the parents of all the kids at Maynooth Drama – you've been brilliant over the years, especially the 'long-termers'.

Thanks to all my writer friends – you're a great bunch and deserve huge success: Catherine Barry, Colette Caddle, Dawn Cairns, Denise Deegan, Claire Dowling, Catherine Dunne, Anne-Marie Forrest, Marisa Mackle, Marita McConlon McKenna, Jacinta McDevitt and Annie Sparrow. Special thanks to two other wonderful writers: Sarah Webb, who gave me her agent's number (forever grateful!) and Martina Devlin (who knows that if she gives up the writing she can be my PR woman anytime!).

To the gang at the *Evening Herald* for all the help with the last book – thanks a million, guys.

Thanks to the bookshops, especially Eason's, and most especially to Adrienne in Liffey Valley – you've no idea how much pleasure it gives me to see the books as I pass by. I'm mostly too shy to sign them!

Thanks to the Adoption Board for their help with my research and to Helen Scott at the Adopted Parents Association for her frank and honest observations of the adoption process. Thanks to everyone who gave me an insight into adoption. While I know tracing is a lengthy process, for the purposes of the novel I had to speed things up a lot – any mistakes are my own.

Loads of grateful thanks to Ali Gunn, my agent, who worked tirelessly on my behalf to make my dreams come true. Thanks also to my new publishers for having faith in me, especially to Tara Lawrence for her brilliant suggestions and to Joanne Coen for her patience with the editing.

For my lovely family – Colm, Conor and Caoimhe.

And finally – thanks to you for choosing this book. Without readers, I wouldn't be here – enjoy!

Something Borrowed

Prologue

THERE IS A silence. A really bad sort of silence. The kind of silence that makes me want to hide.

Tommy gawks at John.

John stands with his arms folded, surveying me. Then he sort of swaggers a bit. 'Betcha didn't know that now.'

All my cousins are looking at me and I don't know why.

'Ready made,' John says again, sniggering.

Auntie Julia looks at Uncle Dessie.

Dessie is snoring on the couch, an opened bottle of Guinness clutched in his hand and beginning to spill all over the floor.

Auntie Julia wallops him awake then grabs John's arm and wallops him across the head. Then she drags John howling out into the hall. I can hear her slapping him all the way up the stairs.

Dessie blinks and looks slowly around. 'That young fella in trouble again.' His voice is all slurry.

'Let's go home now,' my mammy says in a high, bright voice. 'Time to go now, Vicky.'

Silence as I'm bundled into my coat. It's the nicest coat of all my cousins and they're all dead jealous.

'What did John mean?' I ask.

Mammy looks at Daddy. Daddy turns away.

'We'll explain when you get home,' Mammy says firmly. 'Let's go now.'

That night was the worst of my life.

1

Chapter One

Sixteen years later

EIGHT O'CLOCK, CHRISTMAS Eve. Sal, my flatmate, skidded to a halt beside Toys Galore – the toy shop I manage. She threw open the door of her VW Beetle and yelled at me to 'effing hurry up'.

When Sal tells you to 'effing hurry up', you do. Throwing my case onto her back seat, I leapt into the passenger seat and fastened my belt.

'I've circled the block twice,' Sal moaned, shoving her blonde hair behind her ear and glaring out at the rain that had just started to fall. 'Where the hell were you?'

'It's Christmas Eve, Sal,' I said mildly, unwrapping some chocolates I'd been saving for the journey. 'I work in a toy shop.'

'So?'

'Toy shops sell toys?' I arched my eyebrows. 'Christmas is all about toys.'

'Yeah?' Sal made a face. 'I thought it was about boozing and listening to your rellies singing stupid songs.'

'Mmmm.' Sal has this awful sceptical view of life. 'D'you want some chocolate?' I held out some Cadbury's Roses to her.

Sal shook her head. 'The tissue they're wrapped in kind of spoils my appetite.'

'I only wrapped them in tissue to stop them getting lost in my bag,' I said, exasperated. 'They're perfectly safe.'

3

She didn't bother to reply. I popped a caramel one into my mouth and followed it up with a coffee flavour.

'Why do you always eat the minute you get into a car?' Sal asked, sounding annoyed for some reason. 'I mean, can you not wait until later? We've a four-hour journey ahead, you know.'

'I have crisps for later.' I pulled out a six-pack of Tayto. Then, in case she thought I was a right pig, I explained, 'Bridie and I had a little party for the kids that came into the shop today – you know, a few lollies and crisps and stuff. So this is what's left.'

'So why didn't Bridie take them home?' Sal asked, braking hard and throwing us both forward. 'Bloody traffic. Jesus!'

'Bridie would never eat six packets of crisps,' I quoted Bridie.

'But she'd use them over Christmas?'

'Dunno.' I didn't know. Bridie never talked about her family or friends or anything.

'Yeah, well, you should have left them there,' Sal remarked. 'You're eating too much. I think you've put on weight.'

'Thanks.' She was in a bad mood for some reason.

'You always put on weight before you go home,' Sal continued. 'Are you afraid they won't think you're eating properly up in Dublin if you don't?'

'Don't be stupid.' Now *I* was getting in a bad mood. Maybe because she was edging too close to the bone. I did tend to eat a lot just before I went home. I ate a lot before my leaving cert too. And before I ditched college.

I ate when something made me uneasy.

We made it to Cork in under four hours. Sal drives like a maniac. She drives the way she lives her life, I guess – fast and furious. Knowing where she is going and just wanting to get there. Anyway, she had just pulled away from me in a huge cloud of dust when my mother began legging it down the driveway, her arms out in a huge embrace.

'She's home, she's home,' she yelled out. I guessed she was telling my dad. He soon appeared at the front door, paper in

4

hand, pipe in mouth, and stood beaming at the two of us as we made our way towards him. Another hug from him. 'Welcome home!' He patted my back. 'And how's the toy shop manager today?'

They were inordinately proud of me. I used to be 'The Student' before I flunked out of college, then I became 'The Traveller' for the five years I backpacked about the world, then 'The Flower Girl' for my flower shop job, then 'The Travel Agent' – and now I was 'The Manager'.

'Well?' Dad asked, smiling away at me.

'Fine,' I muttered.

'Will you let the girl breathe.' My mother pushed him out of our way as we entered the hallway. She was breathless from her run to meet me. 'Let her get a cuppa and some food into her before you start quizzing her.'

It was always the same. The dinner, the chat. I was escorted by both of them into the big, stone farmhouse kitchen. Mam pulled out a chair for me at the wooden table and before I had a chance to adjust my seat, a huge slush pile of stew was ladled onto a large plate and slapped down in front of me.

'I'll have some of that.' Dad winked at me as if asking for some food was a risky business.

Mam, only too happy to oblige, gave him even more than she'd given me and made a production of laying it in front of him.

'Ta.' Dad slapped his stomach and began to eat.

Mam pulled down a warm plate from over the range for herself and soon the three of us were eating in silence.

I never talked much in the house. To be honest, ever since I was a kid, I've been sort of scared by it. And it's not because it's old and creaky, though that may have something to do with it, it's more because everything about the house is so HUGE. And I mean *everything*. From the granite stonework on the outside walls to the flags on the kitchen floor. Even the table I'd sat at for years looked as if it was hewn from an enormous oak.

Mam and Dad suited the house. They looked as if they'd been born out of the masonry, both of them tall and brawny and sort of ageless, while I, small and skinny, am like some kind of freak compared to everything around me. I stand out, you know. But in the wrong sort of way.

I've always stood out in the wrong sort of way from the rest of the McCarthy clan. So it was a relief when at twelve I found out that I was adopted. Don't get me wrong; it was an awful shock, but a relief as well. At least I had a reason for feeling that I was always the odd person out – and it wasn't just in the family, it was everywhere. In school, with friends, even in crowds at gigs I've always felt apart somewhat, like I'm not quite anchored.

Stew finished, Mam cleared the table and an enormous strawberry cheesecake was brought from the fridge and dumped in front of me. 'Your favourite.' She smiled delightedly at me. 'I made it specially.'

'Ta.' Oh God, I didn't much like cheesecake. I hadn't ever liked it really. But when I'd returned from my travels, Mam had attempted to make something a bit different. Something to show me that fancy cuisine could be made anywhere, not just in 'foreign hot places where the women don't even cover themselves up properly'. And I'd raved over the cheesecake – well, I would, wouldn't I, when I'd lived on pennies for a whole month and eaten bits of stale bread to keep me going? A bit like I did now, actually.

Anyway, ever since then, Mam has made me a cheesecake and she and Dad eat a small portion each, protesting that fancy food brings on their indigestion while I gamely shove a quarter or so into me to keep them happy.

'Daddy?' Mam asked, knife poised. 'Would you like a piece?'

Dad rubbed his stomach and eyed the cake suspiciously. 'Oooh, I dunno. Brings on a lot of wind, I find.'

'I find that too,' Mam said, setting down the knife. 'It repeats on a body.'

'Belching and farting, that's what happens when you eat strange food. No,' Dad waved his hand about, 'none for me, thanks.'

'I won't either,' Mam said.

Both of them looked at me.

So now, I was expected to eat something that made them belch and fart? 'A small piece,' I murmured.

'A small piece,' Mam scoffed. 'When was ever anything small in this house? You'll have a piece to fill you up, so you will.' With that she hacked off at least half of the bloody cake and offered it to me.

They watched while I cut into it. They watched as the first piece went into my mouth. They watched as I swallowed. I swear, if they could have seen me digest it, they would have. 'Gorgeous,' I pronounced.

Mam laughed and clapped her hands. Dad lay back in his chair and lit his pipe. 'I think we'll have a cup of tea, Evelyn, and some mince pies.'

Mam jumped up like a jackrabbit to meet his request.

Tea was laid before him. Tea was put before me.

A huge plate of mince pies and a big bowl of cream were laid on the table and while they ate that, I did a Bruce Bogtrotter on the cake.

Tea over, we all retired to the dining room.

This was the part where I had to entertain them with all I'd done since the last time I'd been down. No matter what it was, they thought it was wonderful. It was embarrassing how much they loved me. It poured out of them with every look, every gesture, every smile.

I hadn't much to tell them, which was a bit embarrassing seeing as I hadn't been down in about four months. But Dad was still reeling over the fact that I was a manager. It didn't matter that there was only Bridie and me in the shop, it was still an honour. A *huge* honour.

'O'Neill hadn't anyone else he could pick.' I hated all this false praise. 'There weren't many in for the job.'

'Mister O'Neill,' Mam corrected hastily.

'Mister O'Neill,' I muttered.

'He chose you,' Dad said vigorously, 'because you are so good.'

'I don't think—'

'You're exactly like your mother, too modest by half.' Dad smiled fondly at Mam who flapped him away.

'Tell her.' Dad nodded at Mam.

Mam turned red. 'Well, I—'

'You'll get a surprise when you hear this.' Dad jabbed his pipe in my direction.

'I entered the—'

'This is good now,' Dad nodded. A big beam. 'Just you wait till you hear this.'

'I was in the—'

'It's a good one, mind.'

'I won—'

'She only went and won the parish flower show,' Dad said loudly. He beamed at Mam who beamed back at him.

'I did a winter bloom display,' Mam said to me. 'D'you remember?'

Vaguely. 'Oh yeah.'

'Well, first prize I got.'

'And that's not all, is it?' Dad gave Mam a nudge. 'Go on, tell her the rest.'

'Well, Amanda Sweeney—'

'This is the icing on the cake,' Dad interrupted.

'Amanda Sweeney—'

'Amanda Sweeney was so impressed by the winter blooms that she asked your mother to do her daughter's wedding in the summer.'

'No!' Now that was news. Amanda Sweeney was the parish snob, not to mention rich chick. 'You're doing her daughter's wedding?' I gawked at Mam. 'You?'

'There's no need for that tone,' Dad chastised me. 'Your

8

mother is well able for it, aren't you, Evelyn? Go for it, I told her. Show those bloody Sweeneys.'

Mam laughed, flapped her arm at him. She always did that. Sometimes he caught it and they went all lovey-dovey on each other, which was a bit embarrassing.

'Two wonderful women!' Dad looked proudly at us. 'What did I do to deserve such luck?'

In my case, I guess, he'd just forgotten to take his rose-tinted glasses off.

I couldn't sleep at all that night. Coming home is never the return to childhood that other people write about. There's no soothing reassurance in sleeping in my old bed, looking at my patterned wallpaper and hearing the familiar tick of the grandfather clock on the landing. Even though it's always the same, it still never lies easy on me. I normally get up some time in the night and grab a glass of milk from the fridge. I spend the rest of the night watching the dawn creep over the fields beyond the house. It reminds me that there's a big wide world out there and I can disappear into it whenever I want.

Chapter Two

CHRISTMAS DAY DAWNED bright and clear. I was up before Mam and Dad, which wasn't surprising as I'd never actually slept. I got their presents out from my case and laid them under the tree in the dining room. They were all wrapped up in traditional red with big white bows. My mother likes tradition a lot, and despite the fact that she'd told me exactly what dressing gown to buy her, I still had to wrap up her present and pretend that I had a major surprise for her.

Once the presents were under the tree, I poured myself a glass of whiskey and hacked off a lump of Mam's pudding. Feet up, I flicked on the telly and waited for the two to get up.

Dad was up first, which was unusual. Normally Mam beats him to it. He walked in on me just as I was cutting myself another slice of pudding. 'Aw, now, Vic,' he scolded. 'You won't eat your breakfast at that rate.'

He didn't know me very well. I grinned at him and offered him a piece.

'Not at all.' He shook his head. 'I'm saving myself for the fry-up.' He took rashers and sausages and pudding from the fridge and flicked on the grill. I filled up the kettle and began to set the table. I felt a bit guilty that I hadn't thought of it before now.

'That's the girl.' Dad looked at me in approval. 'Now, only a glass for your mother, she's cutting down on the auld tea and coffee.'

'What?'

10

'Aye,' Dad nodded, deftly turning a sausage, 'she says the stuff is bad for her.'

'Since when?' My mother was the world's biggest tea drinker. If she gave it up, half the world's exporters would go bust.

'Since a few months ago,' Dad said. 'She just decided all of a sudden. She only drinks it at night now.'

'Right.' I removed Mam's cup from the table and put a glass there instead. 'So what does she drink instead?'

'Orange juice,' Dad said as if it was some kind of an exotic beverage. 'Imagine replacing tea with orange juice.'

'Is he laughing at me again?' Mam's voice came from the stairway.

'He is,' I called back.

Mam appeared in her oldest dressing gown. That was to make my present seem extra good. 'Happy Christmas, love,' Mam said as she embraced me.

'Happy Christmas, Mam.'

She turned to Dad who took her hand in his and they looked at one another for a few seconds before kissing each other tenderly on the lips. Happy Christmases were exchanged.

I turned away. I always felt weird looking at them – as if I was in the way or something.

'Aw, who's been eating the pudding?' Her annoyed tone made me flinch. 'Sean,' she demanded, glaring at Dad, 'have you?'

He pointed at me.

Her face sagged with disappointment. 'Aw, Vic, could you not wait? I wanted it to be whole for the dinner.'

'Sorry, Mam.'

She 'tisked' a bit.

'Didn't I tell you?' Dad said righteously to me, acting like the big class swot.

'And you could have stopped her.' Mam belted him with her hand.

'Hadn't she half it eaten by the time I came down?' Dad held out his hands in an appealing gesture. 'How could I stop her?'

'I needed something to wash the whiskey down,' I grinned, knowing they'd be shocked.

'Vicky!' they both exclaimed.

'You'll be drunk in mass,' Mam pronounced. 'That's not a fit way to turn up in the house of God.'

'Well, if God laid on a bit more entertainment I mightn't need the drink to get me through it,' I shot back. I knew they'd laugh. They always do. Sort of shocked and horrified yet loving the fact that I'm a free spirit.

That's what they think I am, you see.

After breakfast, we opened our presents and after that we went to mass. It lasted for ages. There was a choir singing and everything. Mam thought that it was beautiful. Dad, like me, had spent most of the time looking around to see who was there. Amanda Sweeney had turned up, her horrible family in tow. The daughter, the one who was getting married, had been in my class in school. We used to be mates until I'd stolen her Barbie doll one year and then her mother wouldn't let her play with me again. Unfortunately I had to shake her hand at one stage during the mass and it was like holding a dead fish. A huge diamond ring glittered like a Christmas light on her left hand.

'A lovely-looking girl,' Dad whispered loud enough for the whole parish to hear, 'that's the one that's getting married.'

'Yeah, Dad. Thanks.'

Mam and Dad loved weddings. Any time someone got married, Mam procured their wedding album and kept it until I arrived home and then I was duly shown photographs of people I didn't know with bright sunny happy smiles on their faces, surrounded by family and friends.

Sometimes I liked looking, sometimes they made me sad. I guess Lisa Sweeney's wedding album would make me very sad, especially for the poor sucker she was getting hitched to.

After mass, I waited in the car while Mam and Dad did the usual hugging and kissing with the neighbours. They also caught

12

up on all the week's gossip. Honestly, that part of Cork was unbelievable for scandal – I don't think anyone slept with his or her actual spouse.

'Well, well, well,' Dad whistled as he started the car. 'Could you credit that?'

'What?' I asked, agog.

'Never you mind,' Mam tutted. 'It's Christmas. It's not spreading scandal about the neighbours we should be.'

'June Crowley slept with Dr Jones.' Dad couldn't wait to get it out. Honestly, he was like a clucking hen. 'Can you credit that now?'

'June Crowley that's married to the solicitor?' I asked.

'The very one.'

'And she's leaving him for the doctor,' Mam added, in case Dad forgot.

'Leaving her husband and two little kiddies,' Dad nodded. 'Isn't that a scandal now?'

'Terrible,' my mother agreed.

And it was, I thought.

'The country is going to the dogs,' Dad said, as he drove at a safe twenty miles an hour home. 'Imagine June Crowley, a married woman, sleeping with Dr Jones.' He shook his head. 'Imagine doing the likes of that.'

'Yeah,' I muttered, 'Dr Jones is a horror.'

'That's not what your father means,' Mam said, totally missing my joke. 'He just can't believe that June would do such a thing. I mean, all she went in for was a check-up.'

'And instead she got something else up,' I grinned.

Shocked expressions before Dad began again. 'You young folk,' he said, carefully avoiding a pothole, 'you take nothing seriously. Marriage breakdown is rife in this society and it's the children that suffer.'

'They don't take marriage seriously any more,' Mam said, nodding vigorously in agreement. 'They don't take relationships seriously any more.'

13

'Yes they do.' I felt I had to stick up for my generation. Mam and Dad were always at this, completely out of touch. Sometimes I felt suffocated by their attitudes. 'Everyone marries for love – no one can see into the future. Things happen.'

'Aye. Things happen.' Mam looked at me. 'They happen because they're let happen. Dr Jones and June knew exactly what they were at, I've no doubt about that.'

'They made a mistake.'

'A mistake that hurt her husband and two children, that's the mistake they made.'

I glared at her. Jesus, they always had the answer for everything. There was never any bend in them. 'Well,' I fired one last shot, 'if my' – I didn't know what to call her – 'my birth mother hadn't made a mistake, I wouldn't be here with you now, would I?'

Mam blinked. Once. Twice.

'That's not what we were discussing,' Dad said quietly.

Naw, they never discussed that, did they?

'And we're glad you're here,' Mam said, in an even quieter voice. 'And you're not a mistake.'

I just stared out the window.

Mam chose that Christmas Day to show me how to cook. I was quite happy to peel a few spuds and chop a few carrots, but Mam had something more exotic in mind.

'You can make the sauces,' she instructed, handing me the flour and butter and milk for the white sauce. 'Now, the first thing is to make a roux.'

No such thing as packet sauce in our house, unfortunately.

Anyway, I made it all lumpy and it burned a bit.

Then I had to cream the spuds.

Too much milk went onto them.

Dad and Mam laughed.

'Hot ice cream,' Dad pronounced as he lifted up a dripping spoonful of spuds. 'Ha, ha, ha.'

Mam giggled and flapped at him. 'Oh, you'll never make a cook,' she muttered fondly to me.

'You don't take after your mother, that's for sure,' Dad said, as he deftly began to slice the turkey. 'Smell that.'

I made a big production of sniffing the turkey and spice-scented air but inside I wasn't even smiling.

I knew I didn't take after my mother.

How could I?

Chapter Three

THE FOLLOWING DAY, Saint Stephen's, was normally spent in Aunt Julia's and this year was no exception. The invites had been sent out months ago, and Dad liked to joke that the RSVP on the invitations meant Respond So Very Positively. You just did not dare to miss Aunt Julia's Christmas party. A family member had a better chance of being forgiven for murder than a 'no-show' at the event of the year.

The party always started at three, when the family, the whole massive extended family, sat around and ate finger food, and normally finished up twelve hours later after the stories and gossip and the jokes had been swapped.

Despite Dad's joke about the invite, it's the highlight of his and Mam's year and it's the curse of mine. All five foot nothing of me sitting around with the towering hugeness of the McCarthy clan. That, plus the fact that I don't get on very well with my cousins. Ever since we were kids, Aunt Julia's two boys, Tommy and John – he's the same age as me, twenty-eight – have teased me. And because they're so funny and witty and everything, all the others tend to side with them. And though I know I should be past all that at this stage in my life, I'm actually not.

Maybe it's just delayed maturity or something.

Anyway, Dad and Mam were dressed in their best. Mam wore her brand-new Christmas dress and the new shoes that Dad had bought her. They didn't match, exactly, but she hadn't the heart to tell him, though how he couldn't see it for himself, I don't know. A green dress with red shoes does look weird, I think.

Dad had his brown suit on, the one he wears to every important occasion. He looked quite handsome in it, actually. But then again, all the McCarthys are handsome, even the women.

I wore a pair of black trousers that I'd worn to Bridie's and my Christmas party. We'd gone to see Joe Dolan because Bridie loves him. And, as I was the manager, I did have to consider what my one member of staff wanted. And Bridie wanted Joe. In fact all the wrinklies there wanted him – it was quite an eye-opener actually to see women that could barely throw a shape on a dance floor throwing their knickers up at a man in a tight white suit.

I swear, I couldn't even eat the dinner I'd been served up.

'You look lovely,' Mam said approvingly as she eyed my very conservative top. 'Green really suits you. It sets off the red in your hair.'

If there was one thing I did not want to draw attention to, it was my red hair. Against the dark looks of the McCarthys it stands out something rotten. Still, there was nothing I could do about it now. 'Ta,' I smiled at her. 'So, are we off now?'

'But where's your coat?' Mam looked horrified. 'You can't go out in just trousers and a light top.'

I held up my black jacket.

'That's too light. You can't wear that. Look,' she held open the front door, 'look at that for rain!'

'Well, it's all I have.'

'You'll catch a nasty cold if you don't put on something a bit heavier.'

'You can't catch a cold from the wet, Mam.'

'Indeeden you can.' Mam looked sternly at me. 'Didn't my own sister, your Auntie Olive, die from getting wet one summer? If she had only dried herself when she came back from the blackberry-picking she would have survived but she thought she knew better.'

'Mam, don't be ridiculous, no one would—'

17

'Coat,' Mam said imperiously.

You just did not argue with her when she spoke like that.

We arrived ten minutes late because no coat I had was warm enough for braving the Corkonian weather. In the end, I'd been forced to wear a see-through raincoat of my mother's. Can you imagine the embarrassment of arriving into a party in a see-through raincoat in front of all your sniggering cousins?

'Nice one, Vic,' Tommy, the most obnoxious of Aunt J's brood, called out when he saw me. 'Is that the fashion now?'

A laugh. At my expense. As usual.

Well, I'd had it with him.

'This?' I pointed to the coat. Nodded. 'Oh yeah.'

He looked a bit thrown. I think it was because I normally ignore him.

I made a big deal of taking the coat off as if every squeaky, sweaty inch of it was precious. 'Is there somewhere safe I can hang it?'

Now they were all gawking at me. Mam and Dad had gone to wish Aunt J a Happy Christmas. 'Well?'

'I'll take it,' Lydia, the youngest cousin, said breathlessly. 'I'll hang it in my room.'

'Be sure and keep it away from fibres,' I told her sternly. 'It tends to pick them up very easily and it'll ruin the line.'

'Sure.' Lydia, who was only ten, walked with great importance out of the room.

'My arse that's the fashion,' Tommy said, grinning.

'Big arses are becoming fashionable all right,' I told him pleasantly.

He laughed.

'And how's Vicky?' Aunt Julia's voice rose as she spotted me. 'Come over and talk to me, child, I haven't seen you in so long.'

I joined my folks at her side, relieved to be getting away from the cousins.

'You've got bonnier,' Aunt Julia said.

18

I presumed she meant I'd put on weight. Aunt Julia had a knack for cloaking her insults in the thick velvet of compliments.

'Hasn't she,' my mother cooed.

Thanks a lot, I wanted to say.

'You've got older,' I said to Julia. And she had. She didn't look as straight-backed as the last time I'd seen her.

Give her credit, she laughed. 'I have, just like yourself,' she smiled. 'Sure aren't we all getting on?'

'Mmm.'

'And how's the job? Your dad tells me you're still in the toy shop.'

'Yep.'

'*Managing* the toy shop, Julia,' Dad said.

'Isn't that nice.' Julia clapped her hands. 'A manager in the family. Your Uncle Ted was a manager.'

'Was he?'

'He was. Very responsible job. Tommy is a manager too.' She shot a smile over at her vile son. 'He manages some kind of big corporation, I don't know all the details.'

'Well, Vicky has her foot on the corporate ladder now,' Dad said, beaming. ''Twon't be long before she's climbing to the top.'

'Aw,' Tommy joined us, 'so that's why she needs the big rain-coat!'

Mam and Dad stared, puzzled, at him.

Aunt Julia tittered. She laughs at him no matter what he says. 'Nothing wrong with a good warm coat,' she said then.

'Nothing at all!' Tommy grinned at me.

I didn't smile back. 'I'll just go get a drink.'

'You do that,' Julia said. 'And after the food, sure maybe you'll give us a song?'

It wasn't a request, it was an order.

I hoped that I could get good and drunk before that happened.

The caterers cleared away the food, pulled Aunt J's table over to the edge of the room and we all sat down to await whatever was going to happen next. There were about thirty of us all cramped together around the table. Everyone was getting relaxed and stories of family outings and family disasters were being swapped. Drink was being swilled down and Tommy and a few of the cousins had started up a game of Twister in another part of the house. Their laughter could be heard all over the place.

'You should go and join them,' Mam whispered to me. 'They sound as if they're having a good time.'

I didn't answer. Up in Dublin, I'd have had no problem making an eejit out of myself in front of a group of people, but here, well, I just couldn't. I know they all thought I was a dry shite and to be honest, I probably was. I just felt so self-conscious in front of them all.

'Vicky's not going anywhere,' Julia said, a bit drunkenly. 'She's going to sing for me. She promised.'

I was hoping she'd have forgotten. 'Well,' I muttered, 'I didn't *exactly* promise.'

'But you will,' Uncle Dan, Dad's brother, grinned at me. 'You know how Julia loves a good song.'

A chorus of 'oh yes' followed and a few bits of clapping and then a cheer arose. I had no option but to get unsteadily to my feet.

'Smile,' Mam hissed at me. 'You look so much nicer when you smile.'

I dunno if the grimace that made its way across my face could have been construed as a smile but I did my best.

A song had to be decided upon.

'Raglan Road' was picked. It's basically a Patrick Kavanagh poem set to music. Luke Kelly of the Dubliners did a great job of it. It was a sad song, full of loss and longing, and I loved it but I hated singing it.

'Up there now, good girl.'

'Give it a belt, there's the girl.'

'Aw, she's a great singer is our Vicky.'

The last from my dad who was well gone.

A big 'shushing' campaign began in earnest as I began to sing.

I was a bit shaky on the first verse but by the middle of the second, I'd forgotten about the whole lot of them. There is something about that song that wraps me up and carries me away. I sang about the queen of hearts making her tarts while I wasn't even making hay, I sang about the snare set by the dark-headed woman and the fact that it didn't matter. Nothing mattered except love.

When the final note died there was a silence. The cousins had even stopped playing their game of Twister to listen. They were all looking at me, looking at me as if I was some weirdo in their midst.

Tommy broke the spell. Turning away from me, he asked loudly, 'Who's on red? Come on, who's the bastard on red?'

That shocked everyone. 'Language, Tomas,' Julia hissed sternly.

Tommy winked at her and she 'tisked' him. Then one of Uncle Dan's lads admitted to being the bastard on red and the Twister game started up again.

Aunt Julia turned from him and smiled at me. Pressed her hand into mine. 'Lovely,' she whispered. 'That was lovely.'

'Ta.'

'Where did you get that voice?' Uncle Dan chortled. 'And the rest of the family like rusty gates every time they open their mouths.'

A laugh.

A bloody laugh.

I don't know if it was the drink or the sheer hell of always being different that finally got to me but I said, really loudly, 'I dunno where I got my voice, Dan. I don't bloody know.'

Then I left the room.

Apparently the party died soon after that. I don't know because I left the house, minus my see-through rain jacket, and just walked and walked and walked. I don't know where I went, I

21

don't even know if I got wet, all I know was that I'd had it with pretending. I'd had it with trying to be a daughter when nothing about me matched with anything about them.

I did love my parents. I couldn't but love them. But I owed it to myself to find my place in the world. To find out where I belonged. To find out where I got my voice from.

I owed it to myself to find my mother.

Chapter Four

'THAT WASN'T A very nice way to treat your Auntie Julia last night,' Mam chastised me the minute I got up. She laid a plate in front of me and asked, 'Toast?'

'Pardon?' My head was banging. My eyes had sandpaper under the lids and all I wanted to do was to get back to the flat I shared with Sal and forget about here for another while.

'I asked if you wanted toast.' Mam quirked her eyebrows. '*And* I also said that leaving Julia's party was very rude of you. *And* as for the way you snapped at Dan, I don't know!' She shook her head and shoved some bread into the toaster. 'You've been very edgy since you arrived. I should have known you were in bad form when you started drinking the whiskey the other morning.'

'Oh for God's sake, Mam, I had a whiskey because it was Christmas!'

'Really.' She sounded as if she didn't believe me. 'And why did you leave Julia's party, so?'

Silence.

'Because,' I bit my lip, 'I just felt like it.'

'You felt like it!' She put her hands on her hips and glared at me. I can honestly say it was the first glare she'd ever given me in the whole of my life. 'Well, you ruined it for us all, do you know that?'

'No.' I stared sullenly at my plate.

'Your dad was worried sick about you. He and Tommy went out in the car looking for you.'

'I'm a big girl, Mam, I don't need people looking for me. Especially not that big cejit!'

'Don't you dare call your father that!'

'I meant Tommy!'

'Oh.'

She didn't say much more after that, just went around making too much toast and too much tea. I ate about ten slices while she began tidying up the kitchen. From outside, the sound of cattle being brought back out into the fields could be heard. The rain was falling, hitting off the kitchen window and making the world appear all grey and sullen. A bit like me, actually. Thank God I was leaving that evening. I figured that I'd tell them just as I was going out the door; that way there'd be no scene, no begging me to reconsider, no well-meant advice.

I was just finishing up the last slice of toast when Dad came in, banging his boots on the step and clapping his hands together to get them warm. 'Aw,' he winked over at me, 'there she is, The Wanderer!'

I smiled briefly and ignored Mam as she crashed a cup into the dishwasher.

'So where did you go?' Dad asked. 'Tommy and I drove up and down the road looking for you.'

'She just felt like leaving,' Mam said then, sounding more exasperated than annoyed. 'Can you believe that?'

'I can,' Dad nodded. 'Sure I've often felt like it myself, only I'd never have the nerve. You're like me like that, Vic,' he grinned. 'Not the one for the big family thingamajigs!'

That did it. In my head, somewhere, I knew he was just trying to cajole Mam into better form. But every other part of me refused to co-operate. It was like, I dunno, a red mist across my real self, and stuff that I'd buried for years erupted from somewhere inside me. 'I am not like you!' I remember that I stood up. I remember the look of shock on his face. But even that didn't stop me. 'I *can't* be, don't you see?' I glared at the two of

24

them. 'You didn't *have* me. You didn't carry me inside you. All that I am, I owe to someone I don't even know!'

Silence.

Mam moved towards Dad. He was still staring, shocked at me.

'Can you imagine how that makes me feel?' I took a step nearer them, trying, I suppose, to make them understand. 'I don't know where I come from. I don't know if I get my curly hair from him or her or my grandfather or maybe an aunt or someone. I don't know if she can sing like me. I don't know if she's small like me or stupid like me or—'

'You are not stupid,' Mam spoke up, loudly. 'Don't say that.'

'And all that you are you owe to us.' Dad spoke in a hard voice. 'We're the ones who' – he gulped and put his arm about my mam – 'we're the ones who kissed you and cuddled you and let you sleep in our bed when you had nightmares as a kid. We're the ones—'

'I know. I know.' I paused. This wasn't coming out right at all. In fact, I hadn't planned on saying it like that. I took a slow breath in and said levelly, 'I know what you mean, Dad, and I am grateful for it. I am. But—' I paused, gulped, tried to think of a way to explain and only ended up with, 'but I have this need to know where I come from – don't you see? I've been thinking about it for ages.'

And I had, I realised. I'd just never admitted it to myself.

'You want to find your birth mother?' Mam spoke softly. 'Is that it?'

I took a look at her soft face and wanted to hug her for saying it for me. 'I *need* to find her.'

They took a moment to digest this.

'It's just to see where I fit in,' I explained, trying not to show how desperate I felt because I didn't want to hurt them. They had never understood my square peg attitude. 'I can never fit in anywhere until I know where I come from.'

Dad thought it was bullshit. I saw it in the way he raised his eyes. But Mam surprised me by catching my hand in hers and squeezing it. 'You're right, Vic. Everyone needs that.' Her voice wobbled a bit. 'You do what you have to do. We'll help if we can. If it makes you happy, then do it.'

'Thanks.' I squeezed her back. Turning to Dad I gave a hesitant smile. 'Dad?'

'You're loved here,' he said, folding his arms and glaring at the two of us. 'That's all I know.'

'I know that,' I said.

'And this is your home.'

I didn't reply to that. Trouble was, it had never felt that way. 'It won't make a difference to how I feel about you both,' I said. Jesus, this was getting a bit sloppy. 'I mean, you'll still get on my nerves and all.'

At least they laughed.

Even if they didn't feel like laughing.

The rest of the day dragged. Conversation was stilted. They didn't know what to say to me and I didn't know how to bridge this distance that had suddenly sprung up between us. It was like all of a sudden they realised that I'd grown up. That I was making my own decisions.

Dad was the worst; he didn't even come to the door to wave me off when Sal collected me, saying that he had to check on the cattle.

Mam walked me to the door, her arm on my elbow. 'You'll ring when you get home?' she asked.

'Uh-huh.'

'You know how I worry with Sally driving.'

'Uh-huh.'

'And about that other thing, I meant what I said. We'll help you in any way we can. Just tell us what information you need and I'll dig it out.' A smile. 'We only want you to be happy, Victoria.'

She always called me Victoria when she was really upset.

'Thanks, Mam.'

A hug.

Then she was gone.

Sal was blasting the horn for all it was worth and making gestures at me to hurry up. And like I said before, when Sal says to hurry, you hurry.

Chapter Five

S AL AND I go back a long way. We met in primary school; she was the sulky kid with the plaits and the 'I-hate-teacher' attitude. I was the awkward, thick-at-maths kid with the 'I-hate-school' attitude. We hit it off straight away and spent our time dreaming up weird and wonderful ways to earn our living once school was over for ever. Secondary school was spent smoking fags and eyeing up the lads. Sal always scored every Friday night at the discos while I wilted like the wallflower I was beside her. I soon learned to spend the slow sets in the loo doing my hair.

To everyone's surprise, including my own, I managed to get enough points in my leaving to do Arts at UCD while Sal, to my surprise, got Journalism in Rathmines. Mam and Dad spent a blissful year boasting about their student daughter while I slowly went mad in a grotty bedsit listening to all the other students rave on and on about how much they loved the student life. In the end, I told Mam and Dad that I couldn't seem to hack it and that maybe some travel would broaden my mind. I got a loan from the bank, then worked my way around most of the world. It was the best and the worst time in my life. Great because I was finally free, horrible because I didn't find anywhere I really wanted to be. So, after five years, I came home to try and find work and pay off my loan.

I've had a selection of jobs culminating in the managership of Toys Galore. And for the first time ever, I really loved being somewhere. It's great seeing kids coming in with their parents, looking for something to buy and going out with smiles plastered to their faces. Or seeing kids choosing presents for their mates, or brothers buying for sisters.

It's dead nice.

And I love toys. Not just dolls and teddies, but everything. The Meccano sets, the wrestlers, the swings and slides.

It's such a happy place to be.

I didn't tell Sal about my decision to look for my mother. It's not that she doesn't know I'm adopted, I think the whole of Cork knows, it's just that Sal doesn't know what to keep to herself and what to blab to everyone else. I guess it comes from working in tabloid land for a living – any bit of news is money in her pocket. Anyway, I decided, there was no point in telling her anything unless I'd actually got something to tell her.

A search wasn't exactly major news.

For the time being, I vowed, I'd find out how to start my search.

It'd be my New Year's resolution.

Chapter Six

'So,' SAL ASKED, the day after New Year's, 'any New Year resolutions?'

Her question startled me, though I have to admit it wasn't entirely unexpected. I'm a great one for the NY's resolutions. I gave a sort of a giggle. 'Resolutions?' I said it as if the thoughts of making some had never even occurred to me. 'Nope. None. I'm not bothering with that this year. In fact, my resolution is not to make any resolutions.' I made a big deal of zipping up my anorak and wrapping my scarf around my neck. I was due into work in an hour.

'Really?' Sal sounded surprised. 'Wow.'

'Yep.' I couldn't look at her. 'Resolutions are a load of crap.'

'They are for you, aren't they?' Sal said matter-of-factly. 'I mean, what was it you were going to do last year? Learn to drive or something, wasn't it?'

'Dunno.'

'And didn't you crash your dad's car and didn't the driving school tell you not to do your test?'

They'd practically *begged* me. 'I'd better go.' I shoved my scarf into my jacket. 'Bye.'

'And you've none this year?'

'I dunno why you're so interested in—'

'Tell you what mine is,' Sal interrupted, lighting up a fag. 'I'm going to be full-time on *Tell!* before the year is out.'

'That's good.' *Tell!* was a magazine that Sal sometimes free-lanced for. A downmarket version of *Hello!*, their whole budget

was spent on writing titbits on the jet set. No one was safe –
that was their slogan. Along with 'If you tell it, we'll sell it!' Sal
did the odd piece for them and got paid handsomely for it.

Her real job, and one she loathed, was working for a local
paper. She was their head reporter and, as such, got the plum
interviewing jobs – she'd done pieces on the local parade being
cancelled due to the mayor having food poisoning, or the local
boy making good in England, or about the joy of having a
twenty-first in the local pub. I thought it was an OK job myself
– all she had to do was sit at a desk and make phone calls or
travel to an interview and claim expenses. But according to Sal,
there was no buzz in it, no thrill of the kill.

She was mental.

'And what's more,' she went on, holding her fag aloft, 'I'm
gonna marry someone rich and famous and they'll buy the magazine for me.'

'And are pigs gonna fly as well?'

'Bitch!' She picked up her cigarette packet and fired it at me
but I managed to leg it out the door before it hit the wall.

It pissed rain all the way from the bus stop to the shop – about
twenty minutes' walk. My scarf, being the vibrant spirit that it
was, unwrapped itself from my neck and danced away down
the street. I just could not be arsed chasing after it, especially
as the rain had managed somehow to invade my waterproof
trainers and I was literally squishing along. My hair, which I'd
blow-dried that morning, frizzed out all over the place. My hair
does that in the rain, believe it or not. In fact, I can actually tell
when rain is on the way because my hair begins to get fuzzy in
advance. On top of all this, my anorak, which was an expensive one, but unfortunately a suede one, got completely and
utterly ruined.

I arrived into work in very bad form.

As you can imagine.

Bridie was there. She always gets in before me. When I first

31

started work, I actually had suspicions that she was sleeping in the place because no matter how early I'd be, Bridie would be there, sitting in her favourite chair and nursing a cup of tea. It was kind of spooky actually. Every morning it was the same, she'd look up at me as I came in, her brown eyes smiling, and say, 'Hello, Vicky, the kettle's boiled,' and scurry around fetching me biscuits and making sure I was looked after.

Groundhog Day for ten minutes every morning.

That day, though, she excelled herself. She made me take off my shoes and socks and put them by the heater. Then she made me tea and told me to drink it up nice and slowly and to relax and get dry.

'You'll catch a cold by getting wet,' she clucked.

I smiled to myself. She was so like my mother that that was scary too.

We sat in silence for a few minutes, her sipping and me sniffing.

'So,' she smiled, 'did you have a good New Year?'

'All right,' I admitted. 'Nothing major.'

'So you didn't go home?'

'Naw, I usually just go home for Christmas.' I didn't want to elaborate. 'You?'

'Oh. You know me,' she looked at her hands, 'I like the quiet life.'

Bridie was the only woman I knew who'd suit being dead. She did absolutely nothing. As far as I could gather, she never went anywhere or had any friends. I sort of felt sorry for her so I always asked her to go for a drink on Friday nights after work. Not that she ever took me up on the offer. 'So what did you do?' I asked. 'Throw yourself a party?'

She laughed at that, a sort of gentle laugh to herself. Bridie laughs at a lot of the stuff I say, which is nice. 'I suppose I did,' she smiled. 'I sat in and watched RTE counting down and then when it was midnight I went to bed.'

'Right.'

I'd gone to a club with Sal and a few of her pals, drunk too much, sang 'Auld Anis Ine' in the middle of O'Connell Street to lots of applause and then got a taxi home.

'Now' – Bridie stood up and I winced as her legs creaked and popped – 'I'll open up. We shouldn't have too many in today, God willing. You stay there and get dry. God knows, we can't afford for either of us to be sick.'

'Ta, Bridie.'

I watched her shuffle out of the room and heard her go out into the main shop and begin unlocking the doors. It was a bit of a nuisance all right, just the two of us. I'd been on to Albert O'Neill, the owner, to get me a third member of staff but he'd snorted and said something about me getting a boyfriend if I wanted to dominate any more people.

I have to say, I was offended at that.

Bridie told me not to worry. 'He's a bit of a moody man,' she said. And I guess she should know, having worked for him for almost thirty years. So I took it on the chin and didn't ask for any more staff after that. I just made myself unavailable whenever he rang looking for me, telling Bridie to say that I was dealing with deliveries or on my lunch.

He could wait, I decided, until I was ready to talk to him. My unavailability would show how busy I was.

And it worked, only not exactly in the way I'd expected.

Chapter Seven

'BRIDIE, WILL YOU go down and keep an eye on the shop, I've, eh,' I indicated the phone, 'to make a call about a delivery.' My face got all hot. I've never been the greatest fibber in the world.

'A delivery?' Bridie frowned. 'Which one would that be now? All our deliveries are coming in Friday.'

I searched my mind for an order. Blank.

'Just one of the Friday ones.' I gave a false smile. 'Have to confirm it.'

'The Barbie one?'

'That one, yeah.'

'I already did it.' Bridie beamed at me. 'I *told* you that.' She gave a bit of a laugh, took another bite out of her egg sandwich and shook her head fondly. 'Honestly, I don't know what's happened you – you haven't been yourself since Christmas.'

'I need to confirm it again.' I kept my voice firm. Jesus, Bridie was way too efficient. 'Please go and keep an eye on the shop, will you?'

She looked a bit put out at that. She replaced her sandwiches in her brown paper bag and, standing up, dusted down her tweed skirt. 'I'm on my lunch,' she muttered. 'It's a terrible thing when you can't even enjoy your lunch.'

'You can come back up once I've made the call.'

'Can't you make it from the shop?'

'No. It's busy. I'll be disturbed.'

Still muttering, Bridie slipped her feet into her spongy shoes and shuffled out the door, clutching her sandwiches in her hand. She'd have no time to eat them; the place was beginning to buzz down there.

Once I was sure she was out of earshot, I closed the door and took a slip of paper from my pocket and dialled the number scrawled across it. Well, tried to dial – my fingers were shaking so much that I mis-dialled twice. When eventually the phone did begin to ring at the other end, my heart started to jack-hammer. I closed my eyes and told myself that what I was doing was no big deal. Thousands of people had done it before. It didn't help. I thought I was going to be sick. What, I wondered, would I be like when I'd actually contacted my mother, if this was the state I was in before I'd actually done anything. I sat weakly down on the chair and waited for my call to be answered.

'Hello. Adoption Board. How can we help you?'

I froze. Completely.

'Hello?'

I wanted to hang up. I was on the verge of putting the receiver back into its cradle when it hit me. If I hung up now, I'd have to make the call at another time. Next week, next month, next year – it didn't matter, I'd have to do it eventually.

'Adoption Board?' the woman spoke again. 'Hello?'

'Hello?' I could barely get the word out, my voice had gone all shaky.

'What can we do for you?'

She sounded so efficient.

'Well . . .' I licked my lips, clenched the phone tighter to my ear. Jesus, I hadn't thought this out at all. 'I'm, er, adopted.'

'Yes?'

Polite interest.

'And, well, I, eh, want to trace my parents.'

Saying it was weird. It made me realise that this was what I'd wanted since I was twelve. All my life, I'd felt as if something was missing and this was it. 'I'd like to trace my birth parents,' I said again.

'I'll put you through to someone,' the lady said, and there was a sudden silence on the line.

More heart hammering.

More clenching the phone really tight.

'Hello?'

And so I began again, slightly more confidently.

'OK,' the man at the other end said, 'well, the first thing you need to do is to formally request, in writing, details of your birth mother.'

'OK. Do I write to yous?'

'No. Write to your placement agency.'

'Sorry? My what?'

'The placement agency – the agency you were adopted from.'

'Oh.' Who the hell were they?

'Your adoptive parents should know it,' the man said, as if reading my mind, 'and if not, we can find out for you.'

'Oh. OK.' Jesus, it'd mean a call to my mother. I wasn't sure if I wanted to do that. I hadn't really talked to them since Christmas.

'When you know where to write,' the man continued, 'you can request two types of information. Non-specific information is the first type. That can be given out very quickly. That includes the name of your birth mother, the place—'

A *name*. I could find out her name. Even that would mean something.

'—up to two years—'

'Sorry, I didn't catch that last bit.' There was a huge chunk in the middle I didn't catch either but I hadn't the nerve to admit it.

'I said that it can take up to two years to trace a birth parent.'

'Two years?' No way.

'People move on,' he said gently, as if sensing my shock. 'Some people might not want to be found.'

'Really?' My voice was small. 'Would that be normal, like?'

The guy's answer was drowned out by the sound of the door

36

crashing open and a booming northern voice yelling, 'I hope you're giving the delivery boys hell, Vicky!' A slap on my back that almost shattered my entire spine. A large, vulgar, expensively dressed man plonked himself onto the seat on the other side of my desk and, spreading fleshy lips, gave me the benefit of his white and gold smile.

How the hell had Albert O'Neill managed to come into the shop without my hearing him? There was no way I could continue my phone conversation now. I cut the nice man off midflow at the other end of the line. 'Well, thank you for your time,' I said, in as crisp a voice as I could, 'I'll have something into you soon.'

'As the bishop said to the altar boy!' Albert gave me a lewd wink, then he laughed. It sounded as if a car bomb had gone off in the street.

I gave a bit of a laugh too as I replaced the phone and folded up the paper I'd been doodling on. The words 'placement agency' were scrawled across it. Shoving the paper into my pocket, I stood up from the desk and held out my hand. 'Hi, Mr O'Neill – Happy New Year.'

'And to you too, Victoria,' he grinned, pumping my arm up and down. It was like shaking hands with a wet dishcloth. 'And to you too.' He let my hand drop and I had to stop myself from wiping it down my jeans.

Albert O'Neill is my boss. Mine and about five thousand other people's. He's one of the most successful businessmen in the country. Probably one of the most successful businessmen in Europe, seeing as how he has toy shops in France, Spain and Italy. He's loud and crude and from all accounts keeps himself fit by chasing women. As far as I could see, he'd be very fit because if they'd any sense, they'd be running very fast in the opposite direction. The man was a horror. Fat. Wobbly in all the wrong places, with a dyed black head of hair on him that was thinning quicker than the ozone layer.

'So' – I gave what I hoped was a businesslike smile. It was

best to play it cool with him – 'to what do Bridie and I owe the pleasure?'

'The pleasure is all mine,' he chortled.

I made a superhuman effort not to look alarmed. 'Oh, now!'

'I have news that should make you both very happy,' O'Neill said, crossing towards me.

'Really?'

'Oh yes. You know how I like to put a smile on my employees' faces.'

I did know and that was why I decided to try and make an exit. 'I'll just get Bridie and tell her that—'

'Stay here!' The order was sharp. The jovial smile was gone. 'I'm telling you, you're the manager. You can pass the news on to Bridie later.'

'Oh, oh, right.' I shrugged, moved back into the office. 'I just thought Bridie—'

'You'll have a new member of staff from next Monday.'

'Sorry?' I thought I'd misheard.

'I said, you'll have a new staff member from next week.' O'Neill shoved his hands into his trouser pockets and gave himself a good scratch. 'Isn't that what you wanted?'

'Well, yes—' I tore my eyes away from his trousers. 'Yes,' I said in a stronger voice, 'that's, that's great. Thanks very much.'

Scratch. Scratch. Scratch. 'Oh, now don't ever say I don't listen to my staff.'

'I'd never say that.'

'Now,' O'Neill went on, 'he won't have much experience.'

'Oh, well, we can train him in.'

'Good.' O'Neill smiled and, his itching over, he began patting down his black hair. 'Work him hard. Make use of him.'

'Definitely.' I allowed him a genuine smile. 'Another staff member is just what we were looking for.'

'I'll be checking up on him from time to time, making sure he's pulling his weight.'

'Aw, well, I'm sure—'

'No son of mine is going to get away with shoddy work.'

'Who? Sorry?'

'My son,' O'Neill nodded grimly. 'Your new employee.'

With that he shook my hand again, his sweaty palm making me cringe, and left the office, booming out his goodbyes to Bridie, who was too awestruck to reply.

I had to sit down.

I could not believe it.

I could not believe that I was going to be stuck with his son as an employee.

For one thing, if he was as bad as his da, I'd spend more time avoiding his advances than actually working and, even worse, what happened if he was totally crap? I could hardly fire him now, could I?

Jesus.

Sal was agog. 'His son?'

'Yep.' I broke open a can of Bud – that was how pissed off I felt. I had made it a rule, some time ago, only to drink at weekends, but I hadn't envisioned this scenario. I deserved a drink. 'His son is coming to work in our toy shop.'

'Wow!' Sal rolled her eyes. 'He's probably loaded – Jesus, if you played your cards right, Vic, you could get in there.'

'Sal, I don't want to get in anywhere. All I want to do is run the shop and I won't be able to do it with the bloody boss's son breathing down my neck.'

'And I thought you said you didn't want to get in anywhere!' Sal rolled her eyes and grinned broadly. 'Jesus, old biddy Bridie will be getting pretty steamed up with that kind of carry-on.'

I had to laugh. 'Stop it!'

Sal turned back to her laptop. 'That's what you'll be saying all right,' she said, still grinning. 'Well, if you're lucky that is!'

Lucky my arse. 'You have not seen the holocaust that is his dad,' I fired back. 'If he's anything like him I—'

'Hey!' Sal interrupted me. 'D'you know something, I think

I've a picture of your boss and his family in a back issue of *Tell!* In fact, I'm sure I have!' She almost knocked over her laptop as she legged it into her bedroom. 'Back in a sec.'

Sal has a great memory for all things celeb. She knows who's married to who, who's living with who, who's having affairs with who. She knows all the members of the royal family and for some reason she has a mad fixation on Dustin Hoffman. The *South Dublin Journal* really didn't use her talents at all. It was no wonder she wanted to be a *Tell!* girl.

I had just opened another can of Bud when she arrived back, waving the magazine about. 'It's this one, I'm sure of it.' She started flipping rapidly through the pages. 'I remember we did a big toy special just before Christmas on the most expensive toys to buy and your boss, I'm positive it was him, agreed to pose for a photo with his family.'

'And he didn't shatter the camera?'

'You are bloody cruel, so you are.' Sal was busy flicking. Then, a sort of recoil before she muttered, 'Ugh, I see what you mean.'

She'd found the page and there, sure enough, was Albert posing with his wife and son. It was under an article entitled *Toys Galore* and it showed Albert and his family in the middle of lots of expensive gear. Albert was dressed casually in a blue shirt and jeans. A stupid Santa hat was perched on his head and it looked as awkward on him as a pair of underpants would on a naturist. Beside him sat his wife, her hand in his. She was a dark, not unattractive, anxious-looking woman. She wore a ridiculously expensive dress.

'John Rocha,' Sal said, drooling. 'It's wasted on her, isn't it?'

In front of the two of them, cross-legged on the ground, was Albert Junior. He was dark like his mother, but he was big like his dad. Big and surly, as if nothing in life made him laugh. There was nothing redeemable in his features at all. In fact, he looked downright scary.

'Mmm,' Sal muttered, screwing up her perfect face, 'maybe it's a bad photo.'

'No maybe about it,' I said.

Sal gawked more closely at the picture as if somehow that would make it morph into something nicer.

'Can you imagine that guy working in a toy shop?' I asked. 'I mean, he'll scare the kids away.'

'I'm more interested in trying to imagine him in bed,' Sal said. 'I mean, looks don't matter in the dark, do they?'

'I'm not interested.'

'Yeah, but I am.' Sal smiled cockily at me. 'You never know, I could call into you one day looking for an intro.' She studied the photo again and groaned. 'Aw damn – he's RFP.'

Ring finger positive.

'Now,' she said, 'isn't that just a bummer?'

Chapter Eight

B RIDIE WAS DRIVING me mad. She thought it was wonderful that O'Neill's son was coming to work with us. 'I'll just go and dust the shelves at the back of the shop,' she twittered, scrimmaging under the counter and locating the feather duster that hadn't been used in my whole eight months as manager. 'It wouldn't do to show ourselves up.'

'He's not a health inspector, Bridie,' I said, grinning. 'He's not going to be interested in the state of our shelves.'

Bridie looked as me as if I'd just crawled out of the swamp. 'He'll be the owner of those shelves one day,' she nodded, 'so he'll want to see that we have respect for them.'

'Respect for a shelf?' I rolled my eyes. 'Suit him better if he's got respect for us.'

'He will if we keep the shop nice.'

And with that gem of pointless logic, off she went, as fast as her legs would let her.

I began flicking through a toy catalogue while all the time she shouted bulletins on her progress.

'Spiders as big as rats!'

'What? As big as O'Neill?'

A shocked silence for a few seconds, then a small titter. 'Oh, Vicky, you are awful. You'll have to stop saying those things when the son comes!'

I allowed myself a grin. Bridie was old school. She simply did not give out about 'the boss' or 'the job' or about anything really. As far as she was concerned, you did your job and got your pay and anything else was a bonus. The manager she'd had before me must have been a slave driver. Bridie had almost fallen off her chair the first morning I arrived and suggested that maybe it'd be nice to have a tea break in the middle of the morning. Then when I'd suggested one after lunch too, she'd shaken her head. 'You take one if you want,' she'd said uneasily, 'but I'll keep working.' So I had to keep working too. Bridie was too conscientious by half. I sometimes wondered who was managing who.

'I'm going to give those shelves a bit of a wash,' Bridie called out. 'A bit of washing-up liquid will do wonders for them.'

'You don't need to do that.' Honestly, I was beginning to feel guilty at her activity. Half afraid too that she'd want me to help her. I hated cleaning at the best of times.

Bridie emerged, flushed, from the back of the shop. 'I do so. You haven't *seen* those shelves. Honestly, they're begging for a good scrubbing.'

'I don't think anyone will notice, Bridie.'

'You young people' – Bridie flapped her hand, reminding me of my mother – 'you *don't* clean so that people will notice. It's about having pride in things.'

'Mmmm.'

'My house, now, I do my windows, inside and out, at least once a week. I hoover every evening when I go home. My brass, now, I do that—'

'Sorry, your what?'

'My brass.'

'You have a special day for washing your bras?'

'*Polishing*, Vicky. You *polish* brass, you don't wash it. It'll tarnish that way.'

'Oh.' I grinned, suddenly realising my mistake.

Bridie continued. 'Brass needs special attention, I find. I always do it on a Monday, after the weekend.'

'Right. So your brass needs special attention after the weekend?'

43

'Yes.'

Lucky Bridie, I wanted to say, but didn't. A little respect, after all. 'Well, look, Bridie, you wash away – I just want to make a quick call, so if someone comes in, you'll look after them, will you?'

'I'll do my best.' She shook her head. 'Those shelves are very dirty.'

I ignored the hint and exited.

In my office, I dialled home. I'd been putting off the phone call all morning but the sooner the better. I told myself that I'd feel relieved when I'd done it.

Dad answered. His 'hello' sounded a bit flustered.

'Dad,' I said, 'it's me.'

Pause. 'Vicky, is it?'

'Yeah. Is anything wrong?'

A bit of a laugh. 'Wrong? No. Why?'

'You just sounded a bit, I dunno, flustered.'

'Well, I'm not,' he said adamantly. 'So, how's my girl? I heard from Sally's parents that you had a great night on New Year.'

'Yeah. Sal and I went to a club.'

'Lovely.'

He didn't mean that. He was always giving out about those *Ibiza Uncovered* programmes, convinced that they reflected life in the clubs of Dublin. If only it were true.

'So what is it you wanted? If it's a chat with your mother, she's not here.'

'Oh, right.' I paused. Bit the bullet. 'Well, maybe you can help me. I'm looking for the name of my placement agency.'

Silence.

'You know, the one where I was—'

'I do know what a placement agency is, Vicky.' His voice had gone all hard and I flinched.

'Oh, well, good. So . . . will you find out for me? It's just that I need—'

'Aaah, do you need to be doing all this, Vicky?' He attempted a laugh. 'I mean, what do you want to go dragging up the past for?'

I gulped. Blinked hard. 'I thought I explained this,' I mumbled. 'I just need—'

'You just need to cop on, that's what you need. There's no point in trying to find—'

'Well, Dad, I think there is.'

If I could have seen him, I reckon his face would have flushed and his hands begun clenching and unclenching. He always did that when he was threatened. Either that or tried to cajole someone to his point of view.

'You think there is,' he repeated slowly.

'Yes, Dad, I do.' My voice caught. I hadn't expected him to be like this. 'I don't want to hurt you, you know that, it's just—'

'I'll see what I can do,' he said abruptly. 'Now, is there any-thing else?'

Even if there was, I wouldn't have had the nerve. 'No. Just say hi to Mam for me.'

'Right.'

He didn't put down the phone.

Neither did I.

Both of us said 'well' together.

He began again. 'Well, bye-bye, Vicky.'

'Yeah. Bye.' Pause. 'And thanks, Dad.'

He mumbled something and hung up.

Chapter Nine

MY DAD DIDN'T contact me all weekend. And it wasn't that he couldn't have. He had my mobile number, my work number *and* the number of the communal phone in the hall of the apartments. He even had Sal's mobile number for some obscure reason. In fact, given the chance, he'd have had the contact numbers of everyone I knew. So for him not to ring was deliberate. I began to wonder if he'd even told Mam that I'd been in contact, but I decided to give him the benefit of the doubt at least until Tuesday. If I didn't hear from him by then, I'd get back on to him.

If I had the nerve.

'Ready?' Sal poked her head in my bedroom door. Long blonde hair, coloured that very day, fell across her face. She brushed it back impatiently and looked at me in exasperation. 'Jesus, Vic, what is the hold-up in here?'

I'd been sitting cross-legged on my bed, headphones shoved in my ears, listening to a CD I'd bought on the way home from work. Between the first track and the fourth, I'd painted my nails and attempted to blow-dry my hair. It hadn't been the most successful of efforts. My hair stuck out everywhere, but then again, it always did.

'You haven't even got dressed yet!' Sal glared at me. 'Mel is on her way over.'

'Sorry.' I jumped up from the bed, my Walkman clattering to the floor. Bits of fluff from the bedspread duly embedded themselves on my wet nails. 'Oh, shit!'

'We're not going to wait.' Sal gave me another of her expert glares and slammed the door.

I stuck my tongue out at the closed door and grumpily began to look through my wardrobe for some inspiration. There wasn't really much point. Sal always outshone me in the fashion stakes. Not that I was in competition with her or anything, it was just that even when I'd made a humongous effort, she still looked heaps better than me.

'Where are we going anyway?' I hoped it was a pub. I had jeans for that.

'Club Zero.'

Great. I morosely discarded the jeans. Club Zero was only the newest, trendiest place in town. It had been opened a month ago by some famous film star or other. Trust Sal to want to spend a Saturday night posing and flirting. I'd be far happier sitting in a pub, drinking a Bud and having a bit of craic. But unfortunately, if I didn't go out with Sal, all I'd be doing was watching TV and wondering if my folks were ever going to ring.

I began a search for trendy clothes. The first thing I found was a tiny black skirt hiding away at the back of the wardrobe. But the fake-tan issue reared its ugly head and I decided against it. A few minutes later, I located a pair of red jeans that I'd forgotten I had. They'd looked good on me the last time I'd worn them. Laying them on my bed, I began a search for a matching top. The only one I had was orange with a big red sun.

Red and orange.

Mmmm.

'Vic? I'm waiting!'

I dressed hastily. Well, as hastily as I could seeing as how I had to lie on the bed to pull my zip up. A cut finger later and I surveyed myself in the mirror. The colours didn't look too bad together actually. At speed, I braided my hair into two plaits to keep it in check and let the side bits fall down around my face. A pair of boots and I was set.

'Are you not wearing make-up?' Sal asked accusingly when I walked out.

'I wasn't sure I had the time,' I muttered. Mel hadn't yet arrived.

'You've always time to put on make-up.' Sal rolled her eyes. 'Honestly, Vic, we're not heading to a grotty little pub here.'

'Yeah. I know.'

'So, put on a bit of make-up, would you. Jesus, your skin is so pale they'll quarantine you when you arrive.'

Red-haired, pale-skinned, that was me. Sal on the other hand had a constant tan from spending all her free time on a sunbed. Her hair was bleached to a bright yellow and she looked every inch a 90210 babe. And, as usual, she'd outdone me in the clothes stakes. A pale blue miniskirt, white, tiny, tight top and powder blue slip-on shoes. Her hair tumbled down around her diminutive shoulders and just looking at her made me feel like a hick.

Who was I kidding? I *was* a hick.

I shoved on some foundation that instantly caked on my face. Yep, I'd forgotten the moisturising trick Sal had taught me. Still, at least I looked healthy. Some eye shadow and lipstick were also applied along with plenty of red blusher.

Mel buzzed up just as I finished.

Sal opened the door to her and there was lots of squealing and giggling and air-kissing. I dunno, maybe I'm just not girlie enough but to me that sort of stuff makes me laugh.

'Hiyaaaa, Vicky,' Mel cooed, waving all her fingers over at me. 'Ready for some fun?'

'She's only putting on her make-up.' Sal rolled her eyes. 'I had to tell her to do it.'

I smiled cheerily over at them.

Mel looked shocked. 'No. No way. You *forgot* to do your make-up?'

'I didn't forget,' I said. 'Sal wanted me to hurry up and it was a toss-up between getting dressed or doing my make-up. I

48

reckon I stood a better chance of getting into Club Zero with clothes on.'

Mel screeched with laughter. Sal tossed her blonde mane and managed to look disgusted. 'Come on, let's go. There'll be a queue a mile long if we don't hurry.'

There was a queue two miles long. Sal hopped from one foot to the other, trying to pretend she wasn't freezing. Mel pulled her fake fur around her and started to tell Sal all about her week in work. Mel worked on *Tell!*; Sal was carefully cultivating her friendship in the hope that it would lead somewhere.

'So,' Mel finished up a story about having champagne with Nicole Kidman at the premiere of some film, 'what did you work on this week? Any interesting pieces?'

She'd done a dead funny one about the rats in the local canal.

'Mmm. Some.' Sal managed a mysterious, casual shrug and changed the subject. 'How long will it take us to get in, do you think?'

'Ages,' I said.

She shot me a withering look.

'This is a great place' – Mel lowered her voice – 'all the celebs come here. Great for gossip too. It's worth waiting ages to get into.'

'Absolutely,' Sal nodded.

There was a silence. Sal took out a cigarette and lit it.

The queue moved forward another inch.

'They all call her Nic, you know,' Mel said then.

'Who?' Sal asked.

'Nicole Kidman,' Mel said. 'All her family.'

'Mine call me Vic,' I offered.

Mel guffawed.

Sal puffed a long stream of smoke into the air.

The queue moved forward a good bit.

'Nearly there,' Mel said.

We were about two feet from the top of the queue when one of the bouncers spotted Mel.

'Mel?' he said. 'Is it you?'

'Oooh!' Mel frightened the life out of both Sal and me by her squeal. She sounded like a pig in its final moments. 'Gregory! Hey, how *are* you.' Air-kiss. Air-kiss.

'You should have come straight to the top,' Gregory said. 'Come on in.'

'And my lovely friends too?' Mel asked.

'This way, ladies.' The bouncer gave Sal an appreciative look as she wiggled on past him.

He barely glanced at me.

Well, I thought, he wasn't worth looking at either.

Club Zero was gorgeous. Called Zero, I guess, because there was very little in it. Minimalist décor – all brushed steel and light wood. Most of the tables were taken when we got in but we managed to find one, right at the back of the room. A glass-topped table with steel legs. We sat on hard steel chairs and Mel offered to buy us all a first round.

Well, I presume she did; it was hard to hear over the music pumping out of the speakers.

'So, a Bud, a tequila and a Red Bull and vodka,' she shouted, taking her tiny, glittery purse out of her tiny, glittery bag. 'Back in a sec.'

Sal and I watched her totter off.

'Isn't this fab?' Sal was busy looking around. 'Honestly, Mel can get into some great places. That'll be me someday.'

I smiled. I had no doubt about it. Sal was a great writer. Her pieces for *Tell!* were hilarious.

'Oh, isn't that your man?' Sal sat up straight in her seat. 'The guy from that new boy band?'

'Where?'

'Just over your shoulder,' Sal said. 'Now don't look too – Jesus!'

I had done a complete swivel about and located the boy band member. He raised his glass to me and I grinned back.

'Did you have to make it so obvious?' Sal snarled when I

turned back. 'Honestly, Vic, you always do that. I tell you not to look and wham, you go and look.'

'Sure he doesn't care' – I shook my head – 'he thinks it's great being recognised.'

'Yeah, well, it's not exactly cool, is it, to go gawping at famous people?'

'Who cares about being cool?' I rolled my eyes. 'Sure we're only having a laugh.'

To prove my point, I turned back to boy band member and gave a little flirty wave.

'Jesus!' Sal glared at me.

It was just as well Mel arrived back with our drinks 'cause I think Sal would have stalked off in a huff. She was dead conscious about her image. I guess it was because she *had* an image. Maybe I did too, only I'm not too sure what mine was. I didn't care about keeping it either. All I wanted was a good time.

'Bottoms up,' Mel said, raising her glass. 'To the girls.'

Now, wasn't that a ridiculous toast?

To the *girls*?

Sal repeated it after her as if she'd just toasted world peace.

I clinked my bottle off their glasses and took a huge slug of Bud. They sipped decorously and draped themselves elegantly over their seats while I leaned elbows on the table to see if I could spot any more famous people.

There were piles of them. A few made their way to our table to talk to Mel. She 'darlinged' them to extinction. Then Sal shook their hands and gave her perfect smile. And giggled a lot. Then I did. Shook their hands, I mean. Then when they left, we all went back to drinking again while Mel explained what they were really like.

'He's mad,' Mel confided to us about one of the stars of a British soap. 'D'you know, on set he won't let anyone sit on his seat. And if anyone does,' she looked at us and whispered, 'he fires them.'

51

'Asshole,' I muttered.

Sal and Mel looked at me aghast.

'It's because he's *creative*,' Mel explained. 'Creative people are like that.'

'Well,' I raised my eyebrows, 'I've never met a *creative* asshole before. Sounds dead promising. Better than any of the fellas I've been with recently.'

Mel guffawed. Sal didn't.

I drank some more.

'Men are assholes, though, aren't they?' Mel said casually. 'At least all the ones I know are.'

'Except Lorcan,' I grinned.

Lorcan was Mel's really strange boyfriend.

'Yes,' Mel agreed, 'except Lorcs.'

I swilled my drink around. Listened to Sal and Mel tear their previous guys to shreds. I dunno what Sal was on about really. Most of the guys she went out with were mad about her. She always did the dumping.

I tended to do the dumping too. But that was because the guys I picked up were complete eejits. The ones that weren't eejits dumped me.

Wasn't that always the way?

'Who was your last fella?'

I became aware that their attention was focused on me. Obviously they'd spilled their emotional baggage.

'His name was Ron, wasn't it?' Sal said. 'Ron the Ride, that's what we called him.'

'Because he worked in Funderland,' I clarified to Mel, who was looking impressed. 'He operated the Bone Cruncher.'

'Lovely,' Mel winced.

'He offered to paint Vic's name on all the carriages, didn't he?' Sal giggled.

'Yep.' I rolled my eyes. 'I mean, can you imagine it – people puking up all over my name?'

Sal and Mel laughed.

I didn't. That suggestion had been the beginning of the end for us and thinking about it still hurt a bit.

'And he even—' Sal was preparing to divulge all the nitty-gritty details of my love life when she noticed that Mel wasn't paying attention any more. I was glad because I knew what she was going to say. And it wasn't Mel's business.

'Hey, Mel, what's up?'

Mel was smiling quietly to herself. She turned towards Sal and said 'Bingo' very quietly.

'Here?' Sal looked confused.

Then Mel looked confused.

Then both of them said, 'What?' together.

Then Sal said, 'What do you mean, "Bingo"?'

Mel 'tisked' as Sal looked contrite.

'See that gentleman over there,' Mel gave a discreet point.

I swivelled once again in my chair. 'The one in the—?'

'For goodness' sake.' Mel's hissed whisper caught me by surprise. This was ferocious. 'Will you just stay where you are!'

Sal glared at me.

'The man in the blue denim jacket and red shirt,' Mel said again to Sal.

'I see him.' Sal looked at her curiously. 'Why?'

Mel winked. 'Tell you Monday,' she said.

'Aw, Mel—'

'No,' Mel said, quite sharply, I thought. Then she flung a look at me.

Then Sal looked at me.

So I knew that whatever it was had to be top secret and that I was in the way.

'I can get out of your way if you want,' I offered.

'Monday,' Mel said, to Sal, ignoring me. 'Gimme a call.'

Sal's face lit up like Sellafield. 'Oh, great, yeah, sure.'

Then they both smiled at me.

'Here's to a great night,' Mel called another toast.

We clinked our drinks.

Chapter Ten

THE NIGHT GOT a bit weird from there. Weird for me, I mean. The way my nights out always tend to be.

It started off with my being abandoned by both Sal and Mel. Mel left to go chat with some weirdos wearing tablecloths and lampshades. There was a lot of drawling and 'Oh yaahing' from them. Along with the obligatory kisses.

Sal then decided to get closer to the red-shirted, denim-jacket man, so off she went to the bar and began to flirt with about half the place. She could bat for Australia. Bat her eyelashes, that is. Before long, she was chatting away to some hunk of testosterone at the bar. I could tell by the way she was touching him ever so casually that she was lining him up to pay for her drinks.

'Hey, you're looking kind of lonely, girl, do you need someone new to talk to?'

It was boy band member. He'd slid in beside me with just about the crappiest chat-up I'd ever heard. I sang back, deadpan, 'Oooh, oooh, I don't want to share the night together.'

Boy band winced. 'Ha!' He tried to make a joke of it. 'Wouldn't have had you down for a Doctor Hook fan.'

'I'm not.' I stared into my drink. Handsome eighteen-year-olds are not my idea of a good time. I was no cradle snatcher.

And besides, I wanted to go home. Now that Sal had decided to flirt, there wouldn't be a guy left in the place for me.

'Oh.' Boy band paused. Flicked his floppy red, gold and brown highlighted hair from his face. 'So you won't like our new single then. That's what we're doing. A cover of "Sharing The Night Together".'

'Great.' I managed to look as if I was pleased for him. 'Good luck with it.' Why on earth was he talking to me? There were plenty of nubile miniskirts his own age about.

He beamed at me. 'Ta.' Then, 'Are you famous or what?'

'Sorry?'

His baby blues studied me intently. 'Are you famous?' He gawked around him. 'I mean, most of the people in here are.' An impressed sigh. 'It's, like, mega, isn't it?'

'Mmm.'

'So?' he looked at me expectantly.

'Well, I can't be that famous – I mean, you don't know who I am, do you?'

Frown. 'We-ell, you look like yer one, you know, the one that does be in the films.' He nodded sagely. 'That's who I thought you were straight away.'

'What one in the films?' Despite myself, I was flattered.

'Yer one, the dark-haired one, what's her name?'

'Sandra Bullock?' I despised the hope in my voice.

He exploded with laughter. 'Naw.' He displayed his American-ised mouthful of teeth. 'She is *gorgeous*. I mean the other one.'

'The ugly one?' I couldn't help it. He'd walked himself into it now.

He missed my irony. 'Not *exactly* ugly.' His face crinkled up with the effort of thinking. 'She's sort of fat sometimes.'

'Oh. Right.' I was beginning not to want to know.

'Not Minnie Driver,' he said. 'You're not Minnie Driver, are you?'

'Nope. I'd be an Audi driver though, given half the chance.'

He laughed in such a way that I knew he didn't really find it funny. It was the sort of laugh that didn't know when to end, so it was all loud and hearty one minute and the next – nothing.

'OK.' He tried to make out that he was holding the chuckles in check. 'Yer wan I'm thinking of has a baby. Have you a baby?'

55

'Nope.'

'Oh.' His handsome face fell. 'So you're not her.'

''Fraid not.'

'So, who are you then?' He looked wonderingly at me.

'Victoria McCarthy.' I said my name as if it should mean something.

Blank. Then, 'Related to the Paul McCarthy?'

Yep. I had an obnoxious cousin called Paul. 'Uh-huh.'

'The singer?' Before I could answer, he said consideringly, 'Yeah, you do look like him, come to think of it.'

He couldn't be serious. I searched his face for some sign that there was a joke going on.

Nothing.

I leaned towards him, waved my glass. 'What's this you were saying about a new single?'

He took the hint. Asked me if I wanted a drink and promised that we'd talk as soon as he came back.

I almost felt guilty but then again, he'd thought I was a fat film star.

It didn't take long to realise that I had just met the thickest guy on the whole planet. If he'd been a magician, he'd have made a fortune because he could swallow everything. I guess I did know a bit about music but hey, I'd never sat in on a Lennon-McCartney recording session. In fact, I was a bit insulted that he thought I was that old. *And* I hadn't ever backed Leonard Cohen up in concert because one of his backing singers was sick. 'They're always pulling that one,' I said airily to him.

'Right,' he nodded, as if picking up life tips from the master. I don't actually think he knew who Leonard Cohen was.

And I honestly expected him to guess I was spoofing him when I told him that I'd once been in a Michael Jackson video.

I was the stand-in dancer.

For Michael.

'Hey,' he said instead, 'that must be where I recognise you from. I just, like, love that guy's videos.'

I'd done it now. Dug myself in so deep that there was no way I could get out without making an idiot of the kid.

And he was so innocent and accepting that I couldn't do that.

So I just kept digging.

His name was Cliff, after Cliff Richard. His hero was Ronan Keating and his favourite song was 'Uptown Girl' – the Westlife version. He was eighteen, had just reached number thirteen in the charts with his cover of 'Sharing The Night Together' and the other guys in his band were all former models. 'But they can sing,' he assured me.

'Great.'

Maybe I could escape to the loo and climb out a window? The guilt was killing me. I mean, I couldn't even look him straight in the face any more.

'So, maybe you'll tell Paul to look out for us?' he asked. His voice had gone a little breathless; the way voices do when they believe that Nirvana is just within reach.

'I don't talk to Paul that much,' I said. The look of devastation on his face prompted me to add, 'About once a month or so, so I'll mention it next time. All right?'

'Ace. Classy.' He nodded and grinned. 'Classy,' he said again. He offered to buy me another drink. 'A Bud, is it?'

'Aw, no.' I shook my head and stood up. There was no way in good conscience I could let him buy me another drink. It was best to get away from the kid now. I'd hide in the toilet until the place closed down or something. 'I'd better go.'

'Suppose you've got a big limo waiting for you,' he said wistfully.

'Nope. Just a plain old taxi,' I grinned.

'Oh, well hey' – he waved wildly at a guy across the room – 'let my manager give you a lift home. He drives us everywhere. Hey, hey, Marti!'

His manager!

'Marti, over here!'

'Aw, no, Cliff, I honestly—'

I saw Marti excusing himself from a group of people and coming towards us.

'Cliff, I'd better—'

Cliff smiled at me. 'Marti, Victoria McCarthy' – 'he stressed the McCarthy – 'wants a lift home. Will you give her one?'

It was on the tip of Marti's tongue to make a rude comment to that. Don't ask me how I knew, I just did. I blushed and he blushed and then we both began to grin.

'She knows Paul McCarthy,' Cliff said then. 'She's related to him.'

'Paul McCarthy?' Marti raised his eyebrows. 'Who the hell is that?'

Cliff looked embarrassed for his manager. 'The Beatles,' he hissed, poking him with his finger.

'That's McCartney,' Marti snorted. 'Jesus.'

Cliff's face dropped.

I smiled as best I could. 'Sorry.'

'And the Michael Jackson thing?' Cliff sounded wounded.

'Sorry,' I said again.

'And, yer man, Leonard Comb?'

'Cohen,' Marti snapped. 'Jesus.'

All I could manage was a 'ha'.

As Cliff slunk off, I was left with Marti.

The manager.

He stared at me. I stared, uncomfortably, back.

'Suppose the lift is out of the question,' I joked feebly. Not that I would have gone with him anyway. With my bad luck, he mightn't even have tried to kiss me.

He grinned. 'Forget the lift, let me buy you a drink to make up for my totally thick lead singer?'

It was an offer too good to refuse.

Chapter Eleven

MARTI WAS THIRTY-FOUR and five foot six. He'd worked with loads of bands and he named them off like a kid would the alphabet. Not that he was boasting or anything, he just told me because I asked him if being a manager was his full-time job. Yep, a stupid question but hey, you try making conversation with a dark, though much smaller version of Brad Pitt. I mean, these type of guys just don't talk to me when Sal is in the room. But the chances were that he hadn't spotted her yet.

'Let's see' – Marti lay back in the hard metal chair and sprawled his legs under the table – 'I started out in the business about five years ago when a band I was in went belly-up. You might have heard of us – we were called Low Life.'

'Naw,' I said. Then to ease the blow, I joked, 'But I've met loads of guys matching that description.'

Marti guffawed. Took a slug of his pint. 'Anyways,' he said, 'I got fed up of the music scene and I decided that I'd take a more background role. So, I found a little band that were going nowhere and I nudged them in the right direction.'

'Really? What band was that?'

He waved his hand about. 'Aw, now, you wouldn't have heard of them. They made it big in Dubai. Never did the business over here. I've a lot of contacts in Dubai.'

'Oh. Right.'

'Hey, don't knock it, Dubai is a good market.'

I wasn't going to knock anything. 'And then?' I asked.

I watched as Marti lifted his pint to his lips. He had nice lips.

Sort of pouty but not in a girlie way. His hair was dark and floppy, cut in this really cool style, all choppy and edgy. His skin was spot-free and had just the right hint of stubble. His eyes though were a mystery 'cause the flashing lights made them look purple. And he was loads taller than me. I liked the way he sprawled about in his chair. It had an easy-going air about it. Marti licked the foam from around his mouth and sighed deeply as if it was the best pint he'd ever tasted.

'And then,' he said, 'I found other bands, did the same thing. I've had a guy, Emilio Byrne, make it big in Nigeria. Now, how many managers have you heard do that?'

'None,' I said truthfully.

Marti nodded in satisfaction. 'There now,' he said, as if he'd just proved his worth as a human being. 'There you are.'

'That's great,' I said.

'Then I got married,' Marti went on.

It took a second for me to digest that bit of information and, before I fully had, he added, 'And then I had a son.'

'A son?' I virtually squealed out the word. 'Great.' My first thought was Jesus Christ Almighty get me out of here. My second one was – no wonder he's chatting me up.

'Then she left me.' Marti added.

I suppose it was some consolation. 'Did she?'

'Holding the baby.'

'Aw, God.'

''Course he wasn't really a baby, he was five. He'll be five and a half now tomorrow.' Marti drained his pint and looked at me. 'What do you think of that?'

I thought it was awful. That's what I thought. I didn't know how he could be so matter-of-fact about it. 'And does your wife ring your little boy or anything?'

'It only upsets him.' Marti banged his pint in front of me. 'So I disconnected the house phone. Only use this now.' He tapped his breast pocket. 'The mobile.'

'Poor little kid,' I said.

60

'She'll come crawling back now that I've made it with Boy Five,' Marti said, wiping his mouth with his sleeve and leaning towards me. 'But she's wasting her time. I don't need her any more.' He thumbed in the direction Cliff had gone. 'Thick as a plate of cold custard but a great voice on him. They'll go far. Tell you what, we'll give Louis Walsh and the boys a run for their money.' He grinned, showing even, white teeth. 'Connections, that's what you need in this business. I brought the boys here to make a few connections. Cliff though wouldn't recognise a connection if it came attached to a plug socket.'

I didn't know if I should laugh.

'Good singer though.'

'He said the song is number thirteen.'

'And rising,' Marti said.

'Congratulations.'

'Ta.'

'Want another beer to celebrate?'

'I wouldn't say no.'

On the way to the bar I wondered if I was stupid. The guy was married, for God's sake. Married but separated, another part of me said. And we were just chatting. OK, he was chatting, I was listening. But I liked it like that. I've never been one for talking about myself.

'So tell us about yourself?' Marti asked.

'Nothing to tell,' I grinned, slugging back my fifth Bud. Or was it my sixth? 'Your average Irish Catholic twenty-something.'

'I like the Irish twenty-something part,' Marti said. 'So two out of three ain't bad.'

I grinned.

'You're not from Dublin?'

'No. I'm not.' More drink. 'Cork.'

'I managed a band from there once. You might have heard of them – the Rosslare Rockers?'

'Nope.' I frowned. 'But isn't Rosslare in Wexford?'

'That was the joke of it,' Marti said.

'Oh.'

'They were pretty big at one stage.'

'Well, I never heard of them.'

'You're probably just not into music,' Marti said knowledge-ably. 'A lot of women aren't.'

'Well, maybe—'

'My wife, now, she wasn't into music. Wasn't into a lot of things, come to think of it.' Pause. 'Which I'd rather not.'

Both of us looked into our drinks.

The silence grew a bit uncomfortable with both of us trying not to think of his wife.

'What do you do?' Marti asked then. In a slightly bitter voice, he added, 'Betcha you're not married.'

'Good bet.'

'Are you here on your own?'

'Well, I came with a flatmate and her friend but they've deserted me.'

'Ouch.'

Shit. I'd made myself sound like a loser. 'Yeah,' I managed a passable scoff, 'they can't stand the competition. With me about they've no chance with fellas.'

Marti smiled. 'I can believe that,' he said, looking at me in a funny way.

Yeah. Right. I drank some more and laughed a little.

'So, what else do you do?' Marti's eyes were still giving me *that* look. 'Besides hook vulnerable guys?' Before I could answer, he held up his hand. 'Nope, don't tell. Let me guess.' He studied my red jeans and orange top. 'You look like the sort of girl that works in a trendy juice bar or something.'

It was said in all seriousness.

'Or a vegetarian place,' he added.

'I work in a toy shop,' I told him.

He laughed. 'Nah.'

'I do,' I said. 'Honestly. Toys Galore in Yellow Halls.'

'Adult toys?' His eyes sparked with interest.

'Well, if you're into Barbie, maybe. Otherwise it's kids only.'

'Aw, that's—'

'Hey, hey, Marti!' A kid, barely out of nappies, was calling Marti over. 'Come here, willya?'

Marti rolled his eyes. 'Can't even chat up a nice-looking girl in peace,' he said, standing up as prepubescent scurried over. 'What's the problem?' he asked.

'I've made a connection, Marti. The editor from *Tell!* is here. She wants to talk to you.'

Marti dusted himself down.

'I know her,' I said.

Marti chortled. 'I'm not as stupid as Cliff, you know.'

'I do know her.'

' 'Course you do,' he winked one of his purple eyes. 'Look, back in a sec. Just let me talk to this woman, will you?' Without waiting for my answer, he turned to the young lad. 'Good work, Robin,' he said.

Robin looked thrilled.

The two walked off together.

To my surprise, he actually did arrive back. Rolling his eyes, he sat in beside me.

'Not the best pitch I ever made,' he muttered, placing his pint back on the table. 'I'll have to do better next time.'

'Hard luck.'

'And speaking of next time,' he grinned at me, 'I'm making a pitch now. D'you fancy coming out with me at some stage?'

I was caught on the hop. I hadn't expected him to ask me out. Granted, we'd chatted most of the night, but he was married, for God's sake. 'Aw, I dunno.' If my folks found out they'd die.

'Please?' His purple eyes looked so appealing. 'OK, maybe I shouldn't have told you about having the wife and the kid, but at least you know what you're getting into.'

That's what worried me. I mean, what if I had to meet his kid? What if his wife was the jealous type?

'Just one night?'

He looked so appealing that I found it hard to refuse him.

'Tickets to see Boy Five live?' He rummaged about in his pocket and pulled out a wad of tickets. 'As you can see, they're going fast.'

I laughed.

'And to be honest, any connection with Paul McCarthy is valuable to me.'

'All right then,' I found myself saying, attracted by his humour. 'Let's see how it goes.'

We swapped phone numbers and he said he'd pick me up the following Saturday at seven.

Chapter Twelve

MONDAY MORNING.
The office was shining.

Bridie, for some bizarre reason, had decided to clean it.

She'd obviously come in appallingly early and now the room reeked with the smell of vinegar and polish. My desk, which up to this had been a dull brown, was now a less dull brown and all my baskets and order forms had been neatly piled one on top of the other. There was even a desk tidy that hadn't been there before and the black filing cabinets glinted with the winter sun pouring in the newly polished window.

Bridie virtually stood to attention as I entered.

'Hey,' I said, 'the cleaning fairies must have been in during the night.' I dumped my bag onto the desk and grinned at her.

'Oh, I just decided to do a bit of housekeeping in the office,' Bride tittered as she removed my bag from the desk with as much tact as possible. 'It'll smear the wood,' she said as she apologetically placed it on the floor.

'Is O'Neill paying you extra to do this?' I asked.

'Oh *no,* and I wouldn't *ask* for it.' Bridie was shocked. 'I just thought with,' lowered voice, 'the son starting that we could put on a decent show.'

'Well I can sing – what do you do?'

'I meant—'

'Let me guess' – I did a big psychic thing on it – 'you are an acrobat. The triple somersault a speciality?'

She gave a weak laugh.

'A lion tamer?'

'Oh now, you're too smart for me, so you are. Too smart.'

We smiled at each other. Bridie began to pack her dusters away in a brown bag. The sight of her frail bent body rummaging about in a tattered bag touched me.

'Look,' I said gently, 'don't be worrying yourself about this fella, *he's* the beginner. He won't know anything.'

She coloured. 'Who's worried? I'm not worried.'

'We'll beat him into shape.'

She ignored me. 'I mean, if I can't polish up without you thinking I'm worried, when can I polish? I'm not the sort that worries. All I want to do is to—'

'Create a good impression. I know.'

'Good.' She folded her arms tightly about herself and stood looking at me. 'What time's he coming anyway?'

'O'Neill said midday.'

'*Mister* O'Neill,' Bridie corrected. 'You can't go about calling him O'Neill when the son is here.'

'Midday,' I said, ignoring her. 'What sort of a time is that to start a job? I dunno. Well, it'll be his last midday, that's all I can say.'

'You wouldn't want to be going getting his back up, now,' Bridie said. 'Creating tension.'

Bridie was creating enough tension for the two of us. I decided to change the subject. I plugged in our white kettle – it had always been a beigey colour before – and asked, 'So, how'd the weekend go? Any mad parties?'

She laughed, as I knew she would. Bridie has a very simple sense of humour. Anything mildly risqué and she titters uncontrollably. 'Oh now, I'm well past the mad party stage. No' – she found a cup and handed it to me – 'I did a lot of cleaning on Saturday night – hoovering and dusting and such like. Then on Sunday, I went to eight mass, bought the papers and sat down for the afternoon. I had a nice bit of chicken for my dinner.

The butcher I go to does a lovely bit of chicken. I could get you some if you like. Very reasonable.'

'Does it come in tin foil with curry sauce and rice?'

'Oh now.' A titter before she straightened the desk tidy. 'And you – how was your weekend? Did you go home?'

'Went to a club with Sal.'

'Is that your reporter friend?'

'Uh-huh.'

'Well, you can tell her from me that her piece on sponge cakes was first-rate.'

Sal? Sponge cakes? She'd obviously cogged it from someone else. 'I will.'

Bridie looked at her watch. 'Well, better get some work done. You finish your tea, don't drink it too fast, it'll burn your mouth. Sit there now and I'll open up.'

She always said that.

I watched her leave.

There were plenty of customers in that morning, which was good. Bridie was showing one boisterous kid the joys of wrestling rings. I wish I'd nabbed him first – the wrestling rings were cool.

Dominic, a small three-year-old, was over playing with the opened box of Lego. His mother hovered around, pretending to look at the shelves but really in the shop for the warmth. The two came in every second day for a couple of hours, having being thrown out of their B&B. The mother, with her tight jeans and crop tops, was a tough-looking woman who never talked much. Dominic was cute, though. Sometimes I'd buy him a lollipop and, if his mother was in good form, she'd let him take it from me. If she wasn't, she'd tell me that she didn't take charity.

I was a bit scared of her, to be honest.

At eleven fifty-five, despite my best intentions, I was getting as edgy as Bridie. At least I'd dressed a bit more upmarket that day. There was no way this guy was going to think Bridie and

I were a couple to be messed with. I'd power dressed and power blow-dried my hair. It now just frizzed out a little.

I'd blind him with knowledge. I'd be brisk, efficient and managerial.

Jesus, I hoped he'd be on time.

I didn't know if I'd have the nerve to give out to him if he wasn't.

The second hand on my watch was ticking off another minute when the phone rang. Thinking it would create a good impression to see me too busy to talk to him when he did arrive, I answered it.

'Hello?'

'Oh, hello, love, it's me.'

It was my mother. 'Mam. Hiya.'

I was vaguely aware of someone coming in the door. I did a quick check and it wasn't the dreaded O'Neill. The someone stood beside the counter and I indicated the phone. He shrugged and, shoving his hands into his pockets, slouched against the counter.

'I'm sorry for ringing you at work, love,' Mam said breathlessly, 'but I think your mobile might be dead or whatever it is they say.'

Damn! I was always forgetting to charge the bloody thing. 'Could be,' I said. My heart began a slow pounding. 'Sooo?' I didn't want to ask why she'd rung. I was afraid it might hurt her feelings. She never rang me in work. Ever. 'How's things?'

'I found that information you were looking for.' Mam ignored my question as she rushed on. 'I just wanted to ring and tell you.'

'Oh.' I didn't know what to say to that. 'Great.' I began to fumble among the junk on the desk for a pen. Papers flew everywhere. Eventually my sweaty fingers found a Biro lodged against the till. 'That's great. Have you the details there?'

I wished the fecker would move away from the counter. If I didn't know better, I'd swear he was earwigging on my conversation.

68

Bridie was signalling me in agitation.

'Well, no.' Mam sounded flustered. 'I sent all the documents up with Tommy. He was down the—'

'Tommy?' I paused. Took a breath. 'You've *told* Tommy?'

'Well, no, love.' She was struggling now. My tetchy tone had upset her. But, hell, how could she have done that? It was my business. *Mine.*

'It's my business, Mam.'

'I know it is, love, but you see, I didn't exactly know what to look for so I just sent it all up to you. Tommy's just delivering it. He won't look at it.'

Tommy of all people. Tommy, my childhood tormentor. My adulthood tormentor, come to think of it. 'He'd better not.' They'd known I didn't like him. How could they have—?

'I just thought it might be safer than posting it,' Mam said then, after a pause. 'I mean, if you came home every weekend I could have held on to—'

'I come home when I can.' I turned away from the guy and muttered furiously into the phone. 'I'm very busy up here.'

Bridie was going red in the face, pointing and gesturing.

'I know you are, love.' Mam's voice was contrite. 'And I'm sorry if I've done the wrong thing.'

'It's fine,' I muttered, though it wasn't. Tommy? For Christ's sake! 'So when will he give it to me?'

'Today, most likely. He said he'd drop it into you in work. He works near you, you see. Just around the corner, he said.'

'Right.'

Bridie was now scuttling towards me. She had a piece of paper in her hand and, covering it, like a kid in school, she shoved it in front of my face. *The son*, it said. A big arrow pointed at the guy at the counter.

I shook my head. Rolled my eyes and pushed her paper away. Honestly, she was getting on my nerves now. 'Bridie, see to this man, will you,' I said.

'I hope it's all there,' my mother was saying. 'If it's not you

69

can ring me on Thursday. I'll be away for a few days.'

'Hiya,' the young guy was saying to Bridie. 'Ed O'Neill.' He offered her his hand.

I dropped the phone.

'Vicky?' my mam was saying anxiously as I picked it up from the floor. 'Are you there?'

'Yeah.' I was staring askance at the fella, willing Bridie to say something instead of staring awestruck at him. 'Listen, Mam, thanks a lot. I've to go now.'

Before she even said her goodbyes, I'd hung up.

'Don't hang up on my account,' Ed O'Neill said, looking at me with these amazing blue eyes. They flicked from one to the other of us. 'I won't tell Dad, you know.'

Bridie gave a false whoop of a laugh that embarrassed everyone.

'I'm Vicky.' I held out my hand to Ed. Determined to ignore his last comment, I said coolly, 'The manager.'

He took my hand in a firm grip and gave a small grin. 'I'm Ed,' he said, nodding slightly. Pointing to Bridie's discarded bit of paper, he added, 'The son.'

Bridie shuddered.

Either this guy took a terrible photo or it was another son. 'I didn't know O'Neill—'

Bridie gasped.

'Mr O'Neill,' I corrected, flushing, 'had two sons.'

Ed shrugged. 'Well he does.' His voice had the slow cadences of the north. 'Only' – he shrugged again – 'I'm the son he doesn't talk about.'

'Oh now,' Bridie gave another slightly hysterical laugh, 'I'm sure he does. Sure he can't deny you anyway – you're the spit of him, so you are.'

Well, that was an insult if ever there was one.

That fat, balding, slobbering Albert O'Neill had ever looked like his son was hard to believe. It was like saying that a big slug of a caterpillar looked like a butterfly. To put it bluntly, Ed

70

O'Neill was a fine thing. Completely different from what I'd been expecting. He looked nothing like his dour brother. The only thing they had in common was their dark hair. However, where his brother had been clean-shaven and manicured, Ed was not. His whole appearance was unruly, from his close-shaven head to the casual way he was dressed. An orange jacket thrown over a black T-shirt with the band Picture House on the front. He wore grey combats and a pair of expensive trainers. His face was handsome though not in a traditional, strong-jawed model way. Cute, I guess would describe him best. Where he resembled his father most was in his eyes. An unusual shade of pale blue. Shiny eyes. But even there, the expression in them was different from his father's.

Ed turned his attention from me to Bridie. He bestowed on her a devastating smile. His voice all warm and creamy, he said, 'You must be Bridie. I've heard about you.'

Bridie melted. I swear, it was like watching a snowman dissolve into a puddle. Her brown eyes were like two saucers in her face as she beamed at him. 'Well,' she gushed, 'I am *so* pleased to meet you. Vicky and I were *so* looking forward to it.'

'Because we're overworked here,' I said swiftly. 'We hope you'll take some of the burden off us.'

Bridie laughed again.

Ed said nothing.

'I've a file here.' I reached in under the counter and took out a yellow file marked *Training*. I'd spent all last week running it up on the computer. I'd made it as long and as easy to follow as possible. I hoped its length would frighten the shite out of him, make him realise how much we did, and that its simplicity would guarantee us an able worker. 'I'd like you to read it.'

His expression told me that its size had the desired effect. 'All of it?'

'Yes.' I was proud of my casual tone. 'Is that a problem?'

'Is there going to be a sequel?'

71

Bridie clapped her hands. 'Ha, ha, ha, ha, ha.' Shaking her head, she muttered, 'A caution. A caution.'

'You can read it up in the office,' I said frostily. 'I'll be up in a bit.'

Ed took the file from me and tipped his forehead in a half salute.

'There's biscuits in the red box,' Bridie called after him. 'You can open the new packet.'

Ignoring the incredulous glare I gave her, she turned her back on me and waltzed back down the shop.

Chapter Thirteen

WHEN EVENTUALLY I got a chance to slip upstairs to the office, I was pleased to see Ed busily reading the training file. To my horror, though, he'd also managed to munch halfway through the luxury biscuits that Bridie had bought in honour of his arrival. He was reaching for another when I came alongside him. It was then I noticed that he was drinking coffee from *my* mug.

'That's my mug,' I couldn't resist pointing out.

He looked at the mug and then looked at me. 'Oh. Sorry. I didn't—'

I waved him away, half ashamed of my childishness, but it had suddenly seemed vitally important to let him know that I was in charge. In charge and in control. For some reason his presence in the shop was freaking me out. I dunno if it was the way Bridie had totally capitulated to him or if it was the fact that now he was here, I didn't quite know where I stood. He was the boss's son, for God's sake. One day he'd own this shop.

How much power did I have over him?

I had to start as I meant to go on.

I sat down opposite him and tried to look managerial. It was hard because I'd never done it before. Clasping my hands together in front of me, the way I'd seen O'Neill do, I began laying down the ground rules. 'You'll have to get your own mug for tomorrow and we have a fund for the biscuits, so you'll have to contribute to that.'

'No problem.' He nodded and indicated the training file. 'I

would've given money only I haven't reached that part yet.'

'And you won't either – it's not in it.'

He laughed slightly. 'Aw well, even if it had been, I probably wouldn't have got to it until next year. I mean, who put this together?' He flipped through the pages of the file, a bemused grin on his face. 'It's like *War and Peace*, for God's sake.'

'I put it together. Actually.'

The grin died on his face. 'Oh.'

'And no one has had any problems with it before.' Which was true, as it happens.

He had the grace to look shame-faced. 'Massive apologies then.' A charming smile. 'Boss.'

I was about to smile back and then decided not to. He might be able to charm old ladies like Bridie but I wasn't such an eejit. 'Now, work starts at nine sharp with an hour for lunch and a tea break in the morning.'

'Do we get an afternoon break?'

'Eh—' I was tempted to say yes, but then had the horrifying thought that maybe he was testing me. 'No,' I managed to gulp out. It was the hardest decision I'd ever made. 'No,' I said more firmly, trying to convince myself, 'one break is enough.'

He didn't look impressed.

'You get one day off a week seeing as there's three of us now. I take Monday' – I allowed myself a little smile – 'because I'm the *boss*. Bridie says she'll have Tuesday so you can take one other day.'

'Thursday,' he said without even bothering to think about it. 'I'll have that day.'

'Well, you can think about it. You don't have to decide—'

'Naw, Thursday's great. Shops are open late in Dublin.'

Well for him, I thought. Spending his daddy's money.

'Good for busking,' he added.

'Busking?'

'Uh-huh,' he nodded. 'Dublin's great for busking and I've done it most everywhere.'

Despite my desire to create a professional image I was seriously impressed. I'd always admired buskers. '*Really?*'

'Uh-huh. Worst place I found was Vienna. I got robbed and beaten. Didn't put me off, though.'

'Wow. So you didn't always work for your dad then?'

He flinched, as if I'd hit him. 'I've never worked for my dad until now,' he said. He held my gaze for a second before glancing back down at the training manual.

'Oh.' I wasn't sure if I'd offended him. He certainly *seemed* offended. 'So what did you do? Just busk?'

'I wish.' He grinned ruefully. 'Nah, I worked in London for a while then I came back here.'

'Oh right.' I waited for him to elaborate and when he didn't, I found myself asking, 'Doing what in London?'

'Work,' he said casually.

Well, that was *me* told. I felt myself flushing madly. So, if he wanted it strictly business, strictly business it would be. I'd blind him with knowledge.

A while later, I offered him a tour.

'Right,' he said, looking a bit dazed at all the information I'd managed to impart. 'I'll, eh, just wash your cup first.' He spent ages washing it and then replacing it in the exact same place he'd found it. 'Lead on.' Slight hesitation. Big grin. 'Boss.'

'My name is Vicky,' I said.

He nodded. Didn't reply.

We'd just got out of the office when Bridie accosted us. She almost bowed in front of Ed and blinded us both with the smile she gave him. 'Oooh,' she said, her voice all quivery, 'did you find the biscuits?'

'Aye. Thanks.'

'I bought chocolate ones especially,' Bridie said to me. 'Men like their bit of chocolate.'

God, she was going to get on my nerves bigtime if she kept looking at Ed like that.

'Do they,' I said. 'That's nice.'

Bridie smiled again.

We both waited to hear what she had to say.

'Bridie,' I prompted, 'what do you want?'

'Oh, oh yeah,' she tittered. 'I only came up to tell you that there's a young gentleman to see you.'

I didn't know any gentlemen. 'Are you sure it's for me?'

'Well' – Bridie blinked rapidly – 'he asked for you. He seems like a nice man.'

Definitely not for me.

'Thanks, Bridie.' I indicated Ed. 'Will you do me a favour? I was about to show Ed around – will you do it?'

'Everywhere?'

'Uh-huh. The shop floor, the stores, the lot.'

'Ed,' she beamed, 'if you'll come with me.'

As I watched the two of them descend the stairs, him making her laugh with some comment or other, I wished that he hadn't come.

'Aw, there she is, my favourite cousin.'

Tommy bellowed it out all over the shop so that heads swivelled to look in my direction. Well, two heads actually – Dominic's and his mother's.

'So this is the place you manage, is it?' Tommy bellowed again.

'Uh-huh.'

'I didn't realise you worked so close to me.' Tommy leaned his elbows on the shop counter as I neared him. 'I'm only over the road.'

'Really?'

'Yeah.' Tommy grinned. 'We'll have to do lunch sometime – hey?'

'Sure,' I smiled, knowing that I'd do a runner quicker than I'd do lunch.

'Anyway' – Tommy dug into the folds of his fancy coat and

took out a brown envelope – 'Auntie Evelyn told me to give you that. Said it was important.'

I snatched the envelope from him and shoved it under the counter. 'Yep. Thanks.'

'She said if it wasn't what you wanted to ring her.'

'Great. Thanks.' I looked over his head to a customer coming in the door. Buy something, I willed. Buy something. Anything to get Tommy out of the shop.

'And John only works in Kildare Street,' Tommy was saying, oblivious of my surliness. 'I'll give him a buzz and see if he's interested in meeting up.'

John was almost as bad as Tommy on the appalling cousin scale. In fact it had been John who'd told me that I was adopted. Well, he'd told me I was a 'ready made', which had hurt even more. And OK, so he'd been grounded for a week and he'd been only twelve, but it had hurt and to be honest, it still did.

'So what's the best time for you?' Tommy asked.

'My lunchtimes vary,' I said as apologetically as I could, 'I probably wouldn't be free.'

'You're the manager, aren't you?' Tommy said. 'Suit yourself. That's what I do.'

I had no doubt about it.

'Here.' Tommy drew out a business card. 'Gimme a ring whenever you want to meet up – eh?' He didn't wait for an answer, assuming that I'd be delighted. 'And ring your mother if that stuff isn't what you want,' he said. 'Talk again.'

Not if I could help it, we wouldn't.

I watched him leave and then turned my attention to the brown envelope. I couldn't wait to get back to the flat and tear it open.

Chapter Fourteen

Dear Sir/Madam,

I was adopted through your agency and I would be interested in having more up-to-date information on my background please. Below, please find my personal details. I listed my name, my date of birth and the address of my parents. I put down my mobile number on the letter in case they wanted to contact me. On the calendar near my bedroom door, I wrote, in massive black marker, CHARGE MOBILE. Turning back to the letter, I read it through. Then, hand shaking, I wrote: *I'd also be interested in making contact with my mother with a view to a meeting.*

I liked the way it looked on the page.

I had a mother.

Somewhere out there I had a mother.

I signed the letter.

Sealed the letter.

And kissed it for luck.

I posted it the next day.

Chapter Fifteen

SATURDAY NIGHT.

Marti was strolling up and down the pathway outside the flat, his hands sunk into black trousers. Black trousers with bright green stripes. A green shirt, open to the chest hair, mercifully covered with a green and black leather jacket. My first and very disloyal impression was that he looked like a clown. I tried to think what he'd worn the night I'd met him in Club Zero and couldn't. 'Hey,' he smiled at me as I emerged. 'You look great!'

'Hey,' was all I could manage back.

The garishness of Marti's clothes sort of swamped him. He looked like he was drowning in a sea of green. I shook the thought away. Clothes were so superficial anyway. Still, I didn't want Sal to see him looking like that, she'd die laughing. She'd nearly died when I'd introduced her to him last Saturday night. 'But he's so *small*,' she'd whispered.

'You – look – stunning,' Marti said, admiring me with what I noticed, in horror, were purple eyes.

'Well,' I joked, trying to salvage some humour from the situation, 'I decided I'd go all out and match your eyes.' I indicated my new purple jeans and red top. And OK, maybe my stuff was a bit off, but I liked it.

He laughed loudly. A little too loudly. He was probably as nervous as I was.

'You're in for a treat this evening,' Marti said as he led me to a black car. 'We've VIP tickets, right at the top of the hall.'

'Eh, great.' I wasn't much into boy bands but it had seemed

a good idea last Saturday. It must have been all the Bud I'd drunk.

'That's why I've got this stuff on,' Marti indicated his clothes. 'People will remember me. The same for the eyes.'

'What?'

'Why I wear the purple contacts. No self-respecting record producer will remember the name Marti Hearty, but they'll remember me because I've purple eyes, see.'

Marti Hearty would be a hard name to forget, I reckoned. Still, I could follow his logic. I just wished he hadn't been so logical on our first date.

'So,' Marti asked, snapping his seatbelt on, 'is this OK by you?' He looked anxiously at me, and I saw that he was nervous. 'I mean,' he went on, 'we could give the concert a miss but the lads need my support and I thought you'd like to hear a good band.'

I tried not to smile. My idea of a good band was drummers and guitarists and singers all sort of working together. 'This is fine by me,' I said and he looked relieved. Sure if nothing else, I thought, I could sit and admire Marti's lovely-looking face, which mercifully hadn't changed from my drunken memories.

It was a sort of showcase for new bands. Boy Five were headlining. 'We can go after they perform,' Marti said, shoving the programme into his jacket pocket and striding ahead of me to the backstage entrance. 'I'll just go and wish them luck.'

In the dressing room four of the lads were sitting around in ridiculous silver cowboy costumes.

'Cost a bomb, those outfits,' Marti informed me before asking the lads, 'where's Cliff?'

'In the jax. Puking,' said one of the guys who I later learned was Keith.

As if on cue, there came the sound of vomiting from the toilet.

'Calm down, man. Calm down,' Keith called.

'But we've never sung live before,' Cliff moaned. 'All we ever did was mime.'

'Jaysus!' Marti rolled his eyes at me and strode over to the toilet door. 'Come out, you twat!' he ordered, hammering on it.

'Aw, Marti, I can't.' Retching sounds.

'Are you such a big blouse that you're afraid of a load of ten-year-olds?'

'Me ma and all is out there. And me girlfriend.'

'Right, eleven-year-olds then.'

The other four lads exploded in laughter.

'Feck off,' Cliff moaned.

'Get out of there or you're out of the band.'

'It's not a band – it's just singers.'

'Mimers,' Keith called helpfully.

Marti scowled furiously at him. Then he began to wheedle. 'Look, Cliff, you're on the crest of a wave here. Number thirteen again in Ireland this week. Who knows what's next? England maybe? Come on, you'll be minted. But fall now and Jaysus, it'll be like Eamonn Coughlan and the Olympics.'

'Eamonn who?'

'Fucking thick,' Marti mouthed to me. Back to the toilet, 'Sonia O'Sullivan then.'

'What was she – a one-hit wonder or something?'

Pause. 'Look,' Marti began again, 'first you were afraid, you were petrified. But now, right, you will survive? D'you get me?'

A man poked his head in the door. 'Ten minutes, folks.'

'Oooh,' Cliff moaned.

The other four lads looked at Marti. Big trusting eyes. I even looked at Marti. I felt sorry for him. This, according to him, was his big chance. But the evil part of me hoped that Cliff would stay in there and Marti and I could go somewhere else.

'If you don't get out of there,' Marti yelled, 'I'll give you such a root up the hole, you won't be able to shag that sweet little girlfriend of yours for a month.'

'She won't let me shag her anyway.'

Laughter.

'Jesus!' Marti began to stomp about the place.

'Cliff, will you bleedin' get out of there!' Now it was Keith's turn to hammer on the door. 'How the hell do you think the rest of us feel? I promise, right, that if you do it, I'll give you the twenty euro I owe you.'

'It's thirty.'

'Right, thirty then. Only come out, for God's sake.'

Silence.

'If I forget the words, you'll jump in and sing them, will you?' Cliff called out.

'Yeah. Yeah, I will.'

'Well, then we're really fucked,' one of the other guys muttered dryly.

From behind the toilet door, Cliff laughed. 'Just let me wipe my face,' he said. 'I'll be out in a bit.'

'Come on,' Marti took my arm. 'We'll sit in the wings so I can push the bastard on if he won't go.'

I laughed, but I don't think it was a joke.

Five minutes later, the drum rolls started. From behind the stage, I could hear the crowd out front going wild. Kids screaming, others hooting. The music getting more and more frantic. The drum roll again and Boy Five standing beside me and Marti and sweating buckets. Cliff was being supported by Keith and one of the other lads.

'Yez look fantastic.' Marti clapped each one of them on the back. 'Super.'

They looked like those cheap white Christmas trees my mother had years ago.

'Don't they look super, Vicky?' Marti asked.

'What can I say?' I spluttered. The whole thing was a gas and, to be honest, I was enjoying the excitement of it all.

'Nothing.' Cliff had recognised me and was scowling. 'It's bound to be a lie, anyway.'

'Now, now,' Marti admonished, 'Vicky is my girlfriend.'

The lads gawked at him.

'And when we meet up again, I'll introduce her properly to you all.'

They didn't seem too thrilled at the prospect. Maybe they were just nervous. The compere was building them up.

'Deep breathing,' Marti said urgently. 'In. Out. In. Out. That's the lads.'

'. . . BOY FIVE!'

A huge cheer tore the place apart.

'Run, acknowledge, take your places,' Marti urged.

The five lads jogged onto the stage, waving and smiling.

Screams. Whistles. Some advanced ten-year-old kept yelling out the word 'Rides' over and over again.

They took their places as the backing track began.

And they sang and danced their way through 'Sharing The Night Together'. Keith tripped up on the fringe of his silver trousers during one very complicated lassoing routine but other than that they went down a storm.

And Cliff was a singer.

Completely wasted in a boy band.

They came off the stage to massive cheering.

'They've made it,' Marti whooped, clapping and cheering along with the rest. 'They're going to be stars!'

And even though I'm a music snob at heart, I liked the way Marti danced about the place. I liked it even better when he hugged me to him. Hard.

And at that moment, I fell a little in love with him.

The lads were elated. They opened the bottle of champagne Marti had had delivered to the dressing room and they generously shared a glass with me. Even Cliff managed a smile. Then a press photographer came into the room and took a few snaps. I had to stand at one end of the group while Marti stood at the other. It was all very exciting.

'So.' Marti put down his glass as the photographer left. 'I'll love yez and leave yez, lads. I'm heading out with Vicky now. See yez Tuesday for a review. Right?'

'Ah, but Marti,' the smallest member of the band spoke up. He had baby blond fluffy hair and a baby squeaky voice. 'Me mudder wants to talk to you about something.'

'Tell her to ring me Tuesday.'

'I told her she'd get you tonight. Aw, Marti, don't go. She'll murder me. You know me mudder.'

'Aw, yeah, you know his mother,' Keith said. 'She'd rip the balls off a prize bull.'

Sniggering.

'Lads, lads.' Marti held up his hand. 'We've a lady in the room.'

'Who? Me?' I said.

The lads laughed again.

Marti sighed. Looked at me. 'D'you mind, Vicky? D'you mind if the lads come with us? You'll understand when you meet Adam's mother.'

The last thing I wanted to do was to sit in a pub with a load of kids and their families. My spirits, which up until then had been rising steadily, sank drastically. How could a guy expect me to spend a first date in a pub with a crowd of teenagers? Sal would break her heart laughing when she found out. 'Maybe I'll go home,' I said. 'Let you get on with the business of managing.' I picked up my bag from a chair. 'You can gimme a call during the week.'

'Aw, now, Vicky, don't be like that.' Marti looked upset. 'You'll have a laugh.'

'I don't think I will.' I looked at the lads. 'No offence, lads.'

'None taken,' Adam squeaked.

Marti grasped my arm. He pulled me about the room. 'You will have fun, you will,' he said, sounding so insistent that I had to smile. It was like when I was a kid and I'd fight with one of my cousins. They'd always say, 'You're not my friend,' and I'd hit them a belt and yell out, 'I am your friend.'

'Look,' Marti went on, 'I'll introduce the lads to you now and we'll all get to know one another. It's important you get on with them, Vicky, I'd like you to.'

I wondered what he meant by that.

'This fella here is Cliff, but you already know him, this is Keith, this is Adam, this is Robin and this is Logan.'

'After Johnny Logan,' the guy said proudly.

I tried not to grin.

'It'll just be this once.' Marti looked at me appealingly. 'Don't get annoyed.'

'I just don't think chatting to mothers and fathers and stuff is quite my thing,' I explained. 'I don't know anything about the music business. I just wanted a quiet drink.'

'My da's a great laugh,' prepubescent Adam called out. 'You won't be bored with him. He works in the zoo.'

Marti nodded. 'Funny stories about animals,' he said jovially. He looked beseechingly at me. 'And anyway, you won't have to talk to them. Promise.'

I guessed it might be OK. The lads seemed nice enough and after all they were number thirteen in the charts – almost pop stars. And to be honest, I found it quite glamorous, being with them and having my photo taken. And Marti was fun and how many times had a fun guy begged me to go anywhere? And Marti made me feel that it would be a laugh – he was all manic energy and enthusiasm. I put my bag down.

'OK.' They all grinned back at me – well, all except Cliff.

'Brilliant!' Marti gave me another hug, which I rather liked, and handed me another glass. 'Drink up now.'

So I did.

The pub we went to was very upmarket. You know the kind of place, no furniture and freezing cold with madly over-priced drinks. 'Important for the lads to be seen in the right places,' Marti said as the bouncer let us in. 'Does wonders for the image.'

We found seats and Marti ordered a round of drinks. The

lads talked among themselves so it *was* kinda like Marti and I were on our own. He told me a bit about each of the lads and about his plans for the future.

'We need another hit single,' he said, 'then the album. After that, we'll do the tours and the rest of it. For now, though, it's important to make it in this country.'

'It must be hard,' I said, 'what with having to look after your little boy and everything.'

He said nothing for a few seconds. Then shrugged. 'That's where family comes in,' he muttered.

'Sorry?'

'My mother lives with us so she minds him.'

'That's good. At least he's not fobbed off on some babysitter.'

His eyes lit up as if I'd just said the most wonderful thing. 'That's exactly how I figure it,' he said. 'Of course it's not the same as having his mother around.'

I guess that was true.

'Still,' Marti shrugged, 'if his mother left him is she any good anyway?'

He had a point. What sort of a mother leaves her kid?

Poor little lad, I thought.

'And how's my boy!' A huge woman with an even bigger husband barged towards us. 'Where's my Cliff?' Cliff was enfolded in a huge hug in breasts that swallowed him whole. 'You were wonderful! Wonderful! I was crying when I saw you.'

'Yeah. Real neat costume, Cliffy.' A young girl punched him on the arm. 'I was bleeding crying too. Laughed my arse off, I did!'

'I'm going to have to do something about that relationship,' Marti whispered to me. 'That girlfriend of his keeps denting his ego all the time. It's no wonder he was sick tonight!'

I was doing my best not to laugh.

More people joined us. Among them Adam's ball-breaker mother. And yep, she was scary. And yep, if I were Marti, I'd never have broken an appointment.

Soon a whole section of the bar was full of proud parents and blushing kids.

He drove me home. Talked more about his band. I was glad of that because I was exhausted. I guess it was from trying to smile and trying to remember who everyone was and trying just to appear *nice*. Being nice was bloody hard work. Especially as I hated crowds and being stuck in the middle of them. And I had a pain in my face from smiling.

'Logan can't get the high notes, I'm gonna have to work on that. And Cliff—'

'Cliff is great,' I said, meaning it. 'Really great.'

'Yeah, but he needs to work on the relaxation. Gets too tense.'

We were outside my apartment by now. Marti cut the engine and turned to me. His hand rested across the back of my seat and I could feel his breath on my face. 'So, how'd you enjoy yourself?' His hair flopped forward over his eye and his mouth quirked upwards in a grin. 'Good, wasn't it?'

'I liked the concert, it was a laugh,' I said.

He looked puzzled.

'And the pub was mostly good,' I went on hastily. 'Except for the extra company.'

He grinned. 'You don't bullshit around, I like that. The next time, there won't be any extra company.'

'Good.' My heart was beginning a slow, heavy beat. He was dead sexy-looking, despite the vertical green stripes.

'So you'll come out with me again?'

'If I'm not too busy.'

He gave a rumble of laughter at that. 'I'll ring you.'

'Do.'

We smiled at each other. I didn't know if I should ask him up. I didn't know what he'd take it to mean. I liked him a lot. He was zany and fun, but I don't sleep with guys that quickly. And besides, if Sal saw him in his green stripes she'd have a field day.

87

The choice was taken from me. Marti smiled ruefully and said, 'Well, I'd better get back to the sprog.'

I liked that he'd said that. 'OK, so.'

Pause.

We looked at each other.

He leaned towards me. I leaned towards him. Our lips met. Softly. Gently. He cupped my face in his palm. Ran his hands through my hair. I moaned slightly because I love my hair being stroked.

'I'll call,' he said.

'Yeah. Great.'

And I meant it too. I reckoned it would be great.

Maybe this was the real thing?

Chapter Sixteen

IT WAS MONDAY of the following week before Sal remembered to ask about Ed. Normally if there was half a chance of Sal meeting a guy with money, she'd have been sniffing around within nanoseconds but her piece for Mel, which I assumed was about the guy in Club Zero, seemed to be taking up all her time.

When we were in school, Sal used to always say that she'd marry for love but that any prospective hubby would have to have money, a good job and a nice car. I used to think that was hilarious. I mean, I used to ask her, what if you fell for a guy that hadn't any of those things? What, like, if he was just nice and kind and considerate? Sal used to look at me as if I was the one that was mad. 'Mr Nice, Kind and Considerate might dry the dishes but the guy I'm looking for will have a state-of-the-art dishwasher.'

I used to think it was all crap until Jorge had come to visit. Jorge was a German guy I'd met when I'd been in Egypt. He'd been a great mate to me over there because Egypt hadn't been lucky for me at all. I'd had my credit card stolen, lost my sleeping bag and, a week later, my tent had gone for a hike. No pun intended. Jorge, for some reason, had found this dead funny and, after dubbing me the 'Egypt Eejit' he'd subbed me, shared his tent and bag with me (it was a double – in case he got lucky) and even cooked meals for me during the two great months we'd travelled together. Eventually we'd split and gone our separate ways – he to Australia and me to South America. We'd kept in touch by e-mail and eventually, when I was settled, I'd invited him to Ireland.

Despite the fact that he was tall, blond and quite passably handsome, Sal hadn't paid any attention to him. As far as she was concerned he was just another weirdo hitchhiker. Only mental people slept in tents, Sal stated. Jorge had been about as interesting to her as a piece of cold cabbage.

Until he mentioned to me that his dad was some big financier in the German stock market. And I, knowing that Sal would be impressed, mentioned it to her. And suddenly Jorge morphed from a piece of cold cabbage into a gourmet meal.

And Sal ate him for breakfast.

My German friend was no longer mine. He and Sal spent the rest of the holiday together and I was suddenly the leftover on the plate.

It was the biggest row Sal and I had ever had.

'Well, you weren't interested in him,' Sal had said in a big bored voice when I'd attacked her for seeing him off at the airport. 'So what's the problem?'

I didn't understand how she had to ask. 'He was *my* guest.'

'So he's not allowed to get off with anyone – is he not?'

'He was my guest.' It was all I could say. I'm useless at fights. I could feel the tears welling up and I blinked really hard to get rid of them. 'I was the one meant to be showing him around. I should have been the one seeing him off.'

'Well,' Sal shrugged, 'he wanted me to – what was I to say? No?'

'Yeah. Yeah actually.'

'That's what I did say.' Sal gave a bit of a laugh and quirked her eyebrows. 'And anyway, we did ask you to come with us and you wouldn't.'

'I don't do gooseberry.'

'Well, you're green enough with jealousy now.'

I, madly mature individual that I am, stormed out of the room. I didn't talk to her for ages. I think her and Jorge e-mailed

90

one another for a while but it petered out. And even though he'd copped off with my friend, he still had the cheek to e-mail me. I never bothered replying and he gave up writing about six months ago.

I think if he'd really wanted to keep in touch, he would have.

Anyway, there I was, flicking through an issue of *Hello!*, my feet curled up on the sofa, when Sal asked, out of the blue, 'Hey, how is rich boy working out?'

She was filing her nails and doing 'the Mel piece' on her laptop. I wasn't allowed to go near it. The whole project was top secret. Anyway, she must have read what she'd written, liked it and decided to file her nails. While filing her nails, she wanted to be entertained. 'Well?' she asked.

How was Ed working out? 'All right,' I muttered grudgingly. 'I mean, he can sell toys better than anyone else I've seen. Bridie likes him.' I paused. Shrugged.

'And you?' Sal prompted.

I shrugged again. 'Dunno.' Pause. 'He's the boss's son, isn't he?' Sal kept staring at me. 'I'm scared he's after my job,' I finally admitted. 'I mean, when you think of it, why else would O'Neill put him in the shop?'

'Because you need an extra worker?'

I half-laughed. 'Aw, come on, Sal, we could pick up an extra worker no problem. This is the guy's *son* we're talking about.'

Sal was silent for a bit. I watched her study her nails and knew she was thinking about what I'd said. Sal was dead wide about business and stuff like that. She was the kind of person who thought things out before speaking. The sort of person that scared me stupid because I tend to jump right in and say what's on my mind. Then regret it. Sal regretted nothing. 'Mmm,' she eventually pronounced. 'Maybe he's just in your place to be trained in from the bottom up. Maybe his dad just wants to give him some experience in a shop before he does anything else.'

'He's come back from *London*,' I said. 'He wouldn't just come

91

back for a crummy old job in a shop. *And* this is his first time to work for his dad.'

Sal looked puzzled. 'London? What was he doing over there? I thought he was working in accountancy or something. At least that's what it said in *Tell!*'

'The guy in our shop is another son,' I explained. 'A younger son. He was in London – he told me. I'm telling you, there's something going on.'

'A younger son?' Sal gawked at me. 'What's he like?'

'I already told you – he's a good salesman but—'

'Naw – is he married?'

'Sal, I'm worried here and all you want to know is if he's married!'

Sal laughed a bit. 'Look,' she said, 'if you're so worried – just ask him or his dad straight out. You're entitled to know.'

'Oh, I couldn't—'

'Well, that's your problem then, isn't it? Now.' She put down her nail file and sat in beside me. 'Go on – is he married?'

'You think I should ask Ed if he's planning on taking over my job?'

'Well, why not? Don't let them think you're a fool. Now, is he married?'

She was right, I suppose. That's what I should do, but the very idea of it made my stomach churn. What if I made a fool of myself? But there was something up, I knew it.

'Vicky!' Sal poked me. 'I've told you what to do – now 'fess up – what's this fella like – is he married?'

'Single,' I answered. 'But not your type.' *What the hell would I say – 'Are you taking over my job?' sounded a bit bald. I'd have to think about it.*

'What do you mean "not my type"? If he's the son and heir of Albert O'Neill, he's right up my street.'

'Yep, but he's living at the wrong end of it – he's the guy with the stubble and the combat jacket.'

Sal made a face. She liked her men well groomed. 'Is he

good-looking? On a scale of Troy to Brad Pitt, where would you place him?'

Troy was our neighbour.

'The Brad Pitt end.'

'Wow!' Sal gawped at me. Thumped me. 'What the hell are you waiting for – get in there!'

'All I want is my job,' I answered. 'And I have a nice man, thanks.'

'That small little fella you went out with on Saturday? Aw, Vicky, come on.'

I ignored the jibe about Marti. 'You go for Ed,' I joked. 'Maybe he might find it harder to do the dirty on me if he's seeing my best friend.'

Sal laughed. 'Who knows – I might just do that. A rich, handsome, single man – if I can't get him, no one can.'

I know she was only joking but she really did believe it. I'd have loved to have her confidence.

'And I'll bet,' Sal went on, in a sort of dreamy voice, 'with that Omagh accent, he sounds dead sexy!'

'Yeah, it's nice,' I admitted. 'There's a bit of London in there now, though.'

Sal tapped her nail file up and down on the palm of her hand. 'Lucky you. How come I never get to work with guys like that? He sounds very fanciable.'

'Huh, if he takes my job, he wouldn't be fanciable if he was dipped head to toe in chocolate.'

'Ugh,' Sal giggled. 'For such a puritan, you've an awful kinky mind.'

I wasn't a puritan, I thought as I left the flat to buy some stuff in the local shop. Sal had promised to help me phrase my 'Are you taking my job?' request if I bought her some fags.

It was beginning to drizzle and immediately, as if I'd been struck with about a million volts of electricity, my hair frizzed out. I hate the drizzle. Give me a good old-fashioned storm any day. At least that way my hair ends up flattened and I don't look like Marge Simpson.

I shoved my hands into my coat pockets and, head down, I began the walk to the top of the road. Even though Sal had been joking, the puritan remark stung. I'd had very few relationships and those that I had had always ended badly. I found it hard to keep interested in a guy once I began to know him. Boredom set in, boredom with a capital ZZZ in front of it. Within every funny, spontaneous guy I picked there seemed to be a slipper-and-pipe man just bursting to get out.

And it wasn't that I didn't want to fall in love and do the whole settling down thing – I did. But the idea of it being so *long-term* revolted me.

'Hey, *coooooool*.' The voice came from behind. 'I didn't know you were a Trekkie!'

It was Troy – the nice but visually challenging guy from our landing. He was a gasman, slightly batty. He was trotting along beside me. 'You rock.' A pair of Bugs Bunny teeth were revealed to me in what I suppose was an admiring smile. 'We can travel together.'

'Sorry?'

'On the bus. To the Trekkie convention.'

'You've lost me, Troy.'

'Trekkie convention?' His eyes flicked up to my hair. Stayed there.

It took a couple of seconds.

Both of us were embarrassed at the same time.

'I've just ruined any chance I ever had with you,' Troy said glumly. 'Beam me up, Scotty,' he chortled, snorting with embarrassment. 'Huh, if only I could – hey?'

Beat him up was more along the lines I'd been thinking.

'Anyway, gorgeous,' Troy nodded, attempting to recover, 'I've got to go. The convention starts in forty.' And off he strode in what I noticed now was a tight gold babygro.

'I hope you get eaten by the Borg,' I yelled after him.

He turned to face me. 'The Borg don't eat,' he said, 'they amalgamate.'

'Well, it'll be the only mating you'll ever get!' I yelled after him.

He laughed loudly and blew me a kiss.

Chapter Seventeen

MY HEART WAS booming as I walked up the stairs to the office the next day. 'The sooner you ask him the better,' Sal had briefed me. 'Otherwise there'll just be bad feeling.' So I'd chosen the very next day – Tuesday – which happened to be the day that Ed and I were on our own in the shop.

'Now be calm and in control,' Sal advised. 'Think before you speak and for God's sake, Vic, don't say anything in the heat of the moment.'

That was fine advice for me. I am a very emotional person. It had got me into trouble my whole life.

'Count to ten,' Sal continued, 'and remember, even if he is going to take your job, it's not personal. Be detached.'

If Ed was going to take my job, I told her, he'd be the one that'd be de-tatched. 'I'll pull the hair out of his head.'

'Classy,' Sal had mumbled.

So, now, here I was, on Tuesday, dressed in my best manager's clothes, looking very efficient with my heart about to explode in my chest. I made myself a cuppa and couldn't drink it. I sat, sweaty-palmed, waiting for Ed to appear.

He arrived about ten minutes later. Dressed in what seemed to be his only jacket – the orange one. 'Hiya,' he smiled at me as he took it off, revealing a navy T-shirt with a denim shirt half unbuttoned. He wore a pair of distressed denim jeans that accentuated the length of his legs and the narrowness of his hips. I love nice hips on a guy. 'Good weekend?' He grabbed his mug from the shelf and poured some boiling water into it.

'Great, yeah.' *Ask. Ask. Ask.*

'How so?' Ed dunked a teabag and squished it out with a spoon.

'I went to a gig.'

'Yeah?' He looked interested. 'Who?'

I wasn't admitting to going to see Boy Five. 'Dunno – can't remember.' My heart was hammering, pounding. I told myself that when he'd poured in his milk and sat down, that I would ask.

'That good – eh?' He grinned and poured his milk and sat down.

I remained frozen.

'Where did you go?'

'Sorry? What?'

'The gig,' Ed prompted. 'Where was it?'

'Oh, eh, the Northside somewhere. Ed, can I ask you something?'

He looked mildly curious. 'Fire away.'

'Eh, well, eh.' *This was it. This was it. Take it easy.* 'Action Men,' I gulped out, sweat glistening on my forehead. 'Where'd you put the Action Men?'

I cursed myself.

'They're on the lower shelf,' he said. 'No need to panic. I just thought that the young kids wouldn't be able to see them where they were so I moved them.'

'Right. Right. Good idea.' Too good an idea, I thought suddenly. He *had* to be after something. 'What are you doing here?' It came out sounding completely hostile.

The hand holding his cup jerked and tea slopped onto his jeans. He didn't seem to notice. He was staring transfixed at me. I dunno if it was the question or the way I'd asked it. 'Sorry?' He laid the cup carefully on the desk and, looking at it rather than at me, he said, 'What was that?'

'You heard me – what are you doing here?' More hostility.

'Drinking tea,' he answered with the grin he'd been using on

97

the customers all week. 'Why?' The nervous look in his eyes belied the grin, though,

'I mean in this shop.' I was going to start hyperventilating. I wanted to know his answer yet I dreaded it. 'Why'd your dad put you here?'

He blinked. Once. Twice. 'To work,' he answered.

I tried to remember what Sal had told me to say in the event of an evasive answer. 'I'm no fool,' I went on, my voice stern. 'If it's my job you want, I want to know.'

He stared incredulously at me. So much so that I felt myself redden. I think I'd just proved myself to be a fool.

'After your job,' he said slowly. 'What gave you that idea?'

'You. Being here.'

A slow smile broke out on his face. 'So that's why you're being so snotty to me, is it?'

'I'm not snotty to anyone,' I said snottily.

He laughed a little, then at my lack of response, he leaned forward in his chair and, sounding really sincere, but still with that grin on his face, he said, 'I'm not here to take anyone's job. I just want to work.'

'But you were working in London.'

He nodded. 'Aye.' His smile disappeared. 'I, eh, left my job over there and it was hard to find another. I was busking but not making a whole lot of money. Dad offered me this.'

'Working under me? And Bridie? And you don't mind?'

He flinched. 'It's work.'

He seemed genuine. But, I wondered, would he actually *admit* if he was taking over? Probably not. Again I felt sick. I'd have to keep an eye on things. 'You being here,' I went on, determined to set some ground rules, 'I suppose you realise that it's awkward on me and Bridie. I mean, you're the boss's son.'

'Yeah.' He nodded, shrugged. 'There's not a lot I can do about it. And Bridie doesn't seem to mind all that much.'

Was he saying that it was *me* that minded? When in doubt, say nothing, Sal had advised. It was hard but I did it.

'I am not a spy,' he went on quietly, his eyes holding mine. 'I just want to work – OK?'

I wished he'd work somewhere else. 'OK,' I muttered, not too sure if I completely believed him though he seemed genuine. 'Just so we know. You work here and no matter what happens it doesn't go back to O'Neill.'

'I won't tell O'Neill a single thing,' he grinned. 'Cross my heart.'

'And you are not after my job?'

He grinned that grin again. 'Looking at you, it's definitely not your job I'd be after.'

I reddened. Half flattered. Half annoyed that he should flirt in what had to be the most stressful conversation I'd ever conducted. Still, I thought, like father, like son. I tossed him the keys. 'Well then, you can open up.'

He caught them mid-air. 'Ta, Vicky,' he said just as he was leaving. 'I'm glad we cleared that up.'

I wasn't too sure anything was cleared up. He was too bright not to want more. Way too bright.

Then it hit me. Ohmigod – I'd called his dad O'Neill.

'Mad,' Ed said, surrounded by bits of a transformer that had just come in. 'How do they expect kids to do it when I can't? Honest, the instructions are crap, Vicky.'

'Maybe it's just you,' I said dryly. He'd suggested that we do a transformer window and, while admitting to myself that it was a good idea, I didn't want to encourage his ideas.

He laughed. 'Maybe,' he agreed good-naturedly.

'Might have to scrap the window,' I said, trying to sound sad about it.

Before he had a chance to reply, Dominic hurtled through the door, determined to make it to the Lego before any other kid got there.

'Slow down, Domo,' his mother called as she followed him. 'It's not a bleeding race, ya know.'

Dominic, still running, turned back to her and ran slap bang into a shelf. He walloped his head and fell face first onto the floor.

'OHHH GOD!' his mother screamed.

'MAMMMYYY!' Dominic screamed.

Ed and I rushed towards them. Dominic was howling as his mother picked him up off the floor and held him to her.

'Is he OK?' I asked.

'No, he's not bloody OK,' she snapped at me, her eyes watering. 'Can't you *hear* he's not OK?'

I flinched.

Ed knelt down beside them. 'Let me have a look,' he said gently. 'Just let me see his face.'

'Noooo,' Dominic cried. 'No, Mammy, don't want to!'

'Leave him alone!' the mother barked, rubbing his back with the palm of her hand. 'Bleeding shelves. What was that shelf doing there anyway?'

I looked hopelessly at Ed.

'Holding up toys,' Ed answered mildly. 'Now, are you going to let me look at him or not? My guess is that he's fine. He'll probably just have a massive bruise, that's all.'

'Dat's all?' Dominic's mother said sarcastically. 'Wonder-bleeding-ful.'

'Better than him having concussion,' Ed said. 'And if you let me look at him, I'll tell you for certain.'

'What? Does this toy shop have its own bleeding doctor now? Are yez going to charge me?'

Ed managed a laugh. 'Dominic,' he said, 'let's see you. Let's see if that bruise looks as if you've been hit by The Rock.'

The Rock was Dominic's favourite wrestler.

Slowly Dominic pulled himself out of his mother's embrace. His bruise was looking pretty big all right.

'Cool!' Ed said in an admiring voice.

'For Jaysus' sake—' the mother snarled.

'Is it big?' Dominic asked half fearfully, half hopefully. He scrubbed his eyes with his tiny fist. '*Really* big?'

'Massive,' Ed answered.

Dominic gave a little laugh and turned to his mother. 'Is it, Ma?'

She nodded, glancing suspiciously at Ed.

'Vic, d'we have an ice pack for this tough guy?' Ed asked, without taking his eyes from Dominic.

'Sure.' Jesus, some manager I was. An ice pack should have been the first thing I'd fetched. I legged it upstairs to the office. In the first aid kit was a chemical ice pack. The one with the liquid and the stony bits that freeze up when you press it.

When I came back down, Ed was still hunkered on the ground beside Dominic and his mother. He was telling her that as Dominic's pupils had not gone small, it was unlikely that he had concussion. 'Just let him hang around with me for an hour or two,' he said. 'I'll keep an eye on him, just to be certain.' Then he added, 'You've not got anything urgent on, have you?'

I smiled. It was nice of him to ask her that.

The mother pretended to consider. 'Naw. Anyway, seeing as that shelf was there, Domo falling was yer fault, so I reckon yez owe us one. You can have him for the couple of hours.'

I handed the ice pack to Ed who winked at me. He told Dominic to hold the pack to his forehead. Dominic, his eyes wide, did as he was told.

'And d'you know what, Dominic, I reckon Vicky there has something dead nice for you under the counter. She's got lolli-pops for kids that hurt themselves, you know.'

'She gives me lollies anyway,' Dominic answered proudly.

'No way!' Ed sounded impressed. 'She must like you, so.'

'Yeah. Yeah.' Dominic smiled. Then asked shyly, 'D'you like me?'

'Absolutely,' Ed grinned and tousled his hair. 'I'll like you even more if you help me stock some shelves.'

'I'll just get my lolly first,' Dominic said.

He followed me back to the counter and I handed him a big green one that I'd bought the previous week but had chickened out of giving to him. His mother helped him unwrap it.

'Would you like a cuppa?' I asked her then, feeling sorry for her. 'You must have got a shock.'

She bit her lip. 'Need more than a cuppa to get me over the shock,' she muttered.

'Oh, well—'

'Black, plenty of sugar,' she said.

'I think I could do with one too, boss,' Ed called after me. 'Let's have an afternoon cuppa just this once.'

'Yeah,' I agreed, trying to sound as if I was torn with indecision, 'I think that's a good idea. We've all had a bit of a fright.'

Ed chortled.

'You've a fan for life there,' I remarked as Dominic left at closing time, his hand clasped tightly in his mother's, a big purple bruise like a beacon covering most of his little forehead.

'Nice kid.' Ed pulled on his jacket. 'Crap life.'

'Is he really all right? I mean, how do you know?'

'Ach, he's fine.' Ed turned in the door. 'Most bumps to the front of the head are harmless. He's grand.'

I nodded, not wanting to thank him but knowing that I had to. 'You did well with him.' I couldn't look at Ed. 'Did you do first aid or something?'

'Aye.' He smiled a little wistfully. 'Anyway, see you tomorrow.'

After he left, I sat down and surveyed the shop. He could sell toys, he could deal with difficult customers, he could calm down hysterical kids – was there nothing he couldn't do?

And then, I did something so completely childish that I surprised even myself. I located the transformer that he'd been working on earlier that day and began to try and figure it out.

I left the shop some time later, the aeroplane/robot proudly sitting beside the till.

Jesus, I was knackered.

Chapter Eighteen

T HERE WAS A letter waiting for me when I got in. I'm one of those pathetic people that love getting letters. Most of the time, they turn out to be bills or organisations looking for my money but I don't care. It's the fact that I've been written to that counts.

'Letter,' Sal indicated the table. 'For you.'

She didn't take her eyes off her laptop as she spoke. Her fingers flew over the keys and I knew better than to disturb her. For some reason she gets really narky if I make a noise in the middle of her writing a sentence. I mean, it's OK for her to tell me I've got a letter but not for me to say 'Where is it?' or anything like that.

I tiptoed across to the table and picked up a white handwritten envelope. My head was so full of gloating thoughts about what Ed would say when he came in and saw my transformer all made up that I ripped the letter open without realising exactly what it was.

It was the non-identifying information on my natural mother.

At least that's what it said. Somewhere in the middle of the first page. The words sort of leaped out at me. Hit me. And jammed themselves back into the sentence. I stood there, paper trembling in my hand, not able to think.

Sal kept typing.

Noises receded and whooshed back again.

The words of the letter danced in front of my eyes before I squeezed them tight shut and told myself to calm down.

I calmed down by folding the pages up and jerkily, it seems to me, walking into my room and shutting the door.

I don't think Sal even noticed.

My hands were trembling as I unfolded the letter again. There were two pages. The first was a note from the Adoption Board, saying that they'd received my request, warning that it could take up to two years to trace a person and that once traced, they advised counselling for all concerned. *Meanwhile*, the letter went on, *please find enclosed some non-identifying information on your birth mother*. The letter finished with a '*Yours sincerely, Valerie Coogan*.'

I placed this on the bed and focused on the second page.

Her name was Barbara.

My birth mother, I mean.

Barbara. I rolled the sound of it on my tongue. Found I couldn't say it without gulping.

She'd been nineteen.

Only young. But old enough to work. Maybe.

Today she'd be forty-seven.

Her hair was red.

My hand stole up to touch my frizzy locks.

I wondered if I looked like her at all.

I couldn't sleep that night. When I was a kid, I used to lie in bed and conjure up images of my mother. She'd be warm and welcoming and smiling. She'd have Barbie's figure and wear cool clothes. We'd go on holidays and I'd meet my dad. The three of us would realise that we belonged together. I'd look around my attic room and know that it wasn't really my attic room. It could have been anyone's.

Now, the image had changed. Now I knew she had red hair and would be forty-seven. She might even have a tooth missing the way I did. For some reason, one of my back teeth had never come up. The dentist at the time said quirky teeth ran in families. I remember my mother saying swiftly that she had all her back teeth and then I remember her looking at me and smiling, sort of sad. As if she'd forgotten that I wasn't really her daughter.

I lay in bed that night and hugged the letter to me. No matter how fragile, it was the first link in a chain that would lead me to her.

That would lead me to who *I* was.

Chapter Nineteen

T HE BUS INTO town the next morning was packed. Hot. And comfortable. Basically, after a night spent tossing and turning, I fell asleep. I woke up when the driver decided to play his music at top volume. Thin Lizzy's 'The Boys Are Back In Town'.

'Jesus!' I jerked awake.

A round, bald guy was peering down at me. 'Sorry, luv, but it was the only way I could wake you. Women dese days are awful sensitive to strange men touching them.'

'I haven't been touched by a strange man in a long time,' I said back as I gathered up my coat and bag from where they'd fallen on the floor. 'Would have made a nice change.'

He chortled good-naturedly. 'Take care,' he said as I left. 'It's raining hard out there.'

Raining hard was an understatement. And the fact that I'd slept past my stop and had to walk almost a mile in the hard rain made it worse.

And then, to arrive in, drenched to my knickers, only to see Bridie fussing over Ed as he tapped away furiously on the computer.

I was virtually ignored as she laid a cup of coffee in front of him and asked him if he'd like a 'special nutty biscuit'.

'Ta.' He didn't even bother to look at her and off she went, filling cups and getting biscuits. All the while she did that she hummed away to herself.

What did he think she was anyway? Some kind of a maid?

'Paralysed, are you?' I asked in a friendly voice, so he wouldn't think I was getting at him. 'Forgotten how to make coffee?'

Both of them looked at me.

'Ed made me a nice cup yesterday, Bridie.'

'Aw' – Ed had a smile in his voice – 'but you said yourself, it wasn't as nice as Bridie's.'

'Ooohh.' Bridie almost wet herself. 'Did she really say that? Did you really say that?' She beamed at the two of us.

I didn't bother to answer.

'I'll make you a cup too, shall I?' Bridie asked me. Then, 'Oh, you're soaking. Oh, take off those wet shoes.'

'I'm fine.' I squelched past both of them and got my own cup down from the shelf. 'Don't worry about me. I'm fine.'

It seemed that they weren't anyway.

'I'll make my own coffee.'

'And how are you coming on there?' Bridie deposited Ed's biscuits in front of him. Without waiting for an answer, she turned to me. 'Ed's working on the computer, doing something fancy, aren't you, Ed?'

'Just showing how best you could use your window display space, Vicky.'

I froze. 'Pardon?'

'Well, see here.' He pointed to our computer screen, which, instead of having a Toys Galore logo dancing across it, was now covered with little diagrams and measurements. 'If you—'

'What have you done to our computer?' I gasped. 'Where have our account files gone?'

'They're still there.' Ed looked slightly amused. 'I only loaded this program onto it this morning.'

'You can't go doing that!' I gawped at him. 'It's a Toys Galore computer system. What happens if—' I sought my computer-illiterate mind for something horrendous, 'if a virus gets into our files? You're putting our files at risk with all your fancy messing about.'

'Oooh yes.' Bridie looked alarmed now and I was glad. 'I never thought of that.'

'The program is safe.' Ed bit into a biscuit and looked at the two of us. 'A mate of mine designed it – he lent me the disk. Yez should be glad of it. It's dead handy.'

'Yeah, well.' I tossed my head. 'We don't need a computer to tell us how best to use our window space. All we have to do is look.'

Ed shrugged. 'So you just haven't bothered to look at it in the last eight months, have you not?'

The nerve! The cheek! 'We've been *busy*,' I said back, flushing. 'Waiting on our new member of staff to arrive.'

'Oooh, yes,' Bridie nodded. 'We've been very busy.'

'Well now you can take a break.' Ed smiled sweetly at me. 'After all, that's why I'm here.' He pointed to the computer. 'And if you'll just look, Vicky, you'll see what I'm talking about.'

I desperately didn't want to look.

'Because,' Ed went on, 'I was thinking last night, that if only I could get that transformer made we could do a mega window on them. And what do I find when I come in today – the transformer all made up.'

'Yeah,' I said airily, 'it was no problem.' To do it in two hours, I should have added.

'So *look*,' Ed indicated the computer, 'you make up the transformers and this is what we can do.'

Jesus, the idea of making up loads of transformers brought me out in a sweat. But if I didn't look, it'd seem petty. 'I'll still have to think about it,' I muttered, crossing towards him.

'Absolutely,' he nodded with enough deference to keep me happy. 'Now, see here—'

To my horror, he began to talk about measurements and depth and horrible mathematicky things. I kept nodding and acting like I understood, but I hadn't a clue. Bridie looked at the two of us proudly before saying that she'd go down and open up.

'We'll have a great shop by the time you're finished with us, eh, Ed,' she giggled before leaving.

She didn't notice the glare I gave her. Neither did Ed, he just smiled absently at her before re-launching himself into the figures again.

Eventually, I had to stop him. 'Who'll do all this work?' I asked.

'Me,' he said. 'It just means pulling out the partition and sticking in a shelf. That way, see, we can get two levels in, whereas before we only had one.'

That made sense. 'OK,' I said, hating that he was right. 'Leave it with me.'

'I'll just do out another proposal,' Ed said, pressing the print button. 'That way you can decide which one you want. OK?'

Jesus, I thought, I hadn't even managed to think up *one* proposal.

The only good thing about Ed working on the computer was that he was upstairs all morning while Bridie and I had the shop to ourselves. If I concentrated very hard, I could just about fool myself that Ed wasn't actually among us at all.

'So,' I asked Bridie as I counted out the bags of small change, 'did you enjoy your day off yesterday?'

'I did.' Bridie was dusting the counters. I'd swear the counter was higher when I'd come here first. Bridie was eroding it with all her cleaning. 'I got up at eight, went to mass and then got all my washing out. Isn't it great when you can get all your washing out?'

'I prefer to have all my nights out, actually.'

I liked to hear her laugh at my jokes. She hadn't bothered all last week since *he'd* arrived. I think she thought he was funnier than me. 'Oh, you're a one,' she said, flicking her duster at me. 'Did you go out last night then?'

'Nah.' I shoved the bags of change into the till. 'But I went out last Saturday.'

109

'With your journalist friend?'

She always called Sal that. I think she thought being a journalist was a big deal.

'Nope. With a man.'

'Boyfriend?'

'I guess he is now.'

'Oooh,' Bridie giggled. She looked at me with glittering eyes. 'Did you meet him in here?'

'Nah, I met him at a nightclub two weeks ago.'

Bridie shook her head, her mouth slightly open. 'Isn't that lovely,' she sighed. 'Just shows how wrong they are – they say nightclubs are the worst places to meet people.'

'Well, mainly they're the places to meet the worst people,' I smiled. 'But he was nice.'

'Well, I'm delighted for you. You haven't been out with anyone since you came here. A lovely girl like you deserves a lovely man.'

I didn't tell her about him being separated or about his little boy. It'd spoil the romance for her. 'Aw, thanks, Bridie.'

We smiled at each other.

'But you'd want to be careful all the same,' she said then. 'I mean, you don't know this chap very well, do you?'

'Careful?'

'You know, make sure you tell someone where you're going when you're out with him. Keep the mobile phone handy. I mean, I'm not one for technology, but the mobile phone is a wonderful thing.'

'And your computer is too.' Ed startled us by arriving down. He looked tired. He was rubbing his eyes and blinking hard. 'Eyestrain,' he muttered as he saw me looking. Then he pushed a few bits of meaningless paper at me. 'For you.'

I felt I'd better thank him. 'Ta.'

Almost as if he knew it choked me to say it, he ignored it. 'I've put in a screening program for e-mail,' he said to no one in particular. 'It's a download.'

Bridie and I looked at each other.

110

What the hell was a download?

'Seeing as you were so worried about computer viruses,' he went on.

Rather than show our ignorance, Bridie said, 'Wow, you certainly know your way around a computer, eh? A download – sounds almost rude.'

Ed laughed.

'So' – Bridie turned her attention back to me again – 'where did you go with this man?'

'A gig,' I answered, flushing. It was one thing telling Bridie about my private life but I wasn't about to announce it to Ed.

'A gig?' Bridie's brow puckered. 'That was unusual, wasn't it? Was it not a bit cold to be out on a horse and cart?'

Both Ed and I cracked up laughing.

Bridie looked confused.

'A music gig,' I giggled. 'As in a concert.'

'So call it a concert.' Bridie puckered her lips, embarrassed. 'A gig, how are you?' She dismissed me and turned to Ed. 'So, how about yourself? Did you go out with anyone the weekend?'

'Just some mates.' Ed was still grinning.

'No girl then?' Bridie asked.

'Girls don't interest me, Bridie,' Ed leaned on the counter and winked at Bridie. 'It's women I go for.'

'And why not!' Bridie giggled like a schoolgirl. 'So, have you a *woman* at all?'

'Unfortunately' – Ed looked dolefully at her, his blue eyes all shiny and round – 'the last time I fell for a woman I hurt myself really bad.'

'No!'

'Aye.' He was grinning. 'Skinned my heart and my knees and everything.'

Oh *please*, I thought.

Bridie was dripping sympathy. 'That's dreadful. Poor you.'

'Aye. So I've no one now at the minute.'

'Can you believe it, Vicky?' Bridie said. 'Can you believe that Ed has no one?'

Yes, yes I could actually. 'No.'

I made it sound unconvincing. Both of them looked at me. 'No,' I said again, brighter.

'Aw, sure, once I can cook some beans and iron a shirt, I'll get by – huh?'

'You won't attract too many women eating beans,' I said.

Ed laughed. He had a nice laugh. Really sunny or something. Worst thing was, though, I hadn't actually meant to be funny.

'And it's great you can laugh at it, too.' Bridie was gushing compassion. 'That's the spirit.'

He laughed again. I had to smile too.

'And have you anyone special yourself, Bridie?' Ed asked, teasing her.

Bridie tittered. 'I'm too old for all that.'

'Ah, you're never too old. I'll bet you're a right raver when you get going.'

'Indeeden I'm not.' She looked thrilled that he thought so, though.

'I bet all the old lads whistle when you walk by!'

'Stop!' Bridie was tittering with laughter. 'Will you stop it.'

'It'd be your legs. You've fine legs, Bridie.'

'Will you stop it!' Giggling, she flapped him with the duster.

'Aye.' He was all bewildered seriousness. 'I don't know what you're laughing at. You wouldn't see better crafted legs on a table, so you wouldn't.'

That cracked her up. I left the two of them and noisily began restacking the Lego sets. Legs like a table. Jesus, it was no wonder he hadn't got a girlfriend.

Chapter Twenty

'OOOH.' MEL BURST into the flat at seven on Saturday, arms outstretched in a big hug. 'Where is she? Where's my girl?'

I presumed she meant Sal.

'In the kitchen.'

I watched her totter into the kitchen on heels high enough to make it as a tall man in a circus. A lot of squealing and screeching followed. I wondered what the big occasion was. I was just shutting the door, about to join them, when Lorcan slithered in. Lorcan was Mel's partner. The first time I'd met Lorcan, I'd been convinced that Mel was having me on. 'Sure he's your boyfriend,' I'd sniggered when Lorcan had gone to the bar to get in a round of drinks. 'Sure he is.'

Mel had turned white. 'Yes,' she'd said, 'of course I'm sure. Why – what have you heard?'

'Oh nothing.' Hastily I tried to backtrack. 'I just—'

'That fling with the actress was just a rumour. You're reading the wrong papers, Victoria.'

And she hadn't talked to me for the rest of that night.

Lorcan was not what you'd expect Mel to go for. He wasn't a human dynamo, he wasn't even borderline good-looking. He was basically a prissy, twitchy, anally retentive snob. And that was when he let himself go. Short, skinny, with thinning brown hair, he favoured polo necks and polyester. OK, so they were BT's polo necks and polyester, but they still did nothing for him. And maybe there might have been a chance I could have liked him, but how do you form a relationship with someone when you hardly understand what they're talking about?

Mel doted on him.

So Sal and I put up with him.

'Hello, Victoria,' Lorcan nodded to me as he came in. His voice was deep and chewy.

'We're on a flying visit – Mel just wanted to offer her congratulations to Sal on her extremely erudite and engaging piece for the magazine.'

'Oh. Right.'

'She loves it apparently.'

More squeals from the kitchen.

'Right. I'd never have guessed.'

Lorcan thought this was funny. He chuckled a bit. Then nodded. Then nodded some more. Then asked, 'Are you going somewhere?' His nondescript eyes looked me up and down. 'You look very fetching.'

'Ta.' I have to say I was flattered. I'd never got a compliment from Lorcan before. So I joked, 'Once I'm not the one *fetching* the pints from the bar.'

He looked blank. 'Oh.' Pause. 'I meant fetching as in—'

'I know.' I felt stupid now. 'It was a joke?'

'Oh.' Weak smile. 'Ha, ha. Very good. Clever wordplay.'

'I'm just heading out for a drink with a guy I met a few weeks ago.' His eyes had already glazed over. Not for Lorcan the mundane everyday lives of others. So I pointed to the kitchen. 'Mel is in there.'

'Marvellous or' – wink, wink – 'should I say *Mel*vellous?' He laughed slightly at his wit, rubbed his hands together and left me staring after him.

Even his walk was odd. He half-hopped, half-loped along, almost as if he was conscious of me looking at him.

I heard him gravely congratulating Sal on her wonderful work and Sal telling them that it was nothing. It was a pleasure. It was what she was getting paid to do.

'And,' Mel said loudly, before taking a deep breath and

pausing dramatically. The air in the flat seemed to vibrate with what she was about to say. I shoved my head in the kitchen door. 'We are running it as our headline piece!'

'Oooh!' Sal almost dropped the bottle of wine she had in her hand. 'No!'

'Yes! Yes! Yes!' Mel did a little jig and blew kisses everywhere. Then she spotted me. 'Vicky, did you hear that? Did you?'

'Congrats,' I grinned in at Sal. I was really pleased for her. She'd worked so hard on the bloody thing. 'Can't wait to read it.'

'Oh' – Mel tapped the side of her nose – 'you'll be reading it all right. Everyone will be reading it.'

'So can we ask what it's about now?'

'No.' Mel shook her head. 'You never know who's listening or who you might tell that will tell someone else and before we know it, the whole world is writing the same thing. Next week. All will be revealed.'

Mel and Sal grinned at each other.

Lorcan sighed dramatically. 'There's no secret so close as that between a rider and his horse.'

We all looked at him.

'Are you calling Sal a horse?' I asked.

'Metaphorically speaking, yes.' Lorcan smiled.

Sal pursed her lips but said nothing.

'Well, I hope you're not suggesting that Mel and Sal are riding one another?' I couldn't resist it.

Lorcan flinched as if someone had just farted; Sal looked at Mel for her reaction before both began to laugh.

'That was a quote from R. S. Surtees – an English sporting journalist and novelist,' Lorcan said, offended. 'I thought you of all people would know that, darling.' He shot an accusing look at Mel.

'Well, I didn't, but I do now.' Mel tweaked his ear.

He blushed and pushed her off.

'Anyway,' I said, 'I must be off.'

115

'Yeah, Vic's got a hot date tonight,' Sal said to Mel.

'Really?' Mel raised her eyebrows. 'So that's why you've' – she made motions with her hands – 'washed your hair, is it?'

I might have taken offence from that, only I knew what she meant. I'd got my hair straightened that morning. It lay all sleek and shiny over my shoulders. Unfortunately it was still red, but my budget didn't extend to colouring it. 'Yep.'

'Anyone special?' she asked.

'Only the manager of some band,' Sal said.

'Boy Five, actually,' I put in.

'Oh, let me guess.' Mel closed her eyes. 'They're five boys who sing.'

I ignored the sniggering from the other two. 'You've met him,' I said. 'He talked to you at the nightclub we went to a few weeks back.'

She looked blank. 'I talk to a lot of people, dearie.' She blew me a kiss. 'It's the nature of my job.'

'Purple eyes?' I said.

'What?' That was Sal and Lorcan.

'He wears purple contacts,' I explained.

I saw Lorcan shiver.

'Oh, yes, I remember him now.' Mel made a face. 'Wanted me to do a spread on his band. I told him we were a celeb magazine not some *Hot Press* outfit.'

'They were number thirteen,' I said. 'Surely they're famous now?'

Mel rolled her eyes. 'Oh, innocence,' she sighed.

I was not staying around to be patronised by Mel. 'Well, I'll bid the horse' – nod at Sal – 'the rider and trainer farewell.' I gave them a little wave. 'I've to get ready to go out.'

'Enjoy!' Mel called after me. 'Make good use of the boys five!'

Huh, they could laugh!

It was so good to be in a relationship again – I'd almost forgotten what it was like. Normally, I'd have had to go out with

116

Sal and Mel and feel like a hick beside them as they talked about deadlines and journalists and editors. Their jobs sounded so important beside mine. I mean, who wanted to hear about how many transformers fitted in a shop window when they could hear about the latest exploits of tabloid hacks with celebs?

The answer, by the way, is fifty. Ed managed to shove fifty transformers into our toy shop window when I finally gave the go-ahead on Friday. Fifty transformers, made up by me on Thursday night – it had taken me hours – fifty transformers transforming into aeroplanes, boats and guns. Ed had worked all day on the window, with Dominic helping him. Dominic had taken quite a shine to Ed and followed him about the shop telling him stories about his B&B. Ed used him to find out what his favourite toys were and made a point of displaying them in the 'Under fives' section. He'd even bought Dominic a little toy for himself. 'It's just a thank-you present,' he explained to Dominic's prickly mother. Bridie kept cooing about how lovely it was of Ed to do that. Huh, I'd been buying the kid lollipops for ages and she'd never remarked on that.

Anyway, Marti called for me at eight. To my relief, he was dressed normally. Well, in tight black leather that squeaked when he walked, but it was better than green vertical stripes. 'How's things?' he grinned when he saw me. 'Thought you might like to grab a beer in town somewhere.'

'Great.' Sounded like my kind of night. I grabbed my coat and flicked on the alarm.

'Lead on.'

'Had a good week this week.' Marti strode ahead of me, towards the lift. 'The lads got a booking doing support to The Chillies so we'll be touring for next week. They're dead excited about it.'

'The Red Hot Chilli Peppers?' I was impressed.

'Naw, The *Chillies*,' Marti replied. 'The man band.'

'Oh.' I didn't want to say that I'd never heard of The Chillies. 'That was short notice, huh? I thought you'd have to book a support act weeks in advance.'

'Aw yeah, well, no one wants to tour with these guys,' Marti said off-handedly, pressing the button to bring us to the ground floor. 'The lead singer is a bit of a wanker apparently. Smashes things up and incites riots at his concerts. Just done to get publicity, you know.'

'Right.'

'So I told my lads, I told them not to get involved in stuff like that. They need a clean image.'

'Good.'

The lift pinged and we both got out. 'And I got my car adapted as befits my status as manager.'

Visions of sleek and sexy flashed before my eyes.

Reality beckoned as I spotted Marti's car underneath an enormous double-sided billboard of Boy Five. The lads' young, fresh faces beamed out from one side of the board while the words *Boy Five – The Best Band Alive* were splashed in lurid red all across the other side.

'Great, innit?' Marti said proudly. Then, without waiting for my answer, he went on, 'I got loudspeakers attached to the roof so that I can play the song as I drive along and everyone gets to hear it. So, what do you think?'

'Well . . .' I bit my lip. 'It'd be great if the lads were going up for election.'

Marti laughed. Then he stopped. His face fell. 'You hate it, don't you?'

'Look, it's your car . . .'

'It's too loud – yeah? It's overboard – yeah?'

'It's—'

'Linda was always telling me I didn't know when to stop,' he muttered. 'Jesus, maybe she was right.' He looked up in anguish at his car. Then he turned his eyes on me. 'D'you still want to be seen in it? I can't take it all down now, it'd cost me a fortune.' He paused. 'We can get a taxi if you like – what d'you say?'

I'd have liked a taxi but he looked so crushed and it was all my fault. 'I don't mind,' I lied, 'just, eh, well, maybe don't play any music – OK?'

A smile lit up his face. 'Aw, no, I wasn't going to anyway.' He caught my hand. Reddening, he muttered, 'I like you, Vicky. You're the first woman I've been out with since Linda left. I don't want to scare you off.'

It was, I learned later, not often that Marti spoke like that, but when he did, he meant it.

'You won't.' I went around to the passenger door of the car. 'Not unless you've a Boyzone tape hidden somewhere in here.'

He laughed loudly. 'No chance.'

It was a perilous journey. Marti's poster seemed to attract a lot of unwanted attention, especially from rough-looking teenagers. Chunks of earth smashed off the sides of the billboards as we made our way into town. Marti's car seemed to be shuddering as each ball of clay made its impact.

'Little useless wankers,' Marti fumed, unable to get the car to go above forty. 'Jealous, that's all they are.'

He manoeuvred his car into a multi-storey car park with inches to spare at the roof and we got out. 'Daly's is a nice pub,' Marti said, locking the car and patting it as one would a pony. 'How about we go there?'

Daly's was nice. It was always good for a bit of a laugh. 'Brill.'

That evening Daly's was packed. There was a sort of karaoke thing on and people were being asked to get up and sing for a pint. A gang of lads beside the door were shoving a guy up as we arrived in. 'Go! Go! Go! Go!' they were chanting.

Marti and I took our seats across from them and Marti went up to the bar to order the drinks.

'And now,' the DJ said, 'we've Ed O'Neill up. Give him a hand.'

The guys beside the door erupted in cheers.

I hardly heard them. It was typical, going into a pub and meeting a guy I could barely stand to work beside. I only hoped he didn't spot me. He didn't seem to. Mouthing the word

119

'fuckers' at his friends, he went up to take the microphone from the DJ.

'I'm told Ed busks around Grafton Street on Thursday evenings,' the DJ went on. 'He's very popular, by all accounts.'

More cheers.

Marti arrived down with the drinks.

'A guy I work with,' I told him.

'Oh, right, great.' Marti took a gulp of his pint. 'Good singer, is he?'

'I have no idea.'

'He'd look good in a mature sort of boy band,' Marti said idly.

I grinned, trying to imagine Ed in a white Lycra cowboy suit.

Ed had decided to sing 'Big Yellow Taxi'.

Another cheer from the lads he was with. Ed grinned down at them and the music began. It was a brilliant performance, helped, it has to be said, by his mates all yelling out the '*Don't it always seem to go, you don't know what you've got till it's gone*' chorus. Soon most people in the pub were clapping and singing along. And Ed just dripped sex all over that stage. Well, to me there is nothing so much of a turn-on as a man with a guitar in his hand. Not that Ed even had a guitar, but if he had, he would have been irresistible.

There was lots of clapping and laughter when he'd finished.

'I think that deserves a pint,' the DJ called.

A Guinness was handed to him to roars of approval from the crowd.

It was on the way down that Ed spotted me. He smiled and crossed towards us. 'Better say hello to the boss,' he grinned.

To my horror, I blushed. 'Yeah, hi,' I stammered out.

'Hey, great song.' Marti thrust out his hand. 'Marti Hearty, manager, Boy Five.'

Ed grinned. 'Ta. They' – he thumbed to his mates who were all staring curiously at us – 'me flatmates, always make me do it when we go out. It's just a laugh, really.'

'You were good,' I said.

'Ta.' Ed grinned at me, indicated his mates again. 'Anyway, I'd better get back.'

'Nice voice,' Marti said to me when he left. 'Pity I'm so tied up with Boy Five 'cause I'd sign him.'

Ed's arrival back at his table was met with a 'whoooo' followed by loads of laughter.

Marti drove me home. This time I did ask him back to the flat and he accepted. As I was spooning the coffee into the cups, he came behind me and wrapped his arms about me. 'Give us a kiss,' he whispered.

I turned around and wrapped my arms about his neck. Slowly he brought his mouth to mine. Soft, gentle kisses. I was just beginning to wish he'd do a bit more when Sal burst in.

'Ooops, sorry, folks.' She grinned hugely. 'Didn't mean to interrupt. I'll get out of your way.'

'Naw, naw, no need.' Marti pulled away from me. 'I'd better go. The sprog will be missing me.'

Sal looked puzzled.

'I'll see you out.' I virtually shoved him out the door.

Then, when he'd gone, after a few more limp biscuit kisses, I legged it into my room before Sal could ask me anything.

Chapter Twenty-one

IT SEEMED THAT everyone in the world got up before I did. As I stumbled out of bed the next day, I heard Sal humming away to herself in the kitchen. I use the word 'humming' very loosely. Sal hasn't a note. And whenever I slag her over it, she always replies that they're not the sort of notes she's interested in having anyway. So there I was, having been in bed by one, feeling completely knackered, and there she was, hardly having been in bed at all, eating breakfast and looking radiant.

How does everyone do it?

Iron tablets?

The 'tonic' my mother was always referring to? 'Vicky, you'd want to get yourself a good tonic.'

'I don't drink gin,' I'd told her.

It had made my dad laugh.

She hadn't looked impressed.

'So,' Sal asked as I shambled in past her, 'how'd the date with Purple Eyes go?'

I stiffened. So far I'd avoided telling her of Marti's marital status. 'Marti,' I corrected. Without looking at her, I popped some bread into the toaster. 'And yep, it went well.'

'Not that well.' Sal sniggered into her bowl of healthy something-or-other. Then made a big deal of looking all around her. 'He's not here this morning, is he?'

She was a great one for measuring the success of a date in terms of how long it took to reach shagging stage. If it didn't happen until the third date it was a mega slow starter.

122

'If he was here this morning,' I said back, 'he certainly wouldn't be here next weekend or the weekend after.'

'Puritan!' Sal scoffed. 'You've been brainwashed by your mother. If he likes you, he'll be back, simple as that.'

I was not getting into the puritan debate again. It had nothing to do with my mother's dire warning of men not respecting me; it was all a lot more practical than that. Sal could take a guy home and shag his brains out and he wouldn't believe his luck. He'd come trotting back the next week to see if it had really happened, whereas if I took a guy home first date he'd think I was desperate. And where would he be the next week? Running for his life, that's where. Or, if he didn't go heading for the hills, he'd start reading more into the relationship than I wanted him to and then *I'd* have to do a runner.

Relationships, for me anyhow, were a minefield. And it wasn't just the love ones.

'He left pretty quick after I came in last night.' Sal was licking her spoon and looking speculatively at me.

'He had to go home.'

'Home?' she scoffed. 'No man goes haring home unless his mammy warns him not to be out late. Now, he's hardly still living with Mammy, is he?'

I didn't answer.

'He *isn't*!'

I didn't like the 'are-you-completely-mental' look on her face. 'She lives with him,' I clarified. 'And she was babysitting his little boy.'

Her spoon clattered to the floor. For a fleeting second I enjoyed her look of shock before she said incredulously, 'Come again?'

'You heard him last night,' I said. 'He had to go home to his little boy.'

'Jesus!'

I felt like I was back in school being grilled for having no homework done. I tossed my hair back in what I hoped was a

123

defiant gesture, before saying nonchalantly, 'Nope, just an ordinary little boy.'

Sal did smile before declaring, 'That is so not something to make a joke about. Oh God!' She pulled an anguished face. 'A kid. How awful.'

She made it sound like AIDS. Seeing as I'd come this far, I decided to go the whole hog. 'He has a wife too.'

'Jesus!' Now she really looked gobsmacked. 'He's *married*.'

'Separated.'

For the first time ever, Sal was speechless. It didn't last long though. 'I take it back. You're not a puritan. You're a gobshite.'

Her words stung. 'He's *separated*.'

'So? He was married, wasn't he? He has a kid, hasn't he? That woman will be in his life for ever.'

'She left them.' I furiously buttered my toast. I didn't want to hear this.

'There'll always be that tie there.'

I shrugged. 'It's not that serious, anyway.'

'It's bloody dynamite!' Sal stood up from the table and brushed by me as she dumped her bowl in the sink. 'There's no future in that. For one thing, he'll always have two houses to support – hers and his.'

'She *left* him.'

'Doesn't make a difference. He'll have no money to make a decent life.'

It always came down to money with her. 'I'm not like you. I don't think of money all the time.' I hoped it would hurt her the way she'd hurt me. I *wasn't* a gobshite. I liked Marti, he liked me. It wasn't as if it was an affair or anything as seedy as that.

'Well' – she fingered my tatty dressing gown and arched a perfect eyebrow – 'maybe you should.' She swished past me, her own silk designer gown fluttering out behind her.

I couldn't eat my toast.

* * *

124

We didn't say much to each other for the rest of the day. She lolled about in her pyjamas, flicking through the Sunday papers and drinking glasses of water. I, after trying to read my latest self-help book and failing, decided to get dressed and go for a walk. The atmosphere in the flat was so bloody cold, I'd have been deep frozen by nightfall.

It wasn't a bad day for February. It was dry and bright and the birds were singing. For the first time that year it looked as if spring was a definite possibility. I decided to head towards the park. Walking alone in the park would look slightly less suspect than tramping the streets of Yellow Halls on my own.

There were a few people milling around in the park. Couples entwined, OAPs with their arthritic dogs, families with kids throwing bread to lethargic ducks. The ducks were the fattest ones I'd ever seen. One little fella was aiming great hunks of bread directly at them and scoring every time.

'Oh, yeah,' he said as he hit one particularly obese duck on the back.

His mother smiled fondly at him.

Little brat, I thought. He reminded me of my Cousin Tommy. It's exactly the sort of thing he would have done. But it was nice the way his mother thought he was great. It gave me a sort of pang to see it. Right in the middle of my chest.

'Vicky!'

The voice startled me.

'I didn't know you were a Sunday stroller!'

What an old-fashioned name. How like a complete dork I sounded. But then again Bridie was an old-fashioned sort of woman. 'Bridie, hi.' I was quite glad to see her. Now, with a person walking beside me, I wouldn't look like such a saddo. She was dressed in her brown tweed coat and old lady button-up boots. Where do old people get stuff like that? Is there some secret shop you only learn about as you get older or something? Anyway, she folded her arms and smiled up at me. 'I'm just taking a stroll while my chicken cooks. It should be ready around

125

half-four, so that gives me just enough time to walk to the swings and back.'

She was the exact same as in work. Everything timed to perfection.

'I like looking at the kiddies in the playground. So I spend about ten minutes there and then I turn back. I live just across that way.' She pointed in a vague sort of way at the trees across the green. 'I always go for a stroll on a Sunday. Do you?'

'Nah.' I began to walk alongside her. 'It's my first time in the park actually. It's nice.'

'It's more than nice. It's a lovely place to blow the cobwebs away. I come here most days. On my day off, I walk the whole park. It takes about ninety minutes. That's what you should do – you'd enjoy it.'

Maybe I would. When I'd been away, I'd walked and walked and thought and thought and there'd come a stage when I'd walked so far that my mind would switch off and that was the best time. Just walking and enjoying the moment. I guess at heart I'm a bit of a loner. I don't mean in an antisocial way or anything, I like a night out as much as anyone, it's just that I always find myself alone at some stage in the night and I enjoy it. I enjoy being a saddo. What I don't like is others *thinking* I'm a saddo.

'Sunday is my favourite day,' Bridie went on, 'going to mass, getting the papers, having a walk, enjoying my dinner, watching the television. Just, you know, relaxing.'

My Sundays were usually spent drinking copious amounts of water to rid myself of the banging headache from the night before.

'So what brings you out here?' Bridie asked.

'Oh' – I made a face – 'my flatmate isn't talking to me.'

'The journalist girl?'

'The one and only.'

'Oh dear.' Bridie made clucking sounds. 'And on a Sunday and everything.'

I don't know what Sunday had to do with it.

'So I came out to get away from her,' I said, trying to sound happy about it. 'If anyone can create a bad atmosphere it's her.'

'Mmm,' Bridie nodded. 'Journalists are very temperamental people.'

I was glad she was on my side.

We walked along side by side until we came to the swings. Well, it was more than swings, it was one of those dinky wooden playgrounds with climbing nets and huge slides and wooden climbing frames. Bridie sat down on a seat and I joined her.

'The kiddies have great fun here,' she said, half wistfully.

'The adults could have too,' I muttered. 'Look at the size of that slide. Betcha it'd be great to go down backwards on it.'

She laughed. 'I'd break every bone in my body.'

I watched the kids running up and down and envied them. 'One day, when it rains and there's no one else here, I'm going to come back and go on that slide,' I said.

Bridie smiled.

'I am. Honest.'

'You'd get stuck halfway down,' she giggled childishly.

I have to say I was insulted. 'I'm not *that* big.'

'No,' she was still giggling. 'I meant with the rain.'

'Oh. Right.'

We didn't say much after that. Just looked at the kids.

'Playgrounds are happy places,' Bridie remarked suddenly. 'That's why I come here.'

'Just like the toy shop,' I said.

She looked at me, surprised. 'Yes, I suppose.'

'That's how I got the job, I reckon,' I told her. 'In my interview they asked me why I'd like to manage a toy shop and that's what I told them. I said that toy shops are always happy. I like happy places.'

'Who doesn't?' Bridie stood up. 'Who doesn't?'

She sounded sad.

I walked her back to the park entrance. She was quiet and didn't say much. I was wondering if she wanted to get rid of me.

Maybe she hadn't wanted me to follow her in the first place? After all, would I want my boss with me on a Sunday? I was about to say that I had to be going when she asked, 'D'you want to come for dinner – I'll have enough for two?'

I hadn't had dinner since Christmas. Not a proper spuds and two veg dinner anyway. But maybe Bridie was only being polite. She was an awful polite person. 'You don't have to,' I protested, 'I know you like being on your own and stuff.'

'Being on my own?' She looked surprised. Then shrugged. 'Well, yes, yes, I suppose I do but, well, with your friend not talking to you, I just thought—'

'Don't worry about me.' *She was having roast chicken. Mmmm.* 'She'll probably talk eventually.'

'There's plenty,' Bridie went on. 'I usually get a chicken big enough to last a few days. That way I can have chicken sandwiches for lunch in work. And I've put on extra potatoes because I was going to make a bit of potato salad, but you can eat them. And I can always put on a few extra peas and carrots. I use the tinned ones, you see.' She sounded as if she really wanted me. And I didn't have anywhere else to go. And I hadn't realised how much I wanted a dinner . . .

'If you're sure,' I said.

'Of course I'm sure.' She smiled at me. 'A bit of company would be nice.'

Bridie's house was a tiny two-up two-down affair. Her garden consisted of grass and rose bushes. Her front door was brown with the brass knob shining like some kind of a homing beacon in a street of tarnished knockers. Inside, her hall was cream and brown and her kitchen was cream and brown. The whole place was clean, but it didn't sparkle. I guess it was because everything looked so brown.

The smell of chicken was lovely, though. And she had potatoes gently boiling.

Sticking a fork into them, she pronounced them almost done.

'Now you sit down and make yourself comfortable while I lay the table and get some vegetables on.'

I sat on one of her brown kitchen chairs. It felt a bit weird to be in Bridie's house but it felt nice as well.

'Can I do anything?' I asked, knowing that if my mother heard me she'd keel over and die.

'No. No.' Bridie waved me off. 'Just relax. I want you going home ready to make up with that friend of yours.'

I felt really awkward as she fussed about, handing me a napkin and a fancy glass.

Then came the dinner. A massive plate for me. Honestly, I'd say she gave me all her lunches for that week.

'Eat up now.' Bridie smiled at me from across the table. 'I don't often get company but when I do I like them to go home full.'

After dinner, she led me into her 'good' room. She didn't say it was good but I knew by the smell of polish and the lonely look of the furniture that it hadn't been used for ages. There were pictures up on the mantelpiece. As Bridie went to get me a coffee, I studied them.

There was one of Bridie taken years ago that still looked like her. She was standing on a beach somewhere with the wind blowing her hair and she had a hand up to keep it down. She was laughing into the lens. Beside her stood a man, laughing too, his hands casually jammed into his trouser pockets. He had dark hair and was quite handsome in a nineteen-fifties type of way.

'Who's that?' I asked as Bridie came in. 'Your husband?'

She put down my coffee and took the photo from me. 'No.' She smiled at the frame. 'He would have been if he'd lived.' I saw her stroke his face.

'Oh. I'm sorry.'

'Not at all. It was a long time ago now.' She put the photo back in its place. 'I just like that photograph. Mainly because I look nice in it – don't you think?'

I grinned at her vanity. 'You're a real babe, Bridie.'

'Legs like a well-made table,' Bridie smiled back.

'Sorry?'

'Ed. He said that.' Bridie giggled. 'He's the funniest lad. I have to admit I was a bit worried at the start but he's working out well, don't you think?'

I was glad she thought so. 'I think he's a bit' – I didn't want her to think I was a bitch or paranoid – 'a bit overpowering.' The word didn't do him justice. 'Back-stabbing bastard' would have done the job.

Bridie looked puzzled. 'Oh no.' She shook her head. 'He's a nice quiet lad and the kids love him.'

'Do they?' That was news to me.

'Oh yes,' Bridie nodded. 'He knows all the PlayStation games and all the wrestlers and everything. I think he does nothing bar watch TV and play computer games in his spare time.'

'And you wonder why he hasn't a girlfriend.'

That was bitchy, I know.

'A boy like that won't be single for long,' Bridie said with a confidence that annoyed me. Then with a bit of a whoop she said, 'And I almost forgot – how did your night out go last night?'

'Great.' I was delighted that she remembered.

'And him?' Bridie asked. 'Do you still like him?'

'Very,' I nodded. 'He's a bit eccentric – you'd think he was odd but he's not. He's' – I looked at her cream ceiling and tried to think of how to describe him – 'colourful. He's got a big loud personality.'

'Oh.' She didn't look too impressed.

'He's not like anyone else I've ever been with. I like that.'

'Well, I'm glad.' She picked up my coffee and handed it to me. 'It's important to be happy, to make good choices.'

She sounded a bit sad as she said it.

I stayed in Bridie's until after seven. She was all set to make me tea but I couldn't hang around any longer. Part of me is ashamed to admit that I didn't want to have to tell anyone that I'd just spent a Sunday with a sixty-year-old woman who wasn't even my mother. I think she was disappointed that I couldn't stay but I pretended to her that I was going out with some friends.

If only.

Instead I pulled up my hood – it had begun to rain – and I walked home prepared to brave the atmosphere.

Sal was surprisingly polite when I came back.

'You had a phone call,' she said tersely, watching me shake all the drops from my mac onto the kitchen floor. 'From the purple-eyed, separated father.'

'I did?' I forgot about my mac and tried to look nonchalant. I figured that if I looked desperate, Sal'd string me along for ages. 'What'd he say?'

'He said that he'd ring you on your mobile.'

My mobile. My very *immobile* mobile. I legged it into my bedroom and, locating my haversack, tore it open. My phone was sitting serenely in its groovy holder, as dead as a Dodo.

The calendar on the wall seemed to mock me with its big CHARGE MOBILE sign. When I emerged from the room, Sal was holding out my charger. 'Figured you'd need this.'

I tried not to grin as I took it from her. Even if she was a cow, she knew me well.

'You'll never have a relationship without a mobile phone,' she warned as she stood behind me.

I said nothing, just plugged in my phone and prepared to wait at least an hour until I could access it.

'Sorry about earlier,' Sal said. 'It was none of my business.'

Apologies from Sal were about as rare as French cooked steak. ''Sfine,' I muttered, trying not to sound too gobsmacked. Uneasily, I wondered what she was up to.

'I mean, if you want a relationship with a married man with a kid, you go right ahead.'

'I will. Thanks for your permission.'

131

'And if I want a relationship with a young, hunky, rich guy, you won't stand in my way either, sure you won't?'

'Nope.'

It was only after she'd waltzed out of the room that I realised what she'd meant. She was going in after Ed.

I wondered what had brought that on.

There were two messages on the phone.

Two voicemail messages.

The missed call part told me that I'd missed a call from Marti and another one from a number that I didn't recognise.

Dialling the number, I attempted to access the messages.

And guess who hadn't topped up her credit?

Chapter Twenty-two

THE FOLLOWING DAY, I broke all records and got up at ten. On my day off!

Normally, I'd lie in bed telling myself over and over that I was going to get up, but the fact that I was unable to access two messages on my mobile was driving me mad. I got up, pulled on my jeans and a yellow sweatshirt, pulled a comb through my hair and, donning socks and trainers, legged it out the door and up the road to the corner shop.

'Call card.' I shoved my money to the guy behind the counter. 'Fifteen euro.'

He seemed to be a slow starter like me. He took my money, looked at it for ages, put it in the till, spent ages looking with narrowed eyes at what he was supposed to do next while I hopped impatiently from foot to foot.

'Hi there.' A face poked itself into mine. Buck teeth gleamed in the dusty light. 'Day off, eh?'

'You got it.' I smiled briefly at Troy, hoping like mad he wasn't going to talk to me.

'Cool sweatshirt.' Troy nodded at my sweatshirt.

'Ta.'

'You always wear big, bold colours, don't you?' Troy leaned his elbow on the counter and poked his face even further into mine. 'I've noticed that about you.'

'That's me, big and bold,' I said. I deliberately didn't look at him. Troy was like a stray dog; if I showed him any interest at all, he'd follow me home and hover about all day.

He was snorting with laughter over my comment and saying that he hoped I wasn't too bold when the guy behind the counter said in a bored voice, 'Was that fifteen euro?'

'Yes.'

A piece of paper with a number was passed over to me. 'There.'

'Ta.' I took it up and shoved it in my pocket. I'd dial once I got out onto the street. My heart had begun to hammer and I felt a bit sick. I told myself it was because I hadn't had any breakfast. 'Bye, Troy.'

'Aw, no, awww, look,' Troy called after me, 'I've to just get a packet of Star Trek cards and I'll walk home with you.'

I pretended not to hear. I took off down the road and crossed into the park, knowing Troy would think I'd gone back to the flat. I sat down on a mouldy-looking seat and inputted my credit number. Once that was done, I dialled up for my messages.

'You have two new voicemail messages. First message. Left Thursday seventh of February.' To my crushing disappointment, I heard my mother say, 'I don't think this auld thing is working at all.' My father's voice rumbled from somewhere in the background. 'I'll leave a message, so,' my mother said a bit narkily. Then, sort of breathlessly, she said, 'Hello, love. It's me. Mam.' A bit of a laugh. 'I've got this new mobile phone from Tommy. He gave it to us, he didn't need it. Anyway, I'm trying it out. Just to tell you that I'm up in Dublin next week. Tuesday. And I'll call into work to see you for lunch. Bye-bye now.' A load more fumbling before it went dead.

The second message came on. I hardly heard Marti as he thanked me for a great night and promised to call me again.

It had been my mother.

The unknown number had been my mother.

All last night, I'd envisioned that it might be the adoption board. That they'd got news for me.

And all along it had been her.

I don't know how long I sat on the bench with the stupid phone to my ear but it was ages.

I was so devastatingly, terribly disappointed.

Chapter Twenty-three

MY MOTHER SAT across from me, tucking into her enormous salad roll. She looked well. She was wearing her green suit, the one she'd bought for Christmas, and a white blouse. Green suited my mother. Most colours did really. On the table in front of her sat the newly acquired mobile phone. 'In case your father rings,' she'd said, placing it reverently beside her plate.

'And why would he?' I asked, amused.

'Oh, no reason.' She gave a short laugh and indicated the phone. 'They're great things, aren't they?'

I hadn't really thought about it. 'Suppose.'

'I mean, if you'd had one when you were on your travels, it would have made things so much easier.'

I ignored that. There was no point in explaining to her about the difficulties of charging a mobile whilst crossing the desert in a tent.

Mam gave her phone another fond look.

I don't know what was so special about it. It was last year's Nokia. 'I would have bought one for you if you'd wanted it,' I said. Then added, 'A new one.'

She rolled her eyes and laughed a bit. 'Don't,' was all she said, but I knew what she meant.

I have a thing about accepting second-hand stuff. 'False pride,' my mam calls it. 'Having too much money,' my dad says. It's neither. I just don't like feeling that I owe someone.

'Don't,' Mam said again. Then, in a wonderful, subtle change of subject, she asked, 'Are the chips nice?'

'Lovely, yeah.'

Silence.

'So, what brings you up here?' I shoved a chip into my mouth to show her that I did like them. 'It's hardly just to see me.'

'I like seeing you,' she said defensively. 'I'd like to see a bit more of you.'

I flinched. 'I'm just busy,' I mumbled.

'I know that,' she said in such an understanding voice that it made me feel like the worst daughter in the world, 'but surely not too busy to come and see us once in a while?'

I said nothing.

Her hand crossed the table and clasped mine. 'What is it?' she said softly. 'Why won't you visit?'

I was caught off-guard. Her hand felt funny on top of mine. It gave me the sort of claustrophobic feeling that the family gatherings did. 'I do visit,' I muttered. What did they want? 'I come home as often as I *can*.'

I don't know what it was I saw in her eyes. They sort of flinched and wavered and then it was gone. She took her hand away. I was glad. 'Well, I hope you'll come down next month. It's your dad's sixtieth and I'm throwing him a surprise party.'

'Of course I'll be there.'

'Good.'

She held my gaze for a bit before turning her attention back to her lunch.

'So that's why you're up here, is it?' I asked, striving for normal once again. 'You're buying Dad a present.'

'Among other things,' she answered.

'Yeah?'

I saw her gulp. 'Well,' she floundered, 'I, eh, I was in the markets looking at flowers for Lisa Sweeney's wedding. They've fabulous colours here. I just want to get an idea of what's available.'

'She's getting married in late *summer*. Those flowers won't be around then.'

137

'They'll be around for the right money,' Mam answered. 'And the Sweeneys said to spend what I like.'

'Well, you'd better not do the flowers too nice or they'll outshine the bride.'

'Stop!' Mam flapped her hand at me and laughed. 'You really are awful!'

'It was just a joke.' For some reason I felt ashamed of myself. 'I didn't mean it.' But I had.

Mam smiled.

There was silence as we began to eat our lunch in earnest. It was nearly two and I had to go back and relieve Ed. No point in giving the guy *excuses* to shaft me.

'So' – Mam poured the last drop of tea from the pot into her cup – 'have you' – she paused and flushed – 'found out anything about your, your' – she bit her lip – 'birth mother?' She busied herself stirring milk into her tea.

God, she was really getting personal today. 'A bit.' It was funny that she'd asked. Like I said before, my folks don't like to bring the issue of my birth into the spotlight. I glanced quickly at my mam and she was giving me this encouraging look, as if she wanted to know, so I gulped out, 'Her name is Barbara.'

'That's a nice name,' Mam whispered.

'Yeah.' I paused. 'And she has red hair.'

Mam laid down her spoon. 'Like yours,' she said softly.

'Uh-huh.' Without thinking, I curled some of my hair about my finger.

Mam smiled a little. Sort of sadly, I think. After a few seconds, she asked, 'Anything else?'

'No.' I studied my fingernails. 'Finding someone can take up to two years, you know.'

'Really?' She made some sort of a surprised gasp. 'I didn't know that.'

I wished she hadn't brought the subject up. All I wanted was for this lunch to end. All the guilty feelings were grabbing me and making me feel awful.

'If you do find out something, will you tell me?' Mam asked then. Her voice was soft and low. 'I'd like to know.'

'Would you?' My eyes unexpectedly filled with tears. I didn't know if I felt awful or relieved or what. 'Really?'

'Yes. Really.' I think she was about to touch me but one of the waitresses came over.

'Are yez finished?' She stood beside us with a cloth in her hand. 'There's a bit of a queue waiting for a table.'

We ignored her. 'OK?' Mam said.

I just nodded.

I couldn't say much.

Sal, of course, chose that day to breeze into the shop in search of love, romance and a big fat chequebook.

'Hiiii,' she said chirpily as she came in. 'How's things?' She sashayed towards the counter in a pair of red jeans and a white Calvin Klein T-shirt that dipped in a plunging V neckline. A tiny red denim jacket clung to her upper body and her light blonde hair tumbled around her shoulders. She looked windswept and vibrant and part of me envied her her easy confidence. She was here to get a man and get a man she would.

'What are you doing here?' I hissed at her. It was bad enough seeing Ed in work and hearing about what a wonderful guy he was from Bridie, without having to listen to it at home too.

She tossed her head. 'I'm looking for a toy,' she said, all mock-innocence. 'What else?'

'A boy?' I virtually shrieked. 'Stop it. Now!'

'Toy,' she repeated, reddening slightly. Then, lowering her voice, she hissed, 'You said you wouldn't care.'

'Of course I care,' I hissed back. 'Jesus, will you get out!'

'Oooh.' Sal suddenly smiled and it was as if the sun came out in the shop. 'Hi, you must be Ed.'

Ed, who had just appeared from the back, dirty and dishevelled, looked confused. 'Sorry, do I know you?'

'I'm Vicky's flatmate.' Sal flicked her razor-straight hair back from her face. 'She's told me all about you.'

'I haven't,' I put in quickly.

Both of them looked at me.

'She says you're an expert on boy's toys,' Sal went on, tittering. 'Can you help me choose something for my nephew?'

'What nephew would that be?' I asked, trying not to grin. Honestly, she was such a cow but she had such nerve.

'My brother's kid, the eight-year-old,' Sal lied charmingly.

'You sure you don't want Vic to show you?' Ed asked, completely oblivious of Sal's intentions.

'She said you're the expert,' Sal twinkled.

Ed shot me a sceptical look, which I returned with a shrug. Then he turned his full attention to Sal. He gave her *the* smile. I had got to call it that because of all the times he used it on the customers. It was a smile that said, 'You are, hand on heart, my number-one priority.' And Sal, not to be outdone, gave him her smile. The one that says, 'Hey, I'm only a helpless woman and I need a man like you to *make* me your number-one priority'.

'This way, Vicky's friend.' Ed was now giving her his wink. 'You'll probably find something suitable back here.'

'It's Sal,' Sal said pertly, using her eyes to dazzle him, 'and yes, I'm sure you're right. I'll bet there's something very suitable back there.'

He grinned and strode on ahead of her, leading the way.

'Cor,' Sal mouthed to me but I pretended not to notice.

She came back about ten minutes later with two PlayStation games and a whole heap of wrestlers and transformers. Ed, depressingly enough, was the best salesperson of the lot of us. The *crap* he persuaded parents to buy for their kids was unbelievable. And it wasn't as if he did a hard sell or anything. He had a sort of easy charm that made you believe he was kosher. All he had to do was recommend something to a customer and it was sold. I think part of it was that Ed loved toys and so he made our customers love them too.

He helped Sal carry her purchases to the counter. 'Honestly,' she was saying to him as she dumped them in front of me, 'you are the most helpful assistant Vicky has ever had in here.'

Like she would know, I thought in amusement.

'And you must be the most generous aunt on the planet,' Ed grinned.

For a second Sal looked puzzled.

'The toys,' I supplied helpfully, 'for your nephew?'

'Oh those,' Sal laughed. 'They're nothing, he deserves all of them. I just love kids.'

I bit my lip to try and stop giggling. 'They'll cost about eighty euro worth,' I said, beginning to cash them up. 'Are you sure you want them all?'

'Sure. Sure I do.' She smiled bravely as I ran them through the till. 'Ed recommended them all.' She smiled at Ed who, completely missing the fact that he was being flirted with, shrugged modestly. 'Here.' Sal handed me her credit card. 'Put them on that.'

Another customer came in. Sal looked meaningfully at me.

'Ed,' I said, 'will you finish this sale while I see to this lady?'

'Ach, no.' Ed shook his head. 'Sure you talk to your friend there, I'll go and see to this one.' He nodded amicably at Sal and sauntered off.

I tried not to giggle.

'Is he thick or what?' Sal hissed, rolling her eyes. She pulled some wrestlers out of the way. 'You can take those wrestlers out. There is no way I'm buying them. They're completely over-priced.'

'And the PlayStation games?'

'Just pretend like I want them. I'll give them back to you—'

'She doesn't want any help.' Ed arrived back. 'Hey' – he looked at the discarded wrestlers – 'what's wrong with them?'

'Oh, nothing.' Sal gave her tinkly laugh. 'I just thought I'd bought two the same.' She hastily began to shove them towards me again.

'Two the same?' Ed shook his head and grinned. I could see Sal melting. 'Not at all. Sure this fella here is Triple H.' He held up my favourite wrestler. 'This other one here is The Rock, he's the one most of the kids love, and the one you just put back, he's . . .'

I walked off and left him discussing the merits of one wrestler versus the other with Sal.

To be honest, if she could survive the conversation, she deserved him.

'I think we should do a wrestling window,' Ed said when Sal finally left. 'The wrestling rings are cool – have you seen them?'

'I ordered them,' I said, a bit snottily. 'I know how good they are.'

'Then you'll definitely have thought that we should do a window at some stage – yeah?'

He looked at me like a kid hoping for sweets.

'I might have,' I shrugged. 'Could never get around to it though.'

'I'll do it if you like,' Ed offered. 'That's what I'm here for, isn't it?' The pale blue of his eyes lit up his face. 'It'll be *great*. I'll put the backstage mayhem and the studio wreckage on each side of the ring. Honestly, they'll sell a bomb once the kids see it. The transformer sales have really picked up – yeah?'

'Yeah,' I muttered with bad grace.

Ed grinned delightedly. 'Told you. And see, the problem with the way we're displaying the wrestlers at the moment is that they're all in the boxes, except for that one over there, and the kids don't see that unless they come in. This way, they'll all come in.'

Of course he was right. And I'd lied, the idea of doing a window had never occurred to me. I gritted my teeth – yet another little defeat in what was turning out to be a bit of a list. 'Fine,' I muttered.

'Don't be so sceptical,' he grinned, 'it'll boost the sales no end.'

I'm glad he took my resentment for scepticism. 'Just make sure Triple H is the one that's winning,' I said gruffly.

He looked at me in surprise. I dunno whether it was because he couldn't believe that I actually knew the name of a wrestler or because I wanted Triple H, The Rock's arch enemy, to be the victor.

'I was going to have—'

'The Rock, yeah, I know, but he's an arrogant shit.' I smiled at him, hoping he'd make the connection between himself and The Rock. 'It's Triple H, the much maligned underdog, or no window.'

A slow grin spread itself across his face. 'Yeah,' he nodded, 'I can see why you'd like wrestling.' Before I had a chance to reply, he said hastily, 'Triple H it is.'

I was horrible enough to hope that the sales of wrestlers would go down.

Chapter Twenty-four

'I JUST DON'T get it.' Sal slugged back her martini and regarded me as if it was all my fault. 'I go in at least once a week and he smiles and laughs and tells me how lovely I look and that's it.'

'The guy is gay,' Mel said with such authority that I almost believed her. 'He has to be. There you are, offering yourself on a plate—'

'I don't "do" offering myself on a plate,' Sal said a little sharply.

''Course not.' Mel blew a long stream of smoke upwards and flicked the ash all over the table. 'Bad, bad choice of words. Anyway, he's gay, that's all there is to it!'

'Why didn't you tell me that he was gay?' Sal demanded of me.

'He's not,' I shrugged. 'Maybe he's just not interested.'

'In *that*?' Mel jabbed her fag towards Sal. 'Of course he is.'

I groaned. This night out was shaping up to be a 'wish I had stayed in and clipped my toenails' type of night. It was meant to have been a celebration of the publication of Sal's piece in the February issue of *Tell!* but instead it was turning out to be an in-depth analysis of Sal's failure to land The Big One. She and Mel had been obsessing over it since we'd left the flat. I dunno why Mel was so bothered; she'd never cared about Sal's love life before. Even the fact that Sal's story was splashed across the front of *Tell!* was no consolation to either of them.

And I mean *really* splashed across the front of the magazine.

Sex Scandal for Soccer Star was the headline. And the piece she had written was about how Denis McCoy, a football sensation in England, had been caught snogging a twenty-year-old beauty while his wife 'played happy housewife in England'. Sal had done her work well. Her descriptions of Denis's mad nights out sounded fantastic. (I wouldn't have minded going on a bender with him.) The pictures that accompanied her story left nothing to the imagination and, unsurprisingly, Denis McCoy had refused to comment on the story. And while Sal and Mel celebrated, I just had an uneasy feeling that though well written, the whole story was just tacky tabloid-ism. Of course, I couldn't say that – I mean, it was Sal's big break and I didn't want to hurt her – but surely she could do better than to wreck someone's life?

'What you want to do,' Mel said, blowing smoke straight into my face as she talked to Sal, 'is to find out what he's interested in and be interested in it yourself.'

I gave a bit of a snort.

They both looked at me.

'Eh, music, wrestling and soccer,' I provided.

'And haven't you just done the exposé on the soccer star!' Mel shrieked, causing people to look over. 'You can talk about that.'

Sal would ruin any chance she ever had with Ed if she told him she was responsible for that piece, I thought in alarm. Ed hadn't been a bit impressed with it. Denis McCoy, a Liverpool player, was one of Ed's heroes. 'Would you look at that?' he'd said to Bridie when the story had been taken up by other newspapers. 'Wouldn't you think a guy's life is his own private business?'

Bridie agreed.

'I mean, a guy makes a mistake, he doesn't need it splashed all over the papers.'

'But he was unfaithful to his wife,' I'd argued, just for the sake of arguing and I guess to be a bit loyal to Sal. 'If he's in

145

the public eye, he can't do stuff like that and not expect to be caught. I mean, people are interested in these things.'

Ed looked at me, his blue eyes narrowed. 'That's not being interested,' he said coldly, 'that's being vindictive. I mean, what is the point in a story like that – hey?'

'I guess the point is that it sells papers,' I said mildly, getting a tiny kick out of annoying him.

'Oh aye, once we sell papers, who cares if we ruin the guy's career?'

'Oh, he'll still play, never fear,' Bridie said lightly. She laughed a bit. 'That's all you're worried about. That it'll stop him scoring for Liverpool.'

Ed threw the paper onto the table. 'Yeah. Yeah, right, Bridie.' He dumped his tea down the sink. 'I'll go down and open up.'

'Oops.' Bridie made a face at me as he left. 'A bit touchy, wasn't he?'

'Mmm.' I grinned slightly. 'I wonder where he tethered it?'

'What?' Bridie asked. 'Tethered what?'

'His high horse.'

She couldn't stop laughing all day.

I grinned as I remembered.

'What are you smirking about?' Sal asked. 'Are you laughing at me?'

'Naw, but I wouldn't tell him you did that story on McCoy – he happens to love the guy.'

'I told you he was gay!' Mel clapped her hands together. 'What did I say?'

'Apparently McCoy is Liverpool's top scorer,' I explained over Mel's triumphant cackles, 'and the whole thing has affected his goal-scoring ability or something.'

'Oh.' Sal looked crestfallen. 'Well, can't he go and cheer on another team?'

'That's not the way it works, apparently.' I slugged down the last of my Bud and sought a way to explain. 'It's like, it's like

146

you being married for twenty years and suddenly deciding to have sex with someone else.'

'Listen.' Mel flicked her ash all over the table. 'A guy I'm married to suddenly loses his scoring ability, I'm outta there, you know what I mean!'

We laughed.

'Look,' I said, when they'd stopped making crude comments, 'why don't you just ask him *out*?' I stood up. 'Anyone want a drink?'

'Just ask him out!' Sal was aghast. 'I've never done that in my life!'

'Tacky,' Mel agreed.

'Well, it's either that or become a soccer fan,' I grinned, 'and I just can't see you as that, Sal.'

'You'd be surprised.' Sal tapped her glass. 'Make mine a double.'

'You'll need it.' I ignored both their exasperated looks and went to the bar.

I got manky drunk. As far as I can remember Mel and Sal had remained sober enough but that's only because they had so much to talk about. They knew the same people and hated the same people. They roared with laughter over stories that I couldn't even understand. And so, for lack of anything better to do, I drank too much.

Sometimes when I drink, things become really clear to me. It's like I can see into the future and into who I really am, inside, underneath all the wisecracks. And as I was sitting there, downing another Bud, it suddenly occurred to me to wonder just what on earth I was doing with Sal and Mel. There they were, two glamorous, career-minded women on the opposite side of the table, laughing and sniggering at everyone. And here I was, a woman who felt about twelve years old, with not a clue of what she was about at all. In my drunken fug I managed to smile every now and again whenever they broke into laughter,

147

but really, I didn't find anything they said a bit funny. Not. At. All.

Before I had a chance to think about it, I rose up. ''Scuse me,' I said, all self-righteous. 'I'm going home. You two just talk crap.'

They laughed.

'Drunk!' Sal said fondly. 'As usual.'

I resented that. 'I re-sent that.'

'Oooh,' Sal and Mel went.

I stumbled off. Got a taxi and came home. 'Vicky,' I thought to myself as I lay down, just before the room began to spin at about a hundred miles an hour, 'you have gotta get out of here.'

Of course, the next morning I woke up with a hammering head and the vague notion that I owed Sal an apology.

And, many months later, I thought that if only I'd listened to the voice of drunkenness, things might have turned out a lot better.

Chapter Twenty-five

I'LL ALWAYS REMEMBER Wednesday 25th February of that year. It's like one of those pop-up cards – everything about the days leading to it and from it are sort of background decoration while this day stands out in 3D, Technicolor. To be more precise, it's about five minutes of that day that stand out.

It was after lunch and I was talking to Dominic, who'd come out of his self-imposed shyness to ask me why Triple H was beating up The Rock in our front window. (Yep, it was going a bomb, the wrestlers were selling out and so I'd reluctantly left Ed's display in place for another month.)

'The Rock is better than Triple H,' Dominic was saying earnestly as my phone began to ring. 'I don't think that it's fair to have him getting all beat up.'

I would swear Ed had put him up to it. He stood at the other side of the shop, leaning against the shelves, grinning broadly over at me.

Dominic's mother was smiling shyly too.

'It's only a window display,' I said in my nice patient voice. 'And Triple H has to win sometime.' I reached under the cash desk to get my mobile out of my bag.

'No, he doesn't,' Dominic said back. 'Triple H could never beat The Rock. Not in a million years. Not ever. Not in this lifetime.' His voice rose. 'Can you smell what The Rock is cooking?' he yelled out all over the place, causing a little baby in a pram to start shrieking.

Ed laughed and Dominic turned and gave him the thumbs up.

'Ed,' I said, 'will you please go into that window and make Dominic happy.'

'Aw, you're so good.' Ed winked at me. He caught Dominic by the hand. 'Come on, Dom, let's show Triple H what The Rock is cooking – huh?'

Dominic squealed.

'That fella is crackers,' Dominic's mother said fondly, looking after Ed. 'I dunno who's de bigger kid.'

'I do,' I smiled.

She laughed. She looked suddenly much younger and nicer.

'Triple H is crap, isn't he, Ed?' Dominic could be heard saying as he looked at Ed moving about the window display.

'He's tragic!' Ed agreed.

'Not quite so tragic as your orange jacket,' I said back, flicking on my mobile.

Ed laughed loudly and I found myself grinning. He never seemed to take offence at anything I said.

'You shouldn't criticise a man's clothes,' Bridie whispered. 'Maybe his dad bought it for him – did you think about that now, miss? You'd want to control your tongue, you'll—'

'Hi,' I said into my phone. I did not want to hear what I should and shouldn't say. She was always telling me off these days.

'Vicky McCarthy?' It was a woman's voice.

'That's me.'

'You shouldn't be on your mobile.' Bridie poked me in the ribs. 'What if Mr O'Neill comes in?'

'Sorry, sorry, I didn't hear you,' I said to the woman as I moved away from Bridie towards the office. 'What did you say?'

'My name is Helen Devine, I work for the Adoption Board. I have some news for you about your mother.'

Time stopped.

It was as if everything receded and still I was walking towards the office.

'Vicky?' the woman said. 'Are you there?'

'Yes, yes.' My voice was feathery. My heart was hammering as if it was going to break up into a thousand pieces. I felt numb. 'My mother.' I closed the office door on Bridie and sat down in the computer chair. 'You have news?'

Beyond the door, Bridie had begun muttering loudly about certain people only wanting to walk into trouble despite her best efforts.

'You've made enquiries about tracing your birth mother – is that right?'

'Yes.'

'Well, it's policy here to ring with any news we have – it's a little more personal, we'll be sending you a letter in a couple of days, OK?'

'Right.' I felt sick, for some reason.

'We have information for you about your birth mother.'

'Yes?' It came out as a whisper.

'We have on file the name of a third party—'

'Sorry?'

The woman's voice was gentle. 'I can tell that this has been a shock for you, hasn't it?'

'I just wasn't expecting—' I gulped. 'So soon.' My voice went a bit wobbly.

'Of course.' Helen stopped and then asked tentatively, 'Have you had counselling?'

'Nope.' Pause. 'What about my, my' – it was weird, saying it – 'my birth mother?'

She ignored me and went on, a bit sternly, I thought, 'From here on in, you should definitely consider getting some counselling. It's not like seeing a therapist or anything, your counsellor will be a social worker who's dealt with these situations before. I'll send you the phone numbers of these counsellors in my letter. It's a big thing this, Vicky. Getting counselling lets you explore your feelings. Helps you think about the what ifs.'

'Yes,' I said, hardly hearing her, 'but my mother?'

151

Helen didn't say anything immediately and when she did begin to speak, it was in a slow, measured way that had me wishing she'd hurry up.

'We have on file the name of a third party,' she began, 'and we have contacted this person and they, it seems, have agreed, in the event of you wanting to make contact with your mother, to act as an intermediary between the two of you.'

I didn't get it. 'What?'

'Your mother nominated this person a long time ago to act as a sort of go-between – carrying messages from you to her.'

I felt as if my heart was being squeezed too hard. 'She doesn't want to know me?'

'No, that's not it at all.' Helen's voice was reassuring. 'It's not uncommon. Your mother might be nervous about meeting you or she might just want to see how she feels about things. It's very rare on first contact to have a full-blown reunion, you know. These things take time.'

I hadn't known that. I felt sick and stupid and naïve and—

'I mean,' she went on, 'you must be nervous at the prospect of meeting her yourself.'

I hadn't actually thought about it. 'I dunno, I never—'

'These are the things counselling *makes* you think about,' Helen said. 'It's important you go.'

'Yes.' I bit my lip, just to feel the pain of it, so I'd know I was really there. 'I guess.'

Silence.

'So what happens now?'

'Well,' Helen said, 'this third party, his name is Jim, has told your mother that you've been in contact. I think she's sending a letter to us to forward on to you.'

So it was to be letters. Letters after this long time.

'In time, you could call her or send photographs.'

'How long does it all take?' I couldn't bear this. I'd waited twenty-eight years already.

'It depends on the people,' Helen said.

152

'But she might never want to meet me!' The words tore out of some part inside me. I couldn't take rejection, not again. 'That's not fair!'

Helen remained calm. 'It's a step-by-step process, Vicky. Just take it that way. Talk to your counsellor. Talk to your parents. And don't forget, you can write back to your mother – OK?'

The tears were starting in the back of my eyes. 'Sure.'

Helen said a few other things but I hardly heard her. In the end, she said, 'It's good news, don't forget that.'

I flicked off the phone. I stared at the computer screen. I didn't know how I felt.

I left work early. I ignored Bridie as she scurried after me enquiring anxiously if I was OK and then Ed as he wondered if maybe I could do with a taxi to get home. I just walked out of that shop, red-eyed, snotty-nosed, and walked and walked and walked. It was drizzling as I found myself in the park. Without thinking I made my way towards the playground. There were very few kids about and so I sat down on a swing and began to go to and fro, to and fro. Soon, I was so high I could see the whole playground spread out in front of me and then I was back down again, among the pebbles and the sand. And then up again. And then down again. That's the way I felt, I realised.

High and low.

And maybe a little bit scared of letting go and falling flat on my face.

Chapter Twenty-six

Vicky,

I've been composing this letter in my head for the past twenty-eight years and yet when I try to write, the things I want to say are coming out all wrong – they either look too formal, too absurd or too pathetic when written down. I don't even know whether to say 'Dear Vicky' or even if I have the right to.

I don't know what it is you want from me and that too makes it hard to write. Whatever it is, I'll do my best. If you want some background on why I gave you up (and I hate that word – I didn't give you up, I never stopped thinking of you all these years) I'll provide it.

I don't want to go on and on in this first letter, I just want you to know that when I heard you'd made contact, I cried for days. You were alive. You were well. My biggest fear was always that by letting you go, something terrible might have happened to you and it would be my fault.

Thank you for doing this – it means more than I can say.

With love,
Barbara

I read that letter over and over, especially the bit about her never stopping thinking of me. I touched the ink, rounded my finger along the words, held it to my face. It was the closest I'd been to my mother in twenty-eight years.

Then I sat down and dialled a counsellor. I was crying and hopeless and beside me on the bed were sheets of foolscap notepaper with letters begun and crossed out and begun again. Like Barbara, I simply hadn't a clue what I wanted to say.

Chapter Twenty-seven

FRIDAY EVENING. THE shop was quiet. Bridie was dusting some shelves while Ed was assembling a swing I had ordered a few weeks before. It was the coolest swing ever – instead of consisting of two ordinary swings and a see-saw, this one had a swing, a see-saw and a roundabout! The roundabout was brilliant. It was circular and could fit up to three kids. Using a handle, the kids could make the roundabout spin up into the air while at the same time spinning around like mad.

Kids were going to go for it bigtime.

'Kids will go for this bigtime,' I'd told Ed and Bridie. 'Wait and see.'

Bridie had agreed but Ed had hummed and hawed and got on my nerves. Then he'd said that the kids wouldn't go for it unless they could *see* it. And I made some smart remark about them being able to see it on the box. And he'd said that that wasn't what he'd meant and I'd said that we hadn't the space for showing off swings. So he'd presented me with some fancy drawings he'd done on the computer (yep – using his mate's wonderful program) demonstrating how the space in the shop could be used much more efficiently if things were moved about a bit.

And I had to give in.

Again.

I'd given him permission to rearrange the whole shop and watched while he sweated buckets lifting stock and rearranging shelves. I wanted him to regret ever suggesting the idea.

'Hand me that nut and bolt, will you, Vicky?' Ed broke into

156

my thoughts as he pointed to some bolts that were on the floor. 'Once I have that in, I'm all finished.'

Oh, if only that were true.

I handed him the things he wanted and he nodded his thanks. Bending over, he began to screw them in.

The only consolation of being upstaged by the assembly of the swing was that Ed had a great-looking backside. It looked so firm and grippable in his black Levi's. I couldn't help myself, I just had to keep peeking at it. It was a pity that such a great ass should be owned by such a great ass, I thought. It was a complete waste. Sort of like a good-looking guy being gay or someone being offered the perfect, salted bag of chips in the middle of the desert or being a big fat juicy pig in the middle of Israel—

'Vicky!'

Marti's voice made both Ed and me jump as it echoed around the shop.

'She's down the back.' Bridie sounded quite disapproving. She's always telling me that she doesn't understand the need for shouting. 'And there's no need for shouting, you know.'

'Right,' Marti boomed as he began striding down towards me. 'Oy, Vicky!' he bellowed, once I was in sight. 'Get the finger out, would ya. I'm double-parked.' Marti had agreed to give me a lift to the bus station. It was my dad's sixtieth that weekend.

I gave him a bit of a wave before legging it up to the office to grab my weekend bag. When I got back down, Marti was admiring the swing. Ed was standing beside him, spanner in hand. 'I'm not sure,' he was saying to Marti. 'You'd have to ask the boss.'

'Ask me what?'

'How much that swing is?' Marti turned to me.

'Five hundred euro,' I said, quoting the staff discount price.

'Mmmm.' Marti made a face. 'Expensive. Still, Leo would love it.'

'And who's Leo?' Bridie asked, coming up behind us.

'Aren't you double-parked?' I cut in before Marti could enlighten her. 'We'd better go.'

'Uh-huh.' Marti strode before me up the shop. 'Bye, folks.'

Behind me I heard Ed and Bridie muttering their 'goodbyes' and 'have a nice weekends'.

It was a relief to get out into the street. I still hadn't told Bridie anything about Marti's circumstances. Well, it wasn't really her business; I mean, it wasn't as if she was my mother or anything. But, then again, I hadn't told my mother either. I hadn't even invited Marti down to the party. Time enough, I kept telling myself. No point in shocking the folks too much.

'I've Leo looking after the car in case I get clamped,' Marti said as he powered along, me running to keep up with him.

'Leo,' I said breathlessly. 'Your Leo?'

'Yep.'

I stopped walking. I soon found myself staring incredulously at his back as he kept up the pace. 'Marti!'

The tone of my voice halted him. He spun around. 'What?' he sounded impatient. 'Come on. I'll be clamped.'

'You can't just drag me into your car and expect me to talk to your son,' I said, not able to believe that he hadn't given it a thought.

Marti looked baffled. 'Why not?'

'I've never met him, for starters. You should have *warned* me. I mean, who does he think I am? You can't just go shoving us both together like this. Will he know that—?'

'He knows you're my friend,' Marti said. 'I told him I've to pick up a friend. He's cool about it.'

'A girlfriend?' This was not happening. I'd planned on giving Leo a little toy or something when we'd meet. Something to buy his affection.

'Girl, boy, doesn't matter. He's only five, for Christ's sake.' He glanced at his watch before grinning hugely at me. 'Now, come on.'

I had no choice but to follow him. I'd never make the bus

158

station otherwise. Dragging my bag, I clumped alongside him, hoping he wasn't parked too far away. As I spotted his car ahead – it was easy to spot, it had the enormous Boy Five election poster thingy up on the roof – my heart began to hammer. Even my palms broke out in a sweat.

Marti seemed oblivious. He crossed to the driver's door, opened it, reached over and popped the lock on my door. 'Park yourself down,' he grinned.

I gingerly climbed into the car, my bag at my feet. I was afraid to look behind at the little boy, scrunched up in a corner.

'Any trouble, bud?' Marti asked Leo as he fired the engine.

'Well,' Leo began and I could sense him looking at me and I still didn't know what to do, 'a man came by and he was putting something on your window so I pretended to be sick, like you said. And I said that you were gone to the chemist to get something for me.'

'Good lad!' Marti chortled. 'Isn't he great, Vicky?'

'Yeah.' I took this as my opportunity to turn around and smile. Even as I did so, I felt my smile wobble all over the place as it was met with a sullen glare from an attractive kid hugging a brown teddy bear.

'Leo and me are going to McDonald's, aren't we?' Marti said then as he overtook a truck to vicious blaring of horns from every motorist in the vicinity.

'Yeah, Daddy.'

'I *love* McDonald's,' I said, my voice hysterically cheerful.

'Well, you can't come,' Leo said, narrowing his eyes. 'It's just me and my daddy.'

There was a silence.

I decided to change the subject. 'I like your teddy.'

Leo held it closer to him and glared at me as if somehow I was plotting to take it away.

'What's his name?'

Silence. Then, 'It's a *her*.'

Dressed in dungarees and a straw hat, the teddy didn't look

much like a her. 'Sorry.' I gave an apologetic smile. 'What's *her* name?'

'Linda.'

It was said with such calculated aplomb that despite feeling as if I'd been punched in the chest, I had to admire the kid. 'Nice,' I muttered, turning away from him. Linda was Marti's wife's name.

'Don't mind him,' Marti whispered, patting my leg. 'That teddy used to be called Marv.'

'Did not!' Leo said.

'Did so,' Marti said back, a bit narkily, I thought.

'That was another teddy!'

Marti slammed on the brakes and threw us all forward. 'Don't you lie to me,' he snapped. 'Don't you dare!'

Leo bit his lip and tears welled up in his eyes.

'Well, I think the name Linda suits her,' I put in, hoping to diffuse the situation. I smiled at Marti. 'Don't you?'

He turned from me and shrugged.

Leo gulped and stared out the window away from me.

I decided to shut up.

Thirty minutes later we arrived at Busarus. Marti pulled into the bus lane and jumped out of the car. 'I'll see you to the door,' he said.

'Can I come, Daddy?'

'It'll only be for a few minutes,' Marti answered. 'You stay here and mind the car. Then we'll head to McDonald's – OK?' He reached in and ruffled the top of Leo's head.

The boy smiled, showing the perfect teeth of his dad. 'OK.'

'Say bye to Vicky.'

'Bye, Leo. It was lovely to meet you.'

His voice was barely audible as he muttered his 'bye-bye'.

'Say it properly,' Marti ordered.

'It's OK—' I began, knowing that the kid would hate me for sure now.

'It's not OK.' Marti glared at Leo. 'He has to have manners. Now say goodbye to Vicky.'

'No.'

'Right. No McDonald's for you.' Marti slammed the car door on his protests. 'Come on, Vicky.'

I could still hear him howling as Marti walked me to the door.

'Sorry about that,' Marti said, looking completely fed up. 'He's been very difficult recently. I don't know what to do with him – he wouldn't go to school for me this morning or anything. Normally he's a great kid.'

'He's probably just missing his mother,' I said. 'You can't expect him to—'

'His mother is gone months now,' Marti said abruptly. 'He should be over it.'

Some people never get over it, I wanted to say, but didn't. 'He's only five.'

'Yeah . . . well . . .' He let his voice trail off and his eyes slid from my face to his feet. He looked defeated. All his cockiness seemed to have deserted him. His eyes met mine. 'Look, have a great weekend, all right?' He leaned over to kiss me. His lips brushed mine and I put my arms about him.

'Bring him to McDonald's, all right?'

His voice was muffled in my shoulder. 'You think?'

'I think.'

He gave me a small smile. Another soft kiss. 'Ta.'

I watched him walk away. There was something sad about him that I hadn't noticed before.

As I walked into the bus station, I heard the jangly sounds of Boy Five being played from Marti's loudspeaker. It made me smile as people groaned all around me.

161

Chapter Twenty-eight

THE PARTY WAS in full swing. Dad, who'd been completely taken by surprise, was dancing with Mam, holding her close and smiling like a lunatic. All he kept telling everyone was that it was 'mighty'. 'This is mighty,' he said, over and over again. All the cousins from both sides of the family were mingling and chatting to one another. Drink was flowing faster than the Nile in heavy rain and the food, which had been prepared by my mother and her army of sisters, was almost gone. The table I sat at sported six empty plates and two miserable cocktail sausages. I sort of felt sorry for the sausages, being rejected and left to grow cold, so I speared the two and shoved them into my mouth.

I washed them down with a mouthful of Bud and watched as my father kissed the tip of my mother's nose. Some part of me remembered Sal saying that it was bad luck to be kissed on the nose and I shivered slightly.

'Hey, has someone glued your arse to that chair?' Tommy, grinning, slid in beside me.

'Yes,' I answered shortly. I did not want to be dragged up onto the dance floor by him.

'Really?' Tommy feigned surprise. 'Have they invented industrial-size Superglue then?'

'Nope.' I regarded him over the rim of my glass. ''Cause if they had, someone would surely have used it on your mouth.'

He laughed. 'You're dead funny, Vicky,' he grinned. He held out his hand. 'Dancing?'

'Drinking.' I held up my glass.

'Aw, come on,' he pleaded, 'one dance.'

The DJ was playing 'La Bamba' and everyone was doing weird things with their bodies. In the centre, my mother and father danced a waltz.

'Maybe later,' I muttered, hoping he'd forget. 'I prefer to look.'

'OK.' Tommy didn't move. Instead he followed my gaze and looked too. He spotted my folks. 'Are they really that happy?' he asked, sounding wistful. 'Or, like, is it for show?'

I was insulted for them. That was typical of Tommy, trying to belittle everything.

'They don't put on a show,' I snapped back, realising it was true. What you saw was what you got.

'No, I guess they don't.' He paused. 'It must be nice for you,' he said then, 'to have happy parents.'

'I never much thought about it.'

'Well, maybe you're used to it.'

There was a silence. I wondered if he was thinking about his dad, who had died years back. Aunt Julia had thrown him out of the house for drinking and a few months later he'd been found dead from alcohol poisoning. He'd been a gentle guy but had spent every penny on booze. Tommy and John had grown up wearing hand-me-downs. Still, I thought, looking at him, he hadn't done too badly for himself. He was dressed that night in really nice gear – the kind of stuff women like men to wear – cream combats and a black Tommy Hilfiger shirt. There was nothing to think that he'd had a hard upbringing.

'And now,' the DJ roared into his microphone, 'everyone up on the floor.'

Tommy jumped up and looked questioningly at me. I wasn't going to follow him until I saw the staff wheeling out an enormous cake in the shape of the number sixty. It was obviously a 'Happy Birthday' moment.

My dad looked gobsmacked at the size of the cake. My mother began pushing him towards it, laughing as she did so.

Dad didn't need a push. He took his place at the top of the room, beside his cake, his face red with pleasure. 'Well,' he said, 'this is mighty.'

People were clapping and I thought his face would split in two from smiling.

'And now,' the DJ continued, in his deep, American voice, 'I've been asked to request his daughter, Vicky, to lead us in "Happy Birthday".'

More cheering.

I wanted the ground to swallow me up. Tommy, roaring, shoved me forward. I plastered a smile on my face and took the microphone from the DJ.

Dad reached out and clasped my hand. I don't think he'd ever looked happier. 'That would be wonderful,' he whispered, so that only I could hear.

I wanted to make it wonderful for him. He'd been cool with me ever since Christmas and I saw this as a way to repair things. I began to sing and it wasn't so bad because everyone joined in. The whole room resounded to the sound of 'Happy Birthday' and 'Hip Hip Hooray'.

More clapping and cheering.

My mother hugged me and hugged my dad and then they both hugged me. It was mortifying. But nice.

'And now,' the DJ said, 'another request has come in for Vicky to sing her dad's favourite song – "Nancy Spain".'

Emotional blackmail, that's what it was.

Dad was beaming at me. 'Go on there now,' he coaxed, 'there's a great girl.'

I rolled my eyes at him and once again took the microphone. I didn't really need it because my voice was quite strong but I took it anyway; I'd feel naked standing up in front of them all with nothing to hold on to.

I didn't understand why everyone always asked me to sing the sad songs. My dad says it's because I look so forlorn singing that it makes people want to listen, my mother says it's because

164

I 'do' sad so well. But I 'do' happy good too. I can belt out a pop tune with the best of them.

Everyone began 'shushing' each other but I started to sing before the whole room was completely quiet. I knew in my heart that they'd become silent once I sang. I wasn't being big-headed, I just knew it from experience. I could make anyone listen to me. My voice has a rough edge, a sort of hoarseness that bleeds into noise and makes it silent. And I sang the song about Nancy Spain and about how impossible it was to forget about her no matter where life led me. I let my voice soar before curbing it. The words of that song have their own music, I couldn't trample all over them.

When I finished, there was a silence.

I hated that silence. In that silence, people look at you differently, as if they've never quite seen you before.

Then the applause, which embarrassed me.

Eventually, I was mercifully able to sit back down at an empty table and resume my drinking.

'You should sing professionally,' the manager of the hotel said as I was leaving.

I smiled politely.

'My brother runs a hotel in Dublin,' he said, thrusting a card into my hands, 'and he's looking for a singer for the weekends to entertain the guests. You'd go down a bomb.'

'Naw.' I attempted to give the card back to him. 'I don't think so.'

'Oooh, Vicky!' My mother poked me in the back. 'You hold on to that card. You could become famous.'

I laughed at that idea. Becoming famous was not something I would particularly want.

'Look,' I explained to both my folks, who were looking chuffed at the very mention of me singing in a hotel, 'doing a stint at a party is completely different to singing professionally.'

'And you'd know, would you?' Dad chortled. 'You who knows all about professional singers.'

Mam tittered.

The hotel manager looked taken aback at my lack of enthusiasm. 'Well, think about it,' he urged. 'The Glen Hotel.'

'Ta.' I shoved the card into my bag, watched by three beady pairs of eyes.

'You'd be fantastic,' the manager called as we left.

'You would too.' Dad slung his arm about my shoulder and one about Mam's shoulder. He smiled at both of us. 'Well, that was a great night. Fantastic. Thanks very much.'

'Yes,' Mam agreed, 'I think everyone enjoyed themselves.'

'And to think I thought you were just bringing me out for a meal!'

We laughed.

'Not that I would have minded that either,' Dad went on. 'My two favourite women in the whole world on either side of me – now what can be nicer than that!' He pulled us closer to him.

The sound of our footsteps was the only thing to disturb the perfect silence of the night. In the sky, pinprick stars peeped down on us.

It was a perfect moment.

The kind of moment when nothing else matters except the silence and being there, exactly where you are.

Then as soon as you begin to think, 'I like this moment', it disappears.

But what matters is that it was there in the first place.

Chapter Twenty-nine

After the usual restless night, I eventually conked out around three and slept until midday. When I awoke, a weak spring sun was doing its best to creep through the room. I lay in bed for a while, warm and snugly under the covers, and thought that of all the things in the world to do, this was my favourite. Just to lie in bed and not to think too much. It was glorious, just savouring the warmth of the sun in the room and the soft silence of an empty house.

Of course, like all lovely things, it never lasted. Five minutes later the front door opened and Mam and Dad entered the hall talking in loud voices about who they'd seen at mass. And who was wearing what and who was not talking to whom. Then Dad went into the kitchen and I heard him pulling on his boots to go check on the cattle. A slam of the kitchen door as he left. Then Mam began rattling pots and pans in preparation for the dinner.

The same thing every week.

I must have dozed back off because the next thing Mam was tapping gently on my door, bearing tea and toast. 'Thought you might like your breakfast in bed,' she said, balancing a big flowered tray on the bedside table. She wiped her hands down her apron before pouring me a cuppa and milking it. 'You're such a big lazy lump in the morning.'

It was said fondly as if being a lazy lump was something rather endearing.

I rubbed my eyes and grinned at her. Pulling myself up in the bed, I took the tea from her. 'Ta.'

She sat down on the bed beside me and watched as I sipped.

'You make the best cuppa in Ireland,' I said. She loved when I told her that.

'So' – she folded her hands in her lap and looked so fondly at me that I had to look away – 'how are you? We didn't get much of a chance to talk on Friday, what with organising the party and everything. How's the shop going?'

'All right.' I didn't want to tell her how I was being upstaged time and again by Ed, because if I was upset, she'd only worry. And she'd tell Dad and then he'd worry. And I'd never hear the end of it. 'We're selling more toys than we did this time last year.'

'Isn't that great?'

'Yep.'

Then I told her about Bridie and her constant cleaning and she laughed and said that maybe I could learn a thing or two from her. I told her about Sal trying to get off with Ed and she clicked her tongue and said that Sal was way too forward and always had been. And I told her about Marti – a sanitised version. She was dead impressed to hear he was a boy band manager. 'Well, at least you've that in common,' she said, 'you're both managers.'

'Yeah.' I managed not to smile too much.

'And—' I put my cup carefully down on the tray and reached under the bed to my haversack. Taking a blue crumpled envelope from it, I nervously held it towards her. 'I got this in the post – from my birth mother.'

My outstretched hand holding the envelope remained between us for what seemed like ages. I could hear Dad coming in downstairs and the tramp of his feet as he walked to the bathroom to wash himself down. The clock on the landing loudly ticked off the seconds and still Mam made no attempt to take the letter from me.

'Don't you want to see it?' I asked. I desperately needed to share it with someone.

'Sure.' Mam smiled a little uncertainly. 'It's just, well, it's a bit sudden, isn't it, I thought—'

I explained about the third party and what the woman in the Adoption Board had said. Not very well, I think, because my words were spinning about all over the place and all I kept worrying about was what if Mam refused to read the letter.

But by the time I'd got to the end of my rambling explanations, Mam had taken the envelope. I watched as she slowly drew out the note. 'Nice writing,' she said, as if it were a compliment to me. She smoothed out the page and began to read. It took her ages; she kept having to go over the words.

'Isn't it a very nice letter?' I asked eventually, dying for some sort of a verdict. 'Doesn't she sound . . . nice?'

Mam looked up at me. Her eyes were bright. She reached out and clasped my hand. Holding it tightly, she said earnestly, 'She's your mother – how could she be any other way?'

I blinked. Once. Twice. Gulped. She just couldn't have said anything nicer. I put my other hand on top of our joined ones. Like the time in the coffee shop, I couldn't speak.

We sat there, like that, for a long time.

Dad made the dinner. While Mam and me were upstairs he'd roasted the chicken, over-boiled the carrots and mashed the spuds. He'd poured us both a glass of wine and announced that dinner was ready by shouting up the stairs for us to hurry on down before it all got colder.

'Sounds ominous,' Mam giggled like a schoolgirl and scuttled from the room.

I got dressed quickly and shoved my feet into a pair of Poochie slippers. I was downstairs just as Dad was taking the carrots from the oven.

'They did too quickly,' he said to Mam and me as he began to poke at them with a knife, 'so I shoved them in the oven to keep them warm but—' Pause. Poke. 'They don't seem too good now.'

169

'A bit on the dry side,' my mother said.

'Like that Sweeney wan,' Dad chortled, tipping the carrots into the bin.

Mam began to examine the chicken, which did look nice, and then she turned her attention to the peas. 'They're cold.'

'Aye.' Dad made a face. 'They did awful quick.'

'He does this every time,' Mam chuckled. 'Every single time.'

Dad looked sheepishly at her. 'Amn't I doing my best?'

'You are, pet, you are.' She tapped his cheek lightly. 'So – what – we have chicken and some spuds and I'll reheat the peas?'

'I'll reheat the peas.' Dad pushed her out of the way. 'You sit and relax, like you were told to do.'

My dad was never what you'd call a new man. All my life he'd tended the farm and done the 'man' things while my mother had cooked and cleaned and washed and polished. As far as I knew they'd been happy in their stereotypical roles but now, for some reason, Dad was branching out and Mam was letting him. It made me admire them in a funny way. I wondered if I'd see her in the tractor the next time I came down and the thought caused me to grin.

'Are you laughing at me?' Dad demanded, pointing to a chair for me to sit down. 'She of the "take-away" mentality.'

'Swear I'm not,' I grinned again.

'Then sit and eat.' Smile. 'Eventually.'

Eventually was ten minutes. There wasn't a sound as we scraped our plates clean. And just when I thought that it wasn't going to make an appearance, an enormous strawberry cheesecake was pulled out from the fridge like a rabbit from a hat.

'And you thought we'd forgotten,' Mam beamed.

'Yeah.' The thing was bigger than ever before.

'I had to buy it,' Mam said, laying it in front of me. 'I didn't have time to be making one, you know, with the party and everything, so I bought this instead. I hope it's all right.'

'You shouldn't have bothered.' She had no idea how much I meant those words.

'Oh no, now, never let it be said . . .' She pulled a knife out from the block on the counter. 'And you'll have a big slice now, won't you, because your father and me, now, we'd never eat that.'

'Cheese in a cake.' Dad made a face. 'It's like putting jelly in spuds.'

I had the uneasy feeling that jelly in spuds would be nicer for me to eat than the bloody cheesecake.

After the dinner, it was show and tell.

So, after a bit of chit-chat, I showed him my letter.

'From her mother,' my mother said. She smiled a sort of brittle smile over at me as he opened the envelope. 'It's a really nice letter.'

Dad opened the page but before he read it, he said, 'Sure aren't you her mother?'

Mam flinched.

'My birth mother,' I said softly.

'Oh aye.' Dad raised his eyes. 'That one.' He sort of spat the words out. 'Well, let's see what she has to say for herself.'

There was no mistaking the tension that had entered the room. It was as if someone had taken all the air out and we were afraid to breathe. As if someone had laid heavy weights on my arms and legs and chest.

Dad was mumbling the words of the letter to himself. Then, he calmly folded up the paper, placed it back in the envelope and handed it back to me. 'Great,' he said. 'Great.'

I took the letter back and glanced at Mam. The indifference hurt.

'She hasn't written back yet,' my mother said with false brightness. 'She's going to see a counsellor.'

'There'd be no need for counsellors if people would be happy with what they've got.'

'Ah, now, Sean—'

'I'm going out.' Dad didn't even look at me as he left, banging the door harder than necessary.

'He didn't mean it,' Mam said quickly. 'You know your father – he takes a while to adjust to things.'

'He doesn't want me to look, does he?' It was a stupid question. Of course he didn't.

'He's not *you*.' Mam knelt beside my chair and looked up into my face. 'He doesn't understand.'

'And you do?'

She shrugged. 'I understand that I want you to be completely happy, Vic. That's what I understand. And if this makes you happy, well then . . .' Her voice trailed off.

'Thanks.'

Like that morning, she caught my hands in hers. 'He'll come around. He always does.'

'I hope.' My lip quivered and I bit down on it.

'He will.' She smiled slightly. 'D'you remember the time, when you pestered him and pestered him to let you drive the car because you'd had lessons?'

'That was—'

'And you wrote off his car?'

'—different.'

'And he swore that he'd never let you near his car again but he did.'

'It was different.'

'He did it because he knew it'd make you happy. That's why the man does everything. He'll come around.' She stood up and ruffled my hair. The subject was closed. 'Now come on, I'll wrap up the cheesecake. You pack your bags and I'll drive you to the bus station.' She smiled. 'Or you can drive me.'

Travelling back to Dublin, the cheesecake at my feet in a freezer bag, I felt guilty.

Guilty that Mam was being so reasonable. Guilty that Dad wasn't.

Guilty that I was going to go my own way anyhow.
Guilty that maybe I'd hurt them.
Guilty because I'd decided that I couldn't handle the guilt.
I'd stay in Dublin as long as I could before going home again.

Chapter Thirty

I WAS LOOKING forward to getting back to the flat. To just dumping my things, grabbing a can and plonking myself down in front of the telly. That way I could forget about the weekend and forget about the fact that tomorrow would be my first meeting with the counsellor. I was kind of regretting calling her now – I mean, I wasn't too sure what to expect. What if she wanted to hear my darkest secrets or something? I could hardly tell her about the time I stole Lisa Sweeney's best Barbie doll, could I? Or the time I ran away from home when I first found out I was adopted? Or—

'Stop,' I told myself as I inserted the key into the lock of the apartment. 'Just take it as it comes.'

'My thoughts exactly,' Troy chortled from behind, so close that he was virtually breathing down my neck. 'I always knew you were my type of girl, Vicky.'

'But you're not my type of boy,' I said back, trying to sound mournful. 'You're too forward for me. I prefer my men quiet and docile so I can boss them around.'

'I quite like the sound of that,' he said as he followed me up the stairs. 'You could be the Captain Picard of the relationship.'

I grinned.

'You could command my machine anytime.' A revolting thrust of denim-clad pelvis.

'And what machine would that be?' I had my hand on the apartment door, ready to leg it. 'Your washing machine?'

I slammed the door to the sound of him laughing.

'That Troy is getting more suggestive every time I meet him,' I yelled out to Sal. She was always in on Sunday nights, finishing off stories for the paper which was 'put to bed' the following day. That's newspaper jargon for finishing something, apparently. I dumped my case on the floor and carried the freezer bag in so that I could put the cheesecake into the fridge.

Sal was in all right, standing at the table, a cuppa in her hand.

But that's not what stopped me dead.

Ed was sitting down at *our* table, nursing a cuppa himself.

'Hiya,' Sal said, smiling broadly. 'How was the weekend?'

I didn't answer. I couldn't take my eyes from Ed.

'I'd introduce you to Ed only you already know each other,' Sal giggled.

'From somewhere,' Ed grinned. He raised his cup to me. 'Cheers, Vicky.'

I still couldn't speak. How had it all happened? There was nothing doing on Friday when I left.

'Ed and I are heading out to the pictures,' Sal said, sitting in beside him.

'Right.' I was shell-shocked. I didn't know if I was pleased or what. 'So . . . what happened . . . how did you . . . ?'

'She asked me out,' Ed said, thumbing to Sally as if I wouldn't know who "she" was. 'Just came into the shop yesterday and asked me to go out with her.'

Sal gave a throwaway laugh.

'Wow!' I smirked over at Sal. 'That is impressive. She *never* asks anyone out, you know.'

'Ha, ha.' Sal stood up abruptly, almost upending her tea. She looked sensational in a long navy denim skirt, split at the sides, which gave flashes of her neat ankles and her tiny tiny feet. A royal blue gypsy top completed the look and she'd tied her long hair back with a blue and navy scarf.

Ed looked good too. Black denims and an orange T-shirt. I reckon he had a bit of a fetish for orange. He wore a gorgeous black leather jacket.

175

'Let's go.' Sal picked up her cup and dumped the remainder of her coffee down the sink. Ed followed her lead.

'Bye, Vicky,' Sal said, almost dancing out the door. 'Don't wait up.'

'See ya, boss.' Ed tipped me a grinning salute.

'You better not be late in in the morning,' I grouched. As soon as I said it, I wanted to kill myself. What was I like?

He laughed. Closed the door.

Bloody wonderful.

Marti rang me later that night. He was in great form. He didn't mention Leo and I didn't ask. 'Listen Vic,' he said, 'the lads are doing another tour this week, I'll be back on Sunday and I'll have a surprise for you – right?'

'A whole week?'

'Yep. Great, isn't it?'

I hadn't meant it that way. 'Suppose.'

'See you Sunday! Listen, have to go!'

He blew me a kiss down the line and was gone.

Chapter Thirty-one

MY COUNSELLING APPOINTMENT was at ten-thirty in the local health centre. It was a bit early, seeing as Monday was my day off, but apparently mornings were all this woman social worker did.

It meant that I had to get up at nine, have a shower, and blow-dry my frizzy red hair, which took *ages* because in order to de-frizz it, I had to blow-dry the roots first and then the outside and then rub some gel into it to keep it that way. I was seriously considering getting it all chopped off and doing a Sinead O'Connor on it. On top of all this, I had to choose my clothes. Now, maybe this sounds mental, but I did not want this woman thinking there was something wrong with me. Not that there was, you understand. But I figured that if I wore my normal attire of red or purple jeans and a bright sweatshirt, she might get the wrong idea about me. I had to pick something that screamed 'sober citizen'. I eventually settled for a pair of navy jeans and a red and navy T-shirt. It looked normal enough. Shoving my feet into a pair of red trainers, I had just enough time to grab a cup of coffee before I left.

'You're up early,' Sal remarked. She was tapping away furiously on her laptop, a big frown on her face. 'Jesus, I'm way behind.'

I said nothing. When Sal was working – and especially when Sal was 'way' behind' – you did not talk. I watched her furiously banging away on her keyboard and I wondered how the night with Ed had gone. He wasn't in the flat that morning anyway, which wasn't a great sign. And gazing at Sal as she pounded the letters with her French-manicured fingernails, I had to admit that she did not look like a woman who'd enjoyed coital bliss with the rich man of her dreams.

Mind you, even if she'd had sensational sex, she'd still be narky. Her mood had been pretty crap recently, mainly because *Tell!* hadn't yet offered her a position.

'What are you looking at?' she snapped.

Definitely no sex.

'Nothing.' I smiled brightly and poured some coffee into a cup. 'Want one?'

She held up her mug. 'Nope.'

More keyboard sounds.

I sat down at the table and began to flick through a magazine. It was one of Sal's. An old issue of *Hello!* with a big feature on Dustin Hoffman in the centre pages. I didn't know what she saw in him. Maybe it was the big nose.

'You ruined my night last night,' Sal said suddenly, startling me. I'd been so determined to read all about Dustin's on-set exploits in order to get this damn counselling appointment off my mind that I hadn't noticed that she'd stopped typing.

'What?'

'I said that you ruined my night last night. Ed wouldn't stay. And I know why.' She leaned forward in her chair and glared at me. 'It's because he didn't want to run into you this morning.'

'Really?' I hadn't known I was that intimidating. It made me feel like a heel. 'Well – I guess that I am his boss and—'

'Yeah, and I was his date.'

My grumpy parting shot to Ed rang in my ears as I stared at Sal's glum face. I felt sorry for her. First Mel messing her about and now this. 'Sorry,' I said meekly. 'You know I—'

'I mean, he came up here and then after a bit he just legged it. It had to be because of you. What other reason would there be?'

'Well, maybe he doesn't want to rush things.'

178

She laughed at that. 'What man, given the opportunity, wouldn't want to rush things?'

'You hardly know each other—'

'Puritan.'

That was it. I turned back to my magazine, determined to ignore her.

'You better hide the next time he comes. I'll pretend you're not in or something.'

Thoughts of cowering away in my bedroom while she and Ed went at it in front of the telly or in Sal's room made me wince. How would I look at them again? 'Why not go to his place?'

'What?' Arched eyebrows, a scornful tone. 'With a pile of guys there? I don't think so.'

'Sorry.' I felt stupid. Sal ignored my apology and crossed to the kettle with her empty mug. I tried to get back to reading about Dustin, but I couldn't concentrate. For one thing, Sal was still glaring at me, and for another, the hand on my watch was slowly creeping towards the ten mark.

'If he'd liked me enough,' Sal said, just as I'd given up my reading and was preparing to leave, 'I reckon he would have stayed, even if you were here. Don't you think so, Vic?'

I shrugged. What did I know? Marti hadn't stayed over yet and according to himself he was mad into me. But, as Sal said, maybe he was just mad, full stop.

'He hardly even kissed me goodbye,' Sal went on. 'Isn't that a bit weird?'

'I *told* you he was weird.'

'No, you told me he was trying to steal your job.'

Same difference as far as I was concerned.

'Then I began to wonder was it something I'd said, the way he rushed out of here last night.'

So it mightn't have been because of me after all. I was a bit annoyed at her trying to make me feel guilty. 'So you don't know that it was my fault?' I asked sweetly.

179

'And I went over everything I'd told him and drew a blank,' Sal continued. 'So it had to be you.'

'Did you tell him that you were the one that wrote the football fella piece?' I asked suddenly. If anything, that wouldn't have gone down well.

'The *Tell!* piece?'

'Uh-huh.'

'The scoop of the year?' Sal said. I think she was a bit offended by me referring to it as the football fella piece. 'That brilliant story that Mel still hasn't hired me for?'

'That's the one,' I said.

'No, I never mentioned it. You told me not to.'

'Good – so it can't be that then.'

'Though I don't know what the big deal is,' Sal continued. 'It was a perfectly honest story about an unfaithful shit . . .' Her voice trailed off. 'Hey, he probably didn't like it because his auld fella got caught a few years ago.' Her face lit up. 'Didn't he have it off with his manageress and didn't she kiss and tell?'

She had too. That must have been awful for the family.

'That was some story,' Sal said, remembering. 'I mean, nothing was left to the imagination, d'you remember?'

'I wouldn't go saying that to Ed.'

'I'm not stupid!' Sal scrunched up her dainty little nose. 'Well, so, I won't tell him I did that piece on McCoy.' She tossed her fab, unfrizzy hair back over her shoulder. 'But he'll have to accept my job sooner or later. I mean, I am who I am.'

'Yeah, well, just make sure he's fallen for you first.'

'Huh, the only thing he seems to have fallen for so far is that cheesecake of yours. He ate practically the lot of it last night.'

'My cheesecake?' I suddenly noticed the box sitting in the bin. And Sal looked as if she wished she'd kept her mouth shut. 'He had no right to eat that.'

Sal gave a false laugh. 'I mean, have you *ever* tried to get romantic when your other half is shovelling strawberry cheesecake into his mouth?' She was deliberately ignoring me.

'He shouldn't have been, though. It was *my* cake.'

'Which you don't eat,' Sal said, sounding pissed off.

'That's not the point.'

'Oh, Vic, don't start. Just don't.' She slammed her mug onto the table and closed her eyes.

'I don't like people taking my things without asking. That's all.'

'So what? He should have woken you at two this morning, should he?'

'Yes. Yes, he should.'

'Oh, come on . . .'

I buttoned my coat up all wrong in my haste to get out. There'd be a row if I stayed. Sal knew I couldn't bear my stuff being touched when I wasn't around. She *knew* it. She'd known it for years and yet she had to go and offer my cheesecake to someone. Yeah, I know, it's all a bit paranoid, but I can't help it. I cling on to practically everything I have. I've stuff dating back years in my room – clothes from when I was a teenager even. I hate throwing stuff out. Even cheesecakes. I would have eaten it.

'I'm going out.'

'It was only a bloody cake!'

'It wasn't a bloody cake. It was a *cheese*cake.'

'Vic . . .'

'You had no right.'

'For God's sake – it was something you didn't like.'

'How would you like if I gave . . .' I searched my mind – 'your laptop away to someone?'

'Completely different,' she said in a big bored voice.

I sort of knew it was. I knew I was being a big kid but I couldn't help it. 'Yeah, well, you'd better watch out.'

And with this stunning comment, I picked up my bag and stalked from the room.

Behind me I heard her going, 'Cop on!'

Once outside, I was suddenly consumed with what I can only describe as terror. The disappearing cheesecake dilemma receded as my heart began to slam about in my chest. Every step I took towards Yellow Halls' health centre made my stomach lurch something awful. I was convinced that great big patches of sweat were forming under my armpits. Even my fringe, which was unfrizzy, was beginning to curl up because of the beads of sweat on my forehead.

I arrived at the clinic five minutes early and found my way to the counsellor's office. Taking a seat, I began to pray feverishly that no one would see me. I did not want anyone to think that I was in need of counselling, even strangers. *Especially* strangers.

At ten-thirty, a small woman, even smaller than me, approached the office. She was dressed in a slate grey tailored jacket and trousers. Underneath her jacket, she wore a white silk blouse. Her dark hair was caught up in a ponytail, which made her appear younger than I'm sure she was. And her smile was gap-toothed. A reassuring sort of a smile that I'm sure she'd practised in front of a mirror.

'Victoria McCarthy?' she asked as she began to unlock the office.

'Vicky,' I said. I hated the name Victoria. It reminded me of some old dried-up prune of a person.

'Vicky, then,' she said. Inside the office, she flicked on the lights. 'Sorry about this, I'm normally in around ten but this morning everything went wrong. I'm Lucy, by the way.' She held out a tiny, manicured hand and I clasped it. It was warm. Her grip was tight. She gestured towards a comfortable green chair. 'Take a seat.'

Well, at least I didn't have to lie on a couch.

I sat gingerly down, right on the edge of the seat, clutching my haversack between my hands the way you'd grab onto a raft in an ocean. I watched as Lucy pulled up the blinds, flicked on her computer and adjusted her chair. Eventually, she clasped her hands together and smiled at me.

I managed a smile back.

'You look nervous.'

I flinched.

'There is nothing to be afraid of, Vicky,' she said gently. 'All we're going to do is have a chat about how you feel about things. It's not therapy or anything like that. It's just so that you know how to deal with all that's happening to you.'

I knew all this. I hoped she wasn't going to go on and on.

'I believe you've made contact with your mother.'

Her directness caught me unawares. 'Yeah. Yeah, I have.'

'And that she's written you a letter?'

'Yes.' I'd brought the letter with me, just in case. 'D'you want to see it?'

'If you want me to. If it's not too private.'

I did want her to see it. I was hoping she'd tell me what to say back. 'It's a nice letter,' I babbled as I opened my bag. 'Friendly.'

She took it from me and had a read. 'It is nice,' she agreed. 'How does it make you feel?'

'What?'

'The letter? How does it make you feel?'

I blinked. Once. Twice. Thought for a bit. She didn't hurry me or expect an instant answer. I'd spent the last while wondering how I felt. I mean, I thought I'd be overjoyed, but it went deeper than that. 'I dunno,' I finally said.

'You don't know?' She paused. 'How about what she says in the letter? How does that make you feel?'

I thought about what my birth mother had said. I knew every word off; I'd read it that many times. In the end I settled for a very inadequate, 'Good, I guess.'

'Good? In what way?'

'Well, you know, it's—' I did some more blinking. 'It's nice to think that she hasn't forgotten me.'

'That's true.'

'And, well, it's good to know that she wants to write to me at all.'

'Why wouldn't she write?'

Because she'd given me away, I wanted to say, but didn't. I just shrugged and looked at Lucy's tiny clasped hands. She had an engagement ring – a solitaire. They're my favourite rings.

'In my experience,' Lucy said, after a bit of silence, 'most mothers never stop thinking about the child they've given up. How could they not? It's a huge thing to have done.'

I didn't answer. I wished I had nice neat hands like Lucy's. Instead I had square hands with huge veins that made kids gawk when they saw them.

'So, what now?' Lucy asked. 'Are you planning on writing back?'

I was forced to look at her. I shrugged and muttered, 'I guess so.'

'You don't sound too sure.'

Her voice was quiet, probing. I bit my lip. My words rushed over themselves. 'I dunno what to say. I mean, I thought I would but, then, well, I couldn't just get it down. That's why I came, you see,' I explained. 'To see if you knew.'

'I can't tell you how to write a letter, Vicky.'

'Oh.' I was back to staring at her hands. What was the use of being here then?

'How long do you think your mother spent writing that?' She pointed at my letter. 'My guess is that she slaved over it too and she still probably wasn't satisfied with the result.'

I hadn't thought of that. Even though it had been one of the things she'd written, I hadn't actually *believed* it.

'My advice is to write what you feel, Vicky. Tell her her letter makes you feel good. Tell her you're glad she hasn't forgotten you. Things you've just told me.'

That made sense. Even to my muddled brain, that did make sense. 'I'll try that.'

'Do.' Then she chatted a bit more about how the letter made me feel. Drew stuff out of me that I hadn't planned on saying.

'Think about things,' she advised at the end. 'Think about where you want all this to go. Think about why you initiated contact in the first place.' She wrote something down on a piece of paper. Then she stood up. 'And that's it,' she smiled. 'It wasn't so bad, was it?'

I shook my head. It hadn't been too bad, but it hadn't been too helpful either. I still had to write the letter when I got back.

'It was lovely to meet you, Vicky, and we'll talk in two weeks, when you've had a chance to think – OK?'

'Sure.'

She held out her hand and we shook again. 'You have my number if you need me during the next couple of weeks, OK?'

'Yeah. Thanks.'

'Bye now.'

'Bye.'

I left her waiting for her next client.

But it had been good to talk.

I hadn't talked about things like that in twenty-eight years.

Chapter Thirty-two

Dear Barbara,

Thank you for writing back and it means a lot that you want to be in contact with me. Your letter and the things you said made me feel good. I know that reads badly but I honestly am finding it hard to express myself properly.

You asked me in your last letter what I wanted from you and the truth is I don't really know yet. I would love some background information on who I am. It's hard going through life not knowing stuff like that – at least I think so.

In time, I guess I'd like to meet you.

I hope this will be possible.

Vicky

Chapter Thirty-three

'HERE.' A BOX was placed under my nose.

'Oooh,' Bridie squealed. 'What's this? A present for Vicky, is it?'

I'd just arrived in, last as usual, and Ed had waited until I sat down before presenting me with an enormous box. He grinned down at me, his eyes made even bluer by the tie-dyed cerulean T-shirt he wore. 'Go on,' he urged, his hands jammed into the pockets of his combats, 'open it.'

'Yes, Vicky, open it!' Bridie nudged me with her elbow, her voice breathless, her eyes out on stalks. 'What could it *be*, I wonder?'

It didn't take a genius to work it out. A white box, tied up with a gold string and bearing the words *Carey Cakes*. I gulped, ready for humiliation.

'Go on.' Ed nudged me lightly with his elbow.

'So you were in touch with Sal,' I said, stalling for time.

'Rang her Monday night,' Ed nodded, a broad grin on his face. 'Seems she's all booked up until Saturday so I'll be seeing her then.'

'You and Vicky's journalist friend?' Bridie looked from him to me. In a teasing manner, she asked, 'Is there something going on?'

'She asked him out,' I said, my finger twiddling with the twine on the box and wondering how I could get out of this. I had a picture of Sal and Ed laughing away over the wobbler I'd thrown over the cheesecake. I could literally feel my guts cringing with shame.

'Well, isn't that great!' Bridie laughed, oblivious of anything but the romance of the situation. 'First you get asked out and then Ed.' A clap of her hands. 'Maybe I'll be next!'

'No maybe about it,' Ed grinned.

Bridie giggled, blushing. She really did love Ed.

'So, are you going to open the box or not?' Ed asked. He sounded amused.

'Oh yes, open it.' Bridie nudged me. 'It looks like a cake we can all share!'

Ed gave a splutter of a laugh but tried to turn it into a cough.

'I know what it is,' I said sullenly to them both. 'It's a cheese-cake, right?'

'Wrong!' Ed smiled delightedly and pulled at the string him-self. 'Da-na-nananh.' He lifted the lid and I saw the most enor-mous chocolate cake, smothered in cream and nuts and bits of flake.

He was grinning like a big kid at me. I gulped.

Bridie literally dribbled all over the place. 'Gorgeous,' she cooed. 'Isn't that lovely, Vicky? Oh Ed, that's so *kind* of you.'

Chocolate cake was my favourite. Sal must have told him that too. I didn't know if he was getting a dig at me or if the ges-ture was genuine.

'It's not kind at all,' Ed said. I sensed that he was looking at me, but I kept staring at the table. 'I ate all Vicky's cheesecake last Sunday and now I'm making it up to her.'

'You didn't have to.' I stood up. It sounded petty when he put it like that.

'Well, it's gorgeous,' Bridie declared. 'Will I put it in the fridge for you, Vicky?' Without waiting for an answer, she picked the box up and toddled towards the fridge.

'I'll open up,' I said, wanting to be out of there before Ed said anything else. To my horror, he followed me out of the room.

'Am I forgiven?' He gave a rueful smile. 'I didn't know the cake was yours, Vicky. Honestly.'

'Joke over.' I walked rapidly in front of him.

'I'm not joking.' There was something oddly arresting in his voice and I turned about to find him staring down on me with an intense look on his face. 'I know it's horrible when someone takes your stuff without asking. It's crap.' He gave a shrug. 'And I apologise.'

Something in me told me he really meant it. Some other part of me said he was only keeping me sweet because he was seeing Sal. 'Apology accepted,' I said. 'Forget about it.'

His smile, warm, lopsided and completely sincere, took me by surprise. I had to turn away.

'Forgotten, boss,' he shouted after me, spoiling everything as usual.

'Here, Dominic,' I said, pushing a plate of cake towards him. He was busy building something completely weird out of the Lego. 'That is for you.'

'Me?'

'Uh-huh,' I smiled at him. 'All yours.'

'Aw, no.' Dominic's mother legged it over towards us. It was as if I'd just offered her kid a plate of arsenic. 'Naw,' she shook her head vigorously. 'Domo doesn't need dah.'

'I know he doesn't need it,' I said, watching poor Dominic's face fall as his mother grabbed the cake from under him. 'But it's just that I got a cake this morning and it's too much for me, Bridie and Ed to eat and it'll be gone off by tomorrow so I thought you and Dominic might like to share it?'

'I *would* like that,' Dominic nodded vigorously. 'I like that cake, Mammy.'

'How'd you know you'd like it?' she spat at him. 'You've never eaten it before.'

Dominic's face crumpled.

'Well, maybe he could *try* it,' I suggested tactfully. I wasn't as scared of her as I used to be, mainly because Ed seemed to be able to get around her and if he could, well, I figured that I could too. 'It'll only go to waste otherwise,' I added.

The woman looked at the plate. Looked at Dominic. And finally, looked at me. 'No more after dis,' she finally said, shoving the cake towards Dominic. 'Dat's enough for him.'

Dominic began to eat it with his fingers, cramming it into his mouth. 'It's nice, Mammy.'

'Is it, luv?'

'Will you have some?' I asked. 'Honestly, Ed bought this enormous cake—'

'He bought a cake for you?'

'Well, yeah.'

She smiled suddenly, showing crooked teeth. 'He likes you, you fucking lucky bitch.'

The poor woman was definitely losing it. 'Well,' I shrugged, 'will you take a piece of cake from this fucking lucky bitch?'

Dominic giggled.

His mother managed a reluctant smile. 'Just a small piece. I'm full after me breakfast.'

Chapter Thirty-four

LATER THAT AFTERNOON, Albert O'Neill paid us one of his unannounced visits. 'Hello! Hello! Hello!' he shouted as he barged through the front door. 'And how's everyone?'

Bridie, the ever conscientious, was first on hand. I heard her answer in a high-pitched, nervous voice that she was 'very well and thank you for asking, Mr O'Neill'.

'And those legs?'

'Very well, thank you for asking, Mr O'Neill.'

'And the boss?'

'Oh, she's very—'

'Right here,' I interrupted, knowing that O'Neill would keep asking Bridie questions until she grew uncomfortable. 'Hi, Mr O'Neill.'

'Albert!' he roared. 'You can call me Albert. How many times do I have to keep telling you?' He boomed out a laugh. Then barked out, 'And where's himself?'

'He's setting up a display in the Football section,' I said.

'Good. Good. Keep him working hard.' O'Neill rubbed his hands together. 'By the way, brilliant window, Vicky.' He jabbed a finger towards the wrestling ring.

'Ed's,' I said shortly. Huh, typical. I'd slaved over the Barbie display and he bloody well hadn't noticed. In fact I don't think anyone had noticed, what with all the wrestling stuff Ed had managed to jam into one tiny slot.

'Oooh.' O'Neill looked surprised. 'Well, I'm sure you had something to do with it?'

I was tempted to say that it had been my idea, but Bridie was there and she'd know I was lying. 'Nope. All your son's.' I gave a forced laugh. 'He's quite the salesman.'

O'Neill's face glowered. 'He's quite a lot of things,' he muttered, rather nastily, I thought.

Bridie and I looked at each other.

'Can I have a word, Vicky – upstairs?' So saying, he dismissed Bridie with a glance.

As usual, the office was a tip. O'Neill almost tripped over the radio as he entered. Papers and files were strewn all over the desk and the computer was displaying a picture of Boy Five which I'd managed to scan in last week.

'Tea?' I asked, knowing O'Neill would forgive the state of the office if he could be persuaded to try a piece of the chocolate cake.

'Were you robbed?' O'Neill said instead, surveying the debris.

I forced out a laugh. 'Chocolate cake?'

'OK.' He sat himself down on the computer chair having removed a pile of files from it. I felt incredibly self-conscious as I made him a cuppa and cut him a generous slice of cake. The man was a lecher; with every glance, I felt as if I was being mentally undressed. I put the tea and cake in front of him and remained standing. I did not want to sit on one of the soft chairs and look in any way vulnerable. I wondered what he wanted. Maybe he was going to warn me that I was to lose my job. Well, I vowed, before he left that evening, I'd ask him straight out.

If I had the nerve, of course.

'Something wrong?'

I jumped, realising that I'd been glowering at him. I readjusted my face into something resembling a smile. 'No.' Pause. 'Nice cake, isn't it?'

'Lovely. Yes.'

I watched as his fleshy lips sucked another bite into his mouth. He chewed like a cow munching on grass. Eventually, finishing up, he sucked all his fingers, one by one, making funny kissing sounds as he did so. Then, fat fingers splayed on brown trouser legs, he said ponderously, 'I wanted to have a word with you about himself.'

My stomach heaved. 'Who? Ed?'

'Yes – how's he getting on?' His blue eyes studied me and I squirmed. His resemblance to Ed was quite striking when you looked closely. O'Neill had probably been a fine-looking man in his youth, before flab and hair loss and bad dress sense got to him. This was it, I found myself thinking in despair. The beginning of the end. 'I want to ask you about him myself,' I heard myself saying, hardly daring to believe it.

His brows came together ominously. 'What's he done?' The words were spat out.

'Nothing,' I said, startled. 'It's, eh, what he's going to do that worries me.'

'Join the club,' O'Neill said bitterly.

'Is he being groomed for my job?'

There was a moment's silence.

'I mean, I asked Ed when he started first and he denied it and I just wondered—'

O'Neill looked at me as if I was a complete moron. 'Groomed for your job?' he asked slowly.

'Yeah, I wondered if he was going to take over—'

'I would not let that son of mine take over on a motorway let alone take over one of my shops.'

'Nice to hear you still think the same of me, Dad,' Ed spoke from the doorway.

Neither of us had heard him and we both jumped.

O'Neill's face darkened.

'And I already told *you*,' Ed went on, looking at me and sounding strangely hurt, 'I told you all I wanted to do was work.'

'Yeah, I know,' I said, feeling terrible and going red. 'It's just that—'

'Oh, don't apologise to him, Victoria,' O'Neill boomed, pushing past Ed. 'It's his speciality, making everyone suffer. Don't mind him.'

'You never did, that's for sure,' Ed said, stopping him in his tracks.

O'Neill whirled on Ed. He was about two inches shorter than his son. 'Don't even go there,' he warned. 'I only financed every bloody thing you wanted to do.' He poked Ed in the chest. 'Computer courses, construction job. Every bloody thing you dropped out of.' He looked at me. 'Medicine – that was the last thing he fucked up.'

'I paid to do that myself,' Ed muttered mutinously.

'Damn right you did. I wasn't throwing any more money away on you. Christ!'

O'Neill, after giving Ed a final prod, stomped off.

'Bastard,' Ed muttered. I think he'd forgotten that I was there. He stood staring after his dad for ages.

I didn't know what to do. So I stayed very quiet, hoping that Ed would go on down.

He didn't. Instead, he turned back to me. 'So now you know,' he muttered. 'I am the O'Neill family fuck-up.'

'Oh no—'

'Oh yeah. Betcha glad you asked about me now.' He took his orange jacket down off its hook.

'Where are you going?'

'Just staying with the habits of a lifetime.'

'You're leaving?'

'Yep.'

I stared, horrified, as he shoved his arms into his jacket. Since he'd been with us, the sales of the wrestlers had tripled. He was a damn good toy seller and all the profit he'd make would ultimately reflect well on me. But over all that was the fact that he'd bought me the chocolate cake. Crap, I know. But I was pathetically grateful to him for admitting he was wrong to take my stuff, for admitting that he didn't like it when people did it to him. For not making me feel weird to be so obsessive. I'd spent most of my life feeling weird. 'You can't go. Don't go.'

He zipped up his jacket. Looked hard at me. Said quietly, 'Tell me one good reason why I should stay.'

'You're a good salesman.'

He laughed slightly. 'That's not much use when you don't trust me.'

'Yeah, well, I know different now. I guess I should have believed you.'

'Yeah, you should have.' Ed pinned me with his stare. 'And that's the problem, see, no matter what I do or say from now on, you'll double-check with me dad.'

'I won't.' He was making me feel guilty. 'I promise I won't.'

'You will.'

'I'm not a liar.'

'Neither am I.'

'I never said you were.'

'You just didn't believe me.'

'How could I?' I snapped. 'I figured if you were eyeing up my job, you wouldn't tell me anyway.'

'So you reckon I *am* a liar?'

'Oh for God's sake, we're only going around in circles here. I can't help the way I felt.'

There was tense silence.

'So how did you feel?' he asked. 'Like what exactly did I do to make you think I was after your job?' He paused. 'I worked my arse off for you, Vicky.'

His eyes bored into me, making me feel even more of a heel.

'Well, think about it,' I muttered defensively. 'It didn't make sense for you to come back from London to take a job working under me and Bridie and you O'Neill's son.'

Ed bit his lip. 'I had nothing else,' he said simply. 'As my dad told you, I ditched med school.'

'Yeah, and how come you never told me that!'

195

He flinched. 'It wasn't your business. And besides, it wouldn't have made a difference. I *told* you all I wanted to do was work. And I bloody well did too. Jesus' – he shook his head – 'if I'd been crap, you'd have been happier – yeah?'

I bowed my head. I could not look into those blue eyes any more. 'Well, you were always making me out to be stupid!'

'How so?' He sounded completely dazed. 'Christ!'

'Doing stuff on the computer, rearranging shelves, being all cosy with Bridie.'

'What?'

'You shoved me out.'

'Shoved you out?' He looked disbelievingly at me. 'Get lost!'

'You did,' I insisted. 'It was always me on my own while you and Bridie talked and laughed. You stole her away just like you were going to steal my job.' My voice had risen and I hadn't meant it to. I was aware of how pathetic I sounded, but damn it, that's the way it was.

'You *really* need to get a life, Vicky.'

He said it as if I was a weirdo. As if he was laughing at me. 'I have a life!' How dare he. He was the one that asked and now he wasn't prepared to face the truth. 'I do have a life.' I searched frantically for something that would impress him. 'I was asked to sing in a hotel.'

He didn't react.

'You're the one that needs to get a life if what your dad says is true.'

My angry words fell into silence.

Ed's face hardened. 'Ta, Vicky.' He turned to go.

I couldn't apologise. I just couldn't. I felt I should but he'd insulted me too.

Bridie came up the stairs, just as he was leaving. 'What is going on up here?' She looked from Ed to me. 'You can hear it in the shop.'

'Bye, Bridie,' Ed said by way of reply. A quick glance at me. 'She's all yours again, Vicky.'

Bridie gawked after him and when the front door slammed she turned to me, horrified. 'Vicky, what have you done? Where's he going?'

I burst into tears.

Chapter Thirty-five

BRIDIE COULD GET no sense out of me. Well, I was hardly going to tell her the full story, was I? I mean, if I told her that I thought Ed had been working so hard and doing so well just so that he could do me out of my job and steal away her friendship with me, I'd sound like one of those sad, obsessive, paranoid people.

As I watched Bridie fussing about, making me coffee and trying to force a huge slice of *that* cake on me, I told myself that we'd manage fine without Ed. I could do windows, I could put up swings. We'd managed before and we would again.

Bridie, of course, was convinced that a huge misunderstanding had taken place. There was no way, according to her, that Ed would have left over his dad wanting to know how he was getting on. He just did not *do* those things. Ed was kind and gentle and funny and charming. Basically, he was heaven on earth. 'He'll be back tomorrow,' she reassured me, 'you wait and see. He loves this job. He told me that only the other day.'

Ed was still AWOL by Friday.

At first, the nasty part of me was glad. I thought it would be like old times, just me and Bridie, working away.

Only it wasn't.

Ed's presence over the last few months had changed things between Bridie and me, or maybe they'd always been that way, I don't know. But I found that Bridie's constant dusting and polishing got on my nerves. At least when Ed was there, I could focus on him rather than feel guilty that I wasn't cleaning along-side her.

And, in the mornings, my eye kept returning to Ed's enormous green mug on the shelf. I wondered how long it would sit there before it became all mouldy. I wondered if I should ring him up and tell him to collect it.

And of course, when a nasty virus threatened to invade our computer system, whom did we have to thank for downloading the anti-virus thingy?

And most irritating of all was that Bridie kept mentioning him. Now that he was gone, I wanted her to forget that he'd been there at all. But she wouldn't. On Friday, she'd spent the morning laughing away to herself because Leeds had beaten Liverpool in some match or other. 'Oh, I wish I could see his face,' she said meaningfully.

I ignored her.

Dominic too wanted to know where he was.

'He's not here any more,' I said to him.

Dominic shrugged, his eyes filling with tears. 'Like Daddy,' he said to his mam.

'Naw,' she said, surprising me, 'he was miles better than your fuckin' daddy.'

But reminders of him were everywhere, not least in the window display, which was still pulling the kids in. It wasn't that I missed *him*, it was more that he was missing, if you know what I mean.

I decided to give him until Saturday before I took action. Though I hadn't a clue what I was going to do.

Of course, when Saturday came around and still Ed didn't show, I lost my nerve. I began to dial O'Neill's number to say that Ed had left, and halfway through I slammed the phone back down. Then, worried and miserable, I had to go back to the flat and watch Sal getting ready for her night out with him. There was no escape.

The guy was haunting me.

I sat on the sofa, pretending to watch a riveting programme about pig prices, while Sal floated in and out of her bedroom in various states of undress. In order to keep him keen, she hadn't talked to him all week, so it was up to me to fill her in or she'd kill me. She was blow-dried, made up and dressed and had just begun painting her nails before I plucked up the nerve.

'I think there's maybe something I should tell you before you go out tonight,' I stammered.

'Yeah?' She wasn't interested. She was holding her nails to the light and trying to gauge if they matched her steel blue trousers or if they needed another coat.

'Well . . .' I licked my lips and took a big, steadying breath. 'Ed has left the toy shop.'

'Oh.' She blinked, confused. 'But he's still coming here, isn't he?'

'I suppose.' That was not exactly the response I wanted. But at least she hadn't blown the top.

'Well then.'

'I'm only telling you so you're prepared for him not staying.' Pause as Sal considered this. 'I mean, we've had a row and he probably won't want to bump into me.' I refocused on Farming Report and waited for the accusations. I tried to look non-chalant but my heart was hammering.

'Him leaving might be for the best,' she eventually pronounced. 'Means you're not his boss any more. Move.' She sat down beside me on the sofa. 'Now, what do you think, do they need another coat?' She shoved her nails under my nose.

I was gobsmacked. Where were the hysterics? 'Eh . . .'

'Oh.' She snatched them away. 'Why am I asking you? Sure you haven't a clue. Where's Mel when I need her?' She studied them again. 'I think they look fine. It's a new non-chip varnish. I'm dying to see how long it'll last.'

That was the sort of stuff Sal found riveting. She even

wrote a beauty page for her paper on stuff like that.

'So, what happened?' she asked, rubbing some hand cream into her nails now that they'd dried to the correct colour. 'Was it over the cake?' Before I had a chance to answer, she went on, 'Honestly, when I told him you'd flipped about the cheesecake, he was so insistent that he get you another one. He didn't even find it funny – imagine?'

'That's because it wasn't funny,' I muttered darkly, cringing yet again.

'She won't appreciate it, I told him, Vicky hates people giving her things. Guess I was right – huh?'

It would have been nice for her to believe that but hey, she was seeing Ed and he was sure to get his slant in on the whole thing and I'd end up looking like a neurotic headcase. 'It wasn't exactly over the cake. He—'

'Aw, well' – Sal snapped her hand cream closed and turned to me – 'something like this was bound to happen. You had it in for him from day one.'

'I did not!'

'You did so.' She stood up and rolled her eyes at me. 'He's trying to take my job, Sal,' she mimicked in my low, husky voice. 'He's not doing what I say.'

'And he wasn't,' I said heatedly. 'He was always trying to undermine me!'

'You think everyone is trying to undermine you,' Sal said back. 'Face it, the guy hadn't a chance. You figured he was trying to steal your job and so you got at him.'

'No, I only asked—'

'It's like the way you are with Mel when we go out. When it's just you and me, we have a blast, but when Mel is there, you think she's taking me over or something.'

'No!'

'You go all out to get drunk, or you make all these smart remarks or you take ages to get ready or—'

'No, I don't!'

'You do. And the time when your German mate came to stay – what was his name?'

I didn't answer.

'Anyway, when he started seeing me, you wouldn't come out with us any more.' She laughed a bit. 'Gee, you flipped bigtime that time.'

'You only went out with him because he had money.'

'You only flipped because you wanted him all to yourself.'

'I'm going out.'

'You want everything all to yourself, Vic.'

'I'm going out!'

'And that's what you always do when you realise you can't have it your way the whole time, Vicky.'

I slammed the door on her.

I had nowhere to go. No money to buy anything. Not, I think, that I could have eaten anything anyway. My stomach was churning, my head was pounding and my throat had a huge lump in it. Sal's remarks had hurt. And what was even worse was that she really believed what she'd said. She hadn't said it in anger or as a joke, but in a sort of amused way. As if I was an amusing oddity or something. As if I was a weirdo. I shoved my hands into the light fleece that I was wearing and began to walk. Ed was due to call for Sal at eight-thirty, which meant that I had thirty minutes to kill before I could go back. It was just as well I had my trainers on; anything else would have crippled me.

I dulled my mind. Tried not to think. Instead, I walked. And walked. And passed flats and roads and roundabouts, schools and shops and the park, which had closed for the evening. I saw couples wrapped around one another, kids playing in their gardens with loads of their little friends, teenagers hanging about in large groups smoking and sniggering, families sitting down to dinner in lighted windows. And I wondered why I'd never been part of a large group. Never. Ever. Not even in school when all the girls had hung about together – there I'd be on the fringes, just watching.

Hovering.

And sort of glad that I was on my own.

I'd always preferred one-to-one relationships. Being part of a gang had never appealed to me. I knew I'd always feel left out. But seeing the kids playing together, I wondered why I'd always shied away from the fun of it. It sure looked like fun. Why had I never—

Because you get scared.

The thought came unbidden and it startled me.

I tried to push it away but it only grew louder. *You don't like crowds because* – I winced as the thought slithered into my consciousness – *because you don't want to have to compete with a group for someone's attention.*

Stop!

I clenched my hands so hard that my nails dug into my palms.

You don't want to compete.

You don't want the rejection.

But so what?

Everyone was different.

And not being part of a team was fine.

Scarily, my disastrous other jobs paraded themselves in front of me. I'd left the flower shop because two new girls had joined. They'd been too cliquey, I'd thought. I left the travel agents because a new boss had brought in new staff and now, well, I'd pushed Ed out.

Maybe not completely intentionally, but I hadn't tried too hard to make him stay after I'd hurt him. OK, so I did think he was after my job, but when I found out he wasn't, what had I done? Accused him of making me look a fool, of trying to steal Bridie. Hurt him by throwing his dad's comments back into his face.

I'd *wanted* him to go.

The chocolate cake *had* earned him some brownie points, but when it came down to it, I'd been glad to see him leave.

But, Jesus, I was the manager.

I was the boss.

I had to have staff. I couldn't go all jealous if the staff happened to get on, could I?

No, some part of me said.

And just because I had good staff didn't mean that they were eyeing up my job – did it?

No.

I saw with a sudden clarity what Ed must have gone through. How it must have hurt to come into the smallest store and be bossed about by the youngest manager. And still, he'd tried to do his best. And what had I done? Never even encouraged him. Never said 'well done' or anything. Because I'd resented him. I'd resented the fact that he was there at all – Daddy's boy with everything to gain. He had it all – looks, charm, a ready-made job, a family, and then he'd topped the lot by making Bridie fall for him. My friend Bridie.

Him leaving was partly my fault.

If I'd really wanted it, I should have been able to persuade him to stay.

I sat down on a wall as the knowledge swept over me.

Sal, with her careless remarks, had opened the door a chink.

And I found suddenly that I couldn't get it closed again.

The lump in my throat dissolved suddenly and I found that I was crying soft, silent tears.

I was a complete fuck-up. Completely weird and alone.

And I didn't know what to do.

Chapter Thirty-six

I WAITED UNTIL Sal went out the next morning before I got up. I'd woken around three a.m. to the sound of voices in the kitchen. There was Ed's unmistakable northern accent as he laughed softly at something Sal had said. It was probably something about me. Anyway, I hadn't been able to sleep until I heard the click of the door as he left the apartment. He mustn't have wanted to face me over breakfast and I cringed in a mixture of shame and relief.

Falling back asleep, I was woken by the sound of the shower. Sal was getting ready for a Sunday afternoon drinking spree with Mel and Lorcan. She'd told me that she hoped it meant what she hoped it meant. Privately, I couldn't see her being offered a job over pints in a pub, but I didn't say that. More importantly, I don't think Mel would have brought Lorcan along if she were discussing business. According to her, Lorcan was pure pleasure.

Like Sal and I *really* believed her.

Anyway, Sal left around twelve and I surfaced. All week, I'd been looking forward to Sunday – well, I had been until I'd rowed with Ed. Marti was due to surprise me. He'd sent me piles of text messages saying how much he was looking forward to seeing me and how well the boys were doing on their first big tour. The audiences had been fantastic, he said, and the only thing that went wrong was when Adam had thrown his cowboy hat up in the air and it had skimmed out over the audience. Some young wan had caught it and had been in tears when they'd made her hand it back. A small piece had appeared in the *Independent* damning the boys but Marti thought it was all publicity. 'How'd you like to lose a hat worth a couple of hundred quid?' he'd texted when I'd told him he should have just left it.

I grabbed a quick breakfast before showering and dressing. Marti had told me to be as flamboyant as I liked. 'It'll be that kind of day,' he said mysteriously. I didn't need to be told twice and I chose my purple jeans, the ones I'd bought for our first date, and a yellow top with Donald Duck on it. I love all the Disney characters. They always look so cheerful, don't you think?

By one, I was presentable, having tamed my hair by plaiting it into two braids.

Marti was on time.

He pressed the buzzer and warbled, '*Something told me it's all happening at the zoo.*' I smiled. '*I don't believe it, I don't believe it's true.*' Then I told him I'd be down in a sec. I glanced in the mirror on the way out. I looked tired, I thought. And there was a frown line between my eyebrows that hadn't been there before. And my eyes were all red so I shoved some powder onto my face, which caked instantly. And Donald Duck looked stupid on me. I was too old for Donald Duck.

I raced back into the bedroom and took out my tie-dyed purple top. Pulling it over my head, making bits of hair stick out all over the place, I left.

Marti was wearing a pair of tight blue jeans and a cream sweatshirt with the words *Boy Five – Five Times Better Than Your Average Boy Bands*. He was sitting behind the wheel of his Boy Five-mobile sporting a pair of cool-looking shades and a navy and cream baseball cap. 'Hey, great to see you.' He leaned over and kissed me as I clambered in.

It was only then that I noticed Leo glowering from the back seat. He had his trusty teddy with him and was holding it tightly. 'Leo,' I said, hoping the shock didn't show in my voice. 'How's things?'

He shrugged and shoved a thumb in his mouth.

'Take that thumb out of your mouth,' Marti said crossly, 'and answer Vicky!'

'Oh, no, it doesn't matter,' I said breezily.

'Then why did you ask it?' Leo said in a bright clear voice.

I ignored him. Marti ignored him. 'Leo's fine,' he said heartily, his hands going white as he clenched the steering wheel. 'And he's looking forward to the surprise too, aren't you?'

Leo shrugged. 'It's the zoo. I heard you talking about it on the phone.'

The zoo?

My surprise was an outing to the zoo?

'The zoo?' I said faintly.

'Sort of.' Marti beamed at me, showing off his gold tooth. 'It's more than that, though.'

'You're shooting the band's video,' Leo chimed in.

Marti gave a loud laugh.

'We're going to the zoo to see the new Boy Five video?' I could not believe this. This was not happening.

'A hard boy to surprise, is Leo,' Marti said through gritted teeth, as he tried valiantly to smile. 'Like his mother, that way.'

'We're going to the zoo to see the new Boy Five video?' I asked again.

'Yep.' Marti beamed at me. 'Isn't that brilliant? I mean, have you ever seen a music video shot?'

'No.' And I really hadn't harboured a secret desire to see one either.

'There you are then.' He looked me up and down. 'And if you want, you can be in it – good-lookers are always needed. We could have you beside the orang-utans – nice contrast with the hair colours.'

'Nah.' I couldn't even muster a grin, that's assuming he was joking. 'I don't think so.' What was happening to my life, I wondered.

'Can I be in it, Daddy?' Leo asked suddenly.

'No!'

'Well, then, I don't want to go.'

Me neither, I wanted to say. I mean, if it had been a video for, say, Juliet Turner or some other brilliant singer-songwriter, I'd probably have been a bit more enthusiastic, but Boy Five?

'What's the new single?' I asked.

'Can't you guess?' Marti took off his glasses and grinned. 'Simon and Garfunkel's Zoo song.'

'Ha. Should have guessed.'

Marti and his crew had hired the zoo especially for the day. When we got there, cameras and lights were being set up outside the lion's enclosure. Boy Five were swaggering around looking very important. They'd been given new hairstyles – floppy blond streaks for two of the lads while Cliff sported an enormous quiff. He looked a bit like a cockatoo. The other two had had their hair completely shorn in order to appeal to the teenagers that liked a bit of rough, Marti later informed me. They were dressed in zookeeper outfits – green overalls that clung in all the right places.

Marti strode on ahead of me, Leo running in his wake. I watched as he clapped the lads on the back and had a few words with the make-up woman. Then he turned to me and beckoned me forward. Introductions were made, the lads nodded briefly at me – all except Cliff who seemed to be a master bearer of grudges.

'Marti,' some fella said then, 'we're ready if you want to go.'

'Uh-huh.' Marti took a seat in a stereotypical director's chair and I sat beside him. From somewhere the music began to boom through the speakers. Boy Five took up their positions in front of the lion's enclosure and proceeded to mime to the song.

'But they're not singing,' I shouted at Marti over the noise.

'Nah, no one ever does on videos,' he said knowledgeably.

The music stopped abruptly. The sound director looked up. 'Too loud.'

The camera guy looked up. 'Too bright.'

Cliff and the lads winced. 'These outfits are too tight, Marti.'

Marti ignored them. 'Back into positions, lads,' he said. A major confab with the cameramen ensued. I sat there, watching the activity going on as the lights were adjusted and the sound was monitored.

Leo trailed around after Marti, who didn't seem to be aware of him.

Eventually they were all ready to go again.

Boy Five took up their positions. They had buckets in their hands and were doing some sort of weird dance routine which involved a lot of jumping over them.

'Action!'

The music blared.

The lads began to mime.

And the lion, which had suddenly arrived on the scene, began to roar. And I mean *roar*. Boy Five jumped about a million miles into the air before legging it. One camera toppled over. Marti yelled out a 'Jaysus' and I had to bite my lip to stop from laughing.

Leo thought it was great.

'Wow, Dad, d'ya hear that! Wow.' He ran up towards the lion to get a closer look. The animal stared at him and then with a disdainful flick of its tail wandered up the hill.

Everything had to be started up again.

And again, just as the lads were about to launch into their dance routine, the lion roared, only it sounded a lot more menacing this time.

'Aw, Jaysus.' Marti glared around at everyone and then glared at the lion. 'Leo, get away from there!' he barked. Leo ignored him. 'Leo!'

Reluctantly, Leo slunk away.

'I only wanted a look,' he muttered under his breath.

'Your dad's afraid you'll get hurt,' I whispered back.

He said nothing.

Marti was striding about the place, wondering what to do.

'Zookeeper,' he pronounced suddenly. 'Maybe the bloody thing is hungry. Get the zookeeper.'

Apparently it was no one's job to get the zookeeper.

'Vicky?' he turned to me. 'Will you go – please?'

'Right.' I stood up. It was better than sitting down and doing nothing. I turned to Leo. 'D'you want to come?'

He glared at me.

'You'll be able to look around the zoo and maybe see some animals?'

He looked uncertain.

'He won't,' Marti hissed, coming over. 'We're on a tight time limit, Vicky. I need you to hurry. This will cost me a fortune.'

I could have strangled the man. Was he completely insensitive to the kid's feelings? Did he even care if Leo liked me? 'I'll bring you around when I come back,' I promised him. 'That's if you'll come.'

He hugged his teddy. 'Will you come too, Daddy?'

Marti gave an impatient sigh. 'Wish I could, Leo, but you can see how busy Daddy is.'

'Then I won't go either,' Leo pouted.

'Fine.' I shrugged. 'I'll just have to go on my own, so.'

'Yeah. After you get the zookeeper,' Marti said, glancing at his watch. 'OK, everyone,' he announced as I walked off, 'take five.'

They took longer than five. I hadn't a clue where a zookeeper could be found. Thirty minutes later, I arrived back with a man smaller than Marti in tow. He hadn't been at all pleased to hear that the lion was roaring. 'I knew this shouldn't be allowed,' he said grumpily as he scampered along beside me. 'I told them that but would they listen?'

I smiled politely and said nothing.

'Now,' he said, as he strode over to where everyone was drinking cups of coffee, 'who's in charge here?'

'I am.' Marti stood up. 'And to be honest, this is not proving to be the most successful of days. The lion, that one there' –

he pointed to where the lion was pacing up and down and glaring at all of them – 'is being very disruptive. I mean, is there any way we can stop it from roaring?'

The zookeeper, whose name was Hugh, smirked. 'I'll open the gates if you want to go in there and try.'

I laughed.

Marti looked offended, though whether it was from me laughing or Hugh's reply, I wasn't sure. 'There's no need for that,' he said placatingly. 'Just shove a few steaks or something in there to keep him busy while we shoot this.'

'That animal is on a strict diet,' Hugh said, somewhat patronisingly, I thought. 'You don't go shoving him a few steaks now and again. What I suggest is that you shoot this somewhere else. You've obviously upset him. I can't have my animals upset.'

'Well, he's upset us,' Marti blustered.

'And I'm sure he's sorry about that,' Hugh smirked. 'But it's not everyone that likes loud music outside their house, is it?'

'So you're saying that that lion has won, are you?' Marti asked.

The lion was lying down now, basking in the unexpected sunlight of the early afternoon. He looked as if he was grinning at us.

'He's smiling,' Leo pronounced delightedly.

'Sure is,' I whispered back.

The child forgot his obvious dislike of me enough to begin to giggle. 'He doesn't like the music – just like my mammy.'

I decided it would be prudent to say nothing.

'So you're not going to do anything?' Marti was still arguing. 'Can't you tranquillise it or something?'

'Move!' Hugh had heard enough. 'Go on now, the lot of yez, move!'

'We've hired the place out,' Marti said back, folding his arms. 'Adam's dad *works* here.'

Adam smiled nervously.

'I don't give a damn if you've *bought* the place out,' Hugh retorted. 'You can't go upsetting the animals – well, not unless you want a huge court case on your hands.'

That did it. Reluctantly everyone began to pack up.

'Well, can you tell us what animals actually like music?' Marti asked, just as Hugh was about to leave.

'That music?' Hugh smirked. 'Animals with severe brain damage, I'd say.'

'So, yourself then?' Marti said, sounding ridiculously polite.

Hugh looked as if he were about to go for him but thought the better of it. 'Excuse me, while I go back to my worthwhile job,' he said instead.

We all watched him saunter off, his small frame looking about a hundred foot high with the swagger he affected.

'Asshole.' Marti raised his eyes heavenwards before turning back to his protégés.

'You ignore that insult, lads. You ignore it. Yez are brilliant. Five thousand pre-teens can't be wrong, sure they can't?'

The five nodded.

They decamped to the monkey enclosure. Once again there began the arduous business of setting up lights and cameras. I really did not want to sit around and watch it all happen. Or not happen as the case may be.

'Marti,' I tugged on his sleeve.

'Yo!' he turned around and bestowed me with a smile. 'What is it?'

'I think I'll just have a wander around. I haven't been to the zoo in years and well . . .' I let my voice trail off. I couldn't say it. I couldn't say that I was dying to look around or that it'd be nice to look around.

'Off you go.' Marti made whooshing motions with his arms. 'You're only in the way here anyway. Enjoy! Enjoy!' He turned back to the make-up woman.

'Now, I want them browner-looking. Brown is sexy.'

'Not if they look as if they've shite smeared all over their faces, it's not,' she grumped.

Marti laughed.

He was still laughing as I turned to go.

I had walked a fair distance away and was heading towards the sea lions when a small voice said nervously, 'Can I come too?'

I was about to smile and say that of course he could come when he added sulkily, 'I mean, I don't want to go with you, not really, but there's no one else.'

'Yeah, well, I don't want to go with you either, but like you said, there's no one else.'

He wasn't sure if I was joking.

But he walked alongside me anyway.

Chapter Thirty-seven

IT WAS QUITE nice having Leo for company, as it happened; at least it took my mind off the fiasco in the shop. It wasn't as if I'd *planned* on thinking about it but it was kind of hard not to. At least with Leo trotting alongside me, I found that I could focus on his hostility, which was heaps better than worrying about O'Neill's impending aggression upon finding out that his problem son had jacked in another job.

'Where d'you want to go first, Leo?' I arranged my face in a big bright contrived smile.

He shrugged and scuffed the ground with his shoe. 'Don't care.'

'How about the sea lions – that's where I was going.'

'Fine.'

'This way, so.' I headed off in what I hoped was the right direction, him trailing behind. Just as we rounded the corner, we came across a sort of mini-playground. I was about to walk past it, when Leo asked shyly, 'Can I have a quick go?'

I was delighted that he'd volunteered an interest in something. 'Yeah. Sure.'

There was a little slide, a swing and a set of monkey bars. I sat down and watched as he made for the slide and scampered up it. Then, in typical boy fashion, he came down head first.

'Don't do that.' I legged it across and caught him just before his head hit the ground. 'You'll hurt yourself. Your dad will kill me if anything happens you.'

'No he won't.' Leo shrugged me off. 'All he cares about is his band.'

214

'Oh now, don't be silly!' I watched as once again he clambered up the slide. 'That's not true.'

'Is so.' He shoved his teddy down before him this time. 'That's what my nana says to him. She says all you care about is the band, you'll want to cop on. And my mammy used to say the same thing.'

'Oh now—' I couldn't finish. He launched himself down the slide head first again, only faster this time. 'Leo!'

'You can't give out to me.' He jumped up and wiped his hands down the length of his trousers. 'You're not the boss of me.'

'I am when I'm on my own with you.' I met his defiant stare with one of my own. Huh, I thought, this kid thinks he's bad, well, he hasn't met me properly yet. 'Now, you can go back to your daddy and the band or you can see the sea lions being fed – it's up to you, but if you come down the slide head first again, then I'm just going to pick you up and bring you back to your daddy.'

'You're too small.'

I don't like being reminded of that. 'Not as small as you, twerp.'

'That's not nice.'

I shrugged. 'Do you want to see the sea lions?'

He stared at his trainers. Black hair fell forward over his face and I thought how much the kid needed a haircut. And he wore a blue sweatshirt that was way too small for him and jeans that were all frayed and faded. Even his trainers were falling apart. I felt a rush of pity for him. Or compassion. Or something along those lines. Without thinking, I reached out and tousled his hair. 'Betcha can't go on the monkey bars without falling,' I grinned.

Leo's eyes met mine. His bottom lip stuck out in a condescending sneer. 'Can so.'

'Let's see you then.'

I used to be the expert on monkey bars as a kid, maybe

because I'd been so skinny that my arms could support my body easily enough. I figured that Leo would be the same.

He ran across to the bars and launched himself onto the first one.

'Keep your body as steady as possible,' I advised and, though he pretended he wasn't listening, he immediately stopped wriggling his legs. 'Now!'

His hand groped for the second bar.

'Steady yourself.'

His other hand groped for the second bar.

'Steady.'

'I know,' he snapped.

Little by little he eased himself across to the other side and when he finished, there was a grin of triumph in his face. 'See?'

'Good man!' I pretended to be amazed. 'That was brilliant.'

He tried not to smile, but it broke through. 'It's hard,' he said nonchalantly, 'hurts your arms.'

'I'd say so,' I nodded. 'Ice cream is good for fixing up sore arms. D'you want one?'

The wary look was back.

'Only if you want one.'

'Well . . . my arms *are* sore,' he conceded.

One ice cream later, we reached the sea lions. Leo had gone back to monosyllabic mood and all my talk about sea lions went nowhere.

'I thought you said they were going to be fed,' he accused.

I shrugged. For some reason it had never occurred to me that they wouldn't be feeding when I arrived to see them. Any poster I'd ever seen of zoos, it always showed the sea lions being fed. I dunno, maybe I thought it went on all day or something.

'Sorry, Leo, I must have got it wrong.'

'Great!' He rolled his eyes and hugged his teddy closer. 'My mammy wouldn't tell lies like that.'

I said nothing, pretending to be fascinated by the lovely blue pool the sea lions were swimming about in.

'She's going to come back, you know.'

'Guess you miss her, huh?' I hadn't planned to say it, the words just popped out.

He eyed me warily. A slow nod.

I crouched down beside him. 'That's good,' I said. 'And I bet she misses you too.'

He bit his lip. 'I don't know.' His eyes pooled with tears and he turned away.

'No mammy ever forgets her children,' I quoted Lucy. I guessed she should know. 'A very important lady told me that.'

'Who?' He turned back and eyed me suspiciously. 'Pink?'

'Eh – no.'

'The Queen?'

'No – just someone who knows all about mammies and their children. She said that no matter where mammies are, they always remember their kids.'

'Really?' His eyes widened and his mouth parted slightly. It was as if I'd just given him the most wonderful news.

'Uh-huh.'

'Dad says she's not coming back.'

'Yeah, well, I don't know about that.'

'Can you ask your important lady?'

I winced. 'Well, she's not around at the moment. Maybe next time I see her.'

Leo nodded. 'OK, so.' His gaze flicked from my face to somewhere over my shoulder. He gave a squeal that made me jump. 'He's coming! He's coming to feed the sea lions!'

The smile, which lit his face, transformed him into quite a beautiful kid and I wondered how any mother could have walked out on him.

On the way back, Marti moaned on and on about whoever said not to work with children or animals knew what they were talking about. 'The monkeys were worse than the lion,' he said, careering across two lanes of traffic. 'One of them kept screeching every time Cliff had to pretend to feed it. And Adam tripped over his bucket just as we were finishing the shoot and we had to take it again. I swear, he's as clumsy as a three-legged racehorse.'

'I went on the monkey bars, Daddy.'

'Good lad.' Marti flashed him a brief smile. 'And then, right, Logan hurt himself with his costume. Said it was too tight and he could hardly stand upright in it.'

Despite Marti's glowering face, I started to laugh.

'It's not funny,' Marti snapped. 'It's been a disaster.'

'Well, Leo and I had a great day,' I chimed in, 'didn't we, Leo?'

He shrugged. 'It was OK. Vicky said that Mammy misses me.'

The car came to a shrieking halt. Someone blasted us from behind. Marti ignored them. 'I don't encourage him to talk about his mother,' he snapped at me, 'and you shouldn't either.'

'What?'

'His mother left him – she's gone. That's all there is to it.'

'He has to be able to talk about it,' I said, remembering the way I never talked about my own mother. 'The poor kid will go mad otherwise.'

'She loves me,' Leo said. 'And she's thinking of me.'

'Shut up!' Marti ordered.

'And Vicky is going to ask if she's going to come back.' Leo's voice shook slightly, but he kept on going. 'She knows an important lady who knows these things.'

'Vicky doesn't know anyone like that,' Marti said.

'She does!' Leo sounded as if he was going to cry.

'She does not!'

'My counsellor,' I interjected. This was fast becoming a nightmare.

'A shrink?' Marti looked appalled.

218

'No.' I swallowed. 'It's a woman I see who's, well, she's helping me trace my own mother.'

'What?' Marti looked confused.

'I'm . . .' I closed my eyes. As far as possible, I'd never admitted to being adopted before. It was, I dunno, shameful to me that my own mother had given me away. A stigma. I know it sounds unreasonable, but hey, I blamed myself. I probably wasn't cute enough or something.

'Well?' Marti said, not sounding that supportive.

'I'm adopted.' I mumbled it. I opened my eyes and stared out at the congested Dublin traffic. 'I'm tracing my mother and this counsellor is helping me find her.'

Silence.

Marti was gawping at me.

'What's adopted?' Leo asked.

'It's when your mammy gives you away when you're born,' Marti explained.

'Like, your mammy leaving you?' Leo asked.

'Oh, a million times worse than that,' Marti said.

'Ta, Marti.'

He shrugged, gave my arm a limp pat. 'Sorry, sorry. I didn't mean—'

'Your mammy left you too?' Leo said, poking his face between the two seats.

I nodded, afraid I'd cry. I always cried when I thought of it.

'Poor you.' He reached out and rubbed his small hand up and down my hair. 'Poor you.'

I gave a shaky smile and gently touched Leo's hand.

Marti studied the two of us for a second and his eyes softened. 'Well, she must've been bloody mad,' he pronounced. 'Leaving a fine thing like yourself.'

I gave a bit of a laugh. I wanted to hug the man.

'My mammy was mad too, wasn't she?' Leo said. 'But she still loves me.'

'She does,' I said firmly, daring Marti to defy me.

219

He shrugged. 'Well, I guess Vicky is the expert,' he conceded. 'Who wouldn't love you, Leo, hey?' He gave his son a broad wink and turned rueful eyes on me. 'Look, Vicky, I'm dead sorry. Talking about Linda makes me angry – I mean she walked out on us – left me with him – I dunno what to do.'

'Leo has to be able to talk about it, Marti.'

'It upsets him.' He inched the car forward and shot a furtive look at Leo, who'd gone back to playing with his teddy. 'It upsets *me*.' Before I could reply, he continued, 'I'm not great with kids. Linda was the one who did all that stuff.'

'Well, learn. It's important.' I bit my lip. 'My folks didn't like talking about my adoption to me. But, like, it doesn't do any good to hide things or ignore things.'

Who was I to talk, I suddenly wondered. Jesus, I was the *expert* in ignoring stuff. But maybe I had a point.

For once in my life.

'You have a point.' Marti gave me his peculiar smile. 'Thanks, Vicky.'

'No,' I said, much to his puzzlement. 'Thank you.'

Chapter Thirty-eight

BRIDIE RANG ME at the flat on Monday to tell me what I'd known would happen all weekend – Ed still hadn't shown. The news, while expected, made my stomach roll. I had tried to ask Sal if Ed had mentioned anything to her about his plans but she was in a big black mood. I took it that Mel still hadn't come up with a job for her.

'I'll be in after lunch to help you out,' I told Bridie. Then, attempting a casual tone, I asked, 'Where does Ed live anyway?'

'Are you going to see him?' Bridie said breathlessly. Before I could answer, she rushed on, 'Oh you should, Vicky. Clear the air and all that.'

'Clear his mug from our office more like,' I muttered.

'Oh now! Oh now!' Uncertain pause. 'You don't mean that. Do you?'

'Just gimme his address, Bridie.'

I heard her tapping some buttons on the computer. 'Here we are now – Apartment five, Abbey Court, Seascape Road, Dun Laoghaire.'

'Ta.'

I put down the phone before she could ask me anything else.

Of course, I hadn't checked to see if he was home. That would have been the sensible thing to do, I realised, as I sat on the dart to Dun Laoghaire. What if he wasn't in? What then? Did I hang about all day in the hope that he'd arrive back? Did I go again tomorrow? Did I ring him up?

221

There was no point in tormenting myself, I decided, once I got off. The main thing to do was to find the place. There'd be time enough to worry when I got there. I shoved my hands into my jacket pockets and bent my head against the breeze coming in from the sea. Nabbing an old man, I asked him if he knew where Seascape Road was.

'Ohh now,' he said, scratching his chin, 'I *do* know the name. In fact a friend of mine only talked about it yesterday. Hang on now while I think.'

I hung on.

'Seaview Road,' he mumbled.

'Scape,' I said.

'Pardon?'

'Seascape Road.'

'Oh well now, I thought you said Seaview.'

'No.' I fixed a smile in place. 'Anyway—'

'Hang on now while I think if I know of a Seacape Road.'

'Seascape,' I said. 'As in e-scape.'

'Oh.' He looked confused. 'Oh now, hang on . . .'

How is it that when you ask someone for directions they always turn out to be dense? He hadn't a clue. He mumbled something about houses going up everywhere so that a person didn't know if they were coming or going and wandered off.

Eventually I found a woman who lived in the area. 'Second left then take the third right and you'll see it after the traffic lights.'

Still managed to get lost.

It was after midday when I found myself staring up at a nice enough apartment block. All sorts of spring flowers danced in beds outside and the gardener was mowing the grass on a ride-on lawnmower. It all looked so peaceful and nice. Or it would have if I didn't think I was going to be sick everywhere. Not since Mrs Sweeney turned up at our door demanding that I give Lisa's Barbie back to her have I been so scared. I hadn't even planned what I should say. All I knew was that I had to say something to fix things. To put things right. To acknowledge to myself that I wasn't the horrible person Sal said I was. I wasn't selfish.

No way.

My finger shook as I pressed the buzzer for 'O'Kane, O'Neill, Mulligan, Brett'.

'Yeah?'

It was him.

'Ed?'

'Aye – who's this?'

I gulped. I could still run if I wanted. 'Me,' I answered in a sort of terrified squeal.

'Vicky.'

There was a pause that seemed to last for ages.

'You'd better come up.'

He buzzed and I pushed open the door. I didn't even notice what the place was like inside, I was so sick at the thoughts of seeing the guy. He lived in a top-floor apartment and I took the lift up, hoping that it'd get stuck.

Of course, it didn't. It announced pleasantly that we were on the fourth floor and with a swoosh the doors opened.

I patted down my hair, licked my lips and straightened my smock top, which had an annoying habit of riding upwards and revealing my belly button. Then, tossing back my mane of frizz, I tried to stride purposefully forward. I figured that if he heard my footsteps sounding so determined, he wouldn't realise how terrified I was.

He had his door open before I got there. 'Vicky' – he gave a clipped grin – 'what a surprise.'

He made it sound like the worst surprise ever.

I walked into a tiny hall and followed Ed into an average-size sitting room. 'I was just about to go out,' he indicated a guitar standing up against the wall.

'Well, I won't keep you long,' I stammered, still not having a clue what to say.

'What d'you want?'

He was barefoot, I noticed. A pair of navy socks and trainers were sitting on the sofa. His T-shirt was unironed and it had some kind of slogan on it. A pair of faded brown cords completed his 'out-of-work' appearance.

'I, eh, came to see if you'd consider coming back.' I knew the minute the words were out that they were the wrong ones.

'No.' His blue eyes looked kinda like his dad's now.

'Oh.' I bit my lip. 'Well, how about,' I took a huge gulp of air, 'if I, well, if I said that I would *like* you to come back. That as a manager I realise that for the good of the shop you should be working there.'

That sounded good, I thought. Not too grovelling. Not too off-hand.

'And I realise,' Ed said, sitting down on the sofa and beginning to pull on his socks, 'as an employee that for the good of the shop, it's better if I don't come back.'

The smart bastard. I resisted the urge to say that and instead squeaked out, 'But why?'

He began to shove his foot into a trainer and lace it up. 'Let's not do this,' he said, sounding weary. 'We'll only say stuff we regret.'

I winced. 'Look, I'm sorry for what I said about you needing to get a life.'

His only response was a nod.

'Ed, will you stop at your shoes and listen to me!'

He hesitated. Laced up his trainer anyway and, resting his elbows on his knees, faced me.

And of course, the minute I had his attention, I didn't know what I wanted to say. Or what I *should* say. I guessed I should make some sort of an apology. I stared up at the ceiling and observed the progress of a huge spider as he scuttled about making a web. That's what I felt I was trapped in right at that moment.

'I'm all ears,' Ed broke into my thoughts. 'Fire away.'

I wished I could *run* away. Never in my life had I to make an apology to anyone. Maybe that sounds arrogant but I guess I'd just never let myself get into this kind of a situation before. If I wanted to, I could have just walked out. I could have placed all the blame on Ed and I reckoned his dad would go for it, but coward and all as I was, I wasn't that bad. And besides, I didn't want to prove Sal right.

'I'm sorry for what I said to you before you left,' I repeated. 'And, also' – big gulp – 'I'm sorry for not believing you.'

Ed shrugged. 'Ta.'

'So will you come back?'

He looked incredulous. 'Nope.' He sounded as if he might laugh.

'Look, Ed,' I said, 'this wasn't easy for me to come here, you know. I'm doing my best to apologise.'

'Well, apology accepted.' Ed stood up to face me, his trainers now fully laced up. 'But, you know, you've nothing major to apologise for. Basically you were suspicious of me, you checked it out – fine. It's me.' He paused slightly and smiled in such a way that I wanted to touch him. It was so full of regret or something. 'I just can't work where I'm not trusted.' A small shrug before he turned to pick up his guitar.

I stood frozen. I'd honestly thought that he'd come racing back.

'Well.' He signalled the door. 'Let's be off.' He stood waiting for me to move.

'It's not so much that I didn't trust you,' I babbled out. 'I was jealous of you.'

'Huh?'

I could not believe what I'd just admitted to. Jesus, the weirdo label was never going to come off now. Might as well go the whole hog and admit what a pig I was. My face grew all hot and my hands went clammy. He, meanwhile, was gawking at me.

'You're good at the job,' I muttered, minus any admiration. 'I, well, I felt threatened, didn't I? Jesus, if I was your dad, I'd let you run the place.'

'Feck off!' There was a smile in his voice.

I looked cautiously up at him. 'No, I would,' I insisted, gaining courage from his smile. 'To be honest, I wanted you to leave. I can't cope with the competition.'

'Competition?'

Oh God. I was walking right into it now. 'You having such good ideas, you being so friendly with Bridie.' I paused. 'Mainly you being so friendly with Bridie.' I cringed at my honesty. But it was something I had to do, something I had to face up to even if he was going to think I was a sad case.

He was looking at me funny.

'It wasn't personal,' I admitted. 'I reckon no matter who'd started, I'd have resented them.'

'So why'd you come here wanting me back? Surely you're happy now?'

'I was *wrong*,' I gulped out. 'I see that now. It's good you're there. I need you in the shop.'

Now it was his turn to look at the ceiling.

'I just *love* that job, Ed. I didn't want to lose it. I didn't want to lose Bridie. I—' I winced, closed my eyes. 'I guess I find it hard to, I dunno, share. I get possessive about stuff.'

'Like the cheesecake?'

'Forget the cheesecake!' Was that cheesecake going to haunt me?

'So, now, you won't be possessive, is that what you're saying?' Ed asked.

'Yep.'

'Really?' He sounded half amused.

'Yes. Really.'

'So you can turn on and off your emotions, can you?'

He was laughing at me. Suddenly I felt like crying. I had totally humiliated myself and for what? 'I didn't come here to be made fun of.' My voice shook. 'I apologised and did *everything* I was meant to do and now it's up to you.'

'What is?'

'Whether you'll come back.'

'I'm sorry,' Ed said, still smiling a bit. 'I shouldn't have laughed.'

'No you shouldn't.'

'I'll come back on one condition.'

It took a moment to sink in. He was going to come back. 'You will?' A huge whoosh of relief surged through me. Tears sparked my eyes and I had to blink hard. 'Really?'

'Uh-huh.' He winked at me and it made me feel weird. Weird in a nice way. 'I'll come back if we have an afternoon break.'

Jesus!

He was grinning now, his hands shoved into his jeans. 'What d'ya say?'

'Well . . .' I tried to sound disapproving but it didn't quite come off. 'If you think it's a good idea.'

'I do.'

'Fine.' I smiled shakily. 'OK, so.'

'Great. Ta, boss.'

I ignored him calling me boss. 'Sooo – will we see you tomorrow?'

'Aw, no, I'll head in now. Sure Bridie is probably run off her feet.' He grabbed his jacket from a chair and hastily patted his hair down.

I was about to tell him that he couldn't wear that T-shirt in when I stopped myself. I was damn lucky he was going in at all. He could have been a bastard about it and said he'd be back next week. Without thinking, I said, 'Thanks, Ed.'

He paused in the act of zipping up his jacket. Turning around, he studied me, his blue-eyed gaze making me uncomfortable, especially as my belly button was clearly on view. I pulled my top down and straightened my shoulders. To my surprise, he held out his hand. 'No,' he grinned slightly, 'thank *you*. D'you know something – no one has ever apologised to me in my entire life.'

227

He said it jokingly but there was something in his eyes, something I couldn't quite make out. I took his hand in mine and he grinned. 'Start over?'

'I'd like that.'

We didn't talk much all the way to the dart, each of us busy with our own thoughts. I kept smiling for no apparent reason and perfect strangers kept smiling back. It was a good feeling and I made a few spring resolutions as I walked along, trying to keep up with Ed's long stride. First off, I was never going to get upset about crowds again. Second, I was going to be nice when Mel and Sal were together. And third—

'Hey, tell me about this singing job you have?'

My blood ran cold. 'What?'

'The hotel you said you sing in?' Ed prompted. 'D'you remember you said it when . . . well.' His voice trailed off. He managed a grin. 'During our free exchange of views?'

'Oh, right!' Jesus! 'That!' I hadn't told him I sang in the hotel, I thought. I'd only said that they'd *asked* me to sing. But he'd taken it up the wrong way and now . . .

'Well, go on.'

He looked so interested and encouraging. He'd think I was a real saddo if I admitted that I'd only blurted it out to make it seem like I had a life. Not that I felt I needed a life or anything, but I just thought that being a singer would make me more interesting to Ed. Make him respect me. And it had. I flirted with the idea of lying and telling him that I'd had to give it up due to a madly busy social life, but well, I'd promised him that this would be a new start. And besides, he was bound to mention it to Sal and that'd be even worse.

'I didn't say that I actually *sang* there,' I began, trying not to cringe in humiliation yet again. 'I only said that I'd been *asked* to sing.'

'Oh.' He looked surprised. 'I thought—' Pause. 'So why *don't* you sing there?'

I couldn't admit that it wasn't *actually* the hotel itself that had asked me, that would sound too pathetic for words. So I tossed my hair back, pulled my top down over my belly button again and muttered some rubbish about being too shy to perform in public.

'You should come busking with me sometime,' Ed grinned. 'That'd cure you.'

'You wouldn't want that,' I said. 'Sure I'd outclass you.'

'Ohhhhh!'

We smiled at each other.

It felt good.

And it had only been a *teensy* lie.

Chapter Thirty-nine

I WAS IN good form when I finally got back to the flat. Collecting the post, I found a brown envelope addressed to me. Opening it, I found a blue envelope addressed to the Adoption Board. I recognised the envelope, the handwriting and the postmark. My mother lived in Limerick somewhere. She used blue envelopes and her handwriting was slanted and uneven.

Somehow I knew this letter was going to fill in a piece of me.

But I didn't rip it open like I thought I would. In fact, it took me ages to pluck up the courage to read it.

Dear Vicky,

Can I say 'dear'? You called me 'dear' in your letter and it was wonderful. I have read and re-read that letter so many times now that I was almost afraid to write back in case somehow by writing I'd break the spell or say something wrong and make you dislike me. I don't want to frighten you off by appearing needy or emotional but yes, I do want to meet you. I want to meet you very much only I'm not sure if it's too soon at the moment. I don't know how I'll be with you and I so much want to create a good impression.

Can you understand that?

You asked for some background information and I'd really like to tell it to you face to face. Maybe it'd be better that way. But since you asked, you were born three weeks early after twenty-four hours of labour. You were the tiniest baby the nurses said they'd ever seen.

Five pounds exactly. All red and wrinkly with blonde-red hair. Have you still got that colour hair? I used to be red too, you see. I remember looking at you and praying that one day we'd meet again.

I gave you up at three months. They told me they had a lovely couple to take you. A lovely couple. I clung on to those words for years. A lovely couple.

Three months with you was not a long time. I mean, what is a few months of you compared to twenty-eight years of your life? In that time, I experienced more emotion than I have ever felt before or since. I loved you, Vicky. I really did, but I couldn't keep you. I remember holding you and kissing you and talking to you. Trying to explain why I had to do what I had to do. Babbling it all out. And I remember you looked up at me with these blue eyes and I felt you knew. At least that's what I told myself. Then they took you from me. And I tried to be good about it. I didn't want to upset you, you see. I kept wondering if I'd cried more or screamed more would they have brought you back to me? Would we have been in each other's lives? But I didn't cry. Not at all. When you were gone, it was as if I was empty. As if someone had died only worse. There was no body, no visible wounds to mourn, just me the same as I had been for nineteen years. My arms ached to hold you.

They ached.

I think I've been crying inside every day since.

Hearing from you has been the best thing to happen to me. You are alive. You are out there.

I want you to have this. I've had it for the last twenty-eight years and parting with it is painful but everyone should have something of their past and this is yours.

Yours, Barbara

A small picture, faded badly, with the inscription *Baby* and my date of birth. The photo was of a tiny baby peering out from the folds of a white blanket. Red-blonde hair stood up in spikes from my head and, I have to say, I looked truly awful. But then again, I'd just spent twenty-four hours descending down a birth canal.

I stared for ages at the picture, trying to come to terms with the fact that it was me. This was my first baby photo, probably taken an hour after I was born. But I felt nothing, only a curiosity as to who had taken the photo and who had held the baby for the photo. Were the hands, slightly visible, my mother's hands or the hands of some nurse? At the back of my head, I wondered how any mother could walk away from something so defenceless.

But looking at the red face and the horrible hair, maybe it wasn't so hard.

Chapter Forty

BRIDIE DECIDED THAT it would be lovely, in the spirit of reconciliation, if the three of us went out for a drink to celebrate Ed's arrival back in the shop. To be honest, I felt a bit stupid celebrating but I was never one to pass up the offer of a night in the pub. I think Ed felt the same way. 'Just let's go for a drink,' he said to Bridie. 'For no other reason than we all like working together.' He grinned over at me and I flushed.

Whenever I thought of what I'd admitted to him in his flat, I cringed.

Bridie clapped her hands. 'Oooh, yes, yes, that's a *nice* reason.'

I tried to stifle my jealousy as she smiled blindly up at him.

I wondered if he had that effect on all women. Certainly Dominic's mother had been thrilled to see him. 'Aw, Jaysus,' she declared, 'you're like all men, just when we're all used to doing without, back you come.'

Ed laughed.

'Domo has something for you,' the woman said then.

Dominic, smiling shyly, had presented Ed with a hand-drawn card as a welcome-back present and Ed positioned it on the shelf behind the counter. *Welcum back Ed from Dominic and Sylvia*.

The next day, Ed solemnly handed Dominic a voucher for McDonald's. 'I know we were meant to tidy the jigsaw shelves and I'm sorry I left you on your own to do it.'

'Vicky helped,' Dominic said, turning the voucher over and over in his hands.

'It's for McDonald's,' Ed said gently, nudging him. Then,

turning to Sylvia, he said, 'You can order a meal there. I hear they're giving away Action Man meals this week.'

Bridie and I held our breath wondering what she'd do.

She folded her arms and studied Ed. Her big earrings jangled as she cocked her head to one side. 'He *was* dead upset,' she said accusingly. 'So, yeah, I think you do owe him one. And he loves McDonald's.' Without saying another word, she pulled Dominic by the arm and hauled him from the shop.

Huh, I thought, if I'd given them a voucher for McDonald's, she'd have told me to shove it. How the hell had Ed managed it?

So, while they went to McDonald's, Ed, Bridie and I headed to the local.

I hadn't dressed up for the night out – I wore a pair of denim dungarees with a wine-coloured top. My hair hung loose around my face and I'd put on the tiniest bit of lipstick, mainly because my lips were chapped. Ed, on the other hand, *had* made an effort, wearing a dark pair of Levi's and a loose blue check shirt. He'd even abandoned the orange jacket in favour of the nice leather one he wore when he was seeing Sal. Bridie wore a black sequinned top and black trousers – slightly dressy for the pub but really lovely on her. She'd scooped her wispy brown hair into an elegant bun and was radiating happiness as she chose a seat for us right at the back of the bar.

'Isn't this a nice change?' she asked, patting the seat for me to sit down. 'The three of us in here instead of all going our separate ways?'

'It's a change all right,' I said brightly, plonking myself in beside her. 'But I'm warning you, Bridie, don't go getting me too drunk – remember what happened at Christmas!'

She laughed. 'That was no one's fault but your own, miss.'

At Ed's questioning look, Bridie said, 'Vicky and I went to see Joe Dolan and—'

'Joe Dolan?' He smirked at me. 'Really?'

'It was my Christmas present to Bridie,' I informed him

quickly. It was bad enough everyone thinking I liked Boy Five without being classed as a Joe Dolan fan.

'So what happened? Did you go mad and throw your knickers up at him?'

'Oh, Ed!' Bridie went into a fit of giggles and flapped at him with her hand. 'Nothing like that. Vicky just drank a little too much and well . . .' She paused and looked uncomfortably at me.

'Bridie had to escort me home,' I finished.

Ed grinned. 'Aw, sure, I'd get drunk too if I went to see Joe Dolan.'

'Would you?'

'Yeah, it'd make it easier to forget.'

I spluttered out a laugh.

'Oh now, that's *awful*,' Bridie said indignantly. Then she recited her Joe Dolan mantra, the one all the brainwashed fans delivered: 'There's no show like a Joe Show.'

'He's a right show all right,' I giggled.

'Oooh.' Bridie glared at me and at Ed, who'd started to grin. 'You young people have no taste.'

'And you old people can't hear properly, isn't that right, Vicky?'

I laughed. He smiled at me. Then he began to laugh.

And Bridie pretended to look disgusted and we laughed harder.

And it suddenly dawned on me that for the first time, it was Ed and *me* laughing together. *Him* and *me*, the way it had been Bridie and him. And it had been so easy.

And it wasn't because we didn't like Bridie or that we didn't want to include her, it was just fun.

Just fun.

Oooh, Jesus!

How on *earth* could I have accused him of trying to get Bridie onside by having a joke with her? Oooh, how could I have done that? My laughter dried up abruptly as I felt my face go a roaring

235

puce red. I couldn't look at him. I couldn't look at either of them. What must he *think* of me?

Jesus.

My sudden descent from laughter to rampant embarrassment wrong-footed him. I think he thought he'd done something else wrong. I think Bridie thought so too. He stood abruptly up from the table, the laughter fading from his eyes. 'Drink, anyone?'

'I'll get this.' I hauled myself up from my seat. I couldn't get away from them fast enough. 'I'm the boss.'

'And I asked first,' Ed said firmly. 'Now?' he turned to Bridie.

'A glass of red wine, please.'

'Vicky?'

I didn't like the way he'd taken over the situation. I was the boss. 'No, I'll get this,' I said again.

'You can get the next one.' He sounded a bit narky. 'Now?' He stared at me as if daring me to argue.

'A pint of Guinness,' I muttered with a bad grace. I was aware of Bridie looking anxiously at us, so I added in a 'please'.

'Great.' In silence, Bridie and I watched him walk towards the bar.

I picked up a beer mat and began to peel it apart piece by piece. It's a habit I have and it annoys the shit out of Sal whenever we go anywhere. I began to put the little torn pieces into the ashtray on the table. I couldn't face Bridie. Jesus, I could hardly face myself.

'He's a nice boy,' she said suddenly.

I glanced up from my beer mat. 'Who? Ed?'

'Of course Ed,' she said sternly. She held my gaze for a bit before adding, 'I don't know what the problem is between the two of you but I hope it'll clear itself up.'

I went even redder and, because I was embarrassed, I snapped out, 'Isn't he back working?'

'For the moment.'

More silence. I don't know what she wanted me to say.

Anyway, I was the boss and it wasn't right to discuss Ed with her. And I couldn't have, anyway.

'You're such a lovely girl, Vicky,' Bridie went on, her voice soft, 'but since Ed's arrived, you've changed.'

I shrugged. Tore the beer mat into tinier pieces.

'I can't be in the middle all the time, Vicky. I like him and I like you and it makes me sad that you both don't get on.'

I made a face.

'I had hoped that tonight would build a bridge.'

'I'm not an architect, Bridie.'

'Now that's just playing with words.' She sounded annoyed. 'You know what I mean.'

It was meant to have been a joke. 'Look,' I said, 'once he sells toys, we'll get on fine.' She didn't seem impressed. 'Haven't we just been laughing together? Haven't we done well this week?'

She sighed and suddenly looked old. She gazed at her tiny birdlike hands and shook her head. 'Oh, Vicky . . .' Her voice trailed off.

She sounded sad and worried and it struck me that she'd probably been worrying about things since the fight, if not longer. And it was my fault that she'd had to do that. My fault because I was a weird wreck of a person. I tentatively touched her shoulder. 'Things will be fine, Bridie.' I gave her a gentle squeeze. 'I promise. Honestly, Ed and I have sorted it. Don't worry – OK?'

'Who's worrying?' Ed startled us as he arrived back. He put his pint of lager down and handed Bridie her wine. 'Well?'

I went red again. I stared at the table.

'Where's Vicky's drink?' Bridie, to my enormous relief, deftly changed the subject.

'I've to get it now. It's not settled yet.'

'Oh, right.'

He stood for a second as if he was waiting for an answer to his previous question.

Both Bridie and I looked blankly at him.

'Drink?' Bridie prompted.

'Oh, yeah. Right.'

We watched him leave.

Bridie and I regarded each other. I smiled awkwardly at her.

'I know you think I don't notice things, Vicky, but I do.' Bridie's voice trembled and she put a hand to her bun and patted it anxiously. 'So far I've kept quiet about it, but please, give him a break. I think he needs one.'

'He needs a break?'

'Yes. I mean, I think so.' She shrugged. 'I don't know. I just get the feeling . . .' Her voice trailed off as Ed arrived back with a lovely creamy Guinness for me.

'There you are, boss.' He placed it on the table, eyeing the decimated beer mat with amusement. 'Sign of nerves, that,' he grinned.

'Yeah, and why wouldn't I be?' I made a humongous effort to grin back. 'I mean, you have never been on the tear with Bridie, have you?'

Bridie laughed and looked gratefully at me. Ed laughed too, his blue eyes crinkling up and shining a brilliant blue. 'Sounds promising,' he said, lifting his pint to his lips.

'Cheers.'

'Cheers.'

'Cheers.'

I bought the next round, Bridie bought the next and soon it was Ed's turn again. And then mine. And then Bridie's. My head was spinning nicely, conversation was coming in witty bursts and already we'd moved from the general to the personal. We were on the subject of families and relationships. Bridie had just told us that she'd never wanted to marry ever since her first love had died in a car accident. 'I couldn't bear to be hurt like that again,' she told us as she ran her finger along the stem of her empty wine glass. 'But sometimes, sometimes, I regret it.'

'Yeah?' Ed, who'd managed thus far to get more information

238

out of her in four hours than I had in the best part of a year, asked, 'Why so?'

'Well, I'm on my own now,' Bridie confessed. 'And it gets lonely.'

We didn't know what to say to that.

'I mean, if I'd taken a chance and fallen in love again maybe I'd be married with children.' Pause. Sniff. 'Oh, I do like children.' She gave us a wobbly smile before standing unsteadily up. 'Now, Guinness again, Vicky? Ed – Carlsberg?'

As we nodded, she wandered off, zigzagging slightly.

'She's had a lot to drink,' Ed observed.

'Too much,' I muttered. 'She'll die when she realises all she's said.'

'Naw, she won't,' Ed shrugged. 'She wants us to know. Anyone that says personal stuff, even if they're drunk, they *want* people to know.'

'Want people to know that you're lonely?' I shook my head. 'Don't think so.'

He shrugged, drank some more.

'I'll tell you something,' I said, jabbing my finger the way I always do when I'm drunk and need to make a point. 'I wouldn't tell *anyone anything* no matter how drunk I was.'

'You wouldn't tell anyone anyway,' Ed replied. 'You're like me.'

Now there was an insult. I sniggered loudly. 'I'm not a *bit* like you!'

He looked me up and down. 'Well, it's true you're not dynamic or sexy or that but—'

'Ha bloody ha!' I raised my eyes to heaven and for some reason my head went down and belted itself off the table. 'Jesus.'

Ed gave a guffaw.

'What?' I knew that even though I couldn't feel the pain, I was going to have a huge bruise in the morning.

'You're nice when you're drunk,' he said.

'*You're* nice when I'm drunk,' I said back.

He laughed again.

239

I drained my pint and sat back in the seat, waiting for Bridie to return. Ed smiled in a drunken lazy way at me. 'This hasn't turned out to be a bad night,' he remarked.

'Yeah, it's been OK.'

'Well, I wouldn't go that far.'

I sneered at him. He'd been making smart arse comments all night. We both were. It avoided any real serious conversations.

'Here we are!' Bridie was back. She put Ed's drink in front of him. 'I'm just getting yours now, Vicky.'

'Ta.'

She left. 'Poor Bridie,' I said mournfully as I watched her jostle her way back to the bar. 'I never realised she was lonely before. But I suppose, if I'd thought about it, I should have known. I mean she doesn't even have a *family*.'

'So?'

'Well, with a family, at least you can visit them and see them and stuff. Even if you don't want to, at least they're there.'

Ed rolled his eyes and sniggered. 'That doesn't mean *anything*.' He leaned towards me and I could smell a sort of yummy aftershave smell from him. 'I mean, just think, right, if you don't get on with your folks, well, that'd be even lonelier, wouldn't it?' He sat back and folded his arms and regarded me.

He had a point. 'Mmm.' Pause. 'Or if they weren't really your folks, say if you were adopted, that'd be lonely too, I guess.'

He looked surprised. Nodded after a bit. 'Suppose.'

'But it's not something I've ever thought about until tonight,' I said hastily.

'Oh, right. Aye.'

Silence.

'Families are strange, aren't they?' I said then, more to break the silence than anything.

'Aye,' he agreed.

Silence.

'How many in yours? I mean, Bridie and I only ever thought there was one until you arrived in the shop.'

He flinched at my words. 'That's what everyone thinks.' Pause. 'There's just me and Al.' He grinned crookedly at me and traced the condensation on his glass with his finger. 'Like I said before – I'm the one they don't talk about.'

'Oh, I'm sure they—'

'It's not like a big major secret,' he interrupted. 'Half of Ireland knows my brother is the golden boy. The toy boy, that's what his wife calls him.'

'That's pretty lame.'

'Yeah, don't you think so?'

'I do. Yeah.'

He grinned and then looked a bit sad. Or so I thought.

'You're better-looking than him,' I said without thinking. 'Me and Sal saw your brother in a magazine and he's . . .' I stopped. Gulped. 'Well, you're just nicer-looking.'

'Your pity is dead touching.'

'Oh no, it wasn't . . .' Me and my big drunken mouth.

'I've given my dad a lot of grief, that's why,' Ed interrupted me. 'Piles of grief. But anyway, he paid me back.'

'How?' I wasn't sure I wanted to hear this.

'Only gets me a job in one of his bloody toy shops.'

'Hilarious.'

Ed grinned and lifted his pint. 'Cheers.'

He'd been telling the truth, though, I thought as I watched him down his pint. He really didn't get on with his dad. The idea fascinated me. Me, who'd been suffocated with love all my life. I didn't know what it was like to fight. 'What sort of grief?' I asked.

'Just . . .' He stopped. 'The usual.'

As if that explained everything.

'Like leaving all your jobs and courses and stuff?'

'Uh-huh.'

'Why'd you leave med school anyway? Had you only started?'

He stared into his glass. 'Nope. I'd qualified.'

'So you could have been a doctor?' I was impressed. I'd known he was bright – hadn't I?

241

'Yep.' He smiled suddenly. 'Scary, huh?'

'Stupid, more like,' I said, with a big exaggerated shake of my head. 'I think it must be brilliant to be a doctor.'

'Yeah, well.' Ed gulped. 'Wasn't for me.'

It was making him uncomfortable, this whole conversation. Drunk as I was, I realised it. 'I gave my folks a lot of grief too,' I said then, in an attempt to cheer him up. 'They still love me to suffocation point.'

He smiled.

'I mean, if I set off a nuclear bomb they'd say something like, "Oh well, the world was overpopulated anyhow."'

Ed guffawed.

'And then they'd worry in case I'd broken a nail pressing the button.'

More laughter. I think he was really drunk.

'And then my mother would offer to file my nails all down to the same size so I'd look good.'

He didn't laugh this time. Instead he remarked softly, 'Must be nice.'

I shrugged.

He hadn't a clue.

The night ended with Bridie getting into a taxi with Ed. He'd offered to see her home, though I doubt if he knew where his own place was, let alone hers. I caught a taxi on my own. I closed my eyes as the taxi driver pulled out from the kerb and smiled to myself.

It had been a good night.

Maybe there was hope for me yet. Maybe I could get used to having a third party in the shop.

Maybe I could begin to move out and make friends.

Maybe.

Chapter Forty-one

LEO WAS WEARING a purple Barney sweatshirt. The sleeves were halfway up his arms and Barney was struggling to cover his belly. His jeans were tatty and his hair was blowing across his face because it was so long. He looked like a kid on one of those TV charity ads.

'Hiya, Vicky.' Marti came abreast of me. I'd been waiting outside the apartment for them. 'Were you waiting long?'

'No.' I still couldn't take my gaze from Leo. Jesus, what was he *like*?

'Are you coming out with us today, Vicky?' Leo asked in his bright voice.

I tore my eyes away from his babyish sweatshirt and managed a smile. 'Yeah, if you don't mind.'

'No,' Leo beamed up at me, a big gap where his front tooth should have been.

'Hey,' I grinned. 'Did you lose a tooth?'

'Nope, it just fell out.'

'And did the tooth fairy come?'

'She forgot.' Leo flushed. 'I dunno why. I left it under my pillow and everything and she didn't come.'

Marti took a fit of coughing. 'I, eh, told him that the tooth fairy is very busy and that sometimes she does forget. He's trying it again tonight, aren't you, bud?'

'Uh-huh.'

'Well, she's a very bold tooth fairy to forget,' I said crossly,

243

glowering at Marti. 'She'll probably give you triple money to make up.'

'Yeah?' Leo looked thrilled.

Marti laughed loudly.

'And just to keep you going,' I said, handing Leo two euro, 'get some sweets from the shop up here.'

Leo pocketed the money, grinning.

'You're spoiling him,' Marti hissed as he let Leo's hand go and Leo scampered ahead of us around the corner to the shop.

'Nope,' I said, 'just trying to buy his affection.'

'Well, you've already done that,' Marti half-grumped. 'The kid thinks you're a bleeding oracle ever since you told him Linda misses him.'

'Which she probably does,' I fired back.

He ignored me.

When we got to the top of the road, we found Leo surrounded by a group of rough-looking kids all chanting 'Baby, baby, baby' and laughing.

'Hey,' Marti shouted, scattering them, 'what the hell is going on here – you lot leave my lad alone, d'yez hear?'

'Big baby!' a stick-thin, freckle-faced kid chanted, sticking his tongue out. 'Crybaby!'

Marti made a run at them and they scarpered.

Leo was crying, big silent tears. I tried to hug him but he pushed me away. 'Hey, hey, bud.' Marti knelt down beside him. 'What happened, hey?'

Leo started to blubber.

'Slow down. Slow down. Tell Daddy.'

He buried his head in Marti's shoulder as sobs shook his little body.

I stood by hopelessly, feeling like a spare part. Marti looked different hugging his kid. I liked the picture the two made.

'I can't understand you, Leo,' Marti said eventually. 'Slow down.'

'Was it the sweatshirt, Leo?' I asked tentatively. I thought I'd heard him say the word 'Barney'.

244

'Baby clothes,' Leo sobbed. 'I'm *not* a baby.'

Marti looked hopelessly at me.

'His sweatshirt, Marti,' I said. 'They were teasing him over it.'

'Were they?' Marti asked Leo, who nodded.

'The little bastards,' Marti declared. He held Leo at arm's length and said fiercely, 'Don't mind them, son, they're just bastards. They're just jealous that they've no sweatshirts like that.'

'Bastards,' Leo formed the new word on his tongue. 'Bastards.'

I didn't know if Marti was handling this quite right, but then again I wasn't a parent.

'A Barney sweatshirt is a bit babyish for a five-year-old, though, isn't it?' I said in an undertone to Marti. 'I mean, does he still *like* Barney?'

'Barney?' Marti frowned. 'Who the hell is that?'

'The dinosaur on Leo's sweatshirt – he's like the equivalent of David Beckham to three-year-olds.'

'Oh right – well, I guess Leo does like him. D'you like Barney, Leo?'

'Barney is a dinosaur, from our imagination, he's six foot tall, farts and all, and he's got constipation,' Leo sang, wiping his tears away and grinning a bit.

'There you are,' Marti said. 'He *loves* him.'

'That's not the Barney song,' I half-giggled and I warbled the real words.

'Hey!' Marti was impressed. 'You can sing!'

'What I'm saying,' I went on, ignoring him, 'is that Leo's sweatshirt is for babies. Sure, look, it's even too small for him. No wonder those kids teased him.'

'So, you're saying it's all right what those kids did?' Marti glowered at me.

'Bastards,' Leo piped up. 'Not kids.'

'I'm just saying that unless Leo gets some new clothes, he'll keep getting picked on.'

'Well, I just won't put that sweatshirt on him any more,' Marti decided. 'We don't want you looking like a baby, do we, Lee?'

245

'D'you not think that maybe he could do with some *nicer* clothes?'

'Women!' Marti rolled his eyes. 'All yez think about is clothes.'

'Have you *actually* bought him any new clothes since, you know, Linda left?'

'New clothes?'

'Yeah, you know the things you buy in shops – trousers and shirts and socks and—'

'I know.' Marti began to shuffle from foot to foot. 'I know what clothes are – I'm not stupid.'

'Well?'

'I dunno.' His eyes met mine. 'I dunno.' A pause before he said, half defensively, 'Well, *I* haven't.'

'In almost a year, you haven't bought your son any new clothes?'

A guilty look crept over his face. 'Well, no, no I haven't,' he muttered. 'Jesus, Vic,' he shrugged, 'I never *thought* to. Linda did all that stuff, I just ran bands. I never thought—'

'All his stuff is too small for him, Marti.'

He was silent.

'He needs new clothes.'

'It's just – well, I never *minded* him before – Christ, in the beginning I even forgot that he went to school.' He laughed slightly, then bit his lip. 'I'm doing my best but it's so fucking hard.'

'And what about your mother?'

He winced. 'She's turned into Linda – always on my case.' He ran his hand through his own perfectly styled hair. 'Jesus, I cannot believe that I haven't bought him any clothes.'

'Neither can I.'

He stared at his Docs, shamefaced.

'Well—' I gave him a push, feeling a bit sorry for him. 'At least you know now, before the kids in school pick on him. It's not too late.'

* * *

Marti decided that very day to do as I advised. 'Well, I might as well,' he declared. 'You're with me – you'd know what to buy.'

How he figured that out, I do not know. I'd never bought loads of clothes for a kid before but God, it was great fun. And I was touched that he took my advice. Nobody *ever* took my advice. We bought piles of stuff for Leo. Mad bright T-shirts, Action Man shirts and jeans, wrestler shorts, Simpsons pyjamas, you name the programme, Leo got an outfit to go with it. It was kinda sad though and a bit embarrassing when we got him his new trainers. 'Wow, Dad,' he announced in amazement as he bounced up and down in them, 'these shoes don't hurt my feet.'

Marti looked appalled and started shushing him. Then he threw Leo's old trainers, which were two sizes smaller, into the bin and let him wear his new ones for the rest of the shopping expedition.

We discovered a small barber shop on one of the side streets and both of us decided at the same time that Leo could do with a haircut. I think Marti realised just at that moment that taking care of a kid was pretty much the same as taking care of himself. I left them to it, telling Marti that he needed some quality time with his son, and arranged to meet them in an hour.

I traipsed around the half-empty shops, fantasising about all the cool stuff I'd buy if I had loads of money. I wandered into toy shops and gazed at their displays. I watched mothers watching their children playing. I bought an Action Man for Leo to match some of the clothes that Marti had bought him.

Then I grabbed a cuppa in Roche's Stores and bought one of their huge meringues to eat. I sat, drinking my tea and thinking about how much I'd enjoyed the day. At least Leo had Marti, I thought, as meringue and cream smeared my face. It was nice to have someone belonging to you.

There were quite a few people in Roche's and most of them were eating horrible healthy things. I looked around for another meringue-eater, hoping I wasn't the only one. My eye caught a babyish handsome face topped by streaked multicoloured hair. Cliff caught my eye at the same time and he flushed. He was with another man, older. This guy was dressed in very smart casual clothes. His back was half angled towards me so that I couldn't see him properly, but he seemed engrossed in what he was saying to Cliff. Cliff said something to him and then they both looked over at me. I nodded to both of them and the man nodded back and Cliff, to my surprise, plastered a smile on his face and gave me a reluctant wave. I felt quite pleased. Maybe he was beginning to forgive me. I was half-thinking of joining them when they began to talk once more and I got the feeling that I wouldn't be welcome. And besides, neither of them were eating cakes.

An hour later, I met up with Marti outside the barber's. 'Where's Leo?'

'Just there.' Marti pointed to a kid I hardly recognised, jumping up and down off kerbs a few feet away. I'd have liked to say that Leo's new haircut made him so beautiful as to be entirely unrecognisable but I couldn't. Leo's new haircut made him look like one of those kids that roam the streets at night with about a million penknives in their pockets. His head had been shaved on either side and marching down the middle was a jet-black two-inch-high mohican.

'Hey, Vicky!' Leo bounded up to me. 'Don't I look cool?' He bent his head to give me the full effect of his new look. The Barney sweatshirt jarred so completely with it that I had to stifle a laugh.

'He knew exactly what he wanted,' Marti said proudly. 'And I said to the man, just give the kid what he wants.'

Father and son beamed at me.

I gulped. Jesus.

'Are you allowed to have haircuts like that in school?' I asked.

Leo shrugged. 'Suppose.' He pulled Marti's arm. 'Can we go to a film now, can we? Can we?'

Marti laughed. 'Yep.' He glanced at his watch. 'It won't be on for another couple of hours – what say we head for a meal?'

After my meringue, a meal was the last thing I wanted.

'How about McDonald's?' Marti looked questioningly at me. Then whispered, 'I know kids like that at least.'

I grinned. There was hope for his fathering skills yet.

'Lead on.'

We went to McDonald's, saw the film, which Leo loved, and then Marti dropped me home. 'I'll get the sprog to bed and pick you up in a while,' he promised.

Just before I got out of the car, I handed Leo his Action Man. 'For you.'

'Me?' He took it from me reverently. Examined the box. Looked at me with shining eyes. I flinched. I couldn't get used to his gorgeous face under such a vicious-looking thatch of hair.

'Thanks, Vicky. You're the *nicest* of my daddy's friends.'

'I'll second that,' Marti chortled.

'I'm going to tell my mammy all about you,' Leo said, ripping open the box.

I winced. I couldn't help it – every time he mentioned her, I did it.

Marti caught my hand. He pressed it firmly, as if telling me not to worry about it. 'See you later – all right?'

'Sure.'

With a mad beeping of the horn, father and son drove away.

Chapter Forty-two

T HE ALARM WENT off at eight-thirty. Bleep, bleep, bleep, it said. I swear, I have the most irritating alarm clock in the world. Its bleep sounds like a nagging mother or something.

'Fuck's sake!' A hairy arm reached over my barely opened eyes and began fumbling about for the clock. 'I thought Monday was your day off.'

Last night came back to me in a blur of hazy colour. Marti had called back for me at nine and we'd gone for a few drinks and on to a band. Someone he was looking at with a view to managing, apparently. They'd been ear-splitting crap and Marti had agreed. 'More talent in Cliff's fingers,' he'd pronounced loudly to all who were around. Then he'd come back for a nightcap and been so grateful to me for all my help with Leo that I found I couldn't resist him when he took me in his arms and started kissing me. The snogging had turned into snogging in my bedroom which had ended up with us in bed. If I'd thought about sleeping with Marti in advance, I'd never have done it, but the drink and the kissing had somehow blurred my reality. Don't get me wrong, I was as nervous as hell. I hadn't slept with a guy in ages, not since Ron the Ride over eighteen months ago. And after that had happened, Ron and I had gone all pear-shaped. 'I'm nervous,' I'd told Marti, as he was sloppily licking my face.

'Don't be,' he'd whispered. 'Just think, in ten minutes it'll all be over.'

I laughed.

But he was right.

Ten minutes later, I lay there, wet and sticky, while Marti grinned into my face.

'Phew,' he winked, snuggling up to me for a final kiss. 'You're fantastic, Vic.'

Then he turned over and conked out.

I lay awake for ages.

Like I always do.

Marti watched me getting dressed. 'Can't you cancel your appointment?' he asked, his blue eyes looking all sad. 'Tell them you've got pressing business to attend to?' He sniggered a bit at his wit.

'No. I can't.' I smiled at him as I reached over him for my jeans. 'It wouldn't be fair.'

'Awww.' He made a face. 'You don't know what you're missing.'

'I do,' I said, as I pulled on my green socks. 'Didn't you give me a demo last night?'

'Aw, yeah. Wasn't it *sensational*?'

I nodded, not sure if he was joking or not. There was silence as I laced up my shoes.

Then he coughed, sort of nervously, and there was something about it that set alarms bells jangling. 'Eh – Vic?'

'What?'

He was staring at the duvet and picking imaginary bits of fluff off it. His face had gone red and he looked as if he was dying with embarrassment or shame or something.

'What?' I asked again, my mouth dry. He was going to dump me, I thought suddenly. Sleeping with him had been stupid. I didn't know if I could bear to be dumped in my own room by a guy sitting in my own bed. I didn't know if I could bear to be dumped, full stop. 'Well?' I asked again, the sick feeling threatening to swamp me. 'What is it?'

'I, eh, wanted to ask your advice. It's all a bit delicate.'

The word wrong-footed me. '*Delicate?*'

251

Another uneasy look. Then he lifted himself onto his elbow and said cagily, 'Well, last night, after I dropped Leo home, I had a phone call.'

'And?'

'Well, it was Linda.'

'Uh-huh.' I couldn't even lift the brush to do my hair. The very mention of his wife was like a slap in the face. I mean, I know she existed but I didn't want to have to talk about her.

'Well, you see, she always rings for Leo and I always slam the phone down. Well, I did before I disconnected it. But, after what you said before about letting Leo talk to her and yesterday and stuff, I got to thinking. And well – should I let him *talk* to her?' He gulped and looked appealingly up at me. 'Maybe he should talk to her – don't you think?'

'Sorry?' I'd been prepared for rejection and now I hadn't even a clue about what I was being asked. 'What?'

'Leo,' Marti said. 'D'you think it's all right for him to talk to his mother?'

He wanted to know if he should let Leo talk to Linda. I mean, that was *all*. He wasn't splitting, he wasn't dumping me. He was asking my advice. As if my opinion mattered to him. I felt all warm and funny and tender towards him. 'Of *course* he should.' I knelt down beside him, grasped his hand and held it to my face. He caressed my cheek.

'You think?'

'She's his mother – it's important for her to be in his life.'

'You think so?' He looked doubtful.

Jesus, he had to be the least empathic man on the planet. 'I know so,' I said. 'No kid wants to think their mother just walked out on them. It'd hurt too much.'

'Is that the way you feel?'

I froze.

Marti groaned loudly. 'Awwww, that was awful bleedin' tactless of me. I didn't mean it. I mean, I don't mean that I think your mother walked out on you, I just meant—'

'Forget it!' I dropped his hand and stood up.

'Aw, Vic!'

I studied my reflection in my wardrobe mirror. I began furiously tying my hair back – it looked awful, all knotted and frizzy and wild. Then I scrabbled about in the drawer for some lip balm.

'Sorry.' I heard the bed squeaking behind me. He crossed to where I was standing. He wrapped his arms about me, his naked body pressed against mine. 'I'm a fuckin' jerk.' He kissed the back of my ear.

'I have to go.' I wriggled out of his embrace, which felt claustrophobic somehow. 'There's cereal in the top press over the sink.'

'Vic!'

'Bye now.'

I knew he watched me as I left.

Lucy was sitting at her desk when I arrived. Dressed in a petrol blue trouser suit, she looked far more together than she had two weeks ago. I immediately felt intimidated. Shy almost.

'Vicky.' She gave me a big bright smile and indicated a chair. 'Sit down. It's nice to see you again. How's things been? Any more letters?'

I produced the letter. 'And she gave me this.' I handed Lucy my baby photograph and she made the appropriate sounds of admiration. I knew she was only putting it on – no one could possibly think I looked cute or adorable with my big red hair and round face.

'So' – Lucy handed me back the photo – 'how does all that make you feel?'

'Dunno.'

Silence. I think she was waiting for something more. 'I just don't know,' I said again.

Lucy cocked her head to one side. 'Well,' she began carefully, 'how did you *think* it would make you feel before you initiated contact? How did you *expect* it to be?'

I shrugged. I wasn't good at expressing myself. Never had been. 'Just, just different.' I knew that wasn't a great answer, so I added, 'I thought I'd be, I dunno, *complete* or something, as if' – I bit my lip – 'as if I'd suddenly found something to make me me.' Unexpectedly my eyes filled with tears. 'Me,' I repeated again.

Lucy muttered a 'Jesus' and began rifling through her desk. 'I can never find bloody tissues,' she hissed as she yanked out a drawer. Pens and papers tipped onto the floor.

'I don't need a tissue,' I said, wiping my eyes on the back of my sleeve. 'Honest.'

'What the hell—?' She pulled a battered box out from somewhere and pushed it across to me.

I pulled one out, just to be polite, but I wasn't going to cry in front of her.

'Now.' Lucy sat back in her chair and smiled ruefully. 'Now that we're set, what was that you said – that you initiated contact to find your, your roots?'

'Uh-huh.' I began peeling the tissue apart. Two little halves.

'And you thought that this would satisfy you.'

'Everyone needs to know who they are,' I said. 'Where they come from.'

Lucy nodded. 'So how much do you think you need to know?'

'Everything,' I said firmly. 'I want to know it all.'

'And if your birth mother can't supply you with all the facts – what then?'

That was a ridiculous question. 'She had me – she should know.'

Lucy blinked. 'You sound angry.'

I shrugged.

'Does being adopted make you angry, Vicky?'

'No.' I'd answered too fast.

'Really?'

I shrugged again. The tissue was now in pieces on my lap. I had nowhere to put it. I began surreptitiously stuffing it into my pocket.

'Do you think you were abandoned? Unloved? Unwanted?'

Each of those words made me wince. Horrible words. It's what Marti thought. 'I dunno – she says she was sad when she gave me up.'

'And she probably was.'

'But she couldn't have been *that* sad.' I'd voiced it. The thing that haunted me. 'No one does stuff that makes them sad.'

Lucy paused. I could see her wondering what to say. Eventually, she said gently, 'I can't answer for your mother, Vicky. All I know is that I've counselled mothers who've given children up and they've never been the same. Part of them has gone, you see. Just like you feel part of you is missing. At the time, it probably seemed the best option to your mother, but we all do things we regret.'

'It's not like getting pissed on a Saturday night though, is it?'

'No,' Lucy said, sharply. 'It's not.'

The way she said it made me feel ashamed. 'Sorry.'

'Don't be.' She urged me to take another tissue, which I again began to demolish. 'You can't help the way you feel. But it's important to examine this anger before you go meeting your mother or before you say things you regret.'

I said nothing. Examine my anger – what a load of Oprah.

'You want to find your mother but at the same time you're angry at her.'

'Yeah, yeah, I am,' I said back. 'I mean, she didn't come looking for *me*.'

'Maybe she felt she had no right?'

'She didn't!'

Silence.

It went on for ages. When Lucy decided that obviously I wasn't going to contribute anything more, she said, 'So, we've established that you've initiated contact to find out about yourself?'

'Yes.'

'And that you'd like to meet your mother?'

'Yes.'

'And that your mother has thought about you and kept baby photos of you?'

I nodded.

'And that you feel angry towards her?'

I shrugged. 'A bit.'

'Why?'

The anger had never been an issue before. Maybe I'd been too anxious to find her. Maybe that had blotted out the other feelings, but yeah, since I'd got my baby photo, a slow anger had sort of crept into things. But I hadn't known until just that moment why. 'Because I was a baby,' I said. I jabbed the photo, which still lay on Lucy's desk. 'Look. Completely defenceless. And she let me go. Just let me go.'

'To a lovely couple.'

'It could have been *anyone*.'

'But it wasn't.'

'She let me go, she didn't love me enough and she let me go to a couple who were probably so desperate for a child that they'd have loved Satan if they'd been given him.' Now the tears were back. 'I was just someone for them to love. Just something.'

'Isn't that the responsibility of any parent?'

'What?'

'To love unconditionally? To accept what they are given?'

'Then why didn't my *mother*?'

'Maybe she did. Maybe she thought she was doing the best for you.'

'No!'

'Think about it, Vicky.' Her voice was soft, as if my growing hysteria wasn't happening. 'To let someone go is to love them too. To love a stranger as your adopted parents did is a great love.'

'To grow up feeling that everything you have is second-hand – is that great?' I gulped. 'To have *borrowed* parents, a *borrowed* life, a borrowed bloody identity – is that *great*?'

'To have a good life, that's great.'

She didn't understand. No one ever could. Vicky the fucking

weirdo strikes again. I was so angry at myself. So angry at her. 'You've everything off, haven't you?' I stood up and glared at her. 'You're like a bloody priest in confession, all good advice but you don't have a clue. A good life.' I rolled my eyes. 'It's not even *my* life. Not really!' I snatched up the photo from the desk and stuffed it in the envelope. 'I'm going now.'

'Vicky.' Lucy sounded upset. 'Don't. All I'm trying to do is to get you to think about things.'

'And I am.'

'I want any meeting with your mother to be a positive experience for both of you. It's natural to be angry and confused and hurt but is it right to let it colour your life and your future and any possible meeting?'

I paused with my hand on the door. 'It won't.'

She ignored that and went on, 'You've an opportunity now to find out everything you want, you've a chance to meet the woman who brought you into the world, you're so lucky that it was an easy trace – just try to take it easy, try to accept things, try to temper your anger and hurt and use it positively.'

'I'm fine.'

Lucy looked hard at me. So hard that I had to turn away. I heard her patting the arm of her chair. 'Come back for a moment, Vicky – you can go then.'

I didn't like leaving on a row. Slowly I turned around. She smiled at me – a sort of smile that said that she'd seen it all before. She wasn't telling me that she didn't understand or that I was weird. I didn't walk towards her though. I just stood with my arms dangling by my sides, feeling stupid.

'Come here.'

I took a small step in her direction, resenting it.

She continued to stare at me, making me feel like a bold kid. Slowly, I walked back to her. I wasn't going to sit down but she didn't seem inclined to speak unless I did, so I perched on the edge of the chair and tried to look nonchalant.

Still she waited before she spoke.

'Well?' I asked.

She smiled again. 'You're angry – it's OK.'

I said nothing.

'But be aware that you are angry, don't try to hide it. Talk with your adoptive parents – tell them the things you told me.'

Yeah, right, I felt like saying.

'It's surprising how they'll understand.'

It'd be very fucking surprising.

'And write to your birth mother, tell her how confused you are, and even if you don't post it, writing it down will clarify things in your own head – it'll get you accepting the way things are rather than fighting it. You can't afford to ignore these things, Vicky.'

I shrugged.

'And I'm sorry if I upset you.'

She was apologising to *me*. This woman who seemed to know everything was saying sorry to me. I felt I had to acknowledge that. 'It's OK.'

'I'm here to help you, not to send you storming off.'

'It's probably my fault,' I admitted reluctantly. 'I'm a bit sensitive over the whole adoption thing.'

Lucy grinned. 'No!'

I managed a smile.

'Some people are happy being adopted,' Lucy said. 'Others like you, well, they have conflicting emotions over it.'

I bowed my head.

'It's normal enough,' she said then.

I liked being told I was normal.

When I got back to the flat, Marti and Sal had both left. There was a note on the table from Marti. *To the nicest girl in the world – I'm sorry – the jerk.*

I smiled. Marti's writing was large and scrawly and decorative. I ran my fingers over the paper, tracing out the large M of his name. I felt suddenly bad at the way I'd walked out on him that morning. I'd probably over-reacted, just as I had with Lucy. Just as I had been doing all my life at little things that I'd perceived as being directed at me. I was folding the note up and preparing to save it in my 'special things' box when there came a knock on the door.

'These came for you.' Troy spoke from behind a large bunch of flowers. 'You weren't here so I said that I'd give them to you when you came back.'

'For me?'

'Yep.'

'For this flat, you mean,' I said, taking them from him, convinced they were for Sal.

'For this flat,' Troy nodded. 'For you.'

'No!'

'I wouldn't act so surprised.' Troy leaned against the doorframe as I searched for a note on the flowers. 'I mean, if I had money, I'd send you flowers too.'

'Aw, well, it's the thought that counts,' I said, grinning. Then I had the horrible thought that maybe they *were* from him.

'That's what I tell myself,' Troy grinned back. 'And I've thought of bringing you out to the best restaurants in town, taking you to see a film of your choice, driving you in a limo everywhere and necking you senseless at the end of the night.'

The envelope was Sellotaped to the plastic on the front. I was half afraid to open it.

'So, how about it?' Troy said. 'Will those thoughts buy me some Vicky time?'

For yesterday, last night and just in case the note isn't apology enough. Marti. xx

I read it again.

For yesterday, last night and just in case the note isn't apology enough. Marti. xx

'Well?' Troy demanded.

Marti had sent them. *Marti.* I bit my lip and gulped hard. 'Sorry, Troy?'

'Aw, hell, I can see I'll have to think harder thoughts.' He smiled ruefully. 'I dunno, you and Sal, yez play very hard to get.'

'Try lowering your standards,' I joked absently, devouring the note again, the smell of flowers filling my nostrils.

'I have, believe me, I have.'

I made a half-hearted rush at him and he was gone, slamming the door and laughing.

I leaned against the closed door and buried my face in the scented blooms.

I wanted to cry.

I don't know why but I was so deliciously happy and so painfully sad all at the one time.

Chapter Forty-three

'**V**ICKY, LOVE, IT'S MAM.'
Guilt hit me like a freight train. But then guilt followed like a bad smell whenever my parents rang. 'Mam, hi.' I forced a busyness into my voice, as if I was under awful pressure.

'Just rang to see how you are – we haven't heard from you in a few weeks.' I could picture her, settling down at the seat in the hall, all ready for a big chat. 'I said I'd better ring, make sure that you're OK.'

She sounded hoarse, as if she had a cold.

'Have you got a cold?'

'Arragh, nothing that a bit of honey and lemon won't cure. So, how've you been?'

'I'm fine, Mam. It's just, eh, I've been really busy.' More bloody lies. 'You know, with work and everything.' Ed, who was doing a window, shot me an amused glance. Work hadn't been busy, not in weeks, mainly due to the unseasonably good April weather we were having. Ed had decided that all the kids must be outside playing and had no need of 'indoor' toys. As a result, he'd suggested an 'outdoor' window. I'd agreed, only slightly annoyed that I hadn't thought of it myself. We'd decided to erect a mini goalpost in the main window. Ed was slotting it together, his gorgeous backside in full view of any prospective customers.

'Work?' My mother asked.

'Uh-huh.'

'And do you work every weekend?'

'Most of them.'

'Probably because you're the manager,' she stated proudly. 'Well, d'you know something – if you can't come down, sure maybe I'll come up for a day. God knows, I could do with a bit of a break from here. I might get Tommy to run me up some Sunday or Monday. He mainly travels on Monday mornings.'

'You don't need Tommy,' I said. 'Sure the bus will drop you up.'

'Yes, and only get me there in time for lunch,' Mam laughed. 'I want to spend the whole day with my daughter. Isn't Monday your day off?'

'Uh-huh.'

'Well then.' She said it as if it was settled. 'So, any more news?'

'Nope.'

I knew what was coming. 'Have you heard from' – she hesitated – 'from Barbara since?'

What a question to ask me in the middle of work! I turned away from Ed, who was pretending not to listen and making loads of unnecessary noise. 'Just a letter with a photo.'

Mam seemed taken aback at that. 'Of herself?'

I barely got the words out. 'No. Of me.'

'Oh.' I could hear her swallowing hard at the other end of the phone. 'Isn't that nice? I'd like to see that.'

'It's a horrible photo,' I snapped. Why did my mother always think everything was 'nice'?

'Oh now . . .' Her voice trailed off. 'Well, I'd still like to see it,' she said.

'And Dad?' I asked, feeling cruel and horrible and not knowing why. 'Would he?'

'I'm sure anything to do with you would interest him,' Mam said staunchly.

She refused to be upset by me. It had been the same when I was growing up – I'd done everything to hurt them and had never succeeded. Which made the shame and the guilt grow and grow and made me do worse things so they'd punish me and lessen the guilt, but they never did. 'I'll show it to you, so,' I said, 'though it's not worth getting excited about.'

'Vicky—'

'Have to go, Mam, there's someone looking for me.'

Ed, obligingly, called out my name.

'Bye.'

'Bye, love, see you in a couple of weeks.'

I put down the phone and pretended to be busy sorting out money. Eventually, when I couldn't stand the silence any longer, I turned to Ed. He was stringing the nets onto the goalposts. 'Ta.'

He looked up from where he sat, cross-legged, in front of the window. 'I wasn't listening,' he said, 'I just heard you say that you had to go. I do that too.'

'Right.' I didn't need a big story from him.

'D'you want some tea?'

Oh God, he was going to drown me in sympathy. 'I'll get it.'

'Milk, no sugar,' he called out after me.

Chancer!

Marti brought me to dinner that evening. I never normally saw him two days in a row, but he'd rung me to ask if I got the flowers and then told me to shove my glad rags on because he was bringing me to dinner.

'To say sorry and to celebrate Boy Five's new single.'

'Aw, Marti, there's no need. I just over—'

'There's *every* need. And women like going for meals, don't they?' He sounded unsure.

'Yeah, yeah, they do.'

'Well, then, that's settled.'

He hung up.

I couldn't believe that we were heading for a meal. A sort of normal date. And Marti turned up looking normal and he'd even hired a taxi so that we wouldn't be driving about in his Boy Five-mobile. The only thing that was abnormal was that Marti didn't seem to be too comfortable in the restaurant. He kept shifting about in his seat and looking around at everyone.

'What's wrong?' I asked.

'Aw, nothing. I just think it's mad paying to eat. Not my thing.'

'Oh.'

'Like, we could have gone to a music bar for half the price and checked out some new talent. Or down to McCoy's to see that new boy band that Louis Walsh has put together. I hear they're—'

The waiter arrived with our soups.

'Doesn't this look lovely?' I tried to change the subject. Marti was obsessive when he began to talk boy bands.

'Yeah.' Marti barely glanced at his bowl. 'Louis Walsh now, I think—'

I picked up my spoon and began to eat. 'Enjoy.'

There was a moment's silence while I ate and he studied me.

'Rumour has it Louis Walsh's band are bringing out another Garfunkel track.'

'Oh, right.'

'And that the video is really high-budget.'

'Rumour has it that if you don't stop,' I half-joked, 'I'm going and you'll have to sit here on your own.'

'Huh.' He rolled his eyes. 'You remind me of Linda, going on like that.'

'What?' My spoon clattered back into the soup, making it splash onto the linen tablecloth.

'Well,' he half-laughed, 'I just meant that she was always giving out about my musical commitments. I swear, she was as jealous. That's what broke us up in the end.'

'I'm not giving out.'

'Yeah. Yeah, I know.'

There was a tense silence. I cut a roll and began to butter it. I remembered Leo saying that his mother had hated the band.

'Linda, see,' Marti went on, 'she resented my involvement with the music industry – told me I should get a better job – but I didn't. She hated that.'

264

'Well, maybe she was worried that—'

'Worried my arse.' The venom in his voice surprised me. 'Huh, she wasn't too worried to leave me, was she? I went out to a gig one night, right, and when I came home, she was gone.'

Oh God, I wished he *was* talking about music. People were looking in our direction.

'Marti—'

'And Leo had been dumped over at my mother's for me to pick up—'

I thought his mother lived with him. 'Doesn't your mother—?'

'So, I figured that the best thing I could do, after she left, was to throw myself into promoting Boy Five. You know, to show her that I wasn't just talking shite. She kept telling me I should get a real job but I've shown her, Vic. I've shown her. Boy Five's success is my "up yours" to Linda.'

The waiter was coming over.

'I have to prove to that bitch that I can do it.'

'Sir, if you'll just lower your voice—'

'And another thing' – Marti turned to the waiter – 'she left Leo, that's my son, with me 'cause she thought, right, that I'd go running to her for advice but I haven't. Ha! And she's as mad as hell about that!'

'Well, that's marvellous, sir, but if you don't lower your voice, I'm going to have to ask you to leave.'

'It *is* marvellous,' Marti went on. 'Have you ever tried to bring up a kid on your own?'

'No.' The waiter looked mildly amused.

'It's not easy.' Marti turned to me. 'There's lots of things to remember – isn't there, Vicky?'

I gave a shrug.

'Clothes, tooth fairies, lots of stuff.'

'Can we expect you to lower your voice, sir?'

'What?' He looked around and suddenly seemed to notice people looking. 'Marti Hearty, manager Boy Five,' he announced.

It was met with a blank silence.

'Always say it as much as you can,' he said to me, 'keeps it in people's heads.' He turned to the waiter. 'Sorry.'

The man nodded. 'Just as long as you stay quiet, sir.'

Marti made a face as the guy left. I ignored him and concentrated instead on my shredded bread roll. Crumbs were all over the table.

There was a lot of silence.

'Did I say something?' Marti asked eventually.

Was he serious?

He pouted. 'You're reminding me of Linda again.' He meant it as a joke. When I began crumbling the crumbs between my fingers, he reached across the table and caught my hand. 'Sorry.'

'For what?'

He flushed. 'Aw, Jesus—'

'For what?'

'For, I dunno, being myself.' He lowered his voice and pressed my hand harder. 'Look, I know I'm loud and all but I thought you liked that.'

I shrugged. I didn't like being made to feel like a freak in a perfectly respectable restaurant.

'I'm sorry, Vic.'

'Yeah.'

'I won't talk about music if you don't want me to.'

'Just for tonight or for ever?'

He grinned. 'Awww, don't be like that. I'm mad sorry, right? I really am, and to be honest, with the money I've spent on me band I can't afford to buy you another load of flowers.' Another grin. 'So go easy on me, right?'

I took a quick glance around the restaurant. People seemed to have forgotten about us; they were eating and talking and laughing. Probably at us but maybe not. 'I don't want any more flowers.'

'Good.'

'Just, just let's enjoy the rest of the meal.'

'No problem.'

He bestowed me with his best Marti Hearty smile and made a big deal of slurping up what had to be his freezing soup. 'Lovely.'

It made me smile. 'Make sure you eat it all now.'

And he did.

It was during the main course that I asked him about Leo. 'How's Leo? Has Linda rung since Sunday?'

'Yep.' He stabbed a chip. '*She*,' he said it as if he was spitting, 'rang this evening, before I went out and before *she* had a chance to do all that crying and stuff, I put Leo on.'

'That was good.'

'Well—' Marti made a face. 'The poor kid cried. And when I took the phone off him, she was crying. And then me mother said it was good what I'd done and she cried.' He looked in bewilderment at me. 'It was a fucking nightmare.'

Despite myself I giggled. 'And how's Leo now?'

'Happier,' he said. Stopped. 'Well – he's happier but sadder too. I dunno.' He shook his head. Winced. 'Can't we talk about something else?'

Marti was like me in that way. I felt sorry for him. 'As long as it's not music.'

He groaned.

'How about Boy Five?'

It took him a moment to get the joke and when he did, he flung a chip at me. So I flung one back at him.

And our 'normal' date ended up with us being asked to leave.

But I laughed. Sometimes it was good to be yourself.

Chapter Forty-four

MEL AND LORCAN arrived in their usual flurried state on Thursday evening. 'Hiiiii,' Mel breezed in, blowing air-kisses in my direction and almost knocking me out with whatever scent she'd sprayed on herself.

'Love the perfume,' Sal cooed.

'Lor-can.' Mel looked fondly at her boyfriend.

He smiled in his smug way. 'It's the new brand from Chanel, I was fortunate enough to be able to get a – what would you say – a pre-smell.'

Mel tittered and Sal gave a strained smile.

I flicked on the television.

'I can't wait to see this new boyfriend,' Mel said, sounding like a giddy kid. 'I hope he's as *gorgeous* as you promised.'

'He is,' Sal said back in an equally childish voice.

'Ed?' I said, surprised.

'Well of course Ed.' Sal rolled her eyes. 'Who else would you expect?'

'Ed's going out with you lot?' Somehow I just couldn't see it. I mean, Mel was fine in an acquired-taste sort of way, Lorcan was a complete poseur and Ed, well, Ed was . . . I tried to think . . . Ed was too straight for their company. I just couldn't see him laughing at Lorcan's jokes or sipping coloured cocktails from big blue glasses the way Sal and I did when we went out with them. Ed would think it a load of pretentious crap and he'd be right.

As if in answer, the door buzzed.

'That'll be him now.' Sal ran lightly to the door, her tiny feet encased in an impossibly high pair of black stilettos. Wherever they were going it was posh.

'So' – Lorcan sat in beside me – 'what are you up to this evening, Vicky?'

'Aw, nothing, just catching up on a few of the soaps.'

'I hate television,' Lorcan said, affecting an American accent. 'I hate it as much as peanuts. But I can't stop eating peanuts.'

Mel laughed loudly.

'Orson Welles,' Lorcan said.

'So why eat peanuts?' I asked. 'I mean, if he hated them and all?'

Lorcan blushed.

'Maybe he hated the idea of eating them,' Mel said sharply. 'I mean, they give you spots, don't they? Maybe the man hated the *idea* of eating them.'

'Just like you hate the idea of eating, eh?' I grinned.

Mel was famous for her liquid lunches. And her grapefruit dinners. Her hips should have been classed as dangerous weapons.

She glared at me, glared at her watch. 'I wanted to be out of here for eight,' she muttered.

From the hallway, there came the sounds of Sal laughing with Ed. In they came and I have to say, whatever about Mel and Sal not being his type of people, he could certainly rise to the big occasion. Dressed in a dark grey suit and black shirt and tie, he looked gorgeous. In fact, it was ridiculous, but I felt a pang at the thoughts that Sal had him for herself. He should have been with someone who really cared about him.

He grinned about, his eyes lighting on me. 'Hey.'

'Hiya.'

We were on much better terms now. Almost a month had passed since the argument and I'd done my best to be nice to him, not just for his sake but also for Bridie's. And the nicer I was, the easier it became. In fact, I nearly got on better with him than Bridie did, mainly because of the afternoon break.

'Well, hello there.' Mel stalked towards him, a catlike creature in a black bodysuit. How on earth would she manage to go to the loo, was all I could think. She was almost purring in pleasure. 'Sal has told us all about you.' She made her voice high and teasing.

Ed didn't seem to notice. 'Aye, and I heard about you and Lorcan from her.' He held out his hand. 'Hiya, Lorcan.'

Lorcan gave his a limp shake. 'Pleasure.'

'Well.' Sal was looking about. 'Will we go? We're heading to Blazes,' she informed me. 'Mel's idea.'

'The hardest place in town to get into,' Mel said airily. 'But hey, the editor of *Tell!* has to eat somewhere.'

'Food comes first, then morals,' Lorcan said. 'Brecht.'

Everyone laughed. Well, Mel and Sal laughed. Ed raised his eyebrows questioningly in my direction. I raised him up my cup of tea. 'Good luck,' I mouthed.

He didn't have it. Luck, I mean. Instead there was a huge row between him and Sal when they came back that night. It woke me up and I lay in bed as she screeched at him and he, after taking all the screeching he could bear, told her calmly to 'find some other idiot to screw with'.

To which she yelled that she'd never even got that far with him.

I covered my ears with the pillow for the rest of it.

But I didn't sleep. All I kept thinking about was how could she row with a guy that had made such an effort to look great so he could go out with her.

God, I hoped she hadn't hurt him too much.

Chapter Forty-five

S AL WAS CALMLY eating her breakfast when I got up the next day. She certainly didn't look as if she'd had her heart broken the night before. In fact she looked so great I reckon she'd been up since five getting herself ready. But maybe it was for show. Sal tended to do that. I, on the other hand, liked the world to know when I felt crap.

'It's OK,' Sal said, without even looking at me, as I stood hesitantly in the door of the bedroom, 'I'm not going to blubber over him.'

'You can if you want,' I said. I poured myself a cuppa and slid into the seat beside her. 'I'm not going to tell him.' I looked sympathetically at her. 'Is it over?'

'Is Peter Maxwell a great journo?'

'What?'

'He owns all the big tabloids!' Sal said impatiently. 'Honestly, Vicky, you're so slow sometimes.'

'And what has he to do with you and Ed?'

'You asked was it over, I answered with – oh forget it!' She bit into a piece of horrible-looking bread. 'Yep, it's over.'

I didn't know what to say. I mean, if she'd been upset or cried, then it would have been a cakewalk. But instead she was scary. I hated her like this. 'I'm sorry,' I ventured.

'Well, I'm not.' She bit another hunk out of her bread. 'And you can bet that he'll be sorry for what he's done. He'll be very sorry.'

'Well, I'm sure he is—'

'I don't mean like that. I mean I'll make him sorry. He's only probably gone and ruined my bloody career, d'you know that?'

'Ed?' I was startled. 'How'd he do that?'

'He made a *show* of me, Vicky. I mean, I'd told him how important Mel and Lorcan were for my career and he just wouldn't go along with it.'

'Go along with what?'

'Aw, you know, humouring them – the stuff we do, laughing at Lorcan's jokes, buttering up Mel. He spent the whole time looking completely bewildered by Lorcan and then' – pause – 'd'you know what he said to Mel?' Without waiting for an answer, she ploughed on, 'He only went and told her that he wasn't attracted to her.'

'No!' My tea spluttered all over the table. 'He didn't!'

'It's not funny.'

'I know,' I said, grinning madly and unable to help myself, 'I know.'

Sal glared at me until my smile died.

Silence.

'So what happened?' I asked meekly. Dear God, I prayed, don't let me laugh.

'Well,' Sal began, eyeballing me, daring me to smile, 'Mel was just being Mel, you know. She was flirting with him, rubbing his arm and doing the usual and he says, really loud' – Sal put on a thick northern accent that sounded vaguely like Ed – ' "Mel, I don't know what your game is, but I'm not attracted to you. Now that wee lad over there" – and he points at Lorcan – "he's with you, isn't he?" '

I bit my lip. 'And?'

'Well, Mel glares at him and goes all red. Then she says that of *course* she's with Lorcan and that she *loves* Lorcan and that she's only having a bit of fun and Ed says that it takes two to have fun and he's not having it. And Mel says that if he's not having fun then he should go.'

'Christ!'

'A real dry shite,' Sal spat. 'So then, right, he says fine and

272

then he says to me that we are leaving.' Sal looked back at her half-eaten bread and then up at me. 'Well – what am I meant to do?'

'Go with Ed?'

At her dark look, I amended, 'Stay with Mel?'

'Exactly,' she said grimly. 'Only Ed couldn't believe that I was hanging on. He starts saying that Mel was *not* having fun, that she was making a pass at him and what did I need a mate like that for? Imagine, in front of Mel and everything.'

Sal was getting upset now. I took a chance and put my hand on her arm. 'D'you want some more tea?'

She pushed her cup towards me. 'Strong.'

'Sure.'

While I was boiling the kettle, she continued, 'So I took him aside and I tried to explain to him that I couldn't afford to upset Mel. That I needed a job in her magazine and then' – she shook her head – 'he asked me what the hell I wanted to write for a crappy tabloid for. A – crappy – tabloid. The bloody nerve!'

I doused the teabags into the cups and carried the cups to the table. 'Here.' I shoved the carton of milk towards her.

Her hand shook as she poured milk into her cup. 'And I told him that we couldn't all be *noble* toy shop workers, only I made it sound like a rubbish job.' She sounded proud of that then realised that I was one of the rubbish-job people too. 'Oh, sorry, Vic.'

'We noble people don't take offence.'

'Well *he* did.'

'Maybe because he was almost a doctor,' I remarked.

'My arse he was,' Sal scoffed. 'Where?'

'Dunno – somewhere in London.'

Sal rolled her eyes. 'Anyway, this almost-doctor-cum-toy-shop-worker had the nerve to tell me, *me,* that I was a snobby using cow so I told him,' she gulped, 'to fuck off and then we got thrown out.'

'No!'

'Yeah,' she nodded miserably. 'I'll never get in there again.

And then, of course, he tried to apologise and at the same time make out that Mel had been all over him and that he wasn't into cheating on his girlfriends. So I told him to grow up and recognise flirting when he saw it and he said that it would be better if *I* did. Imagine, *me?* Grow up? He said that friends who did that on each other weren't worth it and that you'd never do that on me.'

'Oh.' I felt a small thrill. He'd actually said something nice about me. 'Oh.'

'So I told him that you wouldn't because you couldn't stand the sight of him.'

My tea went all over the place again. 'What?'

She shook her head defiantly. 'Well, you can't, can you?'

'Sal, you shouldn't have said that.' I stared aghast at her. 'You really shouldn't have.'

'But sure he knows it.'

'No he doesn't!' I stood up from the table. 'You should never have said that. That was *awful*. I can't believe—'

'Yeah. Well.' She bit her lip. 'I was upset, wasn't I? I mean, what will Mel think of me?'

It was always fucking Mel. 'What about what I think of you? Huh? You can't go saying that stuff about me to him.'

'I — was — upset!'

'And now, so am I.'

She continued to glare. I continued to glare. Eventually, she stood up and pushed past me. 'Work,' she said, picking up her laptop. 'Bye.'

I was speechless. I watched her walk to the door, take down her coat from its peg and leave.

The silence in the flat overwhelmed me.

My horror at what she'd said to Ed overwhelmed me.

For the first time I realised that I *could* stand him.

That perhaps I actually liked him.

Which made what she'd said all the worse.

* * *

'Have you and Ed been fighting again?' Bridie asked anxiously as I arrived into the office.

Ed was nowhere to be seen. I unwrapped my scarf and hung it on the back of a chair, before answering. 'No.'

Bridie looked unsure. 'Well, he's in a funny humour. He wouldn't even have a cuppa this morning. Said he had stuff to do in stores.'

'Oh.'

'It's not like him not to want a cup of tea. I mean, he didn't even have a biscuit. Now, for Ed to refuse a biscuit, that's odd. So I thought that maybe you'd rowed again.' She waited, presumably for my confession. When I remained schtum, she said with a sort of accusing voice, 'And now you say that you haven't been fighting.'

'No.' I didn't sound entirely convincing.

'Are you sure that maybe you haven't said something to him to annoy him?'

'I've said nothing.'

'Well, he's not himself. Not himself at all.'

'Good,' I grinned. 'Maybe we'll get on even better then.'

'And it's those sort of comments that cause rows, Vicky,' Bridie said, agitated. 'I wish you could listen to yourself. I don't know about you but I find it impossible to work in a bad atmosphere. I don't know if I can take any more of it. I was just thinking on the way in this morning how well we were all doing. How the shop is a happy little place to—'

'Bridie,' I interrupted her flow and she flinched. 'I'll talk to him, right. I'll see what's wrong.'

'You can't just go talking to him,' Bridie said, exasperated. 'He's hardly going to tell you things, is he? I mean, he likes me and he wouldn't tell me and he's hardly likely to—'

I closed the door on her.

Ed was moving boxes all over the place in stores. He was dusty and dishevelled. He barely glanced at me as I entered. I sat

275

down on a box containing a swing and bided my time. Well, it was more a case of me trying to work out what to say. In the end, I squeaked out a 'Hi'.

He flicked me a glance.

'I hear it's all over with Sal.'

'Yep.' He threw an empty box onto a pile of other empty boxes.

'I'm sorry.'

'I'm not.'

More throwing and moving and shifting.

'Look,' I said, my voice a high squeak, 'she's always different around Mel and Lorcan. She, eh, says lots of stuff she doesn't mean.'

Finally he paused. Hands on hips he regarded me. 'Well she can say it to someone else.' He looked me up and down. 'Now if you've come to plead her case, you can forget it.'

'I haven't come to plead anyone's case.' Jesus, what did he think I was? Fourteen?

'So what *are* you doing here?'

I didn't have the nerve. 'Just, you know—'

'No.' He gave me a hostile look.

'Well, Sal told me that she said something to you last night and, well, I just wanted to clear it up.' My palms began to sweat.

'Sal said a lot of stuff to me last night, most of which would take a tribunal to clear up.'

'Oh.'

'So – what was this thing she said?'

He was staring at me again. Making me uncomfortable. 'Oh—' I waved my hand about. Gulped. 'Well, it was just the thing about me, you know, not being able to stand the sight of you.' God, it sounded awful. I wanted to die.

'Oh that.' He turned his back to me and began working again. 'What about it?'

'Well, it's not true. I mean, I don't think that.'

'Right.'

He was still working away. I don't know what he was hoping

276

to achieve. Our storerooms were always a mess. 'Just so you know,' I went on, babbling to his back, feeling mortified. 'I do like you. I'd even go so far as to consider you a friend.'

He stopped working and turned to me with a speculative look.

'Of sorts,' I added hastily.

He grinned slightly.

'I, eh, just thought I'd say it in case you, you know, were upset about it.'

'Well, I'm not.' He wiped his hands down the length of his jeans and surveyed the mountain of boxes he'd shoved to one side. 'Boys' stuff,' he said, pointing to the left. 'Girls' stuff,' pointing to the right.

'Handy,' I said, my face burning. Why the fuck had I bothered? Did I honestly think he'd be so upset that he'd disappear to the storeroom? Was I that big-headed to think that my opinion of him mattered to him? 'Well, I'll go get my tea.'

'Yeah, I'll follow you up in about ten minutes. Tell Bridie to stick my name in the pot.'

Trust Bridie to be an alarmist. Jesus, if it weren't for her, I'd never have said anything to him. I'd have been extra-nice just to show him I liked him, but I'd never have humiliated myself like that. 'Make your own bloody tea,' I snapped. 'Bridie's old.'

'Spoken like a true friend,' he shouted after me.

Bastard.

Chapter Forty-six

THE REVIEWS FOR Boy Five's new single were lukewarm. 'That's the Irish media for you,' Marti said as he threw one of the rock mags aside in disgust. 'If I'd made it in England, they'd be bloody afraid to write crap like this.' He picked up the magazine again and rifled through it. 'Yeah, here – look at this.' He jabbed a review and read, 'This group should have been left in the zoo and thrown to the lions.'

'Well, they did praise Cliff's voice.' What they'd actually said was that the high notes Cliff had sung were probably only as a result of the tight zookeeper's outfit he wore in the video. 'In a way,' I amended, seeing the dark look on Marti's face.

'Fuckers,' Marti fumed.

'Well,' Sal said from her corner, 'the job of any journalist is to tell the truth.'

'My fucking arse,' Marti said back.

'Shut up, Sal,' I hissed. Between listening to Marti moaning and Sal bitching about Ed at every opportunity, things were at a huge low. Still, it took my mind off the fact that I'd spent the last few days trying to compose a letter to Barbara. So far, I'd managed a 'Dear Barbara'. Everything else I wanted to say wouldn't come out. Or it came out all wrong. All I wanted to know was who I was but it seemed a bit cold just to demand my history from her. It seemed too scary now to meet her. And that photograph that she'd given me still made me angry. It was shoved right to the back of my sock drawer, way down behind my horrible socks, the ones I never wore but couldn't bear to throw out.

Marti topped up his wine and offered me some more.

'How do the lads feel about the reviews?' I asked, as Marti poured a generous measure for me.

'I dunno if they even understand them,' he said in all seriousness. 'I mean, let's face it, the lot of them are a few notes short of a riff.'

'Marti!' I glanced at Sal. There was no such thing as an 'off-the-record' comment as far as she was concerned. 'You didn't hear that, did you, Sal?'

'I doubt my readers would be interested anyhow.' She held up a huge book with a lurid green and blue scarf on the front. 'The art of knitting, that's the feature piece this week.'

Despite her light tone, I knew she was hurting. Mel and Lorcan had been conspicuous by their absence. I knew she'd rung Mel to apologise, but so far there had been radio silence from the other end.

'It'll get better.'

'Yeah,' she said, 'I really think it will. Jesus, it can't get much worse.' She grinned ruefully.

To be honest, she'd been dead nice ever since the row we'd had over Ed. Okay, she hadn't apologised, but she'd done the next best thing. She'd bought us home a take-away and a bottle of wine. I'd forgive anyone anything for a bottle of wine. Especially a twenty-euro bottle of wine. And just to please her, I'd listened as she'd savaged Ed. Then she'd grilled me on him – wanting me to say horrible things about his other relationships, of which I knew nothing. But I did tell her that his dad didn't seem to like him, which had pleased her. 'Sensible man,' she'd spat and forced me to drink a toast to Albert O'Neill's health.

'And what about me?' Marti asked, poking me in the arm. 'Will it get better for me?'

'Oooh' – I made a face and put on a baby voice – 'yes, yes it will.'

'Right, into the bedroom, so,' Marti joked, clapping his hands together and standing up. 'Excuse us, Sal.'

I pulled him down, giggling. 'Will you stop it!'

A lurid wink, 'I haven't even *started* yet.'

'And you won't be,' I laughed. 'Haven't we to go and collect Leo and bring him out?' We always took Leo out on a Friday night.

Marti suddenly looked embarrassed. He shot a look at Sal. Then he sat back down and gazed at his hands. 'Eh, no, actually.'

'What? Is he sick?'

'Nope.' Marti shot another look at Sal, who was pretending to be engrossed in her history of knitting research. 'He's, eh,' Marti lowered his voice, 'he's gone out with his mother.'

'What?'

'What?'

'I thought you weren't listening,' Marti said crossly to Sal.

'A journalist is always listening,' Sal said back. 'So, what's the story? Did she beg to be allowed to see him or what?'

'Sal!' I glared at her. 'It's Marti's business.' She rolled her eyes.

'So?' I asked Marti. 'How did it happen?'

'I was going to tell you,' Marti muttered. 'I mean, it's no big deal.' He made a face. 'Leo talked to her again last night, like *you* said he should and, well, she asked if she could see him and what the hell could I say? I couldn't disappoint the kid, could I? I mean, I don't want him to think he's after being *abandoned*, do I?'

Was he trying to nail this on me? I didn't mind. I felt quite proud of him actually.

'No.' I gave him a light punch. 'You've done the right thing.'

Behind me Sal snorted but we both ignored her.

'Yeah.' Marti sat back in the chair and nodded vigorously. 'I think so. I mean, you'd want to see how happy Leo was when he saw her. So fucking happy.' He smiled a bit, to himself. 'I'd forgotten the kid could smile like that.'

Sal was now making squeaky violin noises. I mouthed her to 'fuck off' but she kept going.

'And Linda, well, she looked fucking terrible,' Marti said.

I was pleased to hear that.

'She'd lost weight and her face was all pale and her hair all scraggy. She's got hair like yours, lovely and bouncy, but it wasn't lovely and bouncy today.'

Brilliant, I thought.

'And her eyes were red, as though she'd been crying.'

Good.

'And when Leo ran to her, I swear I thought he was going to knock her down. And she held him hard, like as if she was going to strangle him. And she was off crying again and telling him how lovely he was and how she was so sorry and that she loved him and missed him and never stopped thinking about him.'

My mother had written that. But she'd never known me.

'Telling you, Vic, I felt guilty for making her suffer. I bloody did.'

I wanted to say that she'd deserved to suffer but somehow I couldn't. Linda had made a mistake – one that had cost her. And she knew it and was sorry for it. 'You've made her happy now,' I said.

He nodded. 'Yeah. I'm not a man to bear grudges. He's her kid, he should see her. She has her rights.'

And I thought, at that minute, that if Marti could forgive his wife, then I should at least be able to write a letter to my mother. It seemed so simple, the idea of writing to her, forgiving her. I leaned over and planted a little kiss on his cheek. 'Hey' – he was surprised – 'what was that for?'

'For you.' I smiled.

'Excuse me while I puke,' Sal said from behind.

Dear Barbara,

Thanks very much for the photo. It was nice of you to send it and I'm glad you kept it with you all this time. And yeah, I still have the red hair and it's a curse. It frizzes out in the rain and curls up

281

at the ends and I've hated it all my life. I've had it straightened, chopped off and nothing works so I've just had to live with it. I mostly wear it in plaits, just to keep it under control.

I'm sorry you were so upset at giving me up. But if it makes you feel better, whoever told you that I was going to a lovely couple was right. They are lovely. They've been lovely all my life.

Believe me, Barbara, you couldn't have done a nicer thing than to give me to these people. There is no point in beating yourself up over what you did or should have done. In the end, you made what you considered the right decision at the time. That's all that counts.

And I thank you for it.

Vicky

By writing it all down, I felt sort of peaceful. I *did* thank her. For the first time I realised that maybe I had been loved. And like Marti with Linda, I didn't want her to feel bad if I could do something about it.

But still, right at the back of it all was the hole.

The part that I needed to fill.

The part that was my story.

Chapter Forty-seven

MY MOTHER HAD to cancel her visit to Dublin. Dad rang me at eight in the morning to let me know. I swear he'd done it on purpose, knowing that it was my day off.

'Your mother has a cold,' he said, in a clipped voice, 'and she can't come to see you.'

'Oh. Right.' I was taken aback. A cold didn't sound too bad. 'Is she all right?'

'I just told you, Victoria, she has a cold. She can't travel. And anyway' – he sucked in his breath – 'it's you that should be coming to visit her, not the other way around. You haven't been down in months.'

It hadn't been that long. 'I already told Mam, I'm very busy in work.' I was glad he couldn't see me because I went bright red.

'There's always Sunday,' Dad said. 'You don't work on Sundays, do you?'

'Depends.'

'On?'

He was so cold. This was my dad and he was like a stranger. 'Dad,' I stuttered, 'don't be like this, please. I'll come down soon.'

'Well, that would be nice,' he said, still in that horrible voice. 'I think your mother deserves it, don't you?'

'Well, *she's* not the reason I'm staying away.' I could have bitten my tongue out.

He didn't reply.

In a miserable attempt to change the subject, I ventured, 'Has she told you that I have a picture of me as a baby?'

283

'You didn't even come before all this nonsense started,' he said, ignoring me. 'So don't use it as an excuse.'

He was right, of course.

'So I'll tell your mother you'll be down when it suits, will I?'

'Soon,' I said quietly. Guilt. Guilt. Guilt. The feeling that I was horrible hammered into my head.

'I suppose we should be grateful?'

'No.'

'Well, we'll see you when we see you, I suppose.'

I didn't reply.

He seemed to be waiting for me to say something.

'Yeah,' I muttered.

'Bye now, Victoria.'

I waited until the phone bleeped. Slowly I put down the receiver. I don't think, ever in my life, he'd called me Victoria.

Not ever.

Lucy looked quite grave as I took my seat opposite her. There was something in the way she had her hands clasped on the desk in front of her that set the alarm bells jangling. A file, with my name on it, was on the desk. She'd been writing something down, presumably about me.

'What's up?' I asked. I sounded breathless. I tried a smile. 'Looks dead serious.'

Lucy shrugged and patted my file. 'Well, that all depends on the way you look at it, Vicky. It could be good news or it might confuse you.'

'Oh?'

Pause.

'Well?'

She took her time before speaking. It was as if she was figuring out how to tell me. Her words, when they came, were slow and measured. 'Basically, Vicky, I've had a communication from the Adoption Board. Your mother has been in touch with them and apparently she'd like to see you. She feels ready.'

I wasn't sure I'd heard right. 'Sorry?'

'Your birth mother, Barbara, she wants to meet you.'

Time stopped. I stared at Lucy, not knowing what to say. This was what I'd wanted for years. This was why I'd started the search and yet . . . I didn't feel very much of anything. Not joy, or resolution or completion or . . . anything.

Lucy stared back at me. 'Well,' she asked after what felt like ages, 'how do you feel about that?'

'Dunno.' The file in front of her caught my attention. My name, written in blue marker. Victoria McCarthy. Only it wasn't my name, really. 'Why *now*?'

'She wants to meet you,' Lucy repeated softly. 'She says that at the time the letters seemed a good thing but now, what with knowing you're so close, she doesn't want to waste any more time.' Gentle searching of my face. 'I guess it's a normal enough reaction.'

Normal? How could she be normal? Is giving your baby away normal? I nearly laughed but at the same time I was terrified, as if I was standing at the edge of a huge hole. 'So what happens now?'

'Now it's up to you,' Lucy said. 'It's what you want that matters here.'

But I hadn't figured that out yet. 'I know I did want to meet her,' I muttered. 'It's just that, well, talking to you, I realise how big a deal it is.'

She nodded.

'And, like, I wasn't prepared for some of the stuff I felt or thought.' I leaned across the desk. 'I was just thinking the other day, Lucy, what if, right, she wants more than I want to give? What if she tells me my story and I don't want to see her any more? What then?'

'Is that the way you feel?'

'I don't know!' The words tumbled out of me. 'I don't know! But it could happen, yeah?'

'It's common enough.'

285

Well, that was reassuring. I liked being told things I felt were common enough. 'And then,' I continued, growing in confidence, 'what if my mam and dad get upset or hurt? What do I do then?'

'Have you not talked to them?' Lucy looked stern. 'I told you last time to talk to them, Vicky.'

'Yeah, well . . .' I shrugged.

'There's no "yeah, well" about it,' Lucy said, sounding cross. 'You *have* to tell them. I mean they know you're searching so what's the problem?'

I hated admitting it. I'd only half admitted it to myself. 'I'm scared,' I said in a small voice. I looked up at her; she had her encouraging face on. It would have been mad funny if it had been on the telly, but in the real world, it made me feel a bit like crying. 'My dad,' I sniffed, 'well, he thinks I'm being stupid. He thinks I should be happy.' I took a deep breath. 'I don't know what he'll say if he thinks I'm meeting her.'

'Oh, Vicky, Vicky, Vicky,' Lucy said as she began her usual rummage for tissues. Not that I was going to cry. In the end, she handed me a piece of A4 paper. 'Sorry. Bloody tissues are a curse to find.'

I took the A4 and scrunched it up. Then I pretended to dab my eyes so that she'd think I was using it.

'Vicky,' Lucy said, after I'd finished my dabbing, 'you *have* to talk to your parents. And even if they don't agree, it's still up to you. It has to be what you want. If you choose not to meet Barbara, it has to be because you don't want to, not because of your dad or mam or anyone else.' A swift smile. 'Understand?'

I nodded. How the hell did I talk to them?

I wondered if I could meet Barbara without telling them. They'd never have to know. But I knew if I did that, I'd probably collapse under the guilt.

And if I upset them, I'd collapse under the guilt too.

But at least I'd have been honest.

'You don't have to decide now,' Lucy went on. 'Take your

286

time. If it's too soon, wait a while. Don't go rushing into things.'

'Yeah.'

'Now.' She lay back in her chair and regarded me. 'what's this about not knowing what exactly it is you want from Barbara?'

Oh God, I hoped she wouldn't pick up on that. The whole thing made me sound like a selfish cow and I wondered how I could paint myself in a flattering light. 'Well,' I began haltingly, 'I've forgiven her, you know, for giving me up.'

'Forgiven her?' Lucy looked puzzled.

'Well, I'm not as *angry* any more,' I clarified.

'OK,' Lucy smiled. 'Good.'

'But, like, how am I meant to forget that she gave me away? And, like, what if she didn't *have* to give me away? I'll probably resent her for that. And then, I was thinking, what if I met her and just didn't like her?'

Lucy looked a little bemused by all the stuff I'd been thinking. To be honest, I was a bit bemused by all the stuff I'd been thinking myself, but it had all come on me once I'd posted my letter last week. I'd had a feeling that things were hotting up and that there was no going back. I always tend to think deep thoughts when my back hits the wall.

'First off,' Lucy said eventually, 'no one expects you to forget that you were adopted. That's part of you, will always be part of you.'

Yeuch.

'And secondly, if you do feel that you don't want to keep in contact with her, it will hurt her, but it's up to you. And like I said, it has happened before.'

'Really?'

'Really.' She smiled. 'And though it's sad on the mother, she's met her child and that's all some of them want. Just to see their kids, to assure themselves that they are OK. It's a wonderful business when it goes well.'

I guess it probably was.

'And here—' Lucy passed a sheet of paper across the desk.

287

'I got this from the Adoption Board too. It's your mother's phone number.'

Jesus.

'Of course, if you do decide to ring her, you should really have someone with you – especially the first time. If you like, I can be with you or your parents – it's up to you.'

Everything was up to me. Me, whose biggest decision to date had been how many Barbie dolls to order for the Christmas market. Jesus.

'I'll think about it,' I said.

'Good.' Lucy smiled. 'You're getting good at thinking things out, aren't you?'

And I was, I guess. No more jumping in feet first. No more acting on impulse.

'Thanks to you,' I grinned slightly.

'Ring me anytime with a decision,' Lucy said. 'And I'll see you in a fortnight if you want?'

I nodded.

Just as I was leaving, she added, 'Vicky, remember, you can't do this sort of thing without upsetting other people. You'd be surprised at how much upheaval there will be after contact is made. This sometimes is the easy part.'

Christ!

I got back to the flat and drank a can of lager straight down. It was comforting to feel it shocking itself through my body. After that, I lay down on the sofa and let the room spin for a while.

But at the end, I knew I'd still have to think things out some-time.

And I'd have to talk to Mam and Dad sometime.

And I'd have to meet my birth mother sometime.

I closed my eyes and wondered just where everything was leading.

And I'd never wondered about that before either.

Chapter Forty-eight

A LL THAT WEEK I walked around in a complete daze. I thought maybe if I didn't think about the decision I had to make, it would all somehow go away. But it didn't. Despite my best efforts to concentrate on work, on Marti, on the fact that much to Marti's glee his separated wife had thrown a wobbler over her son's haircut, nothing penetrated except the fact that by the next time I met Lucy, I had to have made some sort of a decision. *And* I had to talk to my folks. Every time the thought loomed, my heart would sink and I'd get this awful feeling of dread right in the pit of my stomach.

Marti wasn't a lot of help.

'Meet her?' He looked at me as if I was mental. 'Why would you want to meet her?'

'I already told you,' I said. 'To find out who I am. Who I look like. Why I can sing. Why—'

'Phone her. Get a picture of the auld doll. I'm telling you, I wouldn't want to meet any woman that left me. It's bad enough seeing Linda twice a week.'

'That's a bit different. You don't need her to fill in who you are.'

'Thank Christ!'

He was in great form these days, mainly because Leo was now the manageable boy he used to be. And Leo was like a new kid, all chat and jokes whenever the three of us went anywhere.

It was amazing the difference a mother could make.

'I'd like to meet my mammy if I never met her,' Leo chirped

up from the back seat where he was sloppily eating an ice cream.

'You shouldn't be listening into this,' Marti said crossly. 'You haven't a clue.'

'I do too,' Leo said equally crossly. 'Vicky must miss her mammy. I missed my mammy. We went to the zoo yesterday, Vicky.'

'That was nice,' I said absently.

'And Mammy bought me a donut and Daddy said that she was spoiling me.'

'Now, now,' Marti said quickly, a little too quickly, I thought, 'Vicky doesn't want to be hearing about your trip to the zoo.'

'Did you go too?' I asked. 'Did the three of you go? I thought—'

'I was meant to have a session with Boy Five,' Marti whispered, 'but the kid' – he jerked his head at Leo, as if I wouldn't know who he was talking about – 'begged me to come. What could I do?'

He could have said no, I thought. But if I said it aloud, it would sound really mean.

But Marti and Linda and Leo together at the zoo. It made me uneasy. 'And what did Linda think?' I asked. 'You being there.'

'Don't care.' Marti shrugged nonchalantly. 'I only did it for the kid.'

That sort of made things sound better.

'That's what parents do,' Marti said sagely. 'They look out for their kids.'

'Are you the new parenting oracle?'

He laughed his brash laugh. 'Naw. I'm just saying that any kind of a decent parent puts their kid first.' Pause. 'Did *your* mother?'

'Maybe she did.' I shrugged. 'Anyway, your wife didn't and you've managed to put it behind you.' I smiled sweetly. 'I'm just thinking of following your example.'

He looked chuffed at that. 'Oh, right. OK. Yeah. That sounds reasonable. So, you think you'll meet her then?'

'Maybe.'

After you talk to the folks, a part of my mind reminded me. I felt sick.

Bridie and Ed agreed that I could take a long weekend. Of course, I felt that I had to explain, only I didn't want to tell them the truth, so in the manner of all liars I completely over-explained. 'I haven't been down in months,' I babbled, going red. 'And my dad is freaking out over it and he thinks I don't want to come down, which is completely untrue.'

They stayed silent.

'Completely,' I said cheerfully. 'As if!' I rolled my eyes and snorted a bit.

'Well' – Bridie glanced at Ed, who was giving his irritating slow smile – 'that's nice. To take time off to visit your parents, I think that's nice.'

'Yeah,' Ed agreed, 'I betcha they'll be made up – imagine, who wouldn't? A whole long weekend with Vicky. Three whole days with Vicky. Seventy-two hours of no one but Vicky. They won't believe their luck.'

Bridie giggled.

'Their *bad* luck,' he added casually.

'Ooh, oooh, Ed.' Bridie wanted to laugh and was afraid to. 'Ohh, Vicky, don't mind him.'

I shrugged. 'Seventy-two hours of no Ed,' I said back. 'That's my good luck.'

He laughed. 'Aw, I'm dead hurt. That's not very *friendly* now, is it?'

Ever since I told him I considered him a friend, he'd been dragging the 'f' word into virtually every conversation we had. '"It takes your enemy and your friend, working together, to hurt you to the heart. The one to slander you and the other to get the news to you."' I paused. 'That's from Mark Twain.'

Bridie and Ed were looking agog at me.

I knew that that saying of Lorcan's would come in useful someday. It was the only one I remembered. 'I am both your enemy and your friend, Ed,' I added pleasantly. 'I'm also your boss, so will you ever clean up aisle three.'

'There's nothing sweeter than a girl with a quick tongue.' Ed saluted me. 'That's from Ed O'Neill's disgusting sayings.'

It was the first time I'd laughed that week.

I don't think Bridie understood it though.

Chapter Forty-nine

I CAUGHT THE bus down on Friday night, hoping that the element of surprise would shock my father into accepting what I had to tell him. Well, not that I'd made a firm decision on it, but if he'd been happier about it, yeah, I think I'd have had the courage to meet Barbara.

And it would take courage, I realised. I mean, there was a chance she mightn't like me either.

Every chance.

I mean, I had red frizzy hair, a small skinny body and no boobs. I sure hope she wasn't looking for a supermodel long lost daughter. And that, I realised, was the really scary thing – I'd been rejected once when I was so young that I didn't remember, but now . . . well, I don't know if I could have taken another rejection from her. Of course Lucy had told me that being put up for adoption wasn't a rejection, it was something done out of love or desperation, but hey, Lucy wasn't the one walking about in my head at night.

Anyway, the bus journey was disaster enough to take my mind off things. The fella sitting beside me fell asleep about ten minutes into the trip and his head buried itself in my shoulder. At first I tried to be charitable about it, but in the end, I got tired of not being able to move so I jerked my shoulder really hard to dislodge him and he ended up tumbling out into the aisle and banging his head.

And I got dirty looks all the way down even though I apologised and everything.

It was a massive relief to get off the bus.

On the plus side, I figured that things couldn't be as bad at home.

It was raining as I trudged up the lane to our house. My weekend bag was getting soaked and I cursed myself for not ringing in advance. Dad would surely have driven to meet me. I hefted my bag onto my shoulder and prepared for the half-mile walk home.

I had gone a couple of yards when I heard a car approaching. Its headlights lit up the road before me and I stepped into the grass verge to avoid it. It went by and then came to a screeching halt. A window was rolled down and a dark head poked out. 'Well, hiya, stranger. No one was expecting you tonight.'

Tommy!

Bloody great.

'Hi, Tommy.'

'Get in.' His head disappeared as he reached across and opened the passenger door for me. He grinned at me as I reluctantly climbed in beside him. 'Jesus, you're soaked.'

'Yeah, rain tends to do that.'

He laughed. 'Well, you're lucky I'm heading up your way tonight – Mam has sent me around with one of her crackpot potions for your mother's flu.'

'Flu?'

'Well, whatever she has. A cold or something.' He turned to look at me. 'Jesus, you should have rung me at work, I'd have given you a lift down. I only came down meself this evening.'

'Devoted son,' I muttered.

'Aw, well,' he said easily, not taking offence, 'the mother gets lonely being on her own. I like to keep an eye on her, you know.' He started the car and we didn't talk again until he pulled to a stop in front of the house.

'Ta.'

'No probs. You hang on there while I get an umbrella from the boot.'

'Don't be stupid, sure I'm wet already.' There was no way I was going to let him do me any more favours. I opened the passenger door and was assaulted by sheets of heavy belting rain. I was drenched in seconds.

Tommy was grinning out at me. 'You can get the umbrella for me, so.'

'In your dreams,' I smirked, slamming the door and running as quickly as I could towards the house.

He followed me and waited while I unlocked the door.

'Who's that?' Dad's voice from the kitchen.

'Me and Vicky,' Tommy shouted. 'I've brought medicine from me mother.'

'Did you say Vicky?' Dad appeared at the kitchen door. He was wiping his hands in a towel. From behind, there drifted the smell of coffee and warmth. He saw me and despite the annoyance I'm sure he was feeling towards me, his face broke into a delighted smile. 'Well, well, well. Hello, stranger.'

'Dad.' I felt suddenly shy. And yep, guilty.

'Come on in, the both of you, it's dreadful out there. Did you come down with Tommy?' He was ushering us into the kitchen, which was deliciously warm due to the range being lit.

'Naw, I picked her up on the road,' Tommy answered, placing a brown bottle onto the table.

'Sure you must be soaked, pet.' Dad looked at me in concern. 'We don't want you catching a cold like your mother, now.'

'Where is Mam?'

'Up in bed asleep, thank God. She was up all night with that auld cough. And the pain in her back.' Dad sighed. 'If she's no better tomorrow, I'm getting the doctor for her.' He looked at me. 'Now, take off that coat and I'll hang it up to dry.' He waited patiently as I divested myself of the coat and then he hung it up over the range on a big hook he'd fixed there years ago.

'So, are ye hungry?' He looked at both of us.

'Starving,' I said, sitting down at the table.

'I'll head on.' Tommy indicated the bottle on the table. 'Mam says a spoonful at night – it'll help her sleep.'

'Right, thanks, Tommy.' Dad began to walk out with him. 'Are you sure you won't have anything?'

'Positive.' Tommy looked back. 'See you, Vic. Maybe you'll call over on Sunday to see us?'

'Maybe,' I said, not meaning it. 'I'll be here until Monday.'

Dad looked as if he'd just won the lottery. 'Well, well, that's marvellous. Marvellous indeed.'

I hoped he still thought so in seventy-two hours' time.

He made me waffles and scrambled eggs. 'There now,' he said, dishing an enormous quantity of eggs onto my plate. 'Eat up, there's plenty more.'

'Where did you learn to make these?' I asked. They weren't brown or burnt and they hadn't even stuck to the saucepan.

'Practice,' he nodded, helping himself to some. 'Your mother taught me and I've just got better and better. Sometimes, I put cheese into them or mix salmon through them. Your mother loves the way I cook them.' He beamed at me. 'I've gone very creative in my old age.'

I grinned. He had indeed. There was a time my father wouldn't have even known how to boil an egg.

'We take turns cooking now. Your mother cooks every second day – well, that's providing there's no emergency with the cattle. But we like to have little competitions to see who makes the most imaginative dinners.'

Seeing as all they ever ate was meat, veg and spuds, I'd say the scope for imagination was limited. They both abhorred sauces and dressings and would only eat boiled potatoes. 'Sounds interesting,' I grinned.

He nodded.

'So,' he asked, 'what brings you down? Was it my telephone call the other week? Was I a bit cranky with you?'

'A bit,' I conceded.

296

'Well, I'm sorry about that,' he nodded. 'I was just worried about your mother. 'Twas me wouldn't let her travel and she was in a huff with me and words were said and I think I took it out on you.'

'It's OK.'

'But it's great to see you. And we do realise how busy you are with everything.'

I was tempted to tell him there and then, to say that I had news for him, but somehow the words got stuck in my throat. I think it was the happiness on his face that I couldn't bear to spoil. And I wondered if I was prepared to spoil it. Prepared to ruin what I had for a pipe dream.

I didn't know.

Lying in bed that night, as usual completely unable to sleep, I heard Mam coughing in the other room. It was a harsh, unforgiving cough that sounded pretty scary. Every time she coughed, my whole body would tense up until the fit was over.

I lay awake, long after they'd both gone to sleep, and worried. What if Mam was really sick? What would I do then? What would I do without her?

I got up at three and went into the kitchen. Pouring myself a glass of milk I realised how difficult the next few days would be.

I loved these people.

I couldn't hurt them.

Not for all the birth mothers in the world.

Chapter Fifty

I AWOKE FROM the weirdest dream to the sound of a car pulling up outside the house. At first I thought I'd imagined it, that it was part of my dream, because it was still night. My room was dark and there were none of the usual farm sounds that you associate with early morning.

Then came the sound of my parents' bedroom door being opened and I heard Dad announcing that 'he'd' arrived. Next thing, Dad was pounding down the stairs and pulling open our heavy front door. There was something in the urgent way he'd spoken that immediately set my heart pounding. Jumping out of bed, I pulled on my old dressing gown – the one Mam always left hanging on a hook in my room. I was just in time to see Dad leading the doctor up the stairs.

'What's wrong?' I gasped, frozen at the sight of them. 'Is it Mam? Is she all right?'

Dad indicated the bedroom and the doctor went inside.

'It's just a precaution,' Dad said, crossing to me. He put his hand on my shoulder. 'It's just that she's been coughing virtually all night and she says that the pain in her back is getting worse—'

'Is she all right?' I demanded.

'That's why the doctor's here,' he sighed. 'I don't know.'

My dad normally pretended to know everything. He sounded defeated, baffled.

I didn't know what to do. Nausea crawled in my belly.

'She just sounds so bad,' he whispered then. 'It's not right.'

Then, with a quick rub of my shoulder, he disappeared inside the room.

I stood, like the spare part I was, awaiting the verdict.

She had pneumonia. According to the doctor, it was mainly confined to her left lung and that was why she had the pain in her back. He told us there was a danger of the other lung becoming affected and that in his opinion she should be brought to hospital immediately.

At the 'h' word both Dad and I jumped.

The doctor didn't seem to notice. 'I'll ring for an ambulance,' he said, taking out his mobile. He turned to Dad. 'Can you pack her clothes?'

'I'll do it,' I said. Dad wouldn't have had a clue what to pack. He'd put in dirty nightgowns and mortify Mam in front of the whole ward. And besides, I wanted to feel useful.

Dad smiled gratefully. He was as white as a sheet and trembling slightly. I don't think he'd have been much good at anything he was so frightened. 'Thanks,' he said. He stroked Mam's hair back from her forehead and I gulped as he kissed her tenderly on the cheek. Mam caught his hand.

'There's nothing too much wrong with you,' he pretended to scoff. 'Honestly, trying to frighten us like this.'

Mam smiled and almost looked like her old self. I was glad I hadn't seen her last night because I wouldn't have been able to sleep. She had become terribly thin, had deep shadows under her eyes and, for the first time ever, she looked old. Or maybe vulnerable is the right word. And the cough. It sounded bad through two feet of wall but hearing her cough now, in the same room, was scary. Every time she coughed my eyes would fill with tears and I'd think of all the nice things she'd ever done for me. And of all the horrible things I'd done on her.

'I'll go and wait for the ambulance,' Dad said. 'They mightn't know exactly where to come.'

'You're only doing that to make sure they take me away.' Mam said thickly.

Dad laughed.

Dad went with her in the ambulance. My mother, who towered over me and always looked so strong and capable, was suddenly tiny as she was wheeled away. Dad seemed to have withered too.

'There's food in the press,' he said before they left. 'You'll manage.'

'Don't worry about me,' I advised. 'I'll be fine.' I tried to keep my voice steady, though I wanted to cry.

'And ring Julia – get Tommy to drive you in later. He'll be around.'

There was no way I wanted a lift from Tommy. I'd find a way to go without asking him. 'I'll be in around dinnertime,' I promised.

Dad gave me a brief hug and was gone.

I watched the ambulance pull out of our driveway, flick on its siren and go screaming up the road.

Then I went inside, sat down at the table and cried.

The phone never stopped ringing all that morning. If I'd paid a plane to fly over the town with a banner headline about my mother being in hospital, the news wouldn't have travelled as fast. Aunt Julia was on around eleven. I actually think she needed reassurance that her potion was not the cause of my mother's sudden admission to hospital. When I told her that Mam had pneumonia, she seemed relieved. Then worried. Then she asked me how I was managing for lunch.

'Dad said there was food in the press.'

'Food in the press,' she scoffed in the bossy way that I hated. 'With a shock like you've had, you'll need something warm inside you.'

'Maybe,' I conceded, just to keep her quiet. The only warm

300

thing I had a hope of making with any success was a cup of coffee.

'I'm going to send Tommy around to pick you up and you can have dinner with us.'

'No!' Jesus.

'It's no trouble,' Julia went on, 'and then Tommy can drive you in to visit. I'm sure your poor father could do with some company. The man must be out of his mind.'

'I was going to get a bus.' I did not want to be beholden to Julia. The thought of it made my skin crawl.

'You'll not be getting a bus,' Julia answered sharply. 'Not while we've cars sitting in our driveway. Now, Tommy will be up for you in about' – she had a muttered conversation with Tommy. Then she came back on line – 'about thirty minutes – all right?'

'Honestly, there's no need—'

'There's every need,' Julia said. 'Wouldn't your mother do the same for us? Aren't you family?'

She didn't wait for me to answer and I'm not sure I could have. I was family. She'd said it herself. Even if it wasn't strictly true, it sounded nice.

I held the phone long after she'd hung up.

I showered, dressed and, within the thirty minutes, Tommy was at the front door. I nodded to him and, after locking up, went silently to his car.

'I'm sorry about your mother,' he said after I'd put on my seatbelt. 'I'd no idea she was so bad.'

'No one did,' I muttered, not looking at him.

'Mam has a huge dinner ready for you,' he said, grinning wryly. 'I told her you probably wouldn't be hungry, so don't feel you have to please her by eating it.'

Aunt Julia took it as a personal insult if her food wasn't finished.

I bit my lip.

'I mean, she'll probably badger you about it, but don't mind her.' Another grin. 'I know I don't.'

'Ta.'

He started up the car without saying any more but, for the first time ever, I realised how thoughtful he was.

True enough, Julia tried to force every vegetable under the sun onto my plate. 'Ah, you'll have a bit of cabbage, now, won't you,' she said, shovelling what had to be about two cabbages in front of me. 'Cabbage is full of iron, which is good for shock.'

'She's not hungry, Mam,' Tommy said. 'And if you keep forcing her, she'll be sick.'

'There's nothing wrong with my food.' Julia turned scathing eyes on him. 'She'll not be sick.'

'Honestly' – I pushed my plate away – 'I can't eat it, Julia. I mean, it's lovely and all, but I just want to get to the hospital.'

'Ooooh.' Julia was at my side. 'Of course you do. Of course you do. Tommy,' she barked, 'will you get up off your backside and start up the car. Of course she wants to be with her father and mother. You'll eat something later,' she said, more to re-assure herself than me, 'you'll be in the mood for it after a day at the hospital. TOMMY!'

Tommy jumped. 'Yeah, Mam, I'm ready. Vicky?' He looked at me. There was a hint of laughter in his eyes which I couldn't respond to. 'Ready?'

'Sure.' I pulled on my coat, which I'd hung over the back of my chair. 'Thanks, Julia. Sorry I wasn't able to do dinner justice.'

'Once your poor mother is all right, that's all that matters.' Julia indicated her groaning table. 'That's only food. There's more important things in life than eating a dinner.'

'Right.' Tommy jangled his keys. 'I'll give you a ring from the hospital, Mam. Let you know what's happening.'

'Take your time.' Julia patted her son's arm. In a whisper, which I don't think I was meant to hear, she added, 'And look after Vicky. You know how highly sensitive she is.'

Highly sensitive? Me? I was about to say that I wasn't when

302

Tommy whispered back, 'I know, Ma. I'm not going to say anything to upset her.'

I could feel myself begin to bristle. A smart retort formed in my mind. I was about to snap back that I wasn't easily upset when I realised that I'd just become easily upset.

And that being easily upset didn't matter.

All that mattered was my mother.

Chapter Fifty-one

T HE NURSE ON duty looked sharply at Tommy and me as we walked into the ICU. 'Mrs Evelyn McCarthy,' I asked. My voice was trembling, as if I was going to cry. Even saying my mother's name was such a precious thing. 'She's my mother.'

'She's only allowed one visitor at a time,' the nurse said, looking sympathetically at me. 'Your dad is with her at the minute. I'll tell him you're here.' She turned to Tommy. 'Are you her son?'

'Nah.' Tommy had his arm about my shoulders. 'Just a nephew. It's fine, I'll stay out here and wait.'

The nurse nodded and padded off down the corridor in her white shoes.

'You OK?' Tommy asked. 'Want a coffee?'

'Yeah and yeah.' I reached into my bag to drag out some change, but he was gone, after first pointing me to a seat. I sat, looking up and down the spotless corridor, feeling more alone than I ever had in my whole life.

Dad arrived about five minutes later. 'On your own?' he asked, sitting beside me.

'Tommy is gone to get coffee,' I muttered. 'How is she, Dad?'

'They're giving her antibiotics and they've got her on oxygen.' He gulped and stared at his huge hands, which dangled uselessly between his legs. 'It looks scary, but apparently she's improving.' He shook his head. 'Jesus, she's had that damned cough for so long, I should have made her go to the doctor.'

'She wouldn't have gone,' I answered. 'You know Mam.'

'At the back of my mind, I knew it wasn't right to have a cough like that, but I said nothing. I was scared, you see.'

'She's in good hands now.' I didn't know what else to say to him. I'd never seen him like this before. It frightened me.

'I was scared in case I'd find out she was sick.' Dad ignored me. 'I didn't want her to be sick so I paid no attention to it. And now look.'

'It's not your fault.'

He buried his head in his hands. 'If anything happens to her, Vicky, I don't know what I'll do. She's my life, you know that.'

'Oh, Dad.' I touched his hand. Rough and strong. 'Don't.'

'The pair of you are my life. I build everything around the two of you. If I lost one of you, I'd be all over the place.' He gave a huge trembly sigh.

'Well, nothing will happen. Nothing.'

He wrapped his big arm around me and it felt safe and secure.

Dad ended up drinking the appalling coffee Tommy eventually managed to purchase because they let me in to see Mam around four. Apparently she'd just woken up, her temperature was down and she'd asked to speak to me. I don't know if it was my imagination, but she did look better. 'You look better,' I said, cautiously approaching the bed. I had a mask over my face and I felt faintly ridiculous. 'You've some colour in your face.'

'I feel a bit better,' Mam croaked. She made no attempt to get up; she just lay against her snow-white pillows and smiled at me. 'My back isn't so sore.'

'Good.'

Isn't it funny that no matter how well you know someone, it's always hard to make conversation in a hospital? It always strikes me as weird that the sick person is expected to do most of the talking. And so it was with Mam and me. All I'd come in to see was that she was looking better and, satisfied with that, I would

305

have sat there in silence with her. But she wouldn't let me. She asked about work, so I told her about Ed and Bridie. She'd always liked the sound of Ed and hadn't been a bit impressed when she'd heard he was seeing Sal. Now that they were broken up, she was happy.

'Maybe there's a chance for you,' she said slyly.

'Nah.' I flushed. I still hadn't told my folks about Marti being married and I certainly couldn't now. 'I'm still with Marti.'

'Oh.' Mam looked disappointed. 'Well, you certainly talk about Ed enough – ever since he started work you've brought him into conversation.'

'That's because you've asked about work,' I said back, feeling embarrassed. I shoved a smile onto my face. 'He's nice, but that's all.'

Mam nodded, giving her smile that said she didn't believe me. 'And Barbara?' she asked. 'Tell me.'

I gulped. The nurse was busy writing stuff down on Mam's chart. 'Nothing much,' I lied.

Mam eyed me.

'Honest.' I gulped out a very forced-sounding laugh.

'I know you better than you think,' Mam whispered. She closed her eyes. 'She wants to see you, doesn't she?'

I didn't say anything. I couldn't. How did she know?

'If it was me, I would never have bothered with the letters.' Mam's voice was getting softer. 'I would want to see you.'

I still said nothing. I didn't want to upset her.

'Well?' Mam asked.

She was expecting an answer.

'She does,' I muttered. 'But now it doesn't seem so important.'

Her eyes opened, slowly. She pinned me with her stare. 'It is important,' she said, stressing each word. 'If it makes you happy, it *is* important. You see her.'

'But—'

'Me and your dad want you to be happy. And don't worry about him, I'll talk to him.' She began to cough suddenly. The nurse shoved me out of the way. She fiddled around with buttons and switches while I gawped uselessly.

'Out,' she said sternly to me.

'No,' Mam spoke up, quite strongly. 'Just a few seconds more.'

The nurse glared at me as if it was all my fault.

'Maybe I'd better—' I indicated the door.

Mam beckoned me forward. 'I'll talk to Sean,' she said. 'He'll do anything for me now.' A quick smile.

It was the smile that did it. Love rushed up through me like a spring from the earth.

'You're my real mother,' I said earnestly. 'I don't *want* any other.'

Mam smiled. 'But think of her,' she said softly, 'missing out on you.'

Then she lay back and closed her eyes.

And it struck me suddenly what I'd spent my years missing out on. I'd missed out on this woman's love because I'd craved the love of a woman who'd given me away. Visions of Bridie holding on to her dead lover in the face of all others came to me. Now she was lonely and wished she'd moved on. I'd spent my time wanting what everyone else had, a real flesh-and-blood mother. And because someone who was meant to love me had given me away, I'd been reluctant to become involved with the love my mam and dad had to offer. Which had made me guilty. And lonely. And unhappy. And what was it all for? I was like Patrick Kavanagh in 'Raglan Road' with his unrequited love. And I had to stop it.

I had to accept love where I found it.

And it was then that I knew I could meet her.

And I could cope with her rejection.

But if my family objected, then she'd have to cope with mine.

Chapter Fifty-two

THE HOUSE WAS a state. Dad and I had spent almost every minute of the past week in the hospital and as a result there was dirt and dust and dirty clothes all over the place. On Saturday, I volunteered to spend the day tidying up. Mam was improving rapidly and was off the oxygen and I felt safe in missing a visit. I was busy trying to burn a shirt with the iron when the guy from the local flower shop appeared at the front door. He was carrying an enormous bouquet of flowers. 'Evelyn McCarthy?' he asked.

'My mother,' I said, as he handed me the flowers. There were lilies and roses and some purple ones that I didn't know the name of. 'Wow.' I caught a whiff of fragrant lily. 'She'll be thrilled with these.'

'And there's some here for a Vicky McCarthy?' The guy produced a smaller bunch. Twelve white roses tied with a white ribbon.

'Oh,' I smiled delightedly. 'That's me.'

'Can't have the mother getting flowers and not the daughter, eh?' he joked as he left.

I was still smiling as I brought the flowers into the kitchen and laid them carefully on the table. There was an envelope Sellotaped to each bunch and I decided to open the envelope on my mother's flowers first. It was pathetic, I know, but I wanted to enjoy the suspense of who'd sent me my flowers for a little while longer. I guessed they were from Marti because I hadn't heard from him all week, except a rushed phone call on Tuesday when he enquired about Mam.

Mam's flowers were from Bridie and Ed. *Get well soon from*

your daughter's slaves was written in Ed's large scrawl. I smiled, slotting the card back into the envelope. Ed in a flower shop? Bridie must have forced him into it.

Then it was the turn of the roses.

To the boss – we thought you could do with some cheering up yourself – Bridie and Ed.

Bridie and Ed.

'Bridie and Ed,' I mumbled, staring at the roses, trying to hide my disappointment from myself. 'Wasn't that nice.'

I stared again at the card as if somehow I could change the words. Then I muttered a 'fuck him' under my breath and then a 'fucking bastard'. Then I repeated both a bit louder, only stringing them together.

It made me feel a bit better.

'Yo, Toys Galore?'

I bristled. 'Is that any way to answer the phone?' I asked before I could stop myself.

'Hey!' Ed sounded delighted. 'It's Vicky. How about you? Things must be all right with you, seeing as you're finding find fault with me again.'

Despite myself I grinned. He had a point. 'Just rang to thank you for the flowers.'

'Ach, you didn't have to. We paid for them out of the money in the till.'

'What?'

'That was a joke,' he clarified. 'No, you're very welcome. How's yer ma?'

'Much better, thanks. We think she'll be out next week.'

'Aw, great.' Then he bellowed, 'Oy, Bridie, Vicky's ma is getting released next week!'

He made her sound like a mental patient. I hoped there weren't too many customers in.

The phone was taken off him. Bridie's breathless voice wafted down the line. 'Vicky, it's Bridie. How are you, pet?'

309

I smiled. 'Great, thanks, Bridie. Thanks for the flowers.'

'Not at all. Did your mother like them?'

'Haven't been in yet, but I reckon she will. And you shouldn't have got any for me – honestly – the roses must have cost you a fortune.'

She laughed slightly before replying, 'Not at all, sure they hardly cost anything.' She raised her voice. 'Vicky says thanks for the flowers, Ed!'

'Yeah, I know,' Ed yelled from somewhere in the background.

'She liked the roses,' Bridie called out. She came back to me. 'Well, listen, pet, don't rush back, I've got it all under control here. You take your time.'

'Ta, Bridie.' A sort of wistfulness for work washed over me. I missed them. 'I'll probably be back next week.'

'No rush.'

'Take care.'

'You too.'

'Bye.'

Ed yelled out a 'bye'.

I felt lonely when I hung up.

I felt even lonelier when I turned back to face the ironing.

Tommy and John and a few of the cousins arrived around lunchtime. Tommy had some food from his mother. He handed it to me with an apology. 'Couldn't stop her,' he said. 'She's a mad woman when she makes a stew.'

The others with him laughed.

'Ta.' I took the casserole dish from him and baulked at its weight. 'Jesus, how much did she do?'

'Enough for the lot of us.' Tommy indicated the rest of the cousins. 'We've come to help you clean up.'

'What?' I was stunned. I didn't need their help.

'Well, it's a bloody massive house.' John, without being invited, stepped into the hall. 'We figured you'd need a hand.'

The rest nodded and then at my lack of response looked

anxiously at me. I think they were waiting for me to throw a wobbler. Or do something completely weird like tell them that I would be well able to manage, thank you very much. And I desperately did want to do that. But I knew it wouldn't be very grateful. And to be honest, I hated cleaning. 'I guess I do,' I murmured with a bad grace. 'Come in.'

They didn't need to be told twice.

I guess they thought they were family.

'Just don't go into my room,' I warned. 'That's private.'

John was hoovering. Not very well, but he was doing his best. I wouldn't say he'd ever hoovered in his entire life. He was sitting on the sofa, pushing the hose of the hoover over and back, over and back.

'Great job.' I handed him a cup of coffee.

'Thanks.' He flicked off the hoover and wrapped his big hands around the mug.

'You're all very good to come over,' I babbled. I'd never really had a conversation with this guy. Every time we met, I tended to ignore him. But there was no ignoring him when he had planted his backside on our good sofa.

'It's no bother,' he said. He stared into his mug of coffee.

I made to leave.

'And to be honest, Vicky, I owe you.'

I turned back to face him. He was staring cagily at me, studying me. 'Owe me?'

'Yeah.'

Pause. I wondered if he was talking about . . . but nah, no one remembered stuff like I did. I wasn't going to let him *see* that I remembered.

'I've felt bad ever since that time when I told you you were adopted. You've never really talked to me since.'

'You told me I was ready made,' I snapped back.

He winced. 'Ready made,' he conceded. He was grinning a little at the word.

311

So much for pretending I didn't remember. 'It wasn't nice.'

'No,' he agreed hastily, flicking me a glance. 'I know it wasn't.' He put his coffee carefully on the floor. Then, biting his lip, he said cautiously, 'At the time I didn't *know* just how horrible; I was only a kid and you wouldn't play with us. We all thought you were stuck up. I only said it to get at you, but it was horrible and like, I'm sorry about that.'

I didn't know what to say. The whole thing had happened years ago. His apology made me feel a bit pathetic – I'd been the one that had borne a grudge for sixteen years against a twelve-year-old kid. Maybe I was the one that should be apologising. Only, I was useless at it. So instead, I stammered out, 'I wasn't really stuck up.'

He quirked his eyebrows.

'I wasn't,' I insisted. Again the sceptical look. 'I was scared of yous,' I admitted. 'You were all so tall and dark, and there was me, small and skinny. I didn't feel I fitted in.'

'All you had to do was play with us. We didn't care what you looked like.'

I startled him with a big 'Ha!' Then said smartly, 'Yeah you did. Tommy always pointed at my hair and yelled "Fire!"'

He tried to turn his snigger into a cough. 'Wow, I'd forgotten that!'

Maybe I should have too. Trying to regain some dignity, I said, 'Well, I haven't.'

'Obviously,' he said dryly. Then, in a gentler voice, he went on, 'Vicky, we were kids. All kids do that.'

'Maybe,' I said. 'But it hurt.' At his shamed look, I felt a bit guilty. 'Still.' I shrugged and tried to sound blasé. 'It was all a long time ago.'

I didn't convince him, let alone myself.

We stared at each other a bit more before I again turned to leave.

'We were jealous – right,' John said, sounding almost defensive. 'If you want to know why we did it – we were jealous.'

312

'Jealous?' I almost laughed.

'You had it all. We had nothing.'

The simplicity of the statement startled me.

'Here comes Miss Perfect with her perfect parents, we used to say.' There was a hint of bitterness in John's voice, despite his grin.

'Here come all my cousins with their *real* parents, I used to say.'

His grin faded. 'I'm sorry for telling you, Vicky.'

I was suddenly ashamed of the elephant in me that wouldn't allow me to forget things. OK, he'd been a nasty little brat, but I guess, in his eyes, I'd been a stuck-up, have-it-all unfriendly weirdo. And people changed. Well, all except me, it seemed. I gulped, made a Herculean effort to be nice. 'You did me a favour actually.'

'Huh?'

'D'you ever see that Steve Martin film where he's adopted by these black people and he can't sing or dance and, like, he's *white*?'

John began to laugh.

'And it's driving him mad that he can't fit in?'

John laughed harder.

'Well,' I grinned ruefully, 'that was me.'

'Must've been hell.' John was still smiling, though he looked sympathetic.

I shrugged. No worse probably than having an alcoholic father. No, I realised suddenly, it wasn't even in the same *league* as having an alcoholic dad.

'Friends?' John asked.

I liked the sound of that. But I didn't want to make out that I was dying for it or anything. 'Hoover this room properly and I'll think about it.'

'Deal.'

We shook on it.

* * *

313

The cousins left just before Dad came back from the hospital. It had been the nicest day I'd spent at home in a long time. They'd cleaned, polished and dusted so that the house was gleaming. They told me that if I needed anything just to call them. Tommy told me he'd see me the next day with more food. I waved them off, feeling a sort of happy bubble inside me. A sort of semi-belonging to this crowd of people who'd just invaded the house and seen into every corner of it. Not that I didn't want to repay their kindness sometime. Maybe when one of their parents got sick or . . . Jesus, I shook my head. What was I thinking? I didn't want anyone to be sick. Not anyone. I was just closing the door on Tommy when Dad drove up. He'd come back to see to the cows. A few of the neighbours had done the morning milking but Dad liked to do it in the evening himself. I envied Dad his ability to accept favours from people. He maintained that people felt good when they helped you out so it was a favour to let them.

I dunno if I totally believed that.

'How's my girl?' Dad smiled, half shyly, at me.

'How's Mam?' I asked the question I always did when he came home.

'Much better.' He walked by me into the kitchen, almost singing out, 'She'll be home next week.'

'That's brilliant.'

'Yeah. Yeah, it is.' Dad sat at the table and took off his coat. He slung it haphazardly over a chair and beckoned me forward. He suddenly looked serious. 'Vic, come here.'

I didn't want a heavy conversation. All week I'd been dreading this. Mam had obviously talked to him. 'Tea?' I tried to say lightly.

'No, sit down, Vic.' He patted the table. 'There's something I want to say.'

I stood. 'Yeah?'

'It's about all this business with your—' He stopped, waved his hand about and said quickly, 'The other woman. Your, eh, birth mother.'

314

'We don't have to talk about this now.'

'We do.' The intensity in his voice surprised me. 'Your mother had a word with me.'

'Yeah and she's sick, so it's emotional blackmail.'

'No.' Dad shook his head. Gulped. 'She's right. She told me some home truths and she's right.'

I stared at him. Again, he indicated a chair. I had no choice – I sat down, my hands clenched together in my lap and a sort of mantra running around my head saying, '*Don't fight, please don't fight.*'

Dad's brown eyes met mine. 'I'm not good at all this chat,' he began, flushing. 'But I guess there comes a time when it's time to say things.'

I nodded, not sure why I was nodding.

'There have only been two important things in my life, Vicky,' Dad went on. 'You and your mother.' Pause. 'And I nearly lost your mother because I was afraid to find out if something was wrong with her.'

He stared at me for a few seconds. I couldn't hold his gaze. My eyes dropped to my dirty nails and red hands.

'I'm not a brave man, Vicky,' he said finally. 'I don't like change. I like things to stay the same. I want your mother to be healthy and you to be here. And, well, you looking for this other woman was a lot of worry for me. It was, if I'm honest, rocking my boat a little too much.'

I stole a look at him. He was chewing his lower lip, a sign that he was agitated. When he continued, his voice shook slightly. 'I was afraid we'd lose you, you hardly came home as it was. I was afraid, *am afraid*,' he clarified, 'of you meeting this woman.' He swallowed. 'I mean, she's bound to be younger than us and have more energy than us.'

'So?'

He looked hopelessly at me. 'Can you not see?'

'What?'

'Well, blood's thicker than water at the end of the day. You'll bond with her, want to go with her. You'll—'

'Dad.' I couldn't believe I was hearing this. 'Do you really think I'd drop you and Mam like that?'

'You don't like it here, Vicky, or you'd visit a bit more often.'

Oh God.

Oh shit.

'See,' he said, his face sad, 'you can't even answer me.'

I struggled to find the words to explain. But it was hard when I'd spent years ignoring it myself. 'I do like it here, Dad,' I began. 'But it's hard for me.' He gawped at me, not knowing why it was so hard to live in a comfortable house with good parents. 'See, I know I only landed here from somewhere else and I can't settle anywhere until I find the somewhere else.'

Nothing. He looked blank and hurt and puzzled.

'D'you remember that time, after college, when I went travelling?'

A nod. 'And you were only meant to go for a year and—'

'Well, I did it to see if I could find out where I *should* be.' Pause. 'And there was nowhere I could connect with. Imagine, the whole world and . . .' I gave a shrug. My eyes filled and I whispered, 'Nothing.'

'Aw, Jesus.' Dad shook his head. 'Aw, Jesus, aw, Vic, don't cry.'

'I'm not.' I shook my head. 'It's just hard. I need to know, Dad.'

He bowed his head. Muttered, half to himself, 'I've been so selfish, Vic.'

'That's not what—'

'Yes,' he interrupted. 'All this mess is my fault.'

'No—'

''Twas me that wouldn't let your mother tell you that you were adopted.'

His admission was a hammer blow. I stared dumbly at him.

'She wanted to but I, well, I forbade her to discuss it with you.'

For some reason, I'd thought they'd had an unspoken agreement between them – that by not telling me they could somehow

316

preserve a fantasy that I really was theirs by birth. But his admission sickened me. An order. He'd ordered the other me to be wiped out. My history. He'd wanted me to spend years in Steve Martin limbo. Despite what I'd said to John, finding out after years that I'd been adopted had been horrible. Overnight, my world had crumbled. I realised, to my horror, that I'd lived a lie for twelve years, I'd lived a borrowed life with borrowed parents. My whole story was just a borrowed history. And it was scary, not to know who I was. And that shock could have been prevented.

'I've never thought of you in all this. Well, not properly anyway.'

His words hung in the air. I couldn't think of anything to say to him. In that moment, I wanted to kill him.

He looked desperately at me. 'We were so happy, see, I just didn't want to jeopardise things. But then you found out you were adopted and I've been scared of this moment ever since.'

'Scared?' My dad scared.

'Yes. Because I don't want to lose you, Vic. You're my girl, always will be. But I know I can't stand in your way. Your mother's right – our job was always to see that you were happy and if this . . .' He faltered, coughed and continued, 'So, what I'm saying is, Vic, if you want to meet this woman or whatever, well, I'm not going to stand in your way.'

After that there was a pause. Then he got up from the table and began to put on his jacket.

'I'm scared of change too.' I said it without thinking. 'I'm probably like you like that.'

He smiled briefly but said nothing. He reached for his cap and jammed it onto his head.

'I have my mother's phone number with me,' I blurted out, desperate for him to show that he meant what he'd said. Desperate to show him that there was nothing to be afraid of. 'And before I meet her, I've to ring her.' I swallowed hard. 'Would you be there while I did? Would you like to talk to her?'

I couldn't read his expression. I had the sudden fear that I'd gone too far, expected too much.

'I'm scared of talking to her on my own,' I admitted.

His expression softened. He attempted a smile. 'Well,' he said slowly, 'we can't have that.' He reached across the table and caught my hand. 'We can't have that.'

Chapter Fifty-three

THE PHONE RANG.

And rang.

Slowly, I became aware that it was still dark out. A sliver of light from the landing threw shadows on the floor of my room. It had been a late night. When Dad had got in from milking the cows, we'd talked frankly for the first time in twenty-eight years. He'd apologised again and promised to be right by my side when I rang my mother. I'd told him that I'd never leave him or Mam but that I just couldn't continue to live in a limbo where my past was a huge black hole.

He'd tried to understand, he really had, but despite everything, he didn't get it. He thought that because I was loved that it should be enough.

The phone kept ringing.

I heard the floorboards creak as Dad got out of bed. 'Jesus,' he was muttering as he padded downstairs, 'if this is a wrong number, I'll go fecking mad.'

I grinned and pulled the covers back up around my ears. Poor Dad, just when he was looking forward to a good night's rest, he was being awoken by a bloody telephone.

He would be in awful form in the morning.

Downstairs, he'd picked up the phone. After shouting a bad-tempered 'hello' into it, he'd gone silent.

Completely silent.

Why would he go quiet if it was a wrong number?

And if it was the right number, why would anyone ring us

at – I glanced at the alarm clock – four a.m.?

Uneasily I wondered if anything was wrong.

I waited to hear Dad come back up.

Only he didn't.

He wasn't talking either.

With a sick kind of dread filling me up, I got out of bed and padded towards the top of the stairs. Dad was holding the receiver to his ear and he looked white.

'Dad?'

It took a second before he registered my voice and when he did, he slowly raised his eyes to mine.

'What's wrong?' I could barely get the words out.

'Here.' He held the phone out to me. 'I can't make out what they're telling me.'

I remember every step I took down. It was like I was travelling in slow motion. I wanted to know yet I dreaded it. 'Hello?'

'This is St Anne's Hospital – is that Vicky?'

The hospital? 'What's wrong?' I whispered.

'She was fine today,' Dad said, half to himself. 'Tell them she was fine today.'

'Sorry for ringing so late,' a soft voice spoke from the other end, 'but it's important that you and your father come in. I'm afraid' – she paused and my stomach rolled – 'that your mother has had a stroke. It's very serious.'

'Stroke?' I was falling down, into somewhere. 'I don't understand.'

'She suffered with angina; unfortunately the pneumonia weakened her heart.'

'Angina?'

'Please come as soon as you can.'

I didn't know how we would. Dad was in no state to drive. I couldn't. I cursed the lack of courage that allowed me to back out of learning. 'We'll be in soon,' I said.

The woman told me she was very sorry and hung up.

Neither of us said anything for a moment.

320

Dad was by the door, staring at his hands. Softly, he asked, 'Is she very bad, Vicky?'

'I don't know, Dad.' I bit my lip. 'But I think so.'

He began rubbing his face, over and over.

'We'll have to get dressed and go in,' I said. 'Go up and put some clothes on. I'll ring for a taxi.'

He stood there, shaking his head.

'Dad.' I gave him a gentle push. 'Please go up.'

He began to shamble towards the stairs. I watched him go. When I was sure that he'd gone into the bedroom, I began to leaf through the phone book, looking for taxi numbers. Then I remembered Tommy. It suddenly seemed important to have someone who cared with us. Someone who could look after us. With a shaking finger, I began to dial.

Tommy answered.

'Tommy,' I said. 'Sorry for ringing so early but it's Mam.' And I couldn't say any more. Just that sentence was enough. I didn't want to say 'ill' or 'stroke' or anything that would make the reality any harder. Anything that would make me cry.

'I'll be there in fifteen,' Tommy said. 'You get yourselves sorted, OK?'

'Yeah.'

The line went dead.

In a complete daze, I walked back upstairs.

Chapter Fifty-four

W E WERE USHERED into the IC unit. Mam was hooked up to machines and tubes and all sorts of things that beeped and blinked. Dad and I tried not to look too shocked.

'It was sudden,' the nurse explained sympathetically. 'We had just put a monitor on her when it happened. No one expected this – she was doing so well.'

'And now?' I asked.

The nurse looked nervously at her chart. 'A doctor will talk to you,' she answered.

I watched her scurry away, feeling a sick dread in my chest.

Dad had barely listened. He was holding my mother's hand and squeezing it hard.

'You'll be fine, Evelyn,' he whispered. 'I know you will. And when you come home, I promise I'll do all the cooking. Everything.'

'I dunno if that will entice her to come home, Dad,' I joked feebly.

He laughed. 'As you can hear, Vicky's with me. We had that little chat. The one you asked me to have with her. Sure, Vicky will tell you herself.' He beckoned me over.

It took every bit of courage I had to catch my mother's hand. It still felt warm and soft and the nails were short and filed, just like they'd been every other time in my life. All the millions of times I'd held that hand. It was as familiar to me as my own. She'd guided me across the road, she'd dragged me kicking and screaming into school, she'd hugged and tickled and loved me.

'Hiya, Mam.' Like Dad I squeezed her hand, hoping for a squeeze in return. There was nothing. Her face looked calm and peaceful on the white pillow. I thought of the last time I'd talked to her, of how she'd been making plans to come home and sort out the flowers for Lisa Sweeney's wedding. And now . . .

'Tell her,' Dad urged. 'Tell her about our talk.'

'We talked,' I said, giving her hand another squeeze. 'And Dad says that you and he will be there when I ring Barbara.'

'I did,' Dad said, his jolly tone sounding forced.

'And we sorted a lot of stuff out tonight,' I went on. 'Lots of things. I even told him why I went travelling that time – it wasn't to get away from you or to hurt you. It was to find out where I came from. That way, I can belong – see.'

Dad was staring at me. 'She always knew that,' he said softly.

'And, Mam,' I went on, trying to sound cheerful, 'you won't believe this, and don't die of shock or anything.' I ignored Dad's intake of breath. Mam loved black humour. 'Well, I'm talking to John now. He came and did the hoovering today at the house.'

'Were you not talking to John?' Dad asked, surprised.

'Dawww,' I said. I squeezed Mam's hand again. 'Imagine not knowing that, Mam. You were right, Dad is hopeless.'

Dad pretended to cuff me.

We both laughed a little self-consciously.

Dad turned back to Mam. He gently lifted up her hand and kissed it. 'I love you, Evelyn,' he whispered. 'And even though you bawled the socks off me today over Vicky, I'm glad you did. We're closer now, aren't we, Vic?' He reached over for my free hand.

'Yep.'

And somehow, I get the feeling that that was all she was waiting to hear, because suddenly the little line that was monitoring her heart began to jump about all over the place and alarms began to ring. Dad and I watched in a stupor as nurses and doctors rushed into the room and began shoving us out. We watched through the doors as they worked frantically to bring her back.

We watched as the activity died down and heads were shaken. We held each other because we both knew that she was gone.

'She had angina,' the nurse tried to explain to me. 'But it was under control.'

I looked blankly at her.

'She'd had tests up in Dublin a few months back and they said that it was quite stable,' the nurse went on. 'But anything can trigger an attack and unfortunately . . .' Her voice trailed off.

I got up, not understanding. Dad was sitting, head bowed, in a chair. Tommy had his arm about his shoulders and was trying to coax him to drink something.

'Angina?' I said. 'What's that?'

Dad had been crying. His eyes were red and swollen. Tears had made tracks across his face. I felt a huge rush of protectiveness for him. I caught his hand and he stood up and hugged me fiercely. 'She didn't want you worrying,' he said brokenly. 'It was under control – she had tests done and everything.'

'But – but I don't understand . . .'

'It's like chest pains,' Dad went on, his voice muffled. 'But they don't do any harm to you. She was getting pains and so she had tests.'

'When?' I couldn't take it in. Why hadn't they told me?

'A few months back – before Christmas and then just after Christmas. She was taking it easy.'

Which was why he'd been cooking and cleaning. And I'd never wondered why, just accepted it. 'But I would have wanted to know,' I said. I couldn't even get up any anger.

'You would only have worried,' Dad said. 'And it wouldn't have done anyone any good.'

'I could have come home more often,' I said, horror at the way I'd neglected her suddenly coming into focus. 'I could have rung her. I could have helped her out.'

'You didn't know,' Dad said. 'And she wanted it that way.'

But I'd been so selfish, so self-centred, so obsessed with how I'd felt.

'She wanted it that way,' Dad repeated, hugging me. 'It made her happy that you didn't know.'

I pulled away from him. I pulled way from Tommy. I turned and walked out of the hospital.

I ignored their calls; I just had to be on my own.

Chapter Fifty-five

ALL THAT DAY and the following are blurry. It was as if I stared out at the world from thick syrup, as if every move took an age. My thoughts were muddled, people spoke to me, shook my hand, and when they'd gone I couldn't even remember what they'd said or what I'd said back.

Dad coped by milking his cows and walking his fields. He tried to speak to me but I couldn't answer. Every time he looked at me, guilt for the way I'd behaved swept through me and I'd be angry at him for not telling me so that at least in the last few months I could have made some effort to come home.

And worst of all, I found it hard to accept that I had no second chance. Life had changed and there was no going back. It all seemed very harsh somehow. There was no court of appeal, no page to re-read and understand, just a huge empty hole where my mother once had been.

Around lunchtime, Tommy tapped on my bedroom door. 'Your dad wants to know if there's anyone you'd like to ring,' he said, holding out the cordless phone. 'He says that maybe not everyone looks at the deaths.'

I hated the way he talked like that. Yesterday my mother had been coming home, now she was a few lines in a newspaper.

At my lack of response, Tommy said, 'I can ring people for you if you like – your workmates and that.'

'If you want.'

I didn't care who came.

'Anyone else?' Tommy asked.

Sal would know, her mother would ring her. Marti would probably need a call. I'd have to do that myself. 'Give it here,' I said, reaching for the phone. 'I'll ring my boyfriend.'

Tommy handed me the phone. 'She's coming to the church tomorrow night at five, Vic, and her funeral is eleven the next morning.'

I flinched at his words.

'It's awful hard to believe, isn't it?'

I gulped. I liked that he'd said that.

'Anyway . . .' Tommy made vague motions with his hands. 'I'll make any other calls you need made.'

I barely remembered him leaving.

Marti's mobile rang and rang. I prayed for him to answer. There was no way I was leaving a message. It just didn't seem right. Eventually, some woman with a warm-sounding voice picked up. 'Hi, Marti's phone?'

'Yeah, hi, is Marti there?'

'Eh, no. Is that a reporter? He's expecting a reporter to ring.'

'No, it's Vicky. Can you get him for me?'

'Are you a singer?'

'Please,' I said, 'will you get Marti for me?'

'He's not agenting any more – just in case you're a client.'

'I'm not . . .' I stopped. Marti not agenting?

In the background, a kid yelled out something. The woman said, 'Leo, I'm on the phone.'

Leo began to whinge, 'Mammmmyyy.'

'Kids,' the woman laughed into the receiver. 'So, Vicky, was it?'

I hung up.

My biggest fear in life has been rejection. Any sort of rejection would send me spinning into a depression. When I'd started applying for jobs, I'd curse the boss that sent me the 'sweet-but-no-thank-you' letter. When I failed to get on with the kids in college, I'd hated them all for what I perceived as their rejection of me.

And until I met Marti, I'd steered clear of falling in love. Sure, I'd go out with guys, but the minute they started to get serious I was out of there faster than a hare at a coursing meet. It wasn't that I intentionally set out to hurt anyone, it was just that falling in love for me was akin to bungee-jumping. I'd get far enough to look over the edge of the cliff but I'd never take that final plunge.

Maybe I'd figured that Marti would be a safe bet – I mean, how much commitment can you get from a guy with a kid and an ex-wife? How much can a guy that's so in love with his career give you? But in the end, it wasn't what he'd been able to give me, but what I'd actually been able to give him. For some reason, I'd fallen for him. There was something about him that had attracted me and kept me dangling. I'd even slept with him, for God's sake. And now, just like I'd always feared, I'd been dumped. But the hurt and the sadness weren't there.

Maybe I was just numb.

Maybe I felt I deserved it.

Chapter Fifty-six

T HE CHURCH WAS packed. Mam's coffin, piled with cards and adorned with flowers, stood at the top of the church. As I passed it, I rubbed my hand along its length. I couldn't believe that she was actually in there though I'd seen her myself, lying still and cold in the funeral home the night before. Dad ushered me into a seat at the top of the church, as neighbours and friends looked on.

The night before had been a nightmare – everybody shaking hands with me. Bridie had hugged me and it was the closest I'd come to breaking down. Ed had shook my hand solemnly and then leaned forward and kissed my cheek. 'Hard luck,' he'd muttered before moving on.

Hard luck indeed.

The mass began. Prayers were said. Hymns were sung. I got up and did a reading. I spoke too low, too fast, and I don't think anyone could make head or tail of it, but then again, maybe that was fitting. I certainly couldn't understand why she had been taken from us. From my initial numbness, a slow anger was burning. Anger at the whole world for letting her die.

Dad had persuaded me to sing 'Be Not Afraid' – my mother's favourite hymn at communion time. And I sang it for her, my voice strong. I didn't want her to be afraid all alone. When I'd finished, I'd glared out at everyone.

The priest gave a nice talk, though he told *everyone* that I'd been adopted. I cringed with embarrassment but no one else seemed to notice. Then at the end my father got up and said a few words. His little speech wasn't prepared but he spoke with such love that he could have given a recipe for mince pies and there wouldn't have been a dry eye in the house.

'I'm a lucky man,' he said at the end. 'I've known one of the most wonderful women on God's earth. And I didn't deserve her and I think himself up there finally realised that and decided to take her away.' He paused and I saw him swallow hard. 'But I had thirty-five years with her and even now, when I'm so heartbroken, I don't regret how much I loved her.' Then he took out a handkerchief and dabbed his eyes. When he came down to me, he clasped my hand and smiled.

The graveyard looked nice underneath the spring sunshine. I stared around at all the people that had come and felt a sort of gratitude to them. Bridie and Ed had closed the shop as a mark of respect and were there; Sal and Mel, dressed to kill in short tight miniskirts, were there too. They'd obviously made up their differences and I wondered who'd made the first move. Sal probably. And right beside them, dressed head to toe in tight black leather, was Marti. Even clad in conservative colours, he was attracting a lot of attention. Maybe it was his earrings or his spiky hair. He also looked as if he hadn't attended a funeral in years. He hadn't a clue what was going on and he virtually gawked as they lowered my mother's coffin into the ground. He whispered something to Sal, who rolled her eyes and said something like, 'Well, what did you think the hole was for?'

I resented his presence. How could he come after what he'd done to me? I only hoped he had the sense to make a quick exit.

The priest finished up and announced that a cup of tea would be available back in the house. I had the sudden panicky thought that there was no food laid on until I remembered Aunt Julia and the others working late into the night. It hadn't dawned on me to question what they were doing but obviously they'd been making sambos and cakes and stuff. It was nice of them. Very nice. I felt a lump in my throat at the thoughts of it.

People began to wander away as Dad and I stood side by side accepting condolences.

Bridie and Ed came up. 'Sorry again, luvvie.' Bridie clasped my hand. 'Oooh, I'm so sorry.'

'Dad, this is Bridie and Ed, the people from the shop.'

'Nice to meet you,' Dad said, sounding very formal. 'Vicky has told us a lot about you.'

'Now that *is* worrying,' Ed said wryly and Dad smiled.

'Are yous going back to the house?' I asked.

They looked at each other.

'Please,' I said, and meant it. I suddenly felt that I was closer to these two than anyone else. I barely knew the neighbours and Sal and Mel weren't exactly people you'd turn to in a crisis.

'We will so,' Bridie said. 'We'll see you later.'

'Ta.'

I watched them wander off – Bridie in her brown coat and black headscarf and Ed in his black jeans and jacket.

'What is he doing here?' Sal demanded, arms folded, staring after them too. 'Honestly, as if things weren't bad enough.' She turned to me. 'Vicky, I'm so sorry about your mother. It's terrible.'

'Awful,' Mel agreed, blowing a plume of smoke into the air. 'Sorry about your wife, Mr McCarthy.' She held out her hand with its inch-long fingernails to my bemused father.

'Thank you very much.'

'It's Mel,' Mel said.

'Mel,' Dad uttered, trying not to stare at her fishnet legs.

'We'll see yous back at the house,' Sal said to me. 'It won't be for long though – we've copy deadlines to meet. Sorry to rush. Listen, I rang Marti to tell him, I didn't know if you'd be able to or not. Anyway, he came down with us, so maybe you could get someone to bring him back.'

'Vicky.' Marti arrived over. 'Hey, sorry about your mother.'

He enfolded me in a claustrophobic hug. Sal and Mel slunk away. 'I tried to make it down yesterday but things have been mad.'

'I'll bet they have,' I replied through gritted teeth. How dare he pretend things were normal? I pushed him off and said to Dad, 'This is Marti, a guy I know.'

'Not Marti the—'

'No,' I said hastily. 'Another Marti.'

Marti was looking strangely at me.

'Pleased to meet you, Marti. Thanks for coming,' Dad said.

'No probs, Mr McC.' Marti nodded. His leather squeaked with every movement. 'Hey, Vic, was that Bridie and Ed I saw earlier? I'll catch up with them. Talk later, Vic, right.' He squeezed my hand and was about to kiss my cheek when I turned away.

'Strange sort of fella,' Dad remarked.

'Mmm.' I couldn't say anything.

'And that Mel, she's a bit strange too.'

'D'you think so?'

'She looks like a Dublin girl, that's for sure.'

I smiled. That was my dad all over.

He wrapped his arm about my shoulders. 'We'll be lonely but we'll get through this, Vicky – all right?'

I think he almost believed it.

The house was thronged with people. All I wanted to do was go up to my room and escape them but years of tradition couldn't be ignored. I went from group to group, nodding at their remarks about my mother and only half hearing them. I tried my best to avoid Marti. There was no way I could face him. His loud voice could be heard every now and then floating across the room.

Eventually, I managed to get outside. After the stuffiness and noise of the house, it was a relief to escape into the space and relative silence of the countryside. Beyond the back door, fields of green stretched in every direction. I had a sudden flashback of me as a kid. I'd always run into the centre of a field and turn around and around, until eventually I'd fall with a thump to the ground. Then I'd lie, eyes wide open, and watch the big blue sky spinning like a top and I'd convince myself that I could feel the world turn. Mam used to laugh at me.

So that's what I did. I ran to the nearest field, spun around and around and around, taking my anger and fury out on myself. Eventually, I hit the ground and the world swirled about me. Only it wasn't half the fun I remembered. I thought I was going to be sick. I squeezed my eyes shut to block out the sensation.

'Are you OK?'

Ed's voice startled me. My eyes shot open and Ed's shape was there and was gone. There and gone.

'Oh, Jesus,' I groaned and closed my eyes again.

I was aware of him sitting on the grass beside me. 'Are you drunk?' he asked, his voice a mixture of amusement and concern.

'I'm not about to get drunk at my own mother's funeral,' I snapped. The spinning in my head was slowing down. I took a chance and opened my eyes. Ed was peeling the petals from a daisy and looking into the middle distance. 'Sorry,' I muttered.

'It's OK,' he answered.

'Anyway, what are you doing out here?' I hauled myself into a sitting position beside him.

'Escaping from the dirty looks I'm getting from your friend and my ex-girlfriend.'

'Oh dear.' I allowed myself a smile.

'You?' he asked.

'Just spinning,' I muttered.

'Spinning?'

'Yeah.'

He didn't ask any more and I liked that. 'My mother used to laugh when I'd do it,' I said then, wanting to talk about my mother. Wanting to make her live, I guess. 'So I . . .' My voice trailed off.

'You'll miss her.' It was a statement rather than a question. I nodded.

'I remember you saying that your folks thought everything you did was great.'

'Yeah.' My eyes filled up. 'Maybe it was because I'm adopted.' I waited for him to say something about me being adopted, but he didn't. So I went on. 'No matter what I did, they thought it was great.' My lip wobbled. 'Especially her.'

He shifted uncomfortably. I don't think he wanted me to cry. He attempted to change the subject. 'My ma does that too.'

'Yeah?'

He grinned slightly. 'When my brother and I turned twenty-one, Dad gave us a pile of money. My brother invested it and made a bloody fortune and so when my turn came, it was a big deal, you know.'

'So what did you do?' My tears were receding. I couldn't cry in front of him. 'Buy over our toy shop?'

He laughed a little. 'Naw. I knew I couldn't compete so I didn't bother. I bought a motorbike and went travelling. Saw the world. Came back with nothing but a pair of jeans and my bike.'

'Jesus!' I gulped out a laugh.

'The old fella went spare.' There was laughter in his voice that made me smile. 'Mam told him that travel broadens the mind. Told him I was like the prodigal son in the Bible.'

'Guess you were.'

'Naw.' Ed shook his head. 'The prodigal son got the fatted calf, I just got earache.'

I smiled.

'Still' – Ed looked wistful – 'it was the best two years of my life. Saw everywhere.'

'Travel is great,' I said, wrapping my arms about my knees. 'I did it too. I feel guilty about it now – I hardly kept in touch with the folks at all.'

'Aw, well . . .' Ed shrugged. Paused. 'You can't change the past, I guess. That's what my mother says, anyway.'

334

I didn't reply. All the postcards I could have sent. All the phone calls I could have made—

'Where was the best place you visited?' Ed interrupted my thoughts.

I didn't have to think twice. 'Easter Island.'

He looked stunned. 'Me too. Fucking eerie, isn't it – all those statues!'

'And in the middle of nowhere. That's what I liked about it.'

'Yeah.' He nodded vigorously. 'And food? Where was the nicest place you ate?'

I had to think about that one. I hadn't exactly eaten that well. 'Vietnam,' I eventually pronounced.

'Naw.' Ed waved his hand dismissively. 'Nothing like an Irish breakfast.'

'Oh ye of unadventurous taste buds!'

He grinned.

There was a silence.

'So, they were glad when you came home – yeah?'

'Thrilled.' I bit my lip. 'That's when Mam started making the strawberry cheesecakes – she thought it was cosmopolitan.'

He wasn't too sure whether to laugh or not.

'I'm going to miss her so much, Ed.' My voice had gone weepy again. 'I feel so lonely without her – there is nobody who's going to love me like she did.'

'Ach, you'll find someone.'

'No.' I shook my head. 'You don't understand until it happens to you.' My face crumpled up and big fat tears rolled down my cheeks.

'Hey.' Ed wrapped an arm about my shoulder. 'How come I always manage to make women cry?'

I hardly heard him. 'I think it's because I could be a kid with her, see. I could behave badly or anything and she'd still love me. With her gone, I can't do that any more.' A tear plopped onto my hand. 'Now I'm all grown up and it's so lonely. It feels so lonely. She was always there, see, but now, there'll be no one.'

'Your dad?'

'It's not the same.' Snot was coming out my nose and I had no option but to wipe it on my sleeve. 'It's not the same.'

'Naw,' Ed said softly. 'It's not.' He hugged me to him.

It seemed the most natural thing in the world to wrap my arms about him and cry my heart out.

It felt good to cry. To just let go. Of course, it was madly embarrassing that I had to do it in front of, let's face it, an employee. But Ed wasn't just an employee. He was my friend.

When eventually I stopped, I became acutely aware of his arm about me. Of the way he was rubbing my back. Of the way his chin rested on my hair. I could hear him breathing and I could smell the fresh smell of his aftershave and the clean scent of his clothes. It all seemed a bit too intimate for my liking.

Without trying to hurt him, I gently pulled away. I scrubbed my eyes and laughed, mortified. 'You must think I'm a wreck,' I babbled.

'No.' He looked straight into my face. 'Are you feeling better?'

'A bit,' I nodded. 'Thanks.'

'No probs.' He reached out and brushed some hair away from my face. 'You need to tie up your hair again.'

'Yeah.'

'It looks nice though, that way.'

There was a tender look on his face that made me squirm. I had to turn away and there was silence for a bit. In the distance, I could hear the sounds of cars and animals and music – the world going on as if it was just an ordinary day.

'What's angina?' I asked suddenly. I turned to Ed, who was busy decimating another daisy. 'My mother had it and I never knew.'

'Angina.' Ed lay back on his elbows, his long legs stretched in front of him. He frowned, thinking. 'Well, it's not generally considered hugely serious. Chest pains, basically. Your mother

336

would have been on medication.' He paused and glanced uncertainly at me.

'Go on.'

'Well, it can be a warning of a future heart attack.' And he talked of stable angina and unstable angina. And he made it understandable for me – which was good. I needed to understand things.

'You would have made a good doctor,' I said when he'd finished.

He winced.

'Why did you give it up?'

He looked away from me.

I touched his sleeve. 'It's just, you know, you were so good with Domo that time. And now, explaining to me. And you must have really wanted to be a doctor to pay for it yourself.'

He shrugged. He hauled himself back up to sitting. Pulling up a fistful of grass he began filtering it through his fingers. 'I did,' he mumbled. Then he looked right into my face. It was a strange moment. Sort of like the air before lightning. For some weird reason my heart started to pound as Ed reached out towards my face.

'I—'

'So this is where you got to!' Marti hailed us from the back door of the house.

We both jumped.

'Here's Marti,' Ed said, jumping up and dusting himself down. 'He'll cheer you up.'

'No!' I jumped up too. 'I can't see him today. I can't.'

'What? But—'

'Just, just tell him I'm too upset to talk.'

Without waiting for Ed to reply, I turned about and ran off.

337

Chapter Fifty-seven

I DIDN'T GET back until after five. I walked the farm, something I hadn't done in years. Everything looked so peaceful, so much the same that it hurt me to realise that nothing in the rest of the world was going to change. I wanted to yell out to somebody. I wanted to say, 'Hey, Evelyn McCarthy is dead – don't you realise that?' But even I knew I'd look a complete loon.

The sun was still beaming down as I turned into the back gate. Many of the cars had gone and I was glad. The only ones left were Tommy's and Julia's. As I entered the kitchen, I heard him. Marti was regaling somebody with stories of Boy Five. I didn't notice Dad sitting alone at the table until he said, 'That Marti fella wants to talk to you.'

'Well, he'll have to wait.' I sat down opposite Dad.

'He's been waiting long enough. He even turned down a lift with Bridie and Ed to wait. And if you don't talk to him soon, Tommy won't be able to take him back either.'

'Can't he get the bus?'

Dad stood up. He came across to me and rubbed my shoulder. 'Don't let this make you hard, Vicky. Just remember how wonderful she was. Now' – he looked at me – 'will I bring in your boyfriend and let him talk to you?'

So he knew Marti was my boyfriend.

'I have nothing to say to him.'

'So let *him* talk.' Dad walked towards the door. 'I'll get him. He seems worried about you.'

Worried my arse, I thought. Worried about himself more like. Worried about how poor bereaved Vicky will take rejection. Worried about when to tell her. Well, I'd make it easy for him. I'd dump him.

'Vicky?'

I turned towards Marti as he stood uncertainly by the door. 'What?'

He looked hurt at the way I was behaving. 'I just wanted to talk to you, to say how sorry I was. I didn't get a chance all day and Ed said you were upset so I decided I'd better hang around.'

'There's no need – I've Dad.'

'Yeah, but—'

'And if you want someone to talk to, try Linda.' I hadn't meant to say that – it just sort of spewed out. The anger I felt at Mam dying was a loaded cannon.

'Linda?' he paled. 'What do you mean?'

'She's back, isn't she?'

'No.' Pause as I glared at him. 'Well,' he gulped, 'not exactly.'

'What the fuck does "not exactly" mean?' Before he had a chance to answer, I stood up. 'D'you know what? I don't care. I don't care. My mother has just died and I don't need this kind of shit with you.' He flinched with every syllable. 'Get out!'

He stood his ground.

'Get out, I said!'

'No.' He sat down. 'I have to explain.'

'Why?'

'I wasn't going to tell you – not now.'

'Oooh, that's big of you – so what were you going to do? String me along until I was over all this and then tell me?'

'Aw, Jesus, Vic – I don't think—'

'Get out!'

'She's asked to come back – I haven't said yes yet.' His voice, loud at the best of times, was louder than I'd ever heard it. I'm sure my Dad and Tommy heard him too.

'But you're going to?'

He looked hopelessly at me.

'I mean, you've given up being an agent, you've obviously dumped the lads. Just what Linda wants – eh?'

Marti bowed his head. 'Cliff got a deal on his own – he dumped us.'

That was a bit of a shock; I hadn't expected that.

'And yeah, I've given up the agenting.'

'Because of Linda?'

He glanced at me. 'Leo wants her back. The kid will never forgive me if I don't make a go of it.'

'That's just an excuse.'

'No.' He stared at his hands. 'He's so happy now, Vic, thinking we'll get back together. I can't take it away from him.'

'So you're dumping me, is that it?' The words stuck in my throat.

'Every kid needs a mother, Vic – you're the one that told me that.'

He had me there.

'You'd have liked it – wouldn't you?'

Tears came but I blinked them back. 'I had a mother – a very good one.'

'Yeah.' Marti gulped and looked at me. 'And so had Leo.' He stood up and sighed. 'I was the fuck-up.' It was a few seconds before he spoke again. 'I never told you, Vic, but I remortgaged our house to finance Boy Five. We all would have had to move in with me ma. That's why Linda left.'

I stared at him.

'I owe it to Leo to try to be a good father.'

He was right, of course.

'For once in my life, Vic, I think I'm doing the honourable thing. I think I'm ready to be a dad and I'm awful sorry you have to be hurt.' He paused. Said softly, 'I really liked you, you know.'

I couldn't speak. Now the grief of being dumped was mingling with the grief of being left behind. I'd really liked him too. I dunno why.

'Sorry.'

I nodded, not wanting to cry in front of him. 'Just go.'

He stood uncertainly by the table for a second or two and then turned and slowly began to walk away. I glanced up at his retreating back and felt – I dunno what – regret or sorrow or something, not just for me but for him too. 'Marti,' I said, surprising myself.

He turned back to face me.

'Good luck,' I gulped out.

A small smile. 'Ta, Vicky.' Then he grinned. 'I reckon, with my parenting skills, Leo's gonna need luck more than I will.'

I tried to smile back. There was a silence.

Marti broke it. 'Well, goodbye then,' he said softly.

'Bye, Marti.'

I heard him leave with Tommy about five minutes later.

Dad came in and made me some strong tea. He didn't ask what had happened and I was glad of that.

Chapter Fifty-eight

ONCE THE FUNERAL was over, it was back to reality. In a way, it was a relief. I could, at last, try and get my head together without having to think about funerals and entertaining people. But getting on with things meant that I had to face the fact that she wasn't coming back. And the whole idea of that seemed such a betrayal. I decided to take another week off just to be with Dad. But he said that the sooner he got used to what it was going to be like without her, the better for him and the better for me too.

'And anyway,' he finished, 'you've a shop to run. You're the manager.'

Even through his grief, I could hear the pride in his voice.

'Bridie can do it for me.'

'Not as well, I'll bet.' He patted my hand. 'You go back and get used to things and I'll stay here and get used to things.'

He was braver than I was. 'I'll ring every day.'

He smiled. 'I'd like that.'

Tommy drove me back to Dublin. He hardly spoke on the way up and when he did it was only because I'd spoken first. When we reached the flat, he took my bags out of the boot and asked if I'd be OK dragging them all the way upstairs.

'I'll be fine.' I picked up my suitcase. 'Cuppa?'

'Naw, ta.' He shrugged. 'Maybe we'll do lunch one day?'

'Yeah. That'd be nice.'

'And if you need anything, Vic – just call, all right?'

Jesus, he was such a nice guy. Mam had been mad about him and now I understood why. 'Tommy, thanks,' I said softly. 'You've been great. Aunt Julia has been great. John even.'

He smiled at my inclusion of John. Then in a perfect take of his mother's voice, he croaked, 'Sure, aren't you family?'

I smiled.

'Take care,' he said, giving my arm a brief rub. He climbed back into the car. 'Talk soon.'

As I waved him off, I realised that he was right. I *was* family. Maybe not related by flesh and blood, but in the end, what did that matter? These people loved me. I was beginning to realise just how important that was.

Sal, Mel and Lorcan were in the flat when I got back. Sal and Mel could be heard squealing from the front door. When I actually got inside, I found them poring over some article that Sal had written. Mel was gleefully rubbing her hands. Then, tapping her nose, she said, 'Never let me down yet. I could smell a story in a vacuum.'

'Smells don't exist in vacuums, darling,' Lorcan said laconically. He was lazily flicking through the *Sunday Business Post*.

'No.' Mel folded her arms and glared at him. 'The only thing that seems to exist in a vacuum is our social life.'

'Hiya, folks,' I said, attempting a smile.

There was instant silence.

Sal began shoving her piece into her folder and I have to say, I was insulted. I had more on my mind than her bloody pieces.

'Hey, how's things?' Mel asked, her voice dripping concern.

I made a big deal of putting down my case so that I wouldn't have to answer.

'I am so dreadfully sorry.' Lorcan proffered a manicured hand. 'Losing a parent is a dreadful thing.'

'Yeah. Thanks.'

They all stood looking at me.

343

'Cuppa,' Sal said, seizing on the word like a lifeboat. 'Would you like one?'

She'd never, ever offered to make me tea before. 'Ta.'

I sat down on the sofa beside Lorcan and inhaled a whiff of his noxious aftershave.

'Isn't it funny how we Irish always make tea to console people?' Lorcan said in his slow drawl. 'And to be honest, all it does is keep you awake at night, tossing and turning.'

'That kind of observation we don't need, thank you,' Mel said stiffly.

'Of course.' Lorcan flashed me an apologetic smile. 'Of course.'

Sal handed me my tea and there was more silence. I soon realised that things must have been booming until I'd entered. Sal and Mel, not being the most empathic of people, hadn't a clue what to do. 'I'll have this in my bedroom.' I stood up. 'I'm tired.'

'Oh.'

'Oh, OK.'

'Bye now.'

Their relief was like a tidal wave washing through the room.

Chapter Fifty-nine

WHEN I GOT up for work the next day, I found Sal sound asleep on the sofa, her laptop on with a screen saver zooming to and fro across the screen. It was obviously an important story because normally Sal would never sleep in full make-up. She'd probably spend the whole day exfoliating her skin now.

I tiptoed out of the flat, not wanting to wake her and endure some more stilted conversation.

It was hard walking to the bus stop, getting on the bus and walking to work. Hard to get used to the normality of it. Hard to comprehend that I'd be doing this for ever now without the security of my mother at home. A security I'd always taken for granted. I blinked back tears before unlocking the shop and heading into the office.

Ed and Bridie were there.

'Hi yez,' I said awkwardly.

'Vicky.' Bridie enfolded me in a hug. 'Welcome back. Welcome back. We're delighted you're back – aren't we, Ed?'

'Aye,' Ed nodded. 'We've even got you a present to cheer you up.'

'Ed bought it,' Bridie said firmly. 'It was his idea.'

Ed flushed. 'Ach, it's nothing really – but I know you like them, so . . .' He opened the fridge and produced a chocolate cake. 'Here.' He virtually shoved it at me.

'Oh.' I bit my lip as I looked at the cream and the chocolate swirls. I hadn't eaten well in days and I didn't think I'd even manage a slice of it. But it touched me something rotten. 'Thanks. Thanks a lot.'

'It's OK.' He touched me briefly on the arm.

There was a silence.

'Will I cut it for you?' Bridie asked.

'Yeah. Sure.' I knew I sounded completely flat and unappreciative, but I couldn't help it. It was too much effort to put on a show.

I sat down on the sofa as Bridie cut us three large pieces. The largest she put on my plate. 'There now,' she cooed, 'build you up.'

I had to force it into my mouth, piece by piece. I was afraid I'd hurt them if I left it. Bridie made me some tea and began chattering about events in the shop. Finally, after giving me a rundown from stock-taking to the state of her legs, she said, 'And do you know, Ed ended up in Casualty last week?'

'Jesus, Bridie.' Ed rolled his eyes and stood up. 'I think I'll open up.'

Bridie laughed. 'Crashed into the front window because he was giving some kids a demonstration on the skateboard. Walloped his head.'

Despite myself I grinned. 'Where? The front or the back?'

'Back,' Ed muttered. 'Knocked meself out.'

'Oh, right,' I grinned. 'Because you know most bangs to the front of the head are harmless. A med student told me that.'

'Ha, ha.'

We smiled at each other. My heart gave a slow roll and I felt myself blush. I don't know why – it was his eyes or something.

'Well, we could have done with a med student that day.' Bridie crossed to the sink to wash out her cup. 'I thought I'd have to give him the kiss of life.'

Ed put his hand on his heart. 'If you'd have kissed me, Bridie, I'd have died and gone to heaven.'

'Go away out of that,' she giggled. 'Flatterer.'

Ed winked at me and left.

'Gone to heaven,' Bridie said fondly after him. 'He doesn't even go to mass. Prefers the pub, he says.'

'Probably the wine tastes better in the pub,' I remarked.

Bridie giggled, shocked. Then she flapped her hand at me and the whole thing reminded me so much of my mother that tears pooled in my eyes.

'Aw, Vicky, aw, love.' Bridie crossed to me and wrapped her thin arm around me. 'Don't upset yourself.'

'Sorry.' I wiped my eyes hastily. 'Sorry.'

'There is no need to be sorry, love. No need at all. If you want to cry, you go ahead and cry. It'll take time before you're back to yourself. Losing someone you love is the worst thing in life, I think.'

'It is. I didn't appreciate her, Bridie.'

'Arragh,' Bridie half-laughed. 'What child appreciates their parents?'

'And she wasn't even my *real* mother.'

'I know, luvvie.'

Of course she knew. The bloody priest had told her.

'I've spent my whole life wanting my real mother.'

'Oh, luvvie.' Bridie knelt in front of me. Her knees popped but she didn't seem to notice. 'D'you know, even if she was your real mother, you'd have wanted her to be different. You'd have wanted her to be like your best friend's mother or like the one on the television. That's just the way it is.'

'No. No it's not.'

'It is.' Bridie nodded vigorously. 'Sure, I always wanted my mother to be like Veronica Lake.'

'Who?'

'An actress. Very beautiful. My mother, on the other hand, was small and fat and dumpy.' Bridie looked sad. 'I was so embarrassed by her.'

'And did you feel guilty about that when she died?'

'Part of me did. But I had loved her too – just like you loved your mother.'

347

But when my mother died, I wanted to say, I'd been trying to trace the other woman. I'd been planning to phone her. To get to know her. To meet her.

I despised myself for it.

I flicked off the computer and, after pulling on my jacket, picked up Ed's to bring it down to him. Bridie had left early and there was only Ed and me left. I'd spent most of the day upstairs, inventing things to do because I hadn't felt able to face people. I knew grumpy customers would upset me and as for happy kids with their happy mothers . . .

Ed was on his way up the stairs and we met halfway.

'Ta.' He took his jacket from me. Asked quietly, 'How you doing?'

'Not bad.' I managed a smile. Apart from almost crying in front of Bridie, I wasn't too bad.

'It's great you're back.' Ed began to walk in front of me down the stairs. 'I was going slowly mental on my own with Bridie. Jesus, she kept cleaning stuff all the time.' A bewildered look at me. 'Is that normal?'

I laughed. 'I dunno. You're the doctor.'

He flinched slightly and then tried to smile. 'Not any more,' he said lightly. He turned to unlock the door.

'You never told me why you left,' I said then, suddenly remembering. 'D'you remember, I asked you—'

'Will I put on the alarm?'

I thought perhaps he hadn't heard me. 'Why did you give up medicine?'

A pause, just long enough to be uncomfortable, before he answered, 'Just, you know, decided it wasn't for me.' He walked past me to the alarm and began keying in the code.

'Is that why you left London?'

He froze, one finger on the keypad. I saw him deliberately relax his shoulders before keying the numbers in.

'Well?'

'Well what?' A grin. 'Are we ready to go?'

He didn't wait for me to answer. He pulled open the door. 'After you, boss.'

He wasn't going to tell me and I guess it wasn't any of my business, but there was something weird going on. He'd been brilliant with Dominic, brilliant explaining to me about angina. In fact, his face had lit up just telling me about chest pains and medication. And now, he looked miserable. And I found that I didn't like to see him upset. 'It might help to talk.'

'About?'

'You know what about.'

He stared down at his trainers and bit his lip. 'I'll head off now – OK?'

I watched him leave. I remembered the night in the pub when he'd said that he and I were the same. That we wouldn't tell people things. I'd changed since then, I realised. Sometimes telling people stuff was good. Talking with Lucy had opened me up, made me accept that I was adopted. OK, I still cringed every time someone found out, but I didn't think it was my fault any more. Even if I never met my mother now, meeting and talking with Lucy had made me happier, less paranoid.

I wondered if Ed would ever meet someone he could talk to.

I hoped he would.

I really did.

Part of me was sorry that it wasn't me, though.

Chapter Sixty

FRIDAY EVENING THREE weeks later, Dad and I were watching the last part of *The Late Late Show*. Pat Kenny had just introduced his last guest of the night. A celeb who'd given a child up for adoption when she was just fifteen.

'I think I'll head to bed,' I said.

'This might be interesting.' Dad jabbed the remote at the telly. 'It might help you when you ring your own . . . birth mother.'

'Oh—' I picked up my cardigan and, without looking at him, said, 'I've decided not to bother with all that.'

'What?' He sounded shocked. 'But, but I thought . . .'

'It's better all around,' I went on. 'I mean, she gave me up. You and' – I bit my lip – 'well, you and Mam were my parents – really.'

'Vicky!'

But I was gone.

I got up around one the next day. Dad was downstairs, pottering about the kitchen, probably making himself some lunch. He normally left a sambo for me with instructions as to where he'd be if I needed him.

I pulled my cardigan over my PJs and went downstairs to grab a cuppa and bring it back to bed with me. Every step I took echoed in the hallway below. Jesus, if I'd hated coming home before, it was even worse now. It was as if the house was in mourning for Mam too. All the rooms seemed so empty and big without her to fill them. Dad felt it too, I think, which was why he never seemed to eat in the kitchen any more.

He was in the kitchen when I got down, however. Sitting at the table, with a giant mug in front of him. On a plate beside the mug was a doorstep of a ham and cheese sandwich.

'Thought you'd be up around now,' he said. 'There's tea in the pot, if you want it.'

'Ta.'

As I was pouring the milk into the mug, he said, 'Vicky, about what you said last night—'

'Dad, honestly—'

'Your mother wanted you to do it, you know.' His voice was soft. Whenever he talked about Mam, his voice went like that. 'She told me so herself the day before . . . the day before . . .' He couldn't say it. 'She told me,' he finished.

'Well, I've changed my mind.'

'Can I ask why?'

No, I wanted to say, you cannot. 'Can a person not just change their mind?' I picked up my mug and eyed the sambo he'd made for me. Ham and cheese. 'Thanks for this.' Picking up the plate, I headed towards the door.

'You might want this,' Dad said.

'What?'

'This.' He held out a slim black book. 'Julia found it last week when she was . . . you know . . . going through your mother's things.'

'What is it?' I eyed it suspiciously. I didn't want to get upset. As far as I was concerned, I was doing well at holding myself together. I hadn't made a mistake in work at all that week. Ed and Bridie were being brilliant and I had only thought about Marti forty-two times, which was only seven times a day.

'She wanted to give it to you herself,' Dad said, caressing the little book. 'And I wanted to do it the way she would have done, but with what you said last night and the way you're feeling, I

351

think now might be the right time for you to have it – here.'
Again he proffered the book.

I put down my breakfast things and slowly crossed towards
him. I didn't think a book would change anything. I was not
going to ring my mother, I was not going to meet her. As far as
I was concerned, I had a mother and now she was gone.

'She wanted to give it to you when you were meeting the
other woman,' Dad said as he watched me slowly open its pages.

To Barbara, with love from Evelyn and Sean.

The sight of her handwriting made the now familiar lump
rise in my throat. I realised suddenly that it was a book of me.
A photograph album charting my life from aged three months
to last year. There were pictures of me smiling, of me riding
my first bike, of me in full school uniform, of me making my
communion, my visit to the zoo, my confirmation. On and on
and on. Loads of happy photos of a much-loved kid. Each photo
was marked and dated and, underneath, my mother had written
a short description of where we'd been when the picture was
taken.

'Oh, Dad,' I whispered, turning page after page.

He stood up and put his arm about my shoulder. 'She wants
your mother to know what a wonderful girl you are,' he said.
'To make her feel that she shared her life with you.'

'But—' I took a deep breath to steady my voice. It was no
use, it came out all wobbly. 'But I feel like I'm *betraying* her for
looking.'

'Not at all, not at all.' Dad's reassuring, loving voice made
me begin to sob. 'Sure, you're betraying her by not looking.'

'Nooo.'

'Yes.' Dad caught me by the shoulders and looked hard at
me. His own eyes were glistening now. 'A mother wants her children to be happy. This is her way of making you happy. Don't
throw it away.'

'But you . . .'

'Were a selfish old man.' He shook me gently. 'I want you to

352

ring this lady. I want to be there when you do. I want her to see what a wonderful job Evelyn did when she brought you up. I want her to remember Evelyn as fondly as we do.'

'Oh, Dad.'

He pulled me to him. 'And I want you to cheer up. Cheer up and start living again. That's what she would have wanted, you know. Go back to Dublin and go out and get drunk—'

'Dad!'

He laughed. 'It's what she would have wanted,' he repeated. 'And Jesus,' he went on, a smile in his voice, 'you never did what she wanted when she was alive, so it's the least you can do now.'

I laughed and cried at the same time.

Chapter Sixty-one

MY FINGER SHOOK as I dialled. Sweat made the receiver slippery. Behind me, Dad was pacing up and down the room, breathing heavily. To be honest, I was more worried about him than I was about myself. He hadn't slept at all the night before – I'd heard him going to and from the kitchen – and I reckon this phone call was to blame.

I'd told Lucy to contact Barbara to say that I'd be ringing on Sunday afternoon, so it wasn't as if the phone wouldn't be answered. My heart really started to pound as the final number was pressed. I listened to the tiny clicking sounds on the line as the phone connected with the phone in Limerick.

'It's ringing,' I said to Dad. My voice was shaking. Part of me felt guilty at the excitement I felt.

Dad froze in the act of walking to the window. He came back and laid a hand on my shoulder. I wished he wouldn't. It was making me claustrophobic. I moved slightly so that I could shake him off without him knowing I was shaking him off. With every ring, my heart hammered more and more furiously until I actually thought I was going to get sick.

'Hello?' A tiny voice from the other end. Then a 'Hello?' Slightly stronger.

'Is that Barbara?' I was surprised that my voice worked.

'Yes.' Pause. 'Is that—' There was a sniff. 'Vicky?' My name was whispered.

'Yeah.'

'Oh my God.' The woman at the other end sounded half

afraid. Then, after a small pause, she went on, 'It is so wonderful to hear your voice. It's so wonderful.'

It was almost like a dream. I couldn't quite take in the fact that I was speaking to someone actually connected to *me*. 'I'm glad to hear you too,' I said. 'It's hard to believe actually.'

'It is, isn't it?' Her voice wobbled. 'I just feel so lucky to have you contact me. I've thought about it for so long.'

'Really?'

'Yes. Since I let you go.' Her voice was husky, like mine. 'And your letters,' she went on. 'Your last letter was beautiful. I cried for days after I'd read it.' She was beginning to cry again. 'Your parents sounded like wonderful people.'

I couldn't speak.

'And' – pause – 'I was sorry to hear about your mother.'

'Yeah.'

'Will you pass that on to your father? Tell him I'm sorry.'

I put my hand over the receiver and said to Dad, 'She says she's sorry about Mam.'

Dad nodded and patted me on the shoulder.

'And will you tell him,' Barbara went on, her voice quivering, 'tell him "thank you" for making me so happy.'

'She says thanks,' I said to Dad. 'Thanks for making her so happy.'

Dad nodded. 'OK.' Then, obviously feeling that that wasn't an adequate response, he said, 'Can I talk to her?'

My heart lurched. 'What?'

'I'd . . . I'd like to talk to her,' Dad said.

What the hell was he going to say? We'd decided last night that he wouldn't *have* to talk.

'Eh,' I said to Barbara, 'my dad is here. He wants a word.' Without waiting for her response, I handed him the phone.

'Eh, Barbara,' Dad said, sounding very businesslike, 'this is Sean McCarthy.'

Barbara said something at the other end.

Dad shifted about uncomfortably. 'Thanks,' he responded.

Then, after swallowing hard, he said, 'I just want to thank you too. No one has ever given us anything quite as precious as our Vicky and, well, I want to thank you for that.' Then he handed the phone to me and left the room.

Barbara was still crying, saying how wonderful it was to have Dad say that. Then I started to cry and agree that it was wonderful. In the end, we agreed to meet at a time to be decided by the social workers.

When I put down the phone I was shattered.

Dad was out in the fields, his boots making huge, squelchy footprints in the muddy soil. He didn't hear me as I came up beside him.

'Thanks for telling her that, Dad. You made her very happy.'

Dad turned to me. 'I just asked myself what your mother would have done,' he answered.

Then he put his arm about my shoulders and together we walked the land until the sun began to bleed across the sky.

Only that Mam was missing, it was almost a perfect moment.

Chapter Sixty-two

'GUESS WHAT? GUESS what?' Dominic burst into the shop. He danced in front of us in a pair of shorts about two sizes too small for him. 'Guess what?'

'You're getting cabbage for dinner,' Ed said, causing Dominic to crease up laughing.

'No, silly,' he giggled. 'Me and my mammy are getting a new house.'

Bridie looked anxiously at me and I looked down at the ground. Sylvia was making her way towards us and she had a thing about Dominic telling her 'private business'.

'Isn't that *great*?' Dominic beamed.

'Hey, Sylvia,' Ed called to her. 'Congratulations on the house.'

'Jesus, Ed,' I whimpered, wanting to kick him. 'Will you shut up!'

'So he's told yez.' Sylvia was actually *smiling*. Her earrings jangled as she turned from one to the other of us. 'And I bleeding told him not to.' She pretended to cuff Dominic, who danced away laughing.

'Mammy says that I can have my breakfast there and that I can stay in it.' Dominic chatted cheerfully. 'She says that we will watch TV in it and the TV will be in a different room to my bed. And that I can have my own bedroom. *And* that we might have a garden. And maybe a dog. And—'

'That is wonderful.' Bridie, having gained courage from Sylvia's smile, clapped her hands. 'I think we'll have to get you a big lollipop to celebrate.'

357

'Naw.' Sylvia reached into her big black leather bag, the one she always carried with her. 'I, eh, figured yez might prefer this to celebrate.' A bottle of wine was put in front of us.

'A woman after me own heart.' Ed picked up the bottle and grinned.

Sylvia flushed and stared down at her fake-tanned legs and white stilettos. 'Yez have been so good to Domo and me, letting us come in here, giving Domo stuff. I know I've been a cow but—'

'Not at all,' Bridie said. 'We've loved having you!'

Ed looked sidelong at me and raised his eyebrows. I suppressed a grin.

'Well, I've still been a cow,' Sylvia said. 'But yez know, it's hard when other people think you can't provide for your kid. You feel a failure.' She smiled ruefully. 'It makes you hard, you know?'

'You are a lovely girl,' Bridie lied sincerely. 'We were always delighted to see you, weren't we, Vicky?'

'No,' I said, grinning. 'You used to scare the shit out of me!'

Bridie 'tisked'.

'I had to be scary,' Sylvia explained earnestly, looking for the first time the young twenty-something that she was. 'I was scared yez would report me for not being able to mind Domo properly. I didn't want to lose him to some do-gooder.' She shot a look at Domo, who was describing to Ed what exactly he was going to have in his room when he got it. Her face softened. 'Kids are bleeding great, aren't they?'

Ed was promising Domo that when he got his room, he'd give him his very own wrestlers to put in it.

At that moment, I thought Ed was bleeding great.

'Where the hell is he?'

Albert O'Neill's furious voice made me jump. Down at the other end of the counter, Bridie tittered nervously. 'Oh, Mr O'Neill, you gave us a fright, there.'

O'Neill ignored her. Instead, he turned bulging blue eyes on

358

me. 'Where is he?' he demanded. In his hand, he carried a copy of *Tell!* It was rolled up tightly.

There was something about O'Neill holding a copy of Sal's magazine that made my stomach lurch. 'He's bringing up some stock,' I said, as calmly as I could. 'He'll be with you in a minute.'

'I can't *wait* a minute!' He began to stride towards the storeroom, ignoring the stares of curious customers.

Ed chose that moment to appear, his arms piled high with Bey Blade accessories.

'Put those down!' O'Neill shouted.

A few women who'd been browsing made a hasty exit. I could see sales slumping all over the place. 'Please don't shout,' I called over. 'We are open, you know.'

'Then close up!'

It was an order.

As Bridie scuttled towards the door, I watched as Ed calmly put down the boxes he'd been carrying.

'Yeah?' he asked his dad. There was major hostility in his voice and a sulky look on his face that I'd never seen before.

'You've done it again, haven't you?' O'Neill jabbed the magazine. 'Just when I give you one last chance, you decide you're going to throw it right back in my face, aren't you?'

'I dunno what you're talking about.'

O'Neill began to heavy-breathe. He looked as if he wanted to throw a punch. Ed, meanwhile, stood stock-still, his hands by his sides.

O'Neill seemed to square up to him until they were almost nose to nose.

'I think we'd better go,' Bridie whispered. 'Let them sort it out themselves.'

'We'll be in the pub,' I called out.

Neither of them took any notice.

Bridie and I exited the shop without our coats. As we stepped outside, we could hear O'Neill telling Ed that he was a complete and utter waster.

359

I felt so sorry for him at that moment that I would have gone back to defend him, only Bridie yanked me out the door and slammed it behind us.

We passed a newsagents on the way to the pub. Issues of *Tell!* were splattered all over the window. It was hard for us not to notice the gorgeous picture of Ed that dominated the front cover. It was a recent one – he was wearing his Ireland football jersey and he was laughing into the camera. His teeth gleamed white and his eyes, fringed with dark lashes, were as cute as hell. Underneath was the banner headline – *Is there a doctor in the house?*

'I have to buy that,' I said suddenly. I rummaged about in my purse, found the three euro I needed and barged into the shop. Grabbing a magazine from the rack, I paid for it.

'You must be shocked,' the newsagent said sympathetically. 'Working with him and all.'

Ignoring him, I rejoined Bridie in the street and opened the magazine. More pictures of Ed with an attractive brunette. He looked happy. The headline across the page: *Mental Medic.*

Bridie was peeking over my shoulder. 'Isn't that a nice photo,' she cooed. 'He should be a model.'

He had been a model apparently.

A model prisoner.

As I read the sensational piece, my heart sank. I mean, I was shocked, but at the same time, I felt so terribly sorry for Ed. He was a decent guy despite the magazine's claim that he'd beaten up his hospital boss so badly that the man had needed stitches.

Ed O'Neill, the article read, *was one of the most promising young medics in the renowned Great London Hospital for Children.* There was then a big technical bit about what exactly Ed had been specialising in. *Then, one evening,* the piece went on, *as a dispute arose over how to treat a sick child, Dr O'Neill accused his superior of negligence. The next evening, Dr O'Neill went to his superior's office and witnesses heard a heated exchange of views. There was the sound of a violent fight and Dr O'Neill had to be pulled off his boss. The hospital discharged*

Dr O'Neill and a case was brought against him for assault. He served four months in prison.

Ed O'Neill is the son of toy baron Albert O'Neill and there are reported difficulties in the relationship between father and son . . .

I froze as I read it. I could not believe it.

There had to be some mistake.

'Oooh, there has to be a mistake,' Bridie whispered.

The article was Sal's.

Somehow I knew it would be.

'I'm going home.' I shoved the magazine at Bridie and ran and ran and ran.

Sal was with Mel when I found her. Both of them were drinking tequila slammers in our local.

'Hey!' She patted the seat. 'Come join us.'

'Have a scoop,' Mel said and they both cracked up laughing.

I hated both of them in that instant. But I really, really hated Sal. How could she do that to Ed? OK, he'd made a mistake, but he'd paid for it. Paid for it with four months of his life in an English prison. Paid for it by serving under me in the toy shop.

'You shouldn't have written that piece,' I said, my whole body beginning to shake. 'It was mean and you'll ruin his life.'

Sal looked incredulously at me. 'He ruined it himself.'

'Just because he dumped you—'

'Oh, please!' Mel rolled her eyes and looked at me as if I was a ten-year-old. 'Vicky, I do not use my magazine to settle romantic scores. Please!'

'Well, Sal does!'

Sal eyed me with such disdain that I wanted to curl up and die. People were beginning to look in our direction and I knew they'd think I was the looney one. I told myself to stay calm.

'Vicky,' Sal said, with such smarminess that I could have drowned in it, 'when you told me Ed O'Neill was coming to work in his father's shop as a plain old worker I knew something was up. I mean, what sort of a father does that?'

'So we decided that she should go out with him,' Mel pronounced gleefully. 'Only he was useless, wasn't he, Sal?'

'I mean, I fancied him but, you know, he was just a story at the end of the day. And yeah, he was useless – he refused to talk about his old man. Refused to talk about his old job.'

'Refused to shag *me*!' Mel said indignantly and they both cracked up again.

'So we had to do a little footwork,' Sal went on. 'We talked to every bloody hospital in England and eventually someone said something. And then we located the old girlfriend who gave us photos. And it was easy from there.'

'And Sal is now working for me!'

They clinked glasses.

'Smell a story in a vacuum,' Mel said loudly.

I stood, as if in a vacuum myself, staring at the two of them. A sudden vision of Sal pumping me for info at one stage flashed in front of me. *Oh*, I'd said, *he doesn't get on with his dad.* I felt nauseated. 'You cold bitches,' I said through gritted teeth. 'How could you?'

'Oh, don't get all self-righteous on me,' Sal said scornfully. 'You're not so hot yourself!'

'Sorry?'

'Who's the girl that goes out with guys and dumps them when they get too serious?'

'I *don't*!'

'Oh, yeah.' Sal turned to Mel. 'Ron only got her an engagement ring and she legged it.'

She was twisting the whole thing. 'At least I didn't write about him in a magazine!'

'And who went globe-trotting for five years and didn't even send me a card and then' – Sal turned to Mel again – 'she ended up on my doorstep with her "I'm your buddy" routine. And moved *in*.'

'Not nice,' Mel said as if I wasn't even there.

'And she calls *me* cold!'

I felt as if I'd been slapped and, much as I wanted to run, I couldn't.

'Let's get one thing straight,' Sal said, pinning me with her stare. 'It's my *job* to write stuff about people. OK, I might hurt them, but it's only a job. *You* do it as a personality trait.'

'I do not!'

'You slag off Troy who has the hots for you. I mean, any guy that's worth it, you treat like shit.'

'Fuck off!'

'Now, ladies.' The barman was approaching with an amused grin. 'Put down the handbags!'

'You are a cold bitch, Sal. A cold bitch.'

'No.' Sal raised her glass, mocking me. 'I just know where I'm going. Do you?'

She couldn't have said anything worse. Of course I didn't. I never had. Which was probably why I'd liked being around her. And, in a rare flash of insight, I realised that that's what had attracted me to Marti too. His certainty. His drive. And the realisation of it made all the pining for him disappear. I was suddenly free of him. And free of Sal too.

'I know where I'm going all right,' I said, hating that what I had perceived as friendship should end like this. 'And it's as far away from you vultures as I can get.'

They both cackled loudly as I turned on my heel and left the pub.

I packed everything I had. I cursed and swore as I dumped all my belongings into a small case and five large plastic bags. And I cried. Tears for a friendship that I'd lost. Or maybe it had never been there to begin with – I dunno. I mean, she was right, I had never written to her when I'd been travelling, I hadn't told her about the search for my mother and I hadn't expected her to comfort me when my mam died. What sort of a friendship did we have at the end of the day?

And that made me cry even more.

I rang a taxi after I'd lugged all my stuff into the corridor. There was no way I could carry it back to the shop.

Troy met me on the stairs. He was with some weird-looking girl, both of them dressed in shiny Lycra catsuits. Troy looked like the Spire in O'Connell Street.

'Hey.' He raised a shiny arm in greeting. 'How's the finest thing in the apartment block?'

'Fine.' I smiled weakly. 'How's the space cadet?'

He laughed. 'Not bad. You going away somewhere?'

'Leaving,' I said.

'Aw.' He looked disappointed. 'Gonna miss your smart remarks bigtime. That Sal one is no fun at all.' He held out a hand. 'Good luck and may the force be with you.'

'You too.'

I watched as he and what had to be his girlfriend walked away.

Then I turned and shoved my keys into Sal's letterbox.

I found Bridie back at work. The shop had reopened for business.

'Hi,' she whispered.

'Is O'Neill gone?' I whispered back.

'Both gone,' she said.

'So why whisper?'

Bridie shrugged. 'I don't know. It just seems right. Oh Vicky, what did you think of that awful story?'

'Awful,' I said. I dumped my bag down behind the counter. 'So awful that I've moved out.'

Bridie looked horrified. 'You and Ed?' she said faintly. 'Living together?'

'Oh, Jesus! No!' Despite my shock at the day's events, I began to giggle. 'No! No! No!' I waved my hand about. 'Oh, Bridie!'

She looked confused.

Her confusion made me laugh harder.

'Out of my flat,' I spluttered eventually.

She looked even more confused.

'Sal, the girl who wrote the piece, is my flatmate.'

'Your journalist friend?' Bridie was horrified. 'Oh no!'

'Oh yes.' I sat down. 'Bitch!'

'So where will you go?' Bridie asked anxiously.

I hadn't thought that bit out yet. If the worst came to the worst, I'd bunk down in the shop. 'Dunno. Somewhere.'

'Well,' Bridie said slowly, 'if you like, you can stay with me for a while. I've a spare room.'

'Really?'

'I know we work together but I'll keep out of your way. Now, you've seen my house, it's clean but a bit old, I suppose. I mean, you probably like all this modern furniture and my house isn't like that. Not like that at all.' She raised anxious eyes to me. 'But you'll be comfortable there and, well, I'd like your company, Vicky.'

'And I'd like yours, Bridie.'

She blushed with pleasure. 'Oooh.'

We sealed it with two chocolate muffins.

That evening, after Bridie had cooked us both dinner, we sat inside and watched television. She'd fussed around me all through dinner and then she'd fussed over Ed.

'What'll we say to him if he comes in tomorrow?' she'd asked.

I shrugged. 'Let's see what happens first.'

'But, I mean, do we stand by him?'

'*Of course* we stand by him,' I said. 'You're the one that's always going on about how wonderful he is!'

She took no offence at my sharp tone. Instead she smiled delightedly. 'Oh, I am glad.'

Coronation Street came on. One of the characters was dumping her boyfriend and he was crying and begging her to reconsider. 'Bridie,' I asked suddenly, 'd'you think I'm a cold person?'

Bridie looked confused. 'What?'

'D'you think I'm a cold person?'

'Is it too warm in here? Have I the heating up too high?'

'No.' I bit my lip. 'Forget it. It doesn't matter.'

She peered across the room at me. 'Is something bothering you, pet? You've been very quiet today altogether. I know we've had a bad day and I know you've had a bad time recently but today you've been very quiet and now you feel cold. Are you sick?'

'Sal said that I was a horrible person,' I gulped. 'I just want to know what you think.'

'The cheek of her!' Bridie sounded like my mother. 'And her writing horrible stories in the papers. The cheek of her. You, Vicky, are one of the least horrible people I know.'

Bridie knew hardly anyone.

'If you had a boyfriend and he asked you to get engaged and bought a ring and everything, and you dumped him and he kept ringing you up and crying, wouldn't that be a horrible thing to do?'

Bridie cocked her head to one side. 'Not if you didn't love him. It'd be for the best, I'd say.'

But I had loved Ron. I'd just been terrified of loving him. 'But what if you did love him?'

'Then maybe, yes, it wasn't nice, but everyone has reasons for what they do and most of the reasons are not horrible ones.' She looked keenly at me. 'I'm sure you had your reasons.' She crossed to a sideboard and, opening it, drew out a bottle of whiskey. 'You need a drink.' As she handed me an enormous glass of whiskey, she said softly, 'And you are not horrible, Vicky. For one thing, you make me smile every day and' – she paused and blinked rapidly – 'you make a lonely old woman feel wanted and valued.' She clinked her glass with mine. 'Cheers.'

'Cheers.'

We smiled at each other.

Chapter Sixty-three

NEWS OF ED'S prison escapades was all over the papers the next day. More people crawled out of the woodwork to give their slant on the whole affair. Prisoners who'd done time with him said that he'd been a quiet enough guy that you just didn't mess with. They'd no idea, they said, of who he really was. He played music a lot, they said. More pictures appeared and the journalists seemed to have gone out of their way to find ones of him staring morosely into space. About five or six hacks set up camp outside our shop and refused to budge.

Ed never arrived into work.

I rang his home about midday to be greeted with the answering machine.

'Ed, this is Vicky. Bridie and I just want to say that we don't care what you did in the past. Like, it was a bit of a shock and all' – Bridie frowned at me for saying that, but there was no point in pretending we were OK with it – 'but we still want you to come back.'

At two o'clock, just as I arrived back from lunch, O'Neill rang. 'You and Bridie can hold interviews for a new position,' he said without any small talk. 'Put a note in the paper tomorrow.'

'But Ed—'

'Is gone,' he finished.

'Why?'

'Is that meant to be funny, Vicky?'

'He's the best salesman in this shop,' I said desperately. 'Since he's been here, we've doubled our profits at least.'

'He's a waster. He got a chance and he blew it. I warned him if it happened he was out on his ear. Now' – his voice had a 'don't-mess-with-me' tone to it – 'the last time I looked, I owned the shops. My decision is final.'

The line went dead.

I rang Ed on and off all that day and there was no answer. For some reason, I found that I wanted to talk to him. I couldn't bear the idea that Bridie and I would never see him again. I didn't want him to be just someone who'd passed through my life. With a pang, I realised that I wanted him *in* my life. I wanted to laugh with him, to know what he was up to. I wanted to see his orange jacket and have a laugh with him. I didn't want our friendship to end. The toy shop wouldn't be a happy place without him, which meant that, sooner or later, I'd have to leave.

I think Bridie felt the same.

'Maybe we'll head to his place after work,' I said.

'You go,' Bridie answered. 'I think you might know the right things to say to him.'

I gawped at her. 'If anyone will, you will. Sure he tells you everything.'

She blushed and stared intently at the till. 'Ed is not the sort of man that tells anyone anything,' she said. 'And he's never once told me how cracked he is over you.' She looked up. 'But he is. You go.'

I opened my mouth and couldn't think of a thing to say. Eventually, what came out was, 'That's ridiculous!'

'He never stops talking about you. He buys you cakes. He even bought you those flowers when your mother was ill.'

'What?'

'I only paid for ones for your mother. You told me you got an extra bunch. They weren't from me.'

I suddenly felt scared. 'So?'

'He'll listen to you,' Bridie said gently. 'Call over.'

I wasn't sure I wanted to now.

In the end, the choice was made for me. The phone rang just as we were closing up for the day.

'Hi, Toys Galore.'

I heard someone at the other end swallow hard.

'Ed, is that you?' I turned my back to the gaggle of reporters outside. I'd swear some of them could lip-read.

'Yeah.' He sounded down. 'Listen, I'm sorry about all this hassle. I dunno how you feel about—'

'We want you to come back,' I said. 'I reckon you had your reasons for what you did.'

'Yeah, I did, but they don't sell newspapers.' He laughed slightly. 'Anyway, I just want to apologise. I *was* going to tell you, d'you remember the day of your mother's funeral?'

I gulped. 'Yep.'

'Well, I bottled it.'

'Can we meet?' The words tore out of me. This was not going to be goodbye.

'Aw, I dunno . . .'

'Please?'

He hesitated.

'I'm staying at Bridie's.' I gave him directions. 'We can all meet up there.'

'All?' He sounded taken aback.

'Yeah – you, me and Bridie.'

'I'm not going to be there.' Bridie poked me hard.

I ignored her. I wasn't meeting him on my own.

'I hear Bridie giving out as usual.'

There was a smile in his voice and I pressed the advantage home. 'So?'

He hesitated. 'Naw, I dunno.'

'Please, Ed.'

'Naw. There's no point. Listen, take care – OK?'

'Ed—'

The phone went dead.

For some reason, I knew I'd just failed bigtime.

Chapter Sixty-four

'Is Vicky here?'

Despite my resolve to be strong and firm, my knees suddenly felt very unsteady. Bridie obviously felt the same because there was a slight tremble in her voice as she answered, 'Oooh, Mr O'Neill, it's you.'

'Yes, Bridie,' O'Neill answered ponderously, 'it is indeed me. And I'm quite annoyed at having to call out. I've rung here and none of my calls have been returned. I'm far too busy for this carry on.'

'And we're far too busy to deal with calls,' I said, approaching the counter with what I hoped was an air of serenity tempered with authority. 'There's only the two of us again, you see.'

O'Neill glared at me. 'Not my fault. Three weeks ago I asked you both to place an ad for a new person and that's what I'm here about.'

Bridie and I looked blankly at him. We'd been practising our blank looks in front of her hall mirror.

'Yes?' I prompted.

'Where *is* the new person?' O'Neill asked irritably. 'According to *her*' – he pointed at Bridie, obviously too disgusted to say her name – 'you haven't taken on anyone.'

'It's not from lack of trying, is it, Bridie?'

'Oooh, it's very trying, Mr O'Neill.' Bridie nodded vigorously. I tried to hold back a laugh.

'So you've interviewed, have you?' O'Neill demanded.

'Isn't this a matter for the office?' I asked, eyeing a woman customer who'd just arrived in.

'Have you interviewed or not?' O'Neill thundered, making Bridie flinch.

'Yes,' I said, 'and none of them came up to the correct standard.'

'Standard?' O'Neill scoffed. 'What standard? They're selling toys, for Christ's sake. It's not brain surgery!'

Bridie was offended. 'It's a *skilled* job,' she said snottily. 'As I'm sure you'll appreciate, Mr O'Neill. I mean, if you didn't have skilled people on the ground, you'd make no money, would you?'

Good on you, Bridie. I beamed at her.

O'Neill flushed. 'I'm not insulting you,' he said. 'But what exactly are the two of you after? Surely you can train the person in? I mean, *Ed*' – he spat his son's name – 'learned very quickly, didn't he?'

'He was a natural,' Bridie said pleasantly. 'Like yourself, Mr O'Neill, a wonderful salesman, could charm money from a miser.'

O'Neill wasn't too sure what to make of that.

'Plus,' I went on, 'he had computer skills, which are a requisite for any job.'

O'Neill rolled his eyes.

'He redesigned the shop floor, he knew the toys inside out, he had a flair for window display, he was good with kids, he—'

'Wore a halo?' O'Neill looked sour.

'No,' I said. 'I never noticed anyway.'

Bridie had to leave at that comment. Her shoulders were shaking.

O'Neill looked furious. 'You find someone, Vicky. You find someone fast. A few months ago you were begging for help and now you won't take it.'

'We had help,' I said firmly. I was not backing down.

'That help is now gone.'

'Excuse me.' The woman, oblivious of the atmosphere between us, had arrived over. 'I was just wondering if I could have a look at the new Action Man toy. There was a lovely lad here the last time and he—'

'Fast!' O'Neill snarled before stomping from the shop.

The woman looked horrified.

'Action Man toy?' I beamed at her. 'Of course you can. Have it on the house.'

'Oooh,' she smiled at me. 'Oooh.'

'Call it being in the right place at the right time.'

It was lonely without Ed; I hadn't heard from him since he'd phoned the shop the day after the story broke. Lying in Bridie's spare room at night, I'd often resolve to ring him. I'd frantically try and think of some problem with the computer that could give me an excuse to talk to him, but in the cold light of day, my courage deserted me. The only thing to do was what we'd decided – that come hell or high water, no one was going to take Ed's job. Only thing was, I reckon our jobs would be the next to go if O'Neill didn't get his way soon.

Chapter Sixty-five

THE MEETING WITH my mother was set for the end of August. During the time in between we rang each other. To be honest, it was hard making conversation over the phone. It was stilted, as if we were both holding our emotions in check. I wondered what it would be like when we met face to face. Would it be different or would we be dancing around each other the way we were now?

Lucy encouraged me to be more open with Barbara. Told me to tell her how I was feeling. Bridie agreed. 'If you want an honest relationship, you should start as you mean to go on.'

'Mmmm.'

'Tell her how you feel about meeting her. Ask her how *she* feels. That's the way for things to survive.'

'Well, I don't see why *I* should be the one,' I muttered.

'Because you never *are* the one,' Bridie suggested in a very sarcastic voice.

'Pardon?'

'Oooh . . .' Bridie, obviously regretting her remark, began to wave her arm about. 'Nothing. Nothing.'

I put down my cocoa. We were drinking it before we went to bed. I'm telling you, old woman habits are contagious. 'It *was* something,' I said. 'Tell me.' I put on a mock-sincere voice. 'I'd like an *honest* relationship with you, Bridie.'

'Oh, *very* clever.'

'Well?'

'We work together, Vicky. I don't think we should get personal with each other.'

'Well, you did it by being sarcastic.'

'And I apologise for that.' She drained her cocoa and stood up. 'Now, I'm going to bed. I'll see you in the morning.'

'Pleeeease?'

She turned in the doorway and studied me. Hard. 'For a smart girl, you're very stupid.'

'I don't—'

'If you had really talked to Ed that day he phoned or phoned him since, he'd still be in the shop with us. He'd never have given up so easily.'

'What?' I gawped at her. 'Are you saying his getting fired is my fault?'

'No, all I'm saying is that he was mad about you, Vicky. And suddenly he's not even around. You should have told him how you felt about him.'

'How I felt about him?'

'Yes.' Bridie nodded, matter-of-factly. 'He'd have fought for the job then. Instead, we're fighting a battle we can't win. He's not coming back and you should face it. You let him go.'

'I didn't! I told him we wanted him back! Anyway, if he liked me, why didn't he say so?'

Bridie shrugged. 'He sent you flowers, bought you cakes. Maybe he felt that's all he could do – maybe he felt he didn't deserve you, him after being in jail and all.'

'My arse.' Bridie looked shocked. 'Anyway,' I went on, 'what am I supposed to tell him – that I love him or something, just to make him come back?'

'Don't you?'

'For God's sake—'

'Then ask yourself – why are you so desperate for him to come back? O'Neill is right – it's only selling toys to the public.'

'He should never have been let go!'

375

'But he accepts it. Maybe you should too.' She closed the door quietly.

I'd never accept it. I glared into my cocoa. I didn't like unfairness. That's all.

Hey, I thought, wouldn't it be great if Ed sued his dad for unfair dismissal?

I could maybe ring him in the morning with that one.

Barbara rang me the next evening. Bridie was out at bingo with a lady from the house next door. They'd tried to persuade me to go along but there were some things I just did not want to include in my social life. Anyway, this was Bridie's new friend and I didn't want to play gooseberry.

When the phone rang, I was half tempted not to answer it. It'd just be the usual 'hello' and 'how are you keeping' call that had become embarrassing. Then I realised that if I wanted, I could change it. I could ask Barbara how she was, if I wanted. I could take our relationship to a more personal level. Despite what Bridie had said about Ed, she was right. If I wanted it to happen, I had to do it myself.

'Barbara, hello,' I said, forcing myself to sound different.

'Hi.' She sounded surprised. 'How are you? You sound . . . different.'

Normally I'd have answered with a 'fine', but that night, I took a deep breath and said, all in a rush, 'Well, to be honest, I'm a bit nervous about meeting you.'

That threw her. 'Really?' She paused. I heard her catch her breath. 'Why?'

'Well—' I swallowed hard. 'It's just, you know, we seem to have the same conversation every time you ring and I'm afraid that, you know, we won't know what to say to each other.'

There was silence.

'Barbara?'

'I just like talking to you,' she whispered back.

'I know, and I like talking to you, but—'

'And I'm so happy to have found you that I don't want to scare you off by getting too personal.'

'Oh.'

'I let you go once, Vicky, and I'm so afraid it'll happen again.'

'I'm not going anywhere,' I said. 'I contacted you, didn't I?'

'Yes.' Her voice went all wobbly.

So much for being honest and open.

'Barbara, don't get upset—'

'I loved you, Vicky. I loved you when you were born but I was scared to keep you. I was afraid to go against my parents, afraid of what they'd say. I let you go and it was the biggest mistake of my life.'

'Don't—'

'But I learned from it, Vicky. I learned that when you love something you should fight to keep it. That's why I don't want to upset you or have you resent me. I'm so lucky to be getting a chance to know you. I'm so lucky that it's not too late.'

'No,' I said slowly, 'it's not too late.'

'And I very much want to meet you and even if we sit in silence, just to be there with you will be enough for me.' She gulped. 'But if *you're* unsure . . .'

'No.' I was feeling dazed by what she'd said, by the words she'd used. 'I'm looking forward to meeting you too.'

It was the best and most heart-breaking conversation I'd had with her so far.

I was terrified. Unsure. Completely at a loss as to what to do. But I couldn't live for years hoping to meet him again, could I? I couldn't be like Barbara, hanging around waiting because I'd fucked up.

But at the same time, I couldn't just go up and tell Ed that I loved him. I mean, what if what I felt wasn't *really* love, what then? And what if I had left it too late? What if I made a complete fool of myself? What if Bridie was wrong and he didn't fancy me at all? But the flowers and the cakes and the way he looked at me told me that he at least *liked* me.

Concrete physical proof was thin on the ground, though. A Valentine's card would have been handy. But Ed didn't seem like the kind of guy that would secretly send a Valentine card. And maybe waiting until next February would be leaving it a little too late?

And, just as I'd decided to leave, I began to wonder how I'd feel if we went out for a few months and it ended in tears?

And then I remembered my dad's speech at Mam's funeral. How he'd never regretted a single moment of his love for her, how loving her made the grief worse but that he didn't regret it.

It was all about taking a chance.

Oh Jesus!

Chapter Sixty-six

I BRUSHED MY hair, plaited it. Shoved on some make-up – not very successfully – applied a lipstick which clashed with my hair but which was the only one I had. Then I searched out some clothes. I eventually found a long, gypsy-style asymmetrical skirt and teamed it up with my trusty black Docs. A smock top with long, gothic-style sleeves completed the look, which I hoped would make Ed realise what he'd be missing if he rejected me.

Rejection.

The word made me shiver.

It was bad enough what Marti had done but it was nothing like the bungee jump I was about to attempt.

I couldn't let myself think about it. So I shoved a CD into my Discman and left for the dart.

It was after seven by the time I got to Dun Laoghaire.

Upon reaching Ed's apartment, I hesitated. My finger hovered over the buzzer. I made a silent vow – if he wasn't in, it wasn't meant to be.

'Who is this?' A sharp voice. Definitely not Ed.

'Is Ed in?'

'Who is it?'

'Just a mate from his old job.'

'In London?'

'No, Vicky from the toy shop.'

'Oooh' – the voice changed suddenly. 'The Vicky that's going out with the music manager?'

I was a bit taken aback that this disembodied voice knew who I was. 'Not any more.'

'Well, Ed'll be glad to hear that.' A laugh. 'You can catch him in Grafton Street. He's busking there tonight.'

Thursday. Fuck! Why hadn't I thought of that? Aw, well . . . fate had stepped in.

'OK, thanks. Tell him I called – yeah?'

My heart, which had been hammering like mad, suddenly plummeted, making me feel dizzy and sick.

'Well, you can catch him in Grafton Street if you – hey, don't you have a lift?'

'Nope.'

'Hang on a sec, I'll drive you.'

'No. No. It's fine.'

'If Ed thinks he missed you it won't be fine for me – hang on.'

Five minutes later, a tall, dishevelled guy with a broken front tooth and the weirdest accent came down to meet me. He was jangling some keys. 'Vicky, howya.' He shoved out a massive hand. 'Dermo Mulligan.'

'Hi, Dermo.' He shook my hand vigorously. 'There's no need to do this, you know.'

Dermo looked at me as if I'd just said something incredibly stupid. 'Like I said, if Ed finds out you were here and he missed you, he'd fucking massacre me.'

I couldn't imagine Ed massacring anyone.

'You think he's quiet, yeah?' Dermo began to stride towards a battered-looking Focus. 'But he's not. He's mad, is Ed.' Then, as if he'd said something wrong, he amended, 'But in a good way.'

I managed a weak smile.

Dermo opened the door of his car, which squeaked like mad. 'In you get.'

As I climbed inside, he studied me. 'Ed likes you. A lot. You're not coming to wreck his head, are you? I mean, you don't believe all that crap in the papers, do you?'

'I'm sure he had his reasons,' I offered. Jesus, there was no way I was confiding in Dermo how I felt about his friend.

'Bloody right he did. Fecking asshole doctor giving him grief every hour of the day. Anyway' – Dermo started up the engine – 'this is great. Never thought I'd be heading into town with a gorgeous-looking wan this evening.'

I smiled weakly.

'Ed hates his dad,' Dermo informed me as he pulled up on a double yellow line. 'His dad never bothered with him when he was a kid, you know. Well, not that Ed ever says that, but all you have to do is know the family. I mean, if something went wrong, Ed always got the blame – and it was usually Al's fault.'

Dermo offered me a pack of fags and when I refused, he took one and lit up himself.

'I'd ask if ya minded only it's my car – like.' He laughed a bit.

I indicated the door. 'Well, I'd better—'

'One time, right' – Dermo jabbed his fag at me – 'Ed was going out with this girl – mad into her he was – and Al steals her off him.'

'Really?' My stomach lurched. I didn't need to hear of Ed and other women.

'Oh, he's over her now. Well, ever since he met you, he is.' Dermo sniggered. 'But that's Al all over, hates things not being his. Sure he's even getting the dad's business and all. Ed reckoned a long time ago that he might as well be hung for a sheep as a lamb, so he spent his time driving his dad spare, pretending to want to do stuff and then dropping out. Made the auld lad mad.'

'I'll bet it did.'

'Then, for some, like, *bizarre* reason Ed decided to become a doctor.'

He made it sound as if Ed had grown horns.

'And he wouldn't let the auld fella pay. Said he was going to do it himself and he did. Brilliant, he was. Until what happened happened.'

'Yeah.'

A warden was on her way towards the car.

'Now, out you get.' Dermo virtually shoved me towards the door. 'And go see him. I swear, he'll be made up to see you. Not that he'd ever admit that *either*. I mean, me and the lads used to slag him over you and he'd tell us to fuck off but like . . .' He paused as some memory lit up his face. 'Right, just let me tell you one last thing, right.'

He looked hastily around to see where the warden was. She was busy writing up a ticket for the car behind.

'Ed didn't want to work in that toy shop, right. Only did it because his ma begged him to. Ed swore he was going to fuck off after a week or so but that night, the night he started, he came back to the flat and said that he was thinking of staying. Told us there was a nice-looking wan working there.'

'Oh.' I felt a glow of pleasure, then thought that with my luck he'd been talking about Bridie.

'Loved that job, he did. Tried to impress you like mad. First time he's ever done that for someone. Right. Out.'

The warden had drawn level with the car. I jumped out the door as Dermo screeched off, whooping and laughing. The warden gave me a dirty look, which I tried to ignore.

Someone was singing a Bob Dylan song as I neared the end of Grafton Street. The voice, gravelly yet unusually sweet, carried right down towards me. The strum of a guitar could be heard on the early summer breeze. The song was Dylan's 'Don't Think Twice – It's All Right', one of my favourites. There was a crowd gathered around the singer and they broke into polite applause as he finished up.

I had known it would be Ed. I watched from the fringes as he goaded the crowd into paying up.

'Come on now,' he joked, 'you pay for what you get. There's no such thing as free anything in this world. Dig deep.' He looked around. 'Any requests? Anyone want a special song? Special bargain – two euro.'

Without thinking, I yelled out, 'Big Yellow Taxi.'

He turned in my direction.

A slow smile lit up his face. 'That lady there wants "Big Yellow Taxi".' He turned to the crowd. 'And d'you know what, folks, I don't think I'm gonna charge her because she's just too good-looking.'

People laughed while I blushed furiously.

'Instead, I'm looking for another kind of payment.'

An 'Oooh' went up from the crowd.

'I want her to sing with me. She's got a great voice on her, so she has.'

I wanted the ground to swallow me up. I hadn't sung since my mother's funeral.

'No,' I mouthed.

'Come on,' he mouthed back. 'It'll be fun.'

A cheer went up. Jesus, it'd be even more embarrassing to refuse. Slowly I went towards him. He grasped my hand in his and a shock of pure excitement ran through me.

'Here we go.' Ed let my hand go and began to strum.

He began to sing and I followed.

Our voices fitted beautifully together.

At the chorus, he turned to me. I blushed. It was the reason I'd wanted him to sing the song in the first place – *Don't it always seem to go, you don't know what you've got till it's gone . . .*

He smiled at me again. A lovely warm smile.

I knew, in that instant, that this was going to last.

I stayed with him until his session ended, the two of us having a blast, singing and improvising and entertaining. At ten, he slung his guitar over his shoulder and turned to me. I felt suddenly shy.

'Buy you a pint?'

'Sure.'

In silence we walked to O'Neills, a pub off Dame Street. He found a table, ordered our drinks and, pushing mine across to me, he said, 'So, what brought you into town tonight?'

'A battered car with a guy driving who managed to tell me every secret you ever had.'

Ed laughed a little self-consciously. 'Dermo? How'd you meet him? Did you call to the apartment then?'

'Yep.'

'Why?'

Oh good Christ. 'Just, you know, 'cause I missed you.'

'Yeah?' He looked pleased at that. 'It's good to see you too.'

I swallowed hard. If I didn't take a chance now, I never would. 'And the words of that song I asked you to sing – well, it's true, I, eh, didn't realise how much I liked you until you were gone.'

There was a silence.

Ed's smile faded and was replaced by something else. Something I couldn't quite understand. 'What are you saying, Vicky?'

Jesus. 'That I miss you,' I gulped out, my face reddening. 'That, well, that I liked the flowers you bought for me and the cakes and stuff, and that I want you to keep doing that.'

More silence.

'And the stuff in the newspapers?'

I shrugged. 'You already said you had your reasons – I trust you.'

He smiled shyly. 'Good,' he nodded. Then he bit his lip and his blue eyes clouded over. 'It was over a kid who'd presented with sickness and a temperature,' he began.

'Ed – don't—'

He overrode my protest. 'The mother was a bit of a worrier and every week she'd have that kid in the hospital. There was never much wrong with him but this night, I thought something *was* wrong. The kid was kinda listless, not his usual self, so I recommended some tests be done but my boss overruled me. I did argue but it was no good. The kid was sent home.' Pause. He bowed his head. 'He died of meningitis the next day.'

'Oh, Ed.'

'I flipped. Guess I blamed myself really. I mean, if I'd argued a bit more, done more, I dunno.' He shrugged hopelessly. 'So I took it out on my boss. I didn't get on with him anyway, he reminded me of my dad, always getting on my case, nothing ever good enough. Never being trusted – and I dunno, I mixed it all up in my head and went for him.' He looked up at me. 'I regret it every day of my life. I got the sack, which I deserved – I would have left anyway.'

'Oh, Ed.' Tentatively I touched his hand. 'That was awful.'

He nodded. 'So, there you have it. You see what you're taking on?'

'Yep. A guy I'm crazy about.'

We left the pub. Booked into a hotel. Completely seedy but neither of us could wait until we got back to Dun Laoghaire. And there was no chance of any hanky-panky in Bridie's.

I can't even remember what the room looked like. Except as Ed closed the door behind us, I stammered out, 'I never normally sleep with guys on a first date.'

'Just as well we're not on a date then,' he said back, his eyes laughing.

He crossed towards me, so handsome I could hardly believe he was mine. He touched me on the shoulders and ran his hands down the length of my arms, before bending his head to kiss me.

I couldn't stand the distance between us. I moulded my body to his and he pulled me into a tight embrace. His mouth pressed down on mine, harder and harder, making me dizzy with desire.

'Oh, Jesus, Vicky, I've wanted you from the second I saw you.'

'So Dermo said.'

A splutter of a laugh.

He ran his hands to my hair, stopping to undo my plaits. Over my back, up my blouse. Kissing my neck.

I could feel him through his jeans. My heartbeat went off the scale.

Together we fell onto the bed. A tumble of unbuttoned clothes. It was completely frantic. I just wanted him. He just wanted me.

I closed my eyes and took my chance.

Later, he made love to me again. Slower and easier and just as erotic. Just looking at him turned me on something rotten. Just listening to his voice sent my heart pounding. The slow curl of his smile. Everything, basically. And it dawned on me to wonder if I'd been so threatened by him in the beginning because I'd been so attracted to him. It was probably why I'd gone for Marti – the safe, separated option.

We ordered supper to be sent to the room. 'Why'd you go out with Sal?' I hadn't even intended asking him. At his amused look, I muttered, half embarrassed, 'It's just, you know, you said you liked me from the beginning.'

'She asked me out,' he said, unperturbed. 'I didn't like to refuse her. And anyway,' he grinned, 'you had Marti.'

'More fool me,' I scoffed, munching on a chip. 'I guess you seeing Sal had nothing to do with her being gorgeous-looking.'

'Nothing at all,' he said. 'I didn't even get serious with her.' He shoved a chip into his mouth and grinned. 'I think I love you, Vicky.'

'Betcha say that to all the girls,' I joked, feeling thrilled.

To my surprise he didn't laugh. 'Nope.' He sat down beside me. 'I'm not like my dad,' he said. 'I promise I'm not.'

'That's not what I meant!'

'Yeah, well . . .' He took my hand in his. 'I'm not,' he repeated earnestly.

'I believe you.'

'Good, 'cause I fancied you for ages.'

'Even when we had that row?'

He nodded. 'Which was why I left – I was only there 'cause I liked you and you didn't seem to feel the same back so . . .' He shrugged and smiled that orgasmic smile of his. 'And then you apologised and you looked so cute with your belly button showing and your hair all frizzed out and . . .'

'Stop!'

'I love you.'

That was enough to get me back to bed.

Chapter Sixty-seven

'So, Vicky, this is it.' Lucy rose to meet me. She hugged me briefly before surveying me. 'How do you feel?'

'Nervous,' I said, taking a deep breath. 'But, well, happy too, I guess.' I hugged my photo album to me. 'If only Mam was alive, it'd be even better.'

Lucy looked sympathetically at me. 'You've been through a lot this year, you've done really well.'

'Thanks.'

'And you're sure you're up to this?'

I nodded.

'Good girl.' Lucy smiled at me. 'Your mother is waiting in the room for you. She's on her own. Do you want me to go in with you?'

'No,' I said. 'I'll go on my own, if that's OK.'

I left Lucy at the end of the stairs as I walked up to meet Barbara.

Just as I arrived outside the door, I said a silent prayer to my mother. I thanked her for getting me to this moment.

And then I knocked. And I knew that I could cope with whatever lay behind that door. I didn't have any expectations of Barbara and I didn't harbour any anger or bitterness towards her. Parenthood was a damn hard job and all people can do is their best at the time. And no parent or childhood is ever perfect – I understood that from Marti and Sylvia and Ed.

I realised suddenly that all I wanted from Barbara was to

know where I'd come from, just to fill in the gap in my past. Which was my past. Not my future.

And if she wanted to continue to see me afterwards, well that would be fine too.

Whatever I got from meeting her would be enough.

Lucy *was* right – I had come a long way.

Epilogue

THERE IS A silence. A surprised silence where everyone is looking and pretending not to.

Aunt Julia comes forward. 'This must be Ed,' she says, smiling.

Ed nods, shakes her hand and grins. 'Happy Christmas to you.'

'And you too,' she smiles back. Then adds, slyly, 'Doctor.'

Ed grins at me. Holding my gaze with his blue-eyed one. 'Well, I had to do something, Vic always wanted me out of the shop!'

I laugh and he brings his forehead to touch mine.

Then all eyes turn to my father. He coughs slightly and announces, 'Everyone, I'd like you to meet Barbara. Vicky's, eh, other mother.'

Barbara smiles shyly around before reaching for my hand. 'Aren't they all so *huge*,' she whispers.

I splutter out a laugh.

'Welcome to our family,' Aunt Julia says. 'Both of you.'

Our family – my family.

The best bloody night of my life.